I0764512

THE BLACKSTONE PERFECTION

NOVELS BY DENNIS BOWEN

THE WATER DIAMONDS
Book 1: International Thriller Series

THE BLACKSTONE PERFECTION
Book 2: International Thriller Series

THE BLACKSTONE PERFECTION

Dennis Bowen

The Blackstone Perfection is a work of fiction. Names, characters, places, and incidents are the products of the author's imagination or are used fictitiously. Any resemblance to actual events, locales, or persons, living or dead, is entirely coincidental.

ISBN: 978-0-9881841-5-2

FIRST EDITION

www.DennisBowen.com

www.twitter.com/DBowenThrillers

www.facebook.com/Dennis.Bowen.90

Book Interior Design by 52 Novels

ACKNOWLEDGMENTS

I would like to thank the readers of my *International Thriller Series*. Readers give writers life, a gift of immeasurable magnitude. As with *The Water Diamonds*, numerous people offered suggestions and encouragement during the writing of *The Blackstone Perfection*, and they also deserve my appreciation.

I wish to once again express my deep appreciation to Laura Taylor, my mentor, editorial consultant, and colleague, for her steadfast hand and intelligent mind, and the value they brought to bear. Any errors or omissions in *The Blackstone Perfection*, I claim as my own.

—Dennis Bowen

CHAPTER 1

The smell awakened him. The vanguard drop of water had pushed along the block wall's seam. Those that succeeded it had propelled it to the edge. It paused for a moment, as if having second thoughts, and then plunged over the precipice, falling 192 times its diameter. The drop accelerated the entire twenty-four inches until its obliteration against the smooth flesh of an aquiline nose. The man attached woke with a start. His eyes snapped open, but the darkness defeated any detection of the source of his rude awakening. The nose, expert at sniffing the fine fragrance of a well-balanced Bordeaux, deftly dismantled its component scents.

The single drop signaled that late Autumn had not yet turned to early Winter with the first snowfall. The drop's odorless nature had been adulterated by vehicular essences as it seeped through the asphalt streets of the modern world and down into the dungeon. Although his new residence had existed more than 630 years, no lingering manifestation remained above ground. The head, shoulders, and torso of the Bastille had been razed more than 220 years before, after its fall in 1789. Its bowels, the stone block encasements and ironworks underground, had been left to rot.

Constrained by a bed smaller than his 6'6", 220 pound frame, he rolled over just as the solid iron closure on his 18" by 12" window to the external world screeched open. Since he had pinched out the desk candle after making a diary entry, his world had been pitch black. The sconced gas lamps in the gallery outside his cell provided morning light. The man who peered into his quarters was clothed head-to-toe in 18th Century dress, no doubt intended as an insult. His jailer, of far less aristocratic lineage than himself, bore the title *Compte de Cièrges*. He provided none of the concierge services the antiquated title implied. The fact that the man opened the portal every morning before breakfast and closed it again after the evening meal enabled the prisoner to count the days. Today made eight since being captured at his château. He could thank the American, Magus Crayle, for the assault, and those in the hierarchy above him for the betrayal. And the humiliation.

He dwelled on his transition from a member of France's elite, residing in a centuries-old estate, to a mere captive devoid of any semblance of control over his remaining years. Suicide presented as his most attractive option, but his captors denied him the resources for even that. A brief length of charcoal stick and a writing pad disafforded that option.

One man had done this to him. Magus Crayle, sent to him by American intelligence, had led him to believe there existed a pathway to his goal: to restore intellectual, reasoned, autocratic rule to his beloved France. To replace the hideous, self-destructive socialism. To restore the monarchy of old. And he, historically and genetically perfect for the task, would assume the throne. Part of a strategic plan devised by the genius, Crayle.

What had gone awry? The Illuminé's man-in-the-CIA had provided Crayle for the purpose, yet must have been the one who'd given the assault orders. And Crayle—a mathematician. How could he have led an assault capable of obliterating his vaunted, seasoned defense force? Perhaps the years of training and experience in the

Foreign Legion no longer provided the human resources he required. He pushed aside the enigma. He knew he would die in this place. The French government, having destroyed the economy, needed their greatest detractor incommunicado until death. They had chosen the perfect venue. With its historical significance, the Bastille oozed symbology. His deep thoughts of remorse were interrupted by a now familiar sound. Breakfast.

• • •

She was late. The guard had just begun his shift—already something amiss. It was feeding time for the prison's sole inhabitant and, of all the uninteresting aspects of guarding someone in lockdown security, meals represented the high points.

Ah, there. He heard the light footsteps nearing the cellblock hallway. She would deliver the food and leave. At that point, the guard would call his girlfriend once again and tell her, in a convincing manner, that he would soon leave his wife. The man deprived of all freedoms moved to the side of his cell door, straining to catch a glimpse of this woman, of any woman.

At four meters distance, she emerged from the shadows. The impatient jailer watched the period-attired, petite young woman step into view and move toward him, tray in hand. She wore a dress of white linen, her shoulders covered by a dark, heavy mantel secured by a satin bow at the neck. A white scarf draped to each side of her face completed the picture. The prisoner took notice as she deployed her magic. A slight smile came to her face and point dimples to her cheeks. They juxtaposed the words darling and precious with the words sexy and sexual. Her allure factor exceeded that of the jailer's wife and his girlfriend. No words were spoken.

She set the tray and its undisturbed contents next to the rust-red, iron door and moved her delicious body against his. His newborn lust turned to physical action. Within three seconds, he lifted and embraced and pressed her against the cold, moist stone wall. She locked her legs tight around his waist.

He pushed his lips onto hers. He brought both hands to bear on his masculine appendage, now also imprisoned. She jerked at her dress. They engaged with seemingly equal passion.

The young woman breathed hard for effect. She thrust herself at him with intensity. But, behind his back, she slipped the long, conical thimbles hidden in each palm onto her thumbs. She bit hard into his upper lip. He tried to jerk away, but she held fast. With all her strength, she drove the pointed ends up each side of his spine and deep into his brain.

The girl pulled her thumbs from the thimbles and held the guard as tightly with her arms as with her legs. As he slid to the floor, the rough stone scraped her back, but her emotions were on fire. She felt nothing.

They sat entwined on the floor for seconds. Her breathing slowed as quickly as his breathing ceased. She kissed his forehead, released her grasp, and fell away.

She crawled to where he lay and, with care not to bloody her fingers, retrieved the heirloom murder weapons. She looked up into the flat-iron barred opening that the prisoner called a window. She looked directly into his eyes. She lifted the thimbles, one at a time, to her lips. She licked them clean, removing all traces of red.

But the young woman's goal did not include seduction into cold-blooded murder. It was not, at this time, her sport. She operated under the strictest orders. They required no witnesses to what would soon follow. There could be no finger pointing to her or to those who orchestrated the plot. And there could be no trail as she affected their escape.

She had come for the Bastille's lone captive. She had come for France's number one prisoner.

CHAPTER 2

"*Alles ist in ordnung,*" the doctor shouted into the phone. "Everything is fine, Dr. Rikki. The subject, Magus Crayle, is with me and I'm about to check his memory recoveries." The man in the starched white lab coat loathed being disturbed while *in process,* even by his direct superior. He busied himself on his laptop computer, having already put her on speaker—his soundproof door closed, of course. He took a second to lightly touch the wired harness that led from the computer to the cap on Crayle's head.

"I want a full update on the subject's progress when you finish your evaluation," she instructed. "This project has accumulated important interest since the combat situation in France. I need specifics. Are you in line with that requirement, Dr. Rorschach?"

"Ja, ja." The pressure caused him to lapse into Swiss-accented English, expressing his frustration. "I vill haf it to you before I leaf tonight."

"One more thing, Doctor. Despite your inability to control the subject, we've learned a great deal regarding the impermanence of memories. There is something that I want you to consider for the next phase."

"Und vot iss dot?"

"Restoration. Partial." She rang off.

The doctor returned his attention to the mildly sedated patient and to the electronic cap positioned atop his cranium. The computer displayed, via picture format, a hierarchy of the subject's memories since the initiation of the experiment. A simple tap on an image evoked the content of corresponding memories. He followed Mr. Crayle's progress from initial transport from the underground hospital to the Big Bear safe house and to the violent fray at the Tack Store. Aided by a young woman—quite beautiful—they'd escaped in her car to her ranch a few miles away. The explicit images that followed made the doctor blush. Two assassins dead. Righteous moonlit sex. All in one day. Perhaps the amnesiac subject did not need old memories after all. The doctor thought for a second about replacing his own. But then he thought better and disallowed any cause-effect relationship.

"Hey, Doc. It's me, Jack," came the next interrupting voice. "How's my guy?"

The doctor focused his glower on Jack Sommers, trying to will him away. But, no. Jack, as project manager for the memory recovery project, had protected Crayle *in the wild,* thwarting several attempts to kill him. Of course, he only had Jack's word for the degree of protection. He would answer Jack's questions. Then, Jack would leave.

"Well, when do I get him back?"

"In the forty-three days since his crash, Mr. Crayle has survived five attempts on his life against overwhelming odds, Mr. Sommers. He needs rest, and I must upload all memories since the car accident."

"It was no accident, Doc. We learned at the French château from that Lalumière character that the accident on the PCH—uh, Pacific Coast Highway—was the first attempt. So, six attempts in all … if you're counting."

"Ahhhhh!" yelled the doctor. "He is my responsibility! You must protect him better."

"Gotcha, Doc. When you're done, I'll take him back up the hill to the safe house and I'll watch over him like a mother hen."

The doctor intensified his glower. Jack, unruffled, just smiled and strolled back to the visitor's lounge to watch the rest of *The Island of Doctor Moreau* in HD.

Rorschach conceded that he'd allowed the subject out into the world with his guarded blessing, and the man before him had not only survived, he'd triumphed. Against gargantuan odds and with a minimal mental toolset, depleted by the good doctor himself. Now the debriefing could begin. Rorschach would use the voice-pattern device the subject carried at all times. He would search for memories newly created and test for the re-emergence of memories archived prior to the experiment.

The doctor glanced out the room's four foot by two foot window at the snow-laden trees, reminiscent of his native Swiss village, Bitsch. That made him, in a way, a son of a Bitsch. He smiled at his mastery of the English language. And at the fact that the hospital existed several hundred feet below ground, and that the window was, in fact, a high-resolution video screen. Poised to download the memory set from the study subject, nature called. He set aside his laptop and exited to the bathroom.

When he returned, he stopped, startled. He found the patient seated on the edge of the bed, his hands working feverishly on the computer's touch screen.

"Ahhhhh!" wailed the doctor.

Rorschach rushed toward the study subject. The man, a former operative named Magus Crayle, hurled the doctor over the bed and into the wall. The sedation bag crashed to the floor and burst. Crayle grabbed the mental transducer cap from his head and threw it into the spreading liquid. Sparks flew as the circuits shorted. The computer screen snapped to black. Smoke poured from the keyboard. A second later, Crayle darted out the door.

The doctor struggled to his feet, pulled the panic button from his pocket, and depressed it with both thumbs.

The patient alarm sounded. Men and women dressed in white ran past the hospital room, the doctor in hot pursuit.

"Don't harm him!" he yelled.

CHAPTER 3

As Rorschach rounded another corner, he spotted Crayle near the end of the hall. Nurses and orderlies surrounded him, but none of them dared to close the remaining ten feet. They had been briefed.

A disheveled Rorschach entered the circle. "Please, Mr. Crayle. Return with me to your room. You will not be harmed. I promise."

An orderly, six-four and 220 pounds of muscle, approached Crayle from behind. New to the facility, he apparently considered 'keep your distance' a caution for those of lesser stature.

Crayle whirled and planted a spinning back kick on the man's jaw. The orderly slammed into the nearby wall and crumpled to the floor. Lights out.

The doctor opened his mouth to speak just as another man stepped past him and paused. All eyes focused on him.

Crayle's gaze narrowed with speculation. The so-called mind-experiment subject still looked cocked and loaded.

But Jack, the project manager for the CIA's Subject Crayle memory recovery experiment, raised both hands to shoulder level. He motioned downward.

Everyone, including the doctor, slowly sank to the floor.

"It's okay, Magus. Come with me," Jack said.

Crayle walked past the docile staff and the doctor. He followed Jack down the hall. Before exiting to the garage, Jack threw words over his shoulder. Then, the two disappeared.

The confounded doctor furrowed his brow. "Vot doss he mean, call me ven I haf a new brain hat. Vere doss he sink I get zem, Costco?"

As Doctor Rorschach continued his unnerved tirade against formidable forces, Jack Sommers and Magus Crayle climbed aboard Jack's ambulance shuttle.

"He wasn't quite done, you know," Jack said.

"He talks to himself while he works. I was awake enough to hear him. He was about to press the *Delete* key on the few memories I've acquired since the crash. They're all I have to build on. And I need them to stay alive," the subject responded. "I am ready for the killers if they come again, Mr. Sommers."

"Yeah, well, you cleaned house over at the French château, buddy. You turned their top killer and all of his goons into mush. They won't be back. And the Chinese guy, Chin, is gonna keep to himself. I'm pretty sure of that. So, what say we get you back into the memory recall game, huh?"

Crayle remained silent. He had heard it all, but he'd learned far too much in a short span of time. Since the start of his recovery, he'd killed seven men in self-defense and several more in the attack on Lalumière's château. All that death and destruction squeezed into a mere seven days. Reconciling those lethal survival skills to his government-job title of mathematician and foremost world-conquest planner would take time.

In two minutes, the vehicle elevator ascended to the surface.

• • •

The actual depth of the CIA covert hospital was highly classified. The brilliant leadership at the government agency, known colloquially as the *company*, had decided to spend millions of dollars over the amount a humans-only elevator would have cost. The decision was based first on the ability to transport high impact subjects in a hardened encasement vehicle with on-board life support and heavily encrypted communications capability. Caught in the shaft, the occupants could contact the hospital below or various distant incarnations of *company* assets, by utilizing extra low frequency communications via the elevator's metal superstructure and the surrounding granite substrate. The ELF technology represented an enhancement to the methodology used by navies worldwide for communication with submarines at any depth. The second reason was that the *company* had no budgetary limitation. When congress pushed its nose into CIA territory, the terminal response, *How much is national defense worth?* always worked. The third reason, it gave its creators serious bragging rights at Langley. It was that cool.

The ride terminated with a jolt inside a large, corrugated building. Its surveillance system automatically surveilled the immediate and surrounding landscape and the inside of a rolling door turned green. Without interaction by the ambulance or its occupants, the door rolled up with nary a sound. The short bumpy ride across the compound past huge piles of gravel and sand constituted a brief interlude.

Jack had not picked this day to transport Crayle back to the safe cabin in Big Bear Valley. The day had picked him. A day during which no activity of any manner transpired at the quarry and no personnel of any sort were present. Jack felt it a good omen. Things would go well this time. Things would stay nice and quiet.

The ambulance rolled onto the remote two-lane road at just past noon. The final October sky was as white as the surrounding hills. The winding road up the hill had been plowed, and the driver thanked those in power that this new custom ambulance had drive on all four wheels.

CHAPTER 4

Less than three weeks earlier, Magus Crayle, under heavy sedation, had received his first ambulance ride up California's Highway 18 to the Big Bear plateau. He had mentally bypassed a black ice encounter and near-death experience. This time, he occupied the passenger seat rather than the gurney in back. The thirty-something paramedic sat in back, armed and under orders from his boss at Langley to shoot should the ambulance be attacked. First the passenger, then the driver. Last, he would shoot himself, or utilize the cyanide capsule provided.

The road up to the plateau's valley made the same hundred plus bends, but this time sans snow. The above-freezing temperature rendered no possibility of the deadly black ice. The trip took less than an hour. They passed an *Entering* sign for Fawnskin. Population 380 reported all anyone might want to know about the tiny north shore village. Absent any noticeable threat, Jack turned left into the safe cabin's driveway.

Jack pushed the handle on the cruise control twice, waited a second, then twice more. The garage door slid sideways. Care had been taken not to trap moisture inside the humidity-controlled environment that protected Jack's Cobra.

He pulled in between a black sedan and the parachute-covered sports car. They all exited the vehicle. Jack handed the ambulance keys to the medic. "Go down the road and fill 'er up, son. Then, check the tires. Hang out at the 7-11 if you like. I'll give a call when I need you."

The medic nodded and retraced his steps. A few seconds later, he and the special ambulance disappeared down the driveway. Jack closed the garage door and punched in a code next to the interior door. The two men descended a ladder, walked to the end of a shored-up tunnel, and scaled another ladder. Jack punched in a security code, and they entered the cabin's kitchen.

Crayle crossed the cabin to the large, lake-facing window. The beauty from the lakefront exceeded remarkable. A strong afternoon breeze blew up a westward chop. The strong high pressure system to the east known as the Santa Ana Condition warmed the air and explained the lack of snow in the Valley. Crayle watched fishermen anchored offshore bob and weave in their boats, struggling to get bottles of Bud to their lips. He hoped his life from this point onward would be so carefree.

He glanced around, amazed that there were no signs of the major automatic weapons assault staged by Lalumière's henchmen at this very same cabin just twelve days earlier. Once the double-pane bulletproof windows had been breached by triangulation, machine gun and pistol bullet holes had peppered the interior. Jack's prize collector plates, which had adorned the living room wall, had been shattered into mere shards. Yet, there they were, as if nothing had transpired. The two realities collided in a cognitive dissonance that caused his head to ache. Crayle, the assassination target, was only alive because of the bravery of a very special FBI agent drawing fire while he and the private investigator escaped.

"Jack, I need to find Phoebe. I must tell her something."

"About the Indian woman?" Jack deduced.

Crayle, surprised by his insight, nodded.

"Micmac is keeping track of her for me. She did good in France. I want her back. You're still in the program, subject Crayle, and you two played well together."

Crayle nodded again. Jack referred to Phoebe's bravery and success at protecting him in the cabin attack, and then again at Lalumière's château. He knew nothing about Crayle and Phoebe's sexual repartees at the big house, nor anything about the château garden *ménage à trois* frolic that had included Chin's Black Daughter, Annie Ling.

"Here." Jack fished a set of keys from the wall rack. "Take the Buick over to Micmac's place. Find your way with the GPS *Favorites*. Thank him for providing the logging-truck-on-steroids for the attack in France. He'll track down Phoebe for you."

Crayle took the secret tunnel to the garage, aware that the entry code had not been changed since he and Lenny had escaped Lalumière's men. He fired up the Buick and located Micmac's address on the GPS, noticing that the device predicted a fifteen minute trip to the ex-Navy UDT man's pad. Fifteen minutes later, he pumped Morse code into a door button. Micmac greeted him.

When Crayle entered, the first thing that struck him was that every horizontal surface supported an array of gadgets. Three guitars, labeled Fender, Gibson, and Gretsch, hung from wall hangers and two amplifiers, a Marshall and a beautiful wood-cased Mesa Boogie, graced corners.

"Yeah, gadget central. And music," Micmac confessed. "It's what I do."

"You mean, it's who you are. You seem to have made the trip back alright. Jack asked me to thank you for the transformer logging truck and for adding your combat experience to the château assault. Well done, gadget man."

Micmac chuckled. "A couple of mini-guns at four thousand rounds-per-minute apiece surprised that French guy's army. Kinda etch-a-sketched 'em right off the game board."

"Yes, well, I really came by … I, uh, I need to talk to Phoebe." Crayle found sheepish to be unlike his precise and direct self.

Their conversation was interrupted. The bathroom door opened, and a figure wearing only a wraparound towel stepped out. "Did I hear my name?"

Crayle's jaw dropped. He glanced back and forth at the two several times before commenting. "You two? I was going to … whoa!"

Micmac laughed. Then, Phoebe. "What can I say? The night I saw him at the club … I liked the way his fingers flicked this way and that on the guitar."

Now the ex-Navy man took a turn with embarrassment. His face blazed red.

"Phoebe, I need to speak with you." Crayle turned to Micmac, as if asking permission. "Alone?"

Phoebe seized the opportunity. "I don't want to impose on Mick. He probably wants to clean up the place. You know, repair the bed. And the couch. We'd just be in the way. I'll throw on some stuff, we can drive somewhere."

In her inimitable way, Phoebe reinforced her independence from Magus Crayle. They were now just friends. Close friends. Their previous intimacies? Archived.

In no more than five minutes, they stood beside the black Buick.

"I'll drive," said Phoebe, reaching for the keys. Crayle noticed a short braid, just to the left of her eye, track downward as she canted her head to the left. He knew it was special to her. She rebraided it every day, a memorial to her father.

She headed the car toward the tourist part of the valley and its major town, Big Bear Lake.

"Phoebe, I need to tell you something." He paused a second to gather his courage. "My memory doctor, Dr. Rorschach, has me talking out my feelings when I'm alone." He produced a small recording device. "My dialogs are saved for him to analyze later."

"You mean, I'm on that!" Phoebe accused. Lips pursed, her gaze snapped back to the road.

"No. It only records *my* voice patterns. I left out our time … times together, you know." He turned Micmac red.

"Like in the big house? Like when I thought you could be the one to get me back in the game? And after …" She trailed off.

"Yes, at the château. Phoebe, I don't know what happened to you before the protection assignment with me. Not the specifics. But I know it was pretty bad."

"I'll bet that little worm, Lenny, found out. He told you." Her accusatory tone notched up. Her lips pushed out to their limit.

"Yes."

Her right hand went to her sidearm, as if to place it on alert.

"Phoebe, when you touched me at the big house that day … well, my amnesia left me unprepared for how it felt. I had no memories of ever sharing love with a woman. Only the chemistry inside urging me to be with you."

"It was just sex, huh?"

"Going in, it was just sex. My memory loss limits my vocabulary, so the only word I can think of to describe what it was like with you … is fabulous."

Phoebe's lips de-stressed. "Fabulous! You said, *fabulous!*"

"The woman who saved me at the Tack Store—"

"Uh-oh."

"That night, I fell in love."

Phoebe had witnessed the falling in love. It had taken place naked in the chill of the night in the Indian girl's back yard. "I wanted to kill you that night."

"*What!*"

"Yeah. I saw the whole thing. Night vision. It was nearly your last new memory. I went home instead. I cried a lot."

"I'm sorry." Crayle covered his face with his hands.

"Look, Mag. An Army brat learns to get smacked down and get back up. The rock star guy—the one who raped me a year ago—he's still got stuff coming. But, now, with Micmac and all … I think you should see her. You two looked like an item to me. Right for each other. A match."

"You *are* fabulous, Phoebe Bransfield. I mean it."

"Yeah. You know, the first time I saw Mick that night with the band at the Sugarloafer. It was … wait for the big word … visceral."

"If it hadn't been for the drool, I wouldn't've noticed." Crayle put on his first smile since leaving the hospital.

Phoebe made a face. "Listen, if we weren't both in committed relationships, I'd come after you with a six-pack of Bud Light and a bottle of Lalumière's last-week-vintage château wine."

She entered the cabin driveway. He turned to her. "Phoebe, I think you and I are soul mates."

"That wasn't your soul I felt inside … on two occasions," she kidded.

"Think of it as an extension of my soul."

She grinned and shook her head. "I'm back in protector mode, Mr. Crayle. Let's go inside."

Phoebe stepped out of the car first. She clasped her hands behind her back. One slipped beneath her jacket to grip her trusted Glock. She surveyed the landscape, nodded assent to Crayle, then trailed him into the cabin.

• • •

Crayle was hungry. He turned toward the kitchen just as the onslaught began.

"Happy Birthday!" Jack, Lenny, and Micmac cheered.

"Happy *fucking* Birthday!" followed from the FBI agent as she stepped around him. With the absence of the blue arm sling, courtesy of a bullet she had taken for him, Phoebe gave him a hug. He pushed her out to arm's length. The love they had made on two occasions flew through his mind like data points. No, more than that. He shook his head. Now, she was attached in a meaningful way to Mick Mackay, the former government weapon nicknamed Micmac. The two were perfect for each other, and Crayle intended to support that.

"You're a regular potty-mouth, Phoebe. We're all going to be more professional, starting now. From now on," Jack said as he lifted an empty biscotti jar from the bar top, "five bucks per vulgarity. No exceptions."

"You are fucking kidding," said Phoebe.

Jack unscrewed the lid. Phoebe stoked in the first five. "Any other comments? No? Let's eat!"

Drinks, crunchies, and dip, prepared by Lenny, sat on the bar. "Everyone grab a drink—I propose a toast," cried the diminutive private investigator and perpetual third wheel.

"Uh, oh," Phoebe warned.

"Copy that," Micmac affirmed.

"Here's to the guy that nearly cost us our lives," Lenny Lipschitz intoned. "And to a guy we'd do it all again for … Magus Crayle!"

"Here, here!" They all tipped their glasses and took hearty swigs. Jack tried to stay away from demon alcohol. His celebratory drink was sparkling cider.

"Hey, Jack. What ever happened to that lunatic Frenchman, anyways?" Lenny asked, eyebrows furrowed. "The gendarmes dragged the sucker off before we could interrogate him. You know, with extreme prejudice like you spooks say."

"Listen, I am retired from the spook stuff. I merely run projects now. Okay? Okay. FYI, they carted him off and stuck him in prison. He's awaiting trial, probably for the rest of his life. They don't execute assholes in France."

"Why don't they just try him and get it over with? I mean, he plotted to take over the country, restore the monarchy, or some such garbage. A trial would be a slam dunk."

"One, Phoebe, their laws are Napoléonic, which means they are a lot more flexible. Things are righteously fucked up over in France right now. The new president and his party can't afford to give Mr. Lalumière a forum. We'll just have to wait and see."

Phoebe produced the jar. Jack tossed in a five.

"He did provide information about some of the memories I lost in the car crash, and he told Lenny why his dad was murdered, but, he only did that because he believed our deaths were imminent. I've got a long list of questions. Jack, can't we get at him and drag the rest of the truth from him?"

"Magus, this may surprise you, but I am working on that as we speak. I'll let you guys know as soon as I know. Don't hold your breaths." Jack wanted the topic put to rest. He wanted no more of the Lalumière character. And his boss, Neil Wohlford, had told him that sleeping dogs needed to lie—undisturbed.

"And what about the Chinese man, Chin?" Crayle asked. "The one who knew about my father? The one whom I apparently helped with some kind of strategic plan. He and Lalumière are linked and, as far as I know, nothing has happened to *him*."

"Current intel is that Mr. Chin is making political moves. I think he has his sights set on Beijing. The fortune he gained in the Hong Kong stock market will allow him to make the appropriate bribes and all. The public seems to like him and, with capitalism entrenched, wants to *be* him."

"It just paints a target on him by those in power. I remember, I told him … Omigod! I remember what I told him." Crayle became animated. "Like Lalumière, he plans to topple the government in Beijing and install himself as emperor. A repeat of the first emperor, Ch'in Xihuangdi, in 221 B.C. Ch'in became the most powerful man since Alexander the Great, but I don't remember how he'll bring it off." Crayle set down his drink and grabbed his head. "Jack, he has to be stopped!"

"Easy, tiger. Please, all of you step out on the deck. It's beautiful outside. Phoebe and I will join you presently."

They filed out. Crayle gave the two a quizzical glance before he shut the door.

"Phoebe, how is he doing after all the surprises and scares and violent encounters of the past twenty some days? Is he sleeping well?" came the loaded part of the question.

"You mean after the heavy sex? Mr. Sommers, Mr. Crayle and I are not sleeping together. That would not be professional on my part, would it?" She excluded the wild sex five days after the start of her assignment … and the sex in the château garden a mere seven days ago. Anyway, she and Crayle had moved on. With Micmac warming her from the inside out, she had entered into a true, committed relationship. She couldn't be feeling better.

Jack regretted his implication. He forged ahead. "I meant, does he complain about sleeplessness or bad dreams when you two talk?"

Now the former CIA operative had become a burr under her saddle. "Are you kidding? How can a math wiz not sleep well? What's he gonna do, have nightmares because he can't discover the one big equation that explains the whole fucking universe?" She held out her hands, fingers outward, palms toward Jack. The question marks were all written on her face for emphasis. "I can't see how multiple attempts on his life and a couple of major gun battles could possibly impair a good night's sleep." She fished out another five dollar bill. "I need a raise."

Jack believed that she was not physically entangled with Crayle, but he suspected that she remained emotionally engaged. "Okay, okay. If you notice something where he seems to be going off the reservation, let me know immediately. I'll inform Rorschach." He paused. His expression changed. "And stop calling me Mr. Sommers. It's Jack." His smile indicated that he regarded her on an other-than-professional level. A flirt. Something new.

Phoebe sat back. Just when she felt she had it all figured out. Just when she felt she had achieved love, happiness, and true friendship, and there was order in the whole freakin' world. *This.* How do you tell your boss to fuck off?

CHAPTER 5

The girl introduced herself only as Sandrine. She led Lalumière through the misty darkness to a manmade, subterranean river. It was a vestige of the original sewer system built in the fourteenth century to preclude sewage used to fertilize crops from draining into the Seine River, and contaminating Parisian drinking water. Over 1,300 miles in length, it provided sewage transport to the modern day population of Paris. She pulled a case from a boat tied to a stone stanchion and removed a dark garment.

Lalumière perceived that this diminutive woman, still in period dress, represented his only hope. To avoid snatching defeat from the onset of possible victory, he ceded control of his life to her. For the moment.

He pulled the sweatshirt over his head. It made him invisible, save for his pale skin. She moved behind him, which gave him a start—he had witnessed her capabilities. She stood on tiptoes to position the shirt's hood over his head, before she added a dark, bowler-shaped hat. Opening a tin, she created dark patches on his face. His mother would not have recognized him from ten paces. She motioned him into the boat.

He backed against the stone wall, trembling. "I … I am afraid … the water."

"There is nothing to fear. I am a certified diver and lifeguard. If the need arises, I will provide rescue services. And I saw your face in the jail door, watching us. So, if *that* need arises …" She produced a knowing smile. Given the circumstance, she felt the dimples necessary. To the French, a sexy woman was somewhat normal. However, French men, all men, found this young woman's sexual allure irresistible. She observed him turn captive once again. Her captive.

They entered the boat, she at the bow, he at the stern. He followed her precise orders to navigate the boat through a maze of winding channels and tunnel-like archways until he saw light a distance ahead.

"Pull over here," she instructed in French. "We must sleep now. Winter is coming, and the days are short. In a few hours, I will lead us out into the dark, but free, world. Continue to follow my orders. There are many who would have you dead. Only by pulling golden strings were we able to secure the previous lodging and an extension on your life. If you are caught again, you will be killed. *Comprenez*?" She tied up the boat.

Without responding or asking the prescient question as to the identity of *we*, he curled into the least uncomfortable position possible. He slept until she woke him.

• • •

The River Seine is 482 miles long from its inception at Source-Seine, nineteen miles northwest of Dijon, through Paris and on to its terminus at Le Havre on the English Channel—*La Manche* in French.

The boat, its fugitive passenger, and the diminutive spy facilitator entered the Seine via a clandestine access gate just east of Notre Dame Cathedral. Replete with bait tank amidships, it was progressed at trolling speed courtesy of a small, quiet outboard motor. Due to its small size, dark color, and the dark clothing of its crew, the craft drew no attention. In twenty-five minutes, the lights of Paris' southeastern extent disappeared into the night. Only the luminous hemisphere behind them provided a hint that Sylvain Lalumière and Sandrine had just departed the City of Light.

The girl manipulated the throttle. The open boat lifted up in the water, the bow rising to the point that the diminutive agent moved forward and used a game-controller-like device to control the boat's speed and direction. Only the dim glimmer of lights from the occasional village along the Seine spared them from utter darkness. She guided them between the green banks topped by twelve-foot high trees, barren save for round bundles of twigs approximating birds nests. As they passed under an off-white arched bridge with crenellated sides, it struck him that the beauty of his ancestors far surpassed that of modern times. Further, the small towns opened to flat fields, some green, some turned brown by the late Autumn temperatures. They were divided into plots by tree lines used as windbreaks.

"There is variety and beauty when there are no people, Sandrine. The people—the peasants—are the same. All of them."

"You must be still," she whispered.

The now fugitive Frenchman would have been difficult to recognize even in adequate light. He had smeared additional dark makeup onto his face to approximate an unbathed homeless person. With the black hat and its six-inch wide brim, no one could discern his identity, the next leader of La Belle France and the true French. In essence, he was *La Vérité*.

The girl interrupted Lalumière's vision of himself as The Truth. She snatched a black satchel from the bait tank and passed out sandwiches. Clearly, cold Croque Monsieur would never be anyone's favorite, but the nourishment promised to keep their energy levels high enough to complete the night's journey. Lalumière, in acknowledgement, winced at the first taste, but then nodded his approval to the girl.

She wondered how *he* would taste, although she concentrated on the business at hand. Her marching orders from Washington would require more than a week to complete. With luck, she would be back at her desk in Paris with only a manageable backlog of cover work.

The scenery changed, signifying entrance into a new French *département*. Trees of the same height as before stood side-by-side. Trimmed into spheres, they approximated large green balloons. Lalumière saw the bureaucratic government's hand. No such government interference with nature would be allowed in his homeland, the Vosges.

Just then, Lalumière saw the girl snap to alert, something over the bow in the distance catching her attention. She shouted to him, but the noise of the outboard motor drowned her out. She slacked off the throttle with the remote.

"Quick. A patrol is coming. It is shining a bright light onto all of the boats. They must have discovered your escape. Quickly. Lean over the starboard side. Feign sickness."

Lalumière started to his left.

"No! They will approach on the port side. That way," she yelled as she pointed to his right.

He leaned over the gunwale just as the patrol boat with three gendarmes came alongside.

In French, the head gendarme asked her what was the matter with the man retching over the side in A-list Cannes Film Festival fashion.

"*Oh la la*," she gasped. "My father's stomach is weak. He hates the water. I thought the calm of a river ride would cure him." She gave a hopeless expression, holding the dimples at bay. She wanted them to lose interest and leave. Dimples would be counterproductive.

"Put him ashore up ahead. Three kilometers. You will see the village Romilly-sur-Seine on the starboard side, eh, to the south. There is an all-night clinic that can put him right, and a small *pension* where you can put up for the night. He will be better tomorrow. On dry land." The men-at-arms sailors laughed.

"*Oui. Merci,*" Sandrine said with a sincere, still worried look.

The gendarmes pushed off to continue their patrol back toward Paris.

"Don't stop yet," she whispered. "The sound carries. They will come back."

Lalumière continued to wretch, sure that, at any second, his stomach and intestines would pull free to become fish bait.

They passed a large white, corrugated metal building. Light caste a haze on a sign. Lalumière only made out the second word, *Nucléaire*. He smiled. Yes. Nuclear. Nuclear was the tool introduced to him by Monsieur Crayle. If only …

The landscape turned to rolling hills past Montbard. Yet another segment of his country. More diversity to rule. The challenges of the aristocracy of his forebears struck him. In a twist of fate, his capture had spared him their frustrations.

The remaining hours passed peacefully as they cruised past modern windmills, their 30-foot long blades spiraling in the breeze.

"There," Sandrine said as she smiled at her passenger. The lights of Châtillon-sur-Seine, a village of just under 6,000 residents, shone in the distance. She guided the boat to the riverside at the Seine headwaters just beyond the town. She lashed it to a mooring pole on the shore. Lalumière, ready to depart, paused when she held up a hand to him. She stepped back into the boat and unscrewed a plug at the bottom of the bait tank. As the boat took on water, she stepped to its side and extended her hand to him, like a lady alighting a carriage. She unlashed the boat and watched it slink downriver into deeper waters.

She moved close to her charge, pointing into the distance to a glow that indicated a large town. "Dijon. There will be a police awareness of your escape. We will bypass to the west."

She collected her things and led Lalumière to a detached garage nearby. Inside, they climbed into a faded green Citroën 2CV, the famous *Deux Chevaux*. Reaching up, she secured the ragtop. She placed a heavy black suitcase, also taken from the bait tank, into the tiny backseat. Sylvain's expression conveyed his curiosity about the potential treasures contained within. Perhaps a gun. Soon, he would know.

She by-passed the village and took a country road southwest to Saulieu. There the two caught The Six to Chalon-sur-Saône. "Stay here," she whispered to her charge. She completed the registration for them inside the Best Western St. Regis, keeping the fugitive out of sight.

The night registration clerk showed her and her luggage to a tiny elevator. She placed the bag inside, pushed a button, and motioned Sandrine to stairs that spiraled around the lift. When the clerk had gone, Sandrine gestured for Lalumière to follow her. They ascended to number 8.

Upon entering an outer, then an inner door, Sandrine cleared the room before allowing her charge to enter. As expected, the room was empty. To be safe, she checked under the bed. Empty. She noted that a six-inch mattress over a six-inch box spring would be adequate for entertaining the Frenchman. And the headboard, a quarter-inch from the wall, would produce sufficient noise to convince others that the two were lovers, not fugitives.

She surveyed the room. The writing desk, chair, and stool would be perfect for teaching Lalumière his role. She hoped he would be a willing student.

The outer walls, rather than forming a sharp corner, angled across, enabling a view of the intersection below. Sandrine opened the windowed doors, shutters, and stepped out onto the small balcony. The streets shone the glaze of a light sprinkle. A blue-on-white sign on the next building identified the narrow cross street as Rue Gloriette. Her escape route. A building diagonally across the intersection, embossed with '1899' at the top, dated the architecture. Its stone and artistic embellishments stood in sharp contrast to a modern apartment building in the distance. "New is quantitative. Old is qualitative. Older is better. Isn't that right, Renaissance Man?"

"I must agree. New is how much. Old is how beautiful. You are correct."

"Yes, I am." But there was something more important that the extant of historical disparity exhibited in Chalon. There were no signs or sounds of the police. She relaxed. Having pulled off the impossible felt good.

Her fastidious self—a remnant of her three years in medical school—took over. She arranged the desk top and night stands to her liking, then moved to the bathroom to rearrange the countertop. Wary of the virulent flu strain sweeping the continent, she quickly cleansed the relevant surfaces with a CIA-issue anti-viral wipe. "Sinks, tub, enclosed toilet, bidet. Perfect."

Lalumière now stood at the balcony. In the distance, he noticed a beautiful long river cruise liner. His fear of water diminished, he wished to travel in style his next time afloat. On such a craft.

Sandrine drew back the covers on the double bed. The exhausted Frenchman seemed disinclined to initiate touchy-feely repartee. Her obsession with control took over. She settled on the end of the bed. She leaned forward, and began on him. Thoughts dimmed as she progressed. He viewed her via a four-by-three foot wall mirror, this perspective transforming him into a spectator. She moved atop him, and his totality turned to her. There was no room for anything else. It was just as well.

• • •

A police car, its claxon expressing a Doppler Shift, approached, then passed. It brutally awakened Lalumière to his reality, a country-wide manhunt for him. One misstep, and all would be lost. Sandrine stood between him and a re-incarceration that would, this time, be for life. Of all the people he'd ever known, she was beyond capable. In a twisted sense, she symbolized perfection.

He clicked on the flat-screen TV. He viewed all stations, including English-language BBC World and CNN. The video was heavily pixilated and the sound broken. "It is the storm," he moaned. He understood nothing, turned it off, and headed for the bathroom to clean up. He hadn't seen Sandrine slip an interference sleeve over the television cable. She alone would control the news.

The morning sky remained overcast. Still, the opened corner doors let in welcome fresh, moist air—welcome to Lalumière versus the dank air of the Bastille.

In a blink, it was morning in Chalon. The sunlight bled around the embroidered curtains, casting the room in a soft hue. Unwilling to risk the breakfast salon, Sandrine ordered in. "Two coffees with saucers. Extra saucers for the breads, butter, and jars of jellies." Inventory complete, she served France's number one fugitive.

He sat on the sofa, and she on her heels on the vintage, pastel, Aubusson rug. He watched her. So like a little girl, he briefly reminded himself that she was a well-trained and experienced foreign agent. A spy. And he had seen for himself the deadly part. He must be careful not to over trust her. Too much was at stake.

Breakfast completed, the spy went to the closet and removed the black suitcase. She hefted it onto the bed. The trepidation in Lalumière showed. He opened his mouth as if to say, "No!" No words escaped. She opened the case. He would know soon.

Sandrine reached inside and removed an item encased in a velvet bag. She turned her face to him and displayed her trademark "this is so cool" dimpled smile. Sylvain Lalumière felt his control fragment. He ordered himself to take his eyes from her and to watch what she did with the bag.

"It is time to teach you your role, Monsieur," she said with such a soft voice, he felt lulled. "This is for you." She pulled a heavy item from the bag.

Heavy. Like a weapon. He caught his breath.

"*Voila!*" She displayed the item.

Not a gun. Lalumière resumed breathing.

"It is the iron mask," she declared.

He could tell by its heft that it could be iron. But, why? Why not a plastic mask? Why a mask at all?

"Hmmmmm?" she teased.

It hit him. The Alexander Dumas hero in The Man In The Iron Mask. A mask that had symbolized, for centuries, the imprisonment and maltreatment of a legitimate heir to the throne.

"Why do you bring this fake mask? Do you make a joke? It cannot be real and, therefore, it is a means of humiliating me at this dark moment," Lalumière lamented.

"*C'est la Vérité,*" retorted Sandrine. "It's real."

"*Non, n'est pas possible,*" Lalumière cried. "It has been lost. And even if it is real, why? It makes no sense."

"It makes perfect sense. The boat? The one I caught you ogling? It's our transportation south, to Marseille."

"But why the mask?" he persisted.

"Today, they have most certainly discovered that you have killed the guard and escaped. Your name and your face will be the most recognized in all of France. I have arranged for us to travel south on the *River Royale* with you in disguise. The boat will be full of Americans, Canadians, and Australians. Your English is near perfect. You will have to affect a French accent into your English, but you will be …" She extended her hands out to the sides in a 'ta-da' gesture. "… The Man In The Iron Mask. And I have decided to call you Mitim. It is a beautiful, symmetric name."

"I will wear that … that symbol of torture. Of injustice. Of repression of the ruling class. That …"

"In a word, yes. The publicity is already in place. We will spend the next several hours with your training. You must be ready to perform tonight."

"*Perform?*" Lalumière almost reconsidered his lust for ascendency. He sighed. "Alright."

"Your character is, as I have said, Mitim. You will stay in character at all times in public and not remove the mask. You know the story quite well, I am told."

Lalumière nodded. Sandrine fit the mask and straps to his head. Mask installed, Lalumière provided an accurate synopsis of the fabled story.

"You must focus your attention on the Americans, but you must entertain everyone. Do you understand these requirements, Monsieur Mitim?"

Lalumière started to nod, but the heavy weight of the iron was antithetical to controlled head movement. He would learn to move his head only for rare emphasis and in a slow manner. "*Oui*. Let us begin."

The training proceeded. Lalumière surprised himself. His mastery of the English language, combined with his natural ability to perform, produced a viable replica of an entertainer. He appeared frightened, but ready to "give it a go" as the Brits were wont to say. And he realized at once that the non-European, English speakers would be the least likely in all of France to discern the identity of the man concealed behind the iron mask. It was brilliant. He wanted to give the girl-spy, Sandrine, a kiss and make love to her once again, but she was so like his eldest daughter in age, he discarded the notion in short order.

Lalumière repacked his newfound identity while the girl paid for the room on-line. The duo exited the hotel onto the *Boulevard de La République* through a side door.

CHAPTER 6

They made their way from the hotel to the docks, Lalumière clad in a deep-hooded monastic cloak. He gazed downward so no passerby would recognize his face. The greater disguise was the beard he had grown since his capture. It was just long enough to obviate the need for further camouflage. Sandrine preceded him, making frontal recognition even more difficult, and she provided eyes lest he run into something or fall into the river. She regarded his sighs as the effects of incarceration and the trip by boat. In reality, Lalumière watched her girlish figure, which displayed just enough of her sensual nature to engender lust in his heart.

The boat's hull announced itself as the River Royale. The vessel proved even more striking up close. It seemed quite long, boasting a main deck, one above, and a sun deck on top. It gave the appearance of two long boats melded to form one.

Sandrine believed an external orientation was necessary. "They always dock them facing upstream. On this side of the river, the port, or left, side is against the quay. The aft half of the boat contains three stateroom decks—living quarters. The forward half provides space for a large lounge and, below that, a formal restaurant. There …" She pointed to the upper half. "… is where you, as Mitim, will perform."

Lalumière scanned the Royale from bow to stern. There, in its docile manner, sat the vehicle to his dreams.

They approached the gray metal gangway guided by rows of service lights, but the dock area retained a gloomy appearance. The incessant screeching of waterfowl completed the Poe-like atmosphere. Sandrine led him down, to the left, and then right to closed doors on the boat's starboard side. She knocked twice, then once, then twice. Inside, an older man brushed aside the doors' porthole curtain and inspected the pair. He opened his door a crack, whispering, "Ees thees heem?"

Sandrine responded alike in French-accented English, "Thees ees Meeteem."

The man abandoned the accent. "And you are his attendant, Sandrine?"

The verbal handshake completed in English, the man allowed them inside and fastened the door behind. Sandrine turned and peered through the porthole. She scanned the docks left, right, and center for any sign of followers. She saw no one.

The interior was dimly lit as the older man led them past a registration desk to the middle of the 361-foot boat and up to the Azure deck. On their left, a sign proclaimed the space inside to be the Renoir Lounge. He guided them aft, up a short set of stairs and down a hallway, finally showing them into a large starboard-side room. The only suite on the River Royale, a luxury river cruiser, this accommodation was the only one appropriate for Mitim.

"The suite is sumptuous for a river boat, Monsieur Mitim." The old man addressed the man in the room, as was tradition. "It is, in American terms, 217 square feet."

Mitim glanced about. The drapes of blue, white, and gold vertical panels directly across from the doorway caught his eye. The old man noticed.

"The drapes are drawn for your privacy from the dock. When the sun has disappeared to the west, you may wish to draw them. They hide a floor-to-ceiling sliding door. Perhaps an approximate ten feet of crystal clear glass will provide you a romantic view of the shore lights." He glanced at Sandrine. He mistook her innocent, youthful appearance as that of one to be romanced. She returned his look, her lips laboring to restrain a smile as her mind enumerated the ways and means of dispatching this new witness. She smiled. "Yes, and the sunsets are to die for."

To their right was a partition, no more than a foot on each side, that separated a work area—modern wooden desk, a small round service table, and chair—from the bedroom in which they now stood. To the desk's left, more curtain and, no doubt, more window. A chrome silver ice bucket, replete with chilling champagne, sat atop the short table. It portended a romantic interlude. Sandrine, accustomed to a room that oozed French, felt the warmth on each and every encounter. And she felt the sex. Surely, she thought, a glass of fine French bubbly and an intercourse *hors-d'oeuvre* would relax Mitim for the night's performance—his first. The little spy filed the notion.

She continued her reconnaissance. A medium blue carpet patterned with white stylized emblems covered the floor. The ceiling glowed off-white, the flat surface broken by a sparse collection of recessed lights. Later, when she performed a sweep, she would check them for electronic bugs. She saved the best for last. The bed to her left, large enough to accommodate two lovers in any position, screamed Kama Sutra. The Egyptian white linen had been turned down over a single light brown blanket to a length of three feet. Sandrine loved the stark brightness. Her heart rate escalated. She imagined it painted, Jackson Pollock style, with rich, red human blood. She glanced back at the old man. Her gaze said, "Thank you for your assistance. *Au revoir*."

No additional words were spoken. The man seemed to be genuinely pleased with his new passengers. Lalumière assumed he'd been well compensated. In reality, the boat's cruise director had been duped earlier by the spy with the mission-name Sandrine—no money had changed hands. Future high-spending, American tourists would be directed to the cruise line by the American Embassy in Paris.

Sandrine noted the dead silence that pervaded the boat. "The passengers will not board until later today, but where are the crew?"

"A mysterious and anonymous benefactor arranged for them all to have the morning off in celebration of the new left-wing government. It seems he was overjoyed by the election results." The older man shrugged. Very French.

CHAPTER 7

Sandrine ensured the old man was out of sight before she closed and latched the door. She turned to find Lalumière stretched out on the queen-sized bed, eyes closed, and his body turned away from the curtained window with its murky light spilling through.

Lalumière surrendered to a deep sleep. Sandrine walked to the window and parted the curtains. She unlatched the sliding glass door and took the short step forward to the shallow French balcony afforded cabins on the top deck. She saw people coming their way, boat staff by their attire. They would prep for the embarkation. The 130 additional guests would board in a few hours. She breathed deeply. While the smells and sounds of the river heightened her senses and gave her pleasure, it was not the extreme visceral and sexual pleasure over which she obsessed. Perhaps she would start a bucket list. Perhaps the old man would be first.

Finished with that thought, she closed the door and drapes, and took a seat at the desk. She examined her syllabus for Mitim. She would prep Lalumière once more before his first performance. Tonight.

• • •

It was six in the evening when Lalumière woke with a start. He glanced in all directions, having lost his bearings. Then he saw her.

She heard the commotion and turned. Her pretty little smile bookended by the two cute dimples brought him back. She hoisted the iron mask to complete the context.

There was something else.

"It is only the boat moving," she soothed. "It caused you to nap well. We need to practice once again for your debut."

"I am hungry. I must eat."

As if on cue, a knock sounded. Sandrine admitted the maid, who carried a tray of hot food. Its aroma wafted to the Frenchman. He closed his eyes, this time savoring the smells of *steak haché* and *frites*. Though the chopped steak and fries were covered to retain the heat, he felt certain he could list the ingredients.

"Just set it next to him." Sandrine watched with care to see if the maid recognized France's number one fugitive. She did not. She was allowed to depart.

"We'll eat on the bed. Then, more practice."

• • •

At 7:30, she announced, "It's time, Mitim."

He donned the period clothing of a prisoner and she, the garb of an attendant. At last, she placed the mask over his head.

"The ship's guests have already dined. They are by now assembled in the Renoir Lounge for the captain's greeting and a toast to their trip. We're outta here."

• • •

The lounge, approximately 80 feet by 20 feet, was standing room only. Guests sat on couches and at bar tables. The four-foot high widows that lined the lounge walls were covered by drapes or Roman shades, their red, gold, silver, and bronze colorings oozing warmth and class. Sandrine had arranged for them to be closed.

She leaned close to Lalumière. She whispered, "The furnishings were chosen to create an expectation of royalty. The ambience readies their minds to accept what you *should* be."

Mitim nodded. He observed from his place in the shadows a happy crowd. Typical, he knew, of Americans.

One of the night desk crew, also on the payroll, pushed a centuries-old wheel chair up behind Mitim. Instead of the modern large wheels on each side, it rolled on casters that adorned each of four legs. Its walnut wood spoke of another time.

The timing proved perfect. Just as the captain turned to the doors and announced the special guest, she propelled the chair to a wooden platform in the center of the room. A spotlight illuminated the pair. The ambient buzz of the guests halted. Dead silence.

Sandrine spoke, "*Monsieurs et mesdames*—ladies and gentlemen. I give you Mitim, the *Man* … In The Iron Mask."

In the confined space, the applause deafened. Mitim briefly feasted on the aggrandizement. He rose with affected difficulty. The heavy iron mask strained his neck muscles as he straightened to his full height. He decided to treat his audience as countrymen, practice for the day he would make the speech for real. To thousands.

He hoisted his hands, bound now by the actual rusted iron cuffs and chains of the original. "My dear subjects, I have come, as you can see, in the bonds of the minions of mediocracy." A sympathetic boo came from the crowd. He recognized this manner of behavior from American late night television shows, but the response thrust him even deeper into his role.

"These selfsame denizens of Paris have driven us deeper into debt, have removed any potential for entrepreneurship and growth, and now seem obsessed with driving the stake of bankruptcy into the heart …" He paused. "… of our beloved France."

The Americans cheered. Many stood and applauded. They could relate.

Through her smile, Sandrine whispered, "Keep it short, Mitim. Less is more."

Mitim ramped up. "The day comes when I shall break these chains." Again, he raised his manacled hands for all to see. Again the cheers. "I will travel to Paris. I will have my day. I will … be King."

This time, the crescendo of hoots, hollers, applause, and expletives deafened all present. It drove Mitim over the top. He would, indeed, achieve his goals. He would assault the blackguards of Paris. He would see them all dead for their misdeeds. He *would* be King.

Sylvain Lalumière, still in the guise of the iron-masked captive of old, bowed his head to the crowd. Led by his attendant, he exited the lounge. His authentic chains rattled a sort of arrhythmic drum roll. The cacophony of adulation faded as she guided him to their suite and shut the door.

"I will not sleep tonight, Sandrine. I must plot my next move. I must address Frenchmen. And you, at the direction of my fellow Illuminé, must insure my success."

"Whoa, tiger. Let's not get ahead of ourselves. Everything is planned to the last detail. And I work for one of the top honchos at Langley. What do you mean by Illuminé?"

CHAPTER 8

The view from Victoria Peak at daybreak was, as always, spectacular. When Chin Yao-wu glanced east, he witnessed a glow as the edge of the red disk on the horizon began its day. The visibility of the surrounds increased apace. It gave up the endless sea. And to the south, Mount Stenhouse, which protected the Y-shaped island known as Lamma. His gaze swept west to the island, Lantau, home of the new international airport and larger by half than the one beneath his feet, his home island of Hong Kong. The new airport replaced the old Kai Tak, whose runway still poked a vulgar gesture into Victoria Harbour. Any plane that ventured left or right or landed short, would hit the harbor at over a hundred miles per hour. In this case, Chin noted, change was good.

And last, the view north. There, across the harbor, the infamous runway dead-ended into the mainland metropolis called Kowloon. The city still provided refuge and residence to the millions who'd fled the Communist takeover, only to be handed back by the British many decades later. Chin's ascendency would provide them permanent relief, but courting millions in a country of a thousand millions would be folly.

His eyes dropped to the panoply of commotion in his home city below. Hong Kong's skyscrapers hid only a portion of the human menagerie, and the walls formed by them only intensified the din. Still, he loved it so. Down and to the right, he saw his Dragon Building as the morning light began its liaison with the golden glass that formed its sides. The Dragon had been home and workplace for most of his life. He had amassed his stock market fortune there.

Chin had also acquired and educated his *daughters* in that place. He missed them for short periods of estrangement such as this morning's visitation to the peak. He turned and signaled his pair of outsized bodyguards. The Peak Tramway ride down would be a mere four-point-nine minutes. Then, the car to the Wanchai district, home to the Dragon. On the ride down, he thought of Red daughter and her technical savvy and ambition. At eighteen, she was young but not to be trifled with. Most of all, his thoughts fell upon Black daughter. He knew he could never touch her in a classic meeting of the flesh, but he could not free his mind of her presence.

But enough of his sexual misery. The black limousine whisked him back to the Dragon Building. Thirty seconds later, he was safely ensconced in his office.

"Gold daughter," he called.

Within ten seconds Gold stood before him. "Yes, Father," she said as she bowed her obeisance.

"General Li arrives at noon. Bring him directly here. Tell new Beige daughter that the general will have no time for the relaxation period and de-stressing activity she was scheduled to provide. Inform her that she will engage with him next time. And see to it that I am not disturbed prior to the meeting with Li. Much preparation is required."

Gold bowed and exited through the two large black lacquered and ornately carved doors.

• • •

At precisely noon, the doors opened again. Gold ushered in the general. Since he had been to the office several times, all daughters and bodyguards knew him by sight. Identification validation was not required.

"So good to see you again, Li. You are looking fit and well. Gold, please provide us our usual fare, a fine single-malt Scotch. You may select this time—make it a twenty year cask or better. And do not bother with the Yangtze River water Green brought last time. Make it the Norwegian Voss." For a heartbeat, he lingered on the remembrance of his village of birth at the headwaters of the Yangtze.

Gold bowed and returned with the goods in minutes. Without a word or a glance at the two men, she soon departed.

"I am hoping a toast is in order, Li." Chin poured the requisite three fingers and dollop of arctic water into each glass. "I have waited weeks for good news."

"I understand, Chin. The last major news was the nuclear bombing I affected at the underground facility in central Iran. I must credit our leading edge technology. The radiation sponge sucked all but two percent of the radiation from the explosion. The mini-nuke, as you prefer to call it, became just a compact version of millions of tons of dynamite. No cases of radiation sickness were reported, and the only deaths occurred in the subterranean nuclear hideout of the Iranians. Great credit is due your French associate, whom I met prior to leaving Iran. His water tunnel made it possible."

"Yes. You will meet him again at the appropriate time, General. However, a China-France axis is unknown to anyone at this time, and we must not speak of him. Unless, of course, I bring it up."

"You are careful. I like that. With what we have at stake, great care is a necessary evil. I need not mention that, if we are exposed, we both die."

"We shall succeed, Li. That is the only option. And the explosion exceeded my expectations by far. The entire West, plus the Russians, are just catching their breaths. All doubt that the Iranians had nuclear weapons was destroyed in that blast. The American president, ever the dove, has been forced to lose face and place 350,000 troops in

Iraq and Afghanistan. Both governments feigned protest at the return of Americans, but both fear a nuclear Iran. Another 100,000 troops have been added to America's Qatar and Saudi resources. And we must not forget the fifty-percent increase in logistical support. They prepare for invasion."

Li nodded. He also observed Chin's familiarity with military force deployments, not merely global political and financial realities. "Even the Germans have anteed up a ground and air force. And understand this. Both of these powerful allies told the French and the Italians to stay home. It demonstrates how seriously they take the situation. All allies of the West have experienced the political damage you forecasted."

Chin refilled their empty glasses. It was hard to merely *sip* the whisky under the current circumstances.

"The plan is coming along nicely, Li. The World has taken the bait. All eyes of import are elsewhere. We have forced Beijing to ride a roller coaster of public emotion. Our capitalist-empowered new prosperity class wishes Beijing to cease and desist any atomic energy assistance to Iran, while somehow maintaining a steady resource of crude and refined oil products to support our burgeoning industries."

"Yes. It has been forecasted that we will exceed the United States in GDP in seven years." Li chuckled. "I watch CNBC World now."

"Good. You are paying close attention to financial happenings. As you are well aware, I succeeded beyond my dreams in the financial arena. I promise you, here and now, to engineer your personal wealth to exceed fifty million Yuan within three years."

Li felt stunned. All of his nuclear wheelings and dealings, at lethal risk, had netted him a cool $160,000 U.S. Compared to the average Chinese income of 40,000 Yuan, a mere $6,000 in the People's Republic of America, he had accomplished well. With difficulty, he maintained his demeanor.

"That, on top of your position as head of all Chinese armed forces. I will handle the non-military aspect of governance with assistance from my Red daughter. She has become adept at all computerized aspects of capital formation and utilization."

The general nodded. To a Westerner, he would, indeed, be a difficult read. Not to Chin. He prepared his answer in anticipation of his guest's next question. "Yes, the Red daughter is efficient, adept, and loyal. But, Chin, what will become of Black daughter? I believe you are aware that she prevails on my mind. With all due respect, of course."

"I am aware. Black is elegant, learned, and highly skilled in her own right." Chin omitted details of her adeptness in the deadliest of martial arts. He could only utilize her as bait for a limited time. Li would become demanding. Two facts mitigated the danger. One, Black knew too much for Chin's own good, because he routinely used his *daughters* as sounding boards, mostly in his own expositions. And, two, his long standing policy of graduating daughters at age twenty, celebrating their emancipation from his control, and then having them led away by the eunuchs to be quietly executed.

It solved Chin's political heresy problem and the potential violation of his own celibacy dictum. Truth told, his unfortunate attachment to Black daughter strengthened by the day. He had even degenerated into keeping a chain-of-life for her. One ring of paper for each month remaining in her existence—less than two dozen. Li could never know, of course, and Chin would continue to dangle the possibility of reward at arm's length.

As had her predecessors, Black daughter would die a virgin. It was the perpetual gift of respect that Chin bestowed upon his murdered mother and the rape that had provided him, the next emperor of China, life.

The general changed the subject. "Beijing does not have a clue. Already the protesters camp in Tiannenmen Square. They blame the government for its open support of the Iranian regime. I personally think they're angry that the Americans have turned a cold shoulder to bi-lateral trade, and the protesters can only get knockoffs instead of the real American goods they crave. Beijing tries to please them, but knockoff concerts of Aerosmith and Lady Gaga do not seem to work."

"Yes. Beijing is on the ropes. Now, we must get down to business. You have spent the past three weeks out west in the province of Xinjiang. Is everything in place for our next move?" Chin uncharacteristically displayed his anxiety. It was the make or break second step of Crayle's three-phase design, and it needed to be carried off without error.

Li took a gulp of the Scotch. "Chin Yao-Wu, I have great news. Even better than great. We took the military team to supervise the great water infrastructure build out in the western provincial capital, Ürümqi. The Frenchman supplied the experts, and we instructed the Uighurs—the Muslims—in all of the skills required. They were all quite eager to transform their large state and, I am sure, have hatched a number of backroom plots to turn their semi-autonomous existence into its own Islamic law country. In the process, we slipped in the second of the bombs." Li handed Chin a special universal remote control. "This is identical to the one used by the Frenchman to initiate the Iranian blast. It has access worldwide. Press the Mode button and then the triangle-shaped button marked with an A. You are then ready to detonate the A-bomb. Just press Play." Li pointed to the buttons as he described the process. "Press Stop if you wish to cancel the sequence."

"The Frenchman would say *voilá*, Li. And I can watch it in real-time on my South Korean HD large screen?"

"Just have it on. Everything has been taken care of."

"I am, indeed, pleased. The Iranian bomb was deduced by the world scientists to be particularly unstable. The Uighur bomb will be likewise. It will be deemed to have been of the same ilk, supplied by the Iranians and brought to China to threaten Beijing. To extort independence. I promise you, Li, you shall be present for the event. Perhaps some popcorn will accompany our Scotch. And then there will be relaxation. You must soon travel to Beijing, General, to make the arrangements we spoke of. The trip will be under cover of your interim promotion to Vice Chairman of the military."

"You have guided me and shown a caliber of leadership like none our country has seen since …"

"The first emperor? He who began China. Our country's wonder and greatness have been directed into abeyance these many centuries. I, with you next to me, shall return China and its people to their destiny. Now, go, and go safely. There can be no mistakes. We enter the *home stretch*, as the American Crayle pronounced it, with our very next acts. I will procure the financial necessities by means of the water diamonds the Frenchman sent prior to his capture … and subsequent removal from the European rendition of the Blackstone Strategy."

"Until then." Li rose. Gold appeared from out of nowhere to escort him from the building.

Chin poured a third drink. He motioned at the guards. "Send in Black."

In his beloved mother's memory, he would not defile her body, but Black would pleasure him to grand ecstasy. He would take account of the world situation tomorrow, then schedule another meet with Li. They approached the mid-point in the grand strategy. As the American Crayle had admonished, timing and detail were as crucial now as ever.

CHAPTER 9

The top twelve members of the Hong Kong media had been selected and ushered into the Learning Center in Chin Yao-wu's Dragon Building. They took the stage-facing seats normally occupied by Chin's twelve daughters. Awestruck at the opulence of the room, they gazed up at the hundreds of long silver rods dangling from the ceiling. None knew of the compressed air system hidden in the ceiling, which could fire one or multiple bolts downward upon activation by Chin.

Once they recorded their depictions of the room, the lights dimmed. A bright spotlight played on a lone chair—a throne—on the stage. The curtains at the rear of the stage parted, and Chin made his grand entrance.

"Gentlemen and Ladies. It is good to have you here this afternoon. I hope you find your seating comfortable. As you know, I am quite the private man and this is the first interview I have ever granted. You are the elite of the Hong Kong media, and I trust you will report today's conference with accuracy, devoid of embellishment."

Chin knew the media game well. As soon as they could, these mongrels would scurry for their lairs and try to outdo each other. It was predictable enough for Chin to count on.

"In order that you may stay in touch with the world, I have made a special addition to this room."

Chin's control console rotated from the stage to his lap. He picked up a remote control and pressed a button. Screens lowered from the bolt-free ceiling above the stage on either side of him.

"I have disabled the sound system for obvious reasons. However, should earth-shattering news occur, the sound will break in. Are we ready?"

The media-hawks nodded in unison.

"As all of you know, I have done quite well for myself in the Hong Kong and Shanghai stock markets."

A woman coughed. Chin reached spontaneously for the button appropriate to her location, but caught himself. Curiously, she sat in the same chair as the former Beige daughter. At Beige's insolence, Chin had, indeed, pushed the button. A silver metal bolt had shot from the ceiling and pierced her skull. It would not do to teach the media representatives the same object lesson. At least, not in this venue.

"Beijing has apparently agreed to work with the Devil. A Devil that will drag us into its self-made Hell. A subset of Islam attempts to devour itself by its incessant prodding of the Western superpowers, much as an ignorant child might prod a restive tiger. A Westerner, brilliant in these matters, characterized the situation to me as *assisted suicide* … on the part of the Islamists. It is of note that our China has labored intensively and extensively to build a strong reputation. We are a good neighbor in the East and in the World, as it is now constituted. Such a reputation is slow to be achieved, but quick to be lost. Dear members of the press, Iran has the bomb."

Chin let the thought linger, having cleverly juxtaposed Beijing's aid with the apparent advent of Iranian nuclear proclivity. The media would connect the dots.

"By sharing our technologies for peaceful purposes, I fear we are in the process of a tragic and devastating loss. We and the rest of the world observed the explosion in the central region of that country, an area in which the necessary water supply for nuclear development was thought to be unavailable. World leaders are pointing their fingers, not only at Iran, but at China. That is why it is necessary for me to speak up. Through you."

The media types took Chin's bait. They turned to each other, heads bobbing up and down in concurrence.

"Our leaders in Beijing have tried to explain, but to no avail. They do not understand that the large, far west province of Xinjiang has a majority population of Muslims that could be influenced by the Iranians. They could be persuaded to accept one of these unstable nuclear weapons and use it to extort full independence from China. Unthinkable. Members of the media, our leaders have a great deal on their plates. The United States is forever a threat. And there is the grand influx of undocumented workers across China's southern border. North Korea, our ally, sometimes behaves like a recalcitrant child."

A thirty-ish female member of the media, appointed as interviewer, gathered the courage to pose a question. "You have been quite successful, Chin, within our new financial system of well-being. What would you suggest Beijing do?"

"I am convinced we must change course. I am respectful of those in our top circle in Beijing. The challenge of governance in the 21st Century world has been replayed again and again. First Southern Europe. Now the French and the Swedes. Southeast Asia. Most of Central and South America. Mexico. The riots are a sign of the grief of the masses. With greatest respect for Chairman Mao and his achievements, it appears that Communism has run its course."

His audience gasped as one.

"May I interrupt, Chin? Run its course? It is our way of life. Karl Marx—"

"Mr. Marx specified our current form of governance under the constraint that the evil ideology, Capitalism, would destroy itself. As we have seen, and I am the perfect example, an adequate blend of care for the masses and capitalism will carry the day. We are not there, but enlightened leadership could complete the journey. China's journey. Our journey."

The Chinese media never applauded an interviewee. Were it possible, they would have done so in this instance.

Chin completed his thought. "A necessary and sufficient leader to that purpose will be required."

"But, if not Beijing, who will lead us to the sort of governance Nirvana you have described? Are you suggesting …"

By the interviewer's use of *us*, he had changed the focus of consideration away from the masses. *Us* meant that the media saw its own skin in the game.

"Myself? I feel I have the modern success story in hand. And, while I am highly educated and have a high degree of proficiency in international and domestic affairs, I am afraid I would have to be called to service by the masses. Through your eyes, of course."

"But the masses, except for the usual protests, seem content."

"They are approaching a tipping point. No one has attacked our mainland as America suffered. Recall that the 9/11 event surprised everyone."

The young woman tilted her head. "Do you really believe such an attack could occur here?"

"It is impossible to predict, but if Beijing is viewed as enabling an attack, the masses might respond. Without credible leadership, chaos would ensue. In that circumstance, for the worse, but possibly for the better."

"Your words are strong. As always, you have provided the people with your superior insights and vision," said the interviewer.

"I consider it a precious gift to be able to express my thoughts."

The media spokesperson stood. "Thank you, Chin Yao-wu. We live in a serious world." She spoke to a fixed camera. "Liu Su-mei, signing off from the Dragon Building, Wanchai, Hong Kong, China."

She removed the lavalier mike from her blouse, bowed to the mogul, and was escorted by Green daughter to her ride back to the studio. Chin knew the studio had already collected the remote video via Wi-Fi. It would be replicated and stored with the sanctity and security afforded a roomful of gold bars. Chin's statements were that precious to the people of China. And this was his first video interview … ever.

The people respected Chin's rise from a poor, central China village to his current high position. He gave them hope. The studio would dote on each of his well-chosen, but rapier-sharp words. Absent the current infighting, Beijing would have been outraged. Even so, visiting their wrath upon Chin could precipitate the very unplanned event that Chin had portended. They were trapped by Chin's application of Crayle's simple appearing, but ingenious strategy—between a number of rocks and a multitude of hard places.

"Now would be a good time for all of you to take a break before returning to your offices. You will receive tea service. Please feel free to speak amongst yourselves."

Chin stood and exited through the curtains. Once out of sight, he lifted the remote control device. He pressed the Mode and A setup buttons. Then, Play.

Two screens flashed on. The reporters recognized the International Bazaar that symbolized the 21.8 million citizen, Xinjiang capital, Ürümqi. As the buildings of the city began to shake and fall, the center of the city rose toward the heavens. Chin's $100,000 sound system accurately captured the intensity of the explosion. The room itself, gimbaled for sound isolation, shook from the low frequency subwoofer output. The silver bolts overhead swayed and clanged as they processed the multitude of frequencies. Men and women alike screamed. Some tried to escape, but the huge double doors remained locked.

Let them panic, Chin thought. Soon enough, they would turn their attention to the screens. They'll view the devastation. And, prompted by my words, will extrapolate what has happened into a new danger to China far surpassing any that exists or ever has existed.

It happened just that way. A hush settled over the reporters. They all returned to their seats. The shaking and rumbling faded, leaving the specter of an enormous mushroom cloud rising above the flattened city center. Chin made his re-entry.

"Please, please. Everyone remain calm. I have just been informed of the tragedy in our farthest west province. It appears I spoke none too soon. A nuclear device has been brought into our country. It must have been one of the volatile and unstable Iranian bombs. I am sure Beijing will respond appropriately to demonstrate to the leaders of Iran just how unacceptable and foolhardy their action has been. Everyone has seen this video. You must hurry to your offices and meet your deadlines. I will schedule another conference when I've had time to process this assault on our land. Thank you."

Chin's last two words cued the opening of the doors. The reporters, pushing and shoving, fled. The doors closed after the last person departed. Twelve minutes passed.

Chin sat on the riser and addressed his console. He selected the twenty-four hour news channel, which reported a tragic incident in front of the Wo Fat media station. Regrettably, journalist Liu Su-mei had been killed by a hit-and-run motorist. But, thanks to good fortune, her final interview with Chin Yao-wu was *in the can*. It would be aired at five o'clock, along with a memorial tag for the reporter.

Chin smiled faintly. Liu was a talented young woman. Her loss to the station assured that neither the complete scripting and timing of the interview, or the promise of a beachfront condo in Hawaii and substantial remuneration, would ever come to light. That her violent death provided additional punctuation to the story was not lost on him.

Red daughter had performed well, but her success exited his mind in the next instant. Black daughter appeared backstage. She sank to her knees to give Father what he deserved at this hour of great success.

CHAPTER 10

Crayle sat in one of the unfinished teak chairs on the rear deck of the Fawnskin cabin. Six days had passed since his return. The cabin represented home, because his memories only went back twenty-two days, all told. In that period of time he had travelled to foreign continents, fought several small battles, laid siege to a French château, and discovered his pivotal role in plots to conquer two of the planet's premier nations. In the process, he'd met and become sexually involved with three women, each one beautiful in her own way. His mode of transportation, a sumptuous personal jet Crayle felt certain belonged to the CIA. He had circled the globe, accumulating at least 24,000 frequent spier miles. He made a mental note to ask Jack for the Top Secret Rewards Catalog he felt sure must exist.

He glanced past the free-standing garage at the big house, remembering his intimate encounter with Phoebe. He released a deep sigh and glanced left—to the lake. The terrain down to the lake, sparsely decorated with snow and ice patches, justified the cargo pants and maroon sweatshirt he'd borrowed from Jack's closet to counter the morning chill. Sunlight filtered through the branches of the tall pine in the yard's center. For the first time since his arrival at the cabin, he felt at peace—

"Yo! Magus Crayle, sir. Let's eat!" Lenny yelled as he pushed out the door, bearing a large, carved mahogany tray. He set it on the table with a clatter.

Crayle bade farewell to peace, and he turned his attention to the bacon, eggs, and corned beef hash to be chased with a large glass of fresh-squeezed orange juice. He took a drink, then held the glass away as if it contained something putrid. "What in God's name is that? Orange juice isn't carbonated. I, at least, remember that."

"The bubbles, MC, are some of Jack's finest champagne—*Cristal,* the bottle said. He won't mind. But more importantly, what we have here," he said, clinking glasses, "is fresh-squeezed Mimosas. Yum."

Crayle decided to acquire the taste. Lenny, even in small doses, was best taken with alcohol.

"Oh, I almost forgot!" Lenny jumped up and rushed inside. He returned with an item about a foot long and rectangular in shape. "This is from your carton. The one my dad prepared from your desk at *company* headquarters." He handed it to Crayle. "Here. Put this on. I tried it already. Your belt slips through there and the ties hold it against your thigh."

"It's a slide rule, Lenny. Not something I need."

"Listen to the old P.I., Mag. It's the only physical link you have to your family. That Asian character, Chin, told you your dad was over there in Hong Kong during the Vietnam thing. If you have it touching your body, maybe some of his vibes will seep in. Maybe you'll remember him."

"I don't—"

"Just try it out for a few days. I think that Chin guy knows a lot more than he let on, but we'll probably never see him again."

"We?"

"As far as Jack has told me, I'm still on the case." He plucked a check from his shirt pocket. "They wouldn't pay me if—"

"Lenny, the CIA is government, an entity that pays for things whether they produce or not."

Lenny pushed out his lower lip.

"I'm sorry, Lenny. I didn't mean you. I meant in general. It's just that I've read some of the old papers Jack keeps around the cabin, and I noticed some things. The government has been the champion of the poor forever, but they're still poor. If the government had just given the poor the money, instead of spending it on dozens of worthless projects, the poor would all be rich."

"I feel their pain, MC, but I learned long ago that it's best to avoid that kind of thinking. It just bums you out."

"I suppose you're right." With that, Crayle slipped the slide rule onto his belt and lashed it flush to his leg.

"Okay, Father Crayle," said Lenny, "speak to him."

Nothing. The only sounds for the next several minutes—wind blowing, leaves rustling, and the chatter of a bushy-tailed gray squirrel.

"Be patient, grasshopper. Alona believes in this astrology shit—I'll call her over."

"Forget it. I'll wear the damn thing. If it conjures up anything other than a pain in the ass," he said as he glared at Lenny, "I'll owe you one."

Jack exited the secret kitchen door and plodded toward the two men. "I need to have a private with Magus." Regardless, Lenny followed Crayle inside. "Okay, P.I. Scram! *Vite!*" Jack liked to use the French word for scram as well. A pouting Lenny stalked back outside, took a seat where he could be seen, and attempted to evoke an aura of guilt. Without notice, and apropos of the unplanned nature of the past week, Phoebe and Micmac arrived. Jack, post pleasantries, hustled them out to the deck with Lenny. He also fetched them a cooler of alcoholic liquids and a tray of crudités with Ranch dip. In seconds, the three were mutually engaged in laughter and knee slapping camaraderie. Lenny appeared to be, once again, in his element.

Jack surveyed the perimeter. All looked good. Privacy achieved.

"So, how about that little *to do* at the hospital?" he asked, taking a seat beside Crayle.

"Jack, I needed to be semi-awake for the memory read. I heard Dr. Rorschach tell that to a nurse. Then, he talked, as he does, to no one in particular. He went on about wanting to delete a section of my new memories. Another experiment. He didn't say which ones. Some of the new memories, since the crash, have become precious to me. An adrenalin rush came over me."

"So, you threw off Rorschach's scan cap and ran in order to keep those memories?"

"Yes. It sounds crazy. I wanted the ones in every detail of those people for whom I have feelings, and I needed the ones that are a sight and sound record of all of the attempts on my life."

"You mean the Tack Store and the cabin attack here, the rooftop attack in Hong Kong, the attempt at the chapel, and your assault on the Frenchman's château. Why?"

"Jack, with all my normal memories erased by the crash just a little over forty days ago, I need all the new ones."

"Why, Magus? You survived them all. Why not get those bad memories gone and just keep the good ones? Hell, I'd take that option if it were offered."

"Don't you see? As I recovered from the crash on the Pacific Coast Highway, Lenny figured out that I had been a mathematician for the government. Jack, I bested my attackers with honed firearm and hand-to-hand combat skills. For a mathematician, that doesn't compute."

"Maybe you served other purposes for the government as well." Jack wanted to kick himself. He had launched the dialog into dangerous waters.

Crayle took a long look at Jack, but continued to express his thoughts. "After the Tack Store, I was given an amulet for protection." He held up his right arm to display three half-inch wide leather strips, interwoven to form a bracelet. Embossed in the leather were images of birds in flight. They were painted white and contrasted with the dark brown leather.

"The Indian gave that to you. The Serrano girl."

"I could have died many times, but I survived."

"Oh. I forgot." Jack drew a folded paper from his shirt pocket and handed it to Crayle. "Sorry."

Crayle read the note. "She wants to see me. Look, it's signed *H.*" He showed it to Jack.

"Then get the hell over there. I gotta take a little trip back east. We'll catch up when I return. And remember this one thing. All this," he pointed to his head, "is classified. You can't tell, what's her name, uh, Hekka, anything."

The trio outside on the deck, still fully engaged in laughter and harmless banter, did not realize that they may have seen Crayle for the last time.

CHAPTER 11

Jack Sommers' flight in the Falcon 7X terminated mid-afternoon at Washington D.C.'s National Airport. He had been comforted by a fully stocked bar and drinks served up in perfect fashion by Flori, who served up sex with equanimity. He arrived suitably refreshed and numbed, ready for another of his all too frequent encounters with his boss.

He knew the drill. Get dropped off at the Manassas Bull Run battlefield, enter the bricked enclosure of porta potties behind the visitor center, and—what the hell?

There, standing in front of the only potty with a red *Occupied* indicator showing, wobbled a man, obviously drunk, yanking unsuccessfully at the locked door. It was the potty that Jack required.

"Hey!" No response. Jack tried again. Nothing. Facing away from Jack, the drunk showed no notice of his presence. Jack was nothing if not resourceful. He stepped into the green-indicated potty next door, and then stepped out, holding open the door. He reached over with his free hand and grabbed the drunk by the shoulder. The man turned.

"Here. This one works." He nodded inside.

The man took a second to move the thought through his encumbered brain, then stumbled inside.

With the *Occupied* sign still in full force, Jack's proximity card allowed him entry next door. He followed the ritual urine sample protocol. In seconds, the inner shell raced below ground to the subterranean CIA and its Strategic Situations Office, SSO. Jack felt that his boss, Neil Wohlford, had a thing about the underground. Add these offices to the clandestine hospital in California and ...

"I have found the mole!" Jack intoned. Before he could laugh at his own humor, he heard a soft, effeminate voice from the computerized system. One he recognized immediately.

"Silence in the elevator, Jack," came Neil's aristocratic admonition.

"Sorry."

"Silence, Jack?" came the rhetorical.

He stepped out of the elevator into the psych-ward-painted hallway. As he made his way along, he twirled from side to side, his eyes engaged with the new greener green walls. Chartreuse. Surplus color. Jack pushed a button to remove his sunglasses' tint. He thumbed a wheel under his sunglasses left temple to filter green and yellow. There. Someone had been correct. Everything *was* shades of gray.

In less than a minute, he stood before Neil's carved, French mahogany door. He noticed the door was ajar. And unlatched. He wasn't sure whether to enter without the characteristic "*Entrez*" invitation. The din of a commotion inside decided for him. His boss was in trouble. Time to make points. He rushed in.

There, sprawled across his boss' desk, was a woman whose flaming red tresses were splayed in all directions. That she was completely naked caused Jack's head to pitch forward. That she was covered head-to-toe with Jack's boss, Neil, proved the greater shock.

"Uh, sir? It's time for our two o'clock ..."

Neil Wohlford didn't casually indulge in infidelity. He showed every respect for his French-Canadian wife, Chantal, an elegant woman whose parents topped the list of Quebecois aristocracy. Doctor Monika Teresa Rikki represented the opposite end of the feminine spectrum. She was what a psychiatrist in pre-politically-correct times would have labeled a nymphomaniac. Herself a certified psychiatrist, she had self-diagnosed as a woman with a big and passionate heart.

Neil appeared the aggressor until he stopped pumping and turned his scowling face toward the man leaning against the doorframe. Monika refused to be denied. She grabbed Wohlford's cheeks and pounded him into her, again and again. She began to come, but Neil continued to pierce Jack's eyes with his own. Reinvigorated by his desire to administer severe punishment to the man in the doorway, his hips began again on their own, as if jumpstarted. He pounded and glared, while Jack observed and Monika reached a climax. The whole affair lasted a mere two minutes and twenty seconds.

Dr. Rikki, dressed and departing two minutes later, gave Jack a sly smile as she passed by.

"It's not what you think," insisted a scowling Wohlford. "She took advantage." He put on his perfectly creased and ironed trousers in slow motion. "She …"

"Glad to see you turned the tables there before securing her complete surrender."

"You could have knocked. You could have had the courtesy of ducking out for a bit so I could explain to her how wrong that was."

Jack closed the door and took a quick glance around. "That's new," he said, pointing to a painting on the wall to his left. "Gainsborough?"

Neil looked dumbstruck. How could this Neanderthal of a field operative recognize a Gainsborough? Oh, well. "Yes, Jack. My latest acquisition. Unfortunately, I have far too many pieces of fine art to display at one time."

"Someday you will have your French château, sir. Lots of room for your pictures." Jack always tried to set a positive mood for his meetings with Neil.

"Jack, my dear subordinate. Châteaux do not have *gobs* of anything. Sometimes I fear your education was a waste of time and money, but never mind. Tell me the status of your charge, Magus Crayle." Wohlford finished tucking in his three thousand dollar shirt.

"He's safe and sound at the safe and sound house in Fawnskin."

"Are we keeping Dr. Rorschach happy? All of those mano-a-mano events in Big Bear, Hong Kong, and France came back to me through the doctor's superior, Dr. Rikki. She was quite animated regarding the risk to the mind experiments she sponsors at Dr. Rorschach's hand. As you know, Dr. Rikki and I have a common …" Neil searched his mind for a word other than *superior*.

"Boss. Yeah, I know. We're in good shape, but you might be hearing about a little incident at the hospital. 'Bout a week ago—"

"*What!*"

"Well, Dr. Mindfuck talks when he works. And for the mindfucking to work, the subject can't be too sedated. So Crayle's wearing this electronic skullcap, and he hears the Doc say something about hitting the *Delete* key. Crayle went ballistic. Can't blame him. The few memories he has since the PCH crash are golden to him. He just about tore the place apart. Lucky I was there. I calmed the situation and carted him up the hill."

Jack eye-wandered as he spoke, so he didn't notice Neil grabbing a handful of Advil, chasing it down with Evian water. Jack also missed Neil's consideration of a non-electronic form of *Delete* with Jack on the receiving end.

"Jack, be careful with him."

"The doctor or Crayle?"

"Both. Keep Mr. Crayle on a short leash and out of mischief, or you will face early retirement. Do I make myself clear?"

"Crystal, sir." Jack saw a chance. "You know that these meetings with you once a month or so are invaluable to me. They insure that we are on the same page and give us a chance to bond."

Neil's face glowed red.

"But I can be most effective at looking after him if we just communicate by phone for the time being."

Neil saw through the ploy in the first instant. He knew Jack to be a field man and that Jack absolutely hated these meetings.

"We will meet when I say, Jack, and your obligations in this matter will continue unabated."

"Yes, sir."

"And keep close contact with Dr. Rorschach. Politics being what they are, you must give the good doctor—what is the colloquialism—give the good doctor his head."

Jack interpreted the last statement as *giving him his head* after he, Jack, had cut it off. He suppressed a smile.

"Very well then, Jack. Keep in touch."

With that, a dismissed Jack stepped out the door and breathed a sigh of relief.

CHAPTER 12

While Jack Sommers and his immediate superior, Neil Wohlford, worked at clandestine class warfare at the CIA's Manassas facility, Crayle and private investigator Lenny Lipschitz feasted on sausage, eggs, and hash browns. Crayle, surprised by how well the little P.I. could cook, wondered whether Alona ever cooked for Lenny. He could not know that the only place Alona really cooked was in the bedroom, on the couch, the floor, the coffee table—any flat surface served as her sexual kitchen.

Lenny, mid-mouthful, took a call on his cell phone. He listened the whole time, then flipped it shut.

"That was Jack, MC. He says I'm to make sure you eat well. So, how's the grub?"

"It's wonderful, Lenny." He reached over and touched Lenny's forearm.

"Hey, I'm not that kind of guy," Lenny said in mock disgust.

"No. I need to talk."

"Well, go down to the dock, sit on your butt, and do a dialog for the doctor. That device you carry in your pocket will record it and he can debrief you at a later date."

"I can't get Hekka out of my mind. I think she's right for me. I have no historical basis for these feelings because of the memory loss, but she just seems right. What should I do?"

"You're asking me? If you're just horny, go over and screw Alona—just kidding. Maybe you've got something goin' on, maybe not. Either way, I think you should find out."

"Jack probably got chewed out by his boss. Maybe I should wait until he returns."

"No, Magus. Just go. When he returns and gets upset, apologize. I learned that from my father. Never ask for permission. If you get into trouble, beg forgiveness. It always works."

"Can I take your Buick?"

"No. I may get a distress call from Alona and have to make an emergency run. Take the Cobra."

"I nearly wrecked it last time."

"Versus TJ and his gang's bullets, *nearly wrecked* worked out just fine."

"But Jack—"

"Remember the rule: take the damn car and ask for forgiveness later. Now, as Jack would say, rock and roll!"

Crayle jumped up, excited. He was in such a hurry, he didn't even grab a jacket for protection from the cold, late Autumn day. He walked to the rear of the kitchen and fumbled with the cipher lock, and the door finally opened. He descended the stairs to the covert passageway. Along the way, his mind rummaged for words. What would he say to her? How would he explain the lack of contact for such a long time? How could he tell if she'd replaced him?

He reached the garage and stripped the parachute cover from the Cobra. Buckling up, he hit the starter button. The 351 Cleveland roared its familiar roar. Once the garage door slid sideways enough to allow egress, he spun the tires, spewing gravel from the driveway into the garage. Jack would be pissed. Crayle didn't care.

It took fifteen minutes for the trip via the Stanfield Cutoff. Relaxed, it would have taken twenty. His nerves betrayed the strength of his feelings as he pulled into the ranch drive. He parked, sat for several minutes, and tried to formulate some sort of meaningful dialog. Perhaps he should ask forgiveness.

Hekka Poppi opened the door to his knock. She was as beautiful as ever, but showed no expression of feelings. Typical for her. He did not perceive it as negative. He stepped inside. Her father was seated in his personal chair.

"Father, this is Magus Crayle. I introduced him to you when he was here …" She silently counted. "… seventeen days ago. Do you remember?"

Her aging father spoke softly in Takic, the near-forgotten language of his tribe.

Crayle's face showed recognition of the three prophetic words the man had spoken last time: *man*, *woman*, *water*.

"Yes, I remember this man." Then the three words again. The old man had no specific knowledge of the couple's tryst at the waterfall he had built in his back yard as a monument to his departed wife.

"He is vetting you in his mind. And, in a sense, in his heart. He is protective of me, and he senses the danger you present. Yet, he sees the warrior. And my strength, as well. He senses our bond. He sees permanence. Forever. It is as I see it."

Her father spoke again.

"He says we are not safe in the Valley of the Big Bear. I have reassured him that we are safe, but ever vigilant."

"Please tell him that the man responsible for the violence is now in prison. Far away."

Hekka spoke in Takic to her father, the words single-syllable and coarse.

Crayle observed the skeptic in the old man.

"Magus, we will leave now. I must show you a beauty of the Valley that can only be appreciated from a special viewpoint. You must view the mark that the White people made on it. Then I must take your scalp." Her hand came quickly to her mouth, stifling a giggle. Crayle noted that her father did not experience the humor.

Her father spoke to her in their native language. His beautiful daughter responded.

"He says he will prepare dinner for us. I told him three hours."

"Dinner is not necessary."

"It is. It is customary that he do so, upon accepting you." At times, Hekka Poppi found it convenient to wax creative with regard to Serrano customs. Her father spoke, again in Takic.

"He believes that there are still White man steaks in the freezer. Former boyfriends, who were less than honorable to me."

Crayle feigned the appearance of fear. First to her father, then to Hekka. Both father and daughter stifled smiles.

"Here." She reached into a closet and presented him with a fur-lined, buckskin jacket. "The fur is from the grizzly. You will need it up the mountain."

Crayle, still feeling a chill in his bones from the ride in the Cobra roadster, pulled on the jacket.

"A perfect fit," said Hekka. "You are the same size as my younger brother. He is still in the Middle East with older brother. Still, he would be unhappy if you received any bullet holes in it, so be careful this time." She laughed. Her attempts at humor, reserved and infrequent, eased the burden of running the ranch in her brothers' absence.

Crayle smiled. In his mind, he did not want to subject his new love to violence ever again. He was satisfied that he had kept her out of his life after the Tack Store fiasco. But that was then. He had a new life to live. Peace, harmony, and a lifelong relationship were his watchwords going forward.

Outside, she kissed him on the cheek. "Come, we will add new memories."

Crayle buckled her into the deep racing seat. Since Lenny had been last in the passenger seat, its positioning nicely fit her five-foot-six body. He buckled the six belts at the quick release connector at her abdomen, careful to avoid indiscreet touching. On the way out, he bypassed her cheek and pressed his lips firm against hers. She feigned embarrassment, looking in all directions before she grabbed his head and pulled him nearer for a serious kiss. Her response complete, she fetched lipstick from her shoulder purse and replaced what had been shared.

Crayle felt a quantum better. She had not rejected him as he'd worried she might. And he was certain she would not have kissed him if she had moved on. He smiled to himself as he buckled in and fired the engine.

Hekka, had a destination in mind, directed Crayle back the way he had come. Just two miles short of his Fawnskin cabin, she said, "Turn left."

With a quick glance, he noticed a sign, which announced their entrance into the *Serrano Campground*. He passed an unmanned guardhouse, slipping into a slot reserved for tourists during the summer camping season. At this time of year, the entire campground stood empty. Even the birds flapped away at the Cobra's roar. The two popped their seatbelts and sat there for a few minutes.

CHAPTER 13

Crayle and Hekka absorbed the beauty of the water's edge campground. The two lane next to them continued west two miles to his nominal residence. It seemed far. One look at the lake demonstrated what he felt on his face. The afternoon wind, stirring white caps on the lake surface, bit at his nose and ears. He turned up his collar to mitigate the chill.

"You have probably guessed that these grounds were named after my people," Hekka remarked. "The White people were generous, don't you think?"

"Hekka, I am White. How can you love a White man after what his ancestors did to your ancestors?" Crayle closed his eyes. He found himself making an excellent argument for the woman he loved to cast him into the heap of ignorant, insensitive, White people.

"I am not so sure that you are White. You are absent your own history. The time of growing up is lost to you, and you have not learned the prejudices that all parents, knowing or not, teach their children. So, perhaps you are not as White as you think. A little pale, maybe." She smiled.

He grabbed her by the shoulders and pulled her tight. "Hekka. I may not be sure of much, but I am as sure as the red blood flowing in my veins that this non-white guy loves this non-white girl." They kissed. Deeply.

"Let's make love," Crayle said.

"No." She laughed. "I want you to come … I mean …"

"Hmmm?"

She took his hand, leading him to and then across North Shore Drive to the onset of a trail marked *Cougar Crest.*

"I am going to educate you, but not in the ways of sex. Follow me. I will proceed slowly because we are at altitude, and I don't want you to become sick."

A quarter of a mile up the trail, Crayle pulled in each breath deeply. He became aware of the paucity of oxygen above 6,000 feet. And the chill of each breath inside his lungs produced a paradoxical burning sensation. Hekka, meanwhile, seemed unaffected.

The first bullet arrived just ahead of its sound. It struck a boulder next to Hekka. Crayle grabbed her arm, pulling her down as subsequent rounds banged off the rocks around them. Hekka, unused to firefights like her brothers, peaked over a rock. Over the men yelling below, she related what she saw.

"Five men. They all have weapons. Now that we are out of sight, they are trying to run up the trail."

"Christ, Hekka. I'm sorry." His eyes pleaded for her forgiveness.

"One of them looks strange. He is yelling the orders. His jaw. It is big and pointed."

Crayle listened, but didn't believe. "That's not possible. He … TJ's dead. As dead as a man can be."

"Look for yourself."

Crayle's head popped up over a boulder. He saw four men running up the path below. Then, he saw the man Hekka had described. In that instant, his eyes met those of the man who had been his nightmare. The man who had tried to kill him on five occasions. Sylvain Lalumière's premier henchman. *TJ.*

But there was something different. This one possessed the same look, but he appeared noticeably larger. A brother? A twin?

"We must go. Follow me, but keep down. We will find temporary safety around the bend in the trail."

They ran crouched as bullets slammed the boulders and rocks around them. They could hear the men, who ran ahead of their leader, shout curses and epithets in their native French.

As the pair rounded the corner, a man slid down the embankment to their right with a thud. He landed on his feet and produced a fighting knife, its four inch blade protruding from a five inch handle. A folder.

By instinct, Crayle grabbed at the holster strapped to his leg. The slide rule.

Hekka's knife flashed out. She leaped ahead of Crayle like a mother mountain lion in defense of her cub.

The man swung first. She fended off the strike with her left arm. His blade sliced a nasty gash across her forearm. Unshaken, the young woman replied with her ten-inch Bowie to the killer's rib cage. The lethal blade sliced his heart in half. He died before the next second ticked. She pulled it free, using her wounded arm as leverage, and then, to be certain, thrust it up through the killer's throat, palate, and into his brain. Down he went.

Hekka crouched next to his body. She cut away the dead man's pant leg. She cut chunks of bloody flesh from his thigh and wrapped them in the cloth.

"The others! They're getting closer!" yelled Crayle. He realized that Hekka, as at the Tack Store where they'd first met, never got rattled. No matter how sudden the surprise, no matter how deadly the encounter, she was a rock.

She tugged at Crayle's arm. "Come!"

He followed her, quickly moving up the trail. As they proceeded, she dropped pieces of still warm, bloody flesh behind them.

"What …"

"An invitation to the cats. The big ones will come first. They will take the warm meat before they will attack us. Their keen sense of smell will guide them down the trail, on a collision course with our pursuers."

"How …"

"You are surprised by my plan, Magus?"

"The surprises in my life beget more surprises."

The first signs of the mountain lions showed over the hillside on their right. As the pair continued up the trail toward the crest, they heard the cat sounds shift.

In less than two minutes, they heard screams. The cats, in attack mode, rendered the killers' long guns useless at close quarters. In just ten seconds, all sounds stopped. No cats. No men. Only the wind.

Then, *"Merde!"* echoed up the mountain. The sole surviving assassin—the leader—had begun where TJ had left off. And like his brother, he would report failure.

"Hekka, it's still not safe. I know how they work. They never deploy their full force, and their leader always drops back and watches the battle, ready to fight another day."

"Then we continue up. I have a special place."

CHAPTER 14

Hekka led Crayle to the hilltop. They checked frequently, but spotted no killers in pursuit. She pointed to the ridgeline, and then guided them east through the tall pines that guarded the hilltop. From time to time, she would stop, to scan the forest below and behind them. After several minutes of rough trail, she turned to him, putting her hands on his chest.

"We will stop here. It will be cold soon. We must make a shelter."

Crayle, hands in his fur-lined pockets, shivered. "It's cold already. A lot colder than down there," he said, nodding at a sliver of lake visible between the pines.

The Indian woman bent down to the forest floor and pushed aside pine needles. "At this altitude, they are feet thick. Follow what I do and do the same. We will make shelter."

Crayle sat on the needle covering. He started to help, but something impeded his progress. He withdrew the slide rule from its scabbard.

"This belonged to my dad. It's for mathematics. Lenny said I needed to keep it with me. It might help." He pulled out the slide and touched its edge. "Ow!"

Blood oozed from the wound on his thumb. He looked at the slit in his flesh and then at the blood track on the rule. It was a weapon. What kind of scientist, what kind of man, had his father been? Hekka seized his hand, brought it to her mouth, and sucked the thick crimson fluid. She then pressed her thumb against the wound to stop the bleeding.

"Does this make us one?" Crayle quipped.

"I will feed you to the cats if you make any more Indian jokes." She smiled. "The wound must be closed. The cats will sense the smell as a sign of weakness." She withdrew a can of Sterno from her backpack and lit it with a World War II vintage Zippo.

"Hekka, I'll be fine. It's a flesh wound." Crayle prayed for mercy.

She ignored his comment and cut a tree branch. She cleaned it and smoothed the bumps. "You must not bleed on brother's coat." She produced a scarf from her neck and wrapped the branch.

Crayle observed every move. "How about we just bind the wound with the scarf?"

She returned to kneel by his side. "Here. You will bite down on this while I perform the wound closure ceremony."

"Ceremony? Hekka, my dear … my … my love. I … I'm fine."

Undeterred, she withdrew her Bowie knife from its scabbard. She held the point close to the flame.

"Your hand …"

Crayle proffered the damaged hand with trepidation. He had exhibited no fear during the attacks on his life. Still, he felt uncertain of his courage in this woman's presence.

She brushed the debris from the wound and gently licked away the blood. She didn't explain that her saliva would aid the process.

He bit hard on the branch.

The hiss and resultant smell lasted no more than two seconds. Crayle emitted a muffled "Ummmh!" The closure was complete.

Hekka cleaned the knife in the soil and returned it to its scabbard. She observed the solid, honest, brave man before her. There had been no crying out. Not even a whimper. Magus Crayle was all the man she could want.

"It will take a moment for it to cool. I will build a shelter. You will explain your recent past—during your absence from me."

She began gathering and placing. Crayle took a deep breath. Her request trumped Top Secret.

"I left your ranch after we …"

"Made love?" she supplied when he paused.

"Yes. I was attacked again by a Frenchman's gang. At my cabin. My protector, an FBI agent named Phoebe Bransfield, saved my life. Hekka, she put hers on the line for me."

"Then I am grateful to her. Continue."

"I was her assignment for protection after my crash." He omitted their intimacy. "Hekka, I discovered a link to my past. In China. I travelled there to find and interrogate a wealthy man named Chin. Somehow, he knew my dad during the Vietnam War. I learned that I had met this man before. He had something to do with the people who wanted me dead."

"Dead? What did you do to him—to them?"

"I created a strategy for him. And for the Frenchman."

"I suggest you discontinue these strategies," she commented, only half in jest.

"My contribution to their plot to conquer China is classified by our government above Top Secret."

"And you knew this? You didn't tell me?"

"I didn't know." He sensed her exasperation. "Not then. The man in charge of my memory recuperation, Jack, told me after you and I … parted."

"Go on." She glanced out over the Valley, searching for the unknown. She felt perplexed about this man, her disjointed emotions desperate to reconnect in her mind.

"I found him. In Hong Kong. I confronted him. He directed me to France, but I was attacked. I nearly died."

"In France?"

"No. In Hong Kong. Not by this man, Chin, but by the same gang that had attacked me in Big Bear. Sent by the Frenchman. One of Chin's twelve daughters, Ling An-yee, saved me."

"Did you know her …" She broke off the obvious question. He would explain if he felt it necessary. "That man has many daughters. As in ours, sons are important in that culture. Did he have no sons?"

"Not only does he have no sons, the young women aren't really his daughters." Crayle regretted descending into minutiae.

"I am confused. We can skip details of the daughters. Then?"

"France. Northeast. More battles, at a church and then at the Frenchman's château. I survived. I confronted him to plead for answers before the authorities took him away. He revealed little."

She touched the amulet on his wrist.

"Yes. I know. I can't explain, but I know. And now I've returned. To you. I feel complete." He glanced into her eyes. Her eyes completed the connection. To him.

• • •

Building their shelter took less than half an hour. They moved inside, settling upon the remaining thick matting of pine needles that provided a comfortable floor. She removed her oversized, fur-lined buckskin coat and motioned Crayle to do the same. Then she removed her blouse and bra.

"I understand now," he said. "You're crazy."

"Our insanity is protected by *your* laws." She gleamed.

She pushed his hands aside and removed his shirt in one motion. She slid her coat over her naked torso. Crayle followed suit. As he was about to zip it closed, she stopped him. She connected her zipper to his jacket and his to hers. As they lay down, the heat between their bodies intensified. It overwhelmed the cold of the night.

As the outside temperature descended to freezing, a breeze blew through the opening. Every cell came alive. They rolled from side to side as they made love, alternating from hot to cold and back. Their heat, confined within the buckskin and fur, crescendoed into simultaneous explosions of mutual ecstasy.

They lay together in the aftermath, the searing heat between them subsiding to merely warm. Crayle didn't want their embrace to end. He devised a tactical plan. He whispered in Hekka's ear. She smiled, then nodded agreement. They rolled onto one side and extended their top legs. Then, they rolled to the other side, extending the remaining legs. A final half-roll to upright. Still embraced and ensconced, they sat facing one another.

Over her shoulder, Magus Crayle caught a glimpse. The glimmer of a slice of moon reflected from the distant lake's surface. He recalled the words her father had spoken that first night at the ranch, and again this day. "Man, woman, water." The terse, bare words faded quickly as the heat ignited a fervor. The renewed lovemaking that followed generated the warmth necessary to remove the day's stress. And to keep them alive.

• • •

The next morning, the rays of the rising sun awakened Crayle. The memory of the previous night's lovemaking inside the parkas muted the danger they'd survived. Hekka's body remained pressed to his and, for the first time in a long while, he felt at peace.

Hekka woke to the sound of a voice. Alerted, she reached for her Bowie. She recognized his voice. His back to her, he sat at the shelter opening, facing the lake and naked save for the fur-lined coat. She realized that he had unzipped the jackets, then re-zipped hers. He had covered her bare legs with pine needles. Crayle continued his dialog.

"That said, Doctor Rorschach, I believe Lenny has good intentions in his heart, but they filter through his enigmatic mind. And don't present well." Crayle paused, recognizing his gross understatement of the P.I.'s social syndrome. "I know some of his history—his father was killed because of my assignments overseas.

"Jack? Jack did his best with us, but I fear he received vacillating direction from his boss in Washington. I feel that Lenny and I were directed to Hong Kong to remove us from American soil. I now realize that Lalumière's men knew our destination. It was necessary for them to have attacked me the first night. How could they know, Doctor?"

Hekka held back. He obviously needed to speak freely, but now she heard more than he had shared with her.

"Doctor, the FBI Agent, Phoebe, is an outstanding woman. She has powered through the most daunting of circumstances. She has kept me alive. Your experiment continues because of her. I thought … I thought there was something … she has her perfect man, now. Me? I know that I love someone. She sleeps in her beauty … right behind me."

Hekka attacked, throwing her arms around Crayle. They tumbled several yards beyond the shelter. She yanked open her coat. Then, his. They recreated their cocoon and made love again.

• • •

"We are safe now, Magus. The killers were themselves killed by the mountain lions or gave up. They were Caucasians, so they will assume we died up here in the cold."

"You're probably right." He looked into her eyes. "They would not know that their two fugitives made love last night like nothing else mattered. Listen to me, Hekka Poppi. I may have lost my old memories, but right now I know one thing for absolute certain. I love—"

An owl hooted its morning cry, muting his third word. They smiled into each other's eyes.

"Come. We must leave. The cats will be out soon in search of food."

They unzipped their coats, releasing themselves from their voluntary bondage.

"There are some Indian techniques that may aid you in the future. We will utilize one of them today in order to descend the mountain."

Crayle's eyes brightened. "I want to learn them."

"Listen very carefully. When you take squirrel excrement ..." She pointed at droppings amongst the pine needles. "... and rub it on the pine tree, it leaves a permanent yellow stain. In the past I learned this technique and have marked the way down."

Crayle picked up the droppings and rubbed them on the tree. Nothing.

Hekka giggled, her hand across her mouth. She turned to run.

"I have the keys," he said. He reached into his pocket. Then looked up.

She took off down the hill like an antelope, holding the keys aloft. Crayle pursued, but soon lost sight of her. He checked the trees as he walked out at a quick pace. No yellow spots. In his two deadly encounters, the young woman had powered through them with courage and intellect. The aftermaths were memorable in their intimacy, grace, and satisfaction. She inspired by just being herself. Not a phony bone in her beautiful body. The embodiment of truth. Except for the squirrel shit. He grinned.

Guided by the slivers of lake he could see through the trees, he picked up his pace. He was determined to catch her, capture her, and tickle her into submission. Then he heard it. The roar. She had the Cobra. His quick pace became a run as he neared the bottom portion of the tree line. He checked in all directions, then sprinted across North Shore Road to the campground. The car was powerful to the extreme and she was a novice relative to supercars. She'd kill herself.

"Ah," he breathed. The Cobra still sat there, the only car in the parking lot. It seemed untouched. There sat Hekka in the passenger seat, her expression saying, "You finally made it, White Man." She was playful regarding their respective races, but seriously proud of her dual heritage.

Crayle carefully checked the car, just the same. He made sure their assailants had not planted a bomb or a tracking device.

Clear, they set off for her ranch. A shower and a warm fire would get them both back into good working order. They both scanned the scenery for black Chargers or anyone who paid undue notice. Of course, a race red Cobra with white racing stripes attracted a degree of head-snapping attention, but Crayle felt safe for the moment. His life, however, was undergoing a serious change. When he was finished with Lalumière's assassination squad, he knew he had major plans to make—and they included this woman who had twice saved his life.

CHAPTER 15

Crayle drove the distance from the Serrano Campground on Big Bear Lake's north shore back to the ranch. He hoped for safety there, a change of clothes, and some warm time with Hekka. He pulled the Cobra into the place where Phoebe had witnessed their lovemaking, not far from the house. Hekka took Crayle's hand as they approached the door. She stopped.

"I will tell father I am in love. Not with a Serrano, but with a White man. The one he met after the Tack Store violence. He still carries a grudge for White men after they destroyed his ancestor's tribal grounds and drove away the big bears from which the valley took its name. I will tell him everything, Magus. I will tell him about the dangers, and I will tell him you are not like your ancestors. You are a good man. He will trust my feelings. I am sure. He knows that my love and respect for him are eternal. Remember, I do all the talking."

"My lips are sealed."

"Remember."

She reached for the door, but it already stood open. She looked at Crayle, then led him inside. Sitting in the same chair he'd occupied when Crayle had first met him was her father.

Hekka screamed. She ran to the chair, falling to her knees before her father. His face was scarred with deep cuts and bruises. His neck had a dark red ring around it, and his shirt was soaked in his blood.

Crayle started to speak, then thought better. He heard as much as saw the tears well in her eyes. Yet, not a single one spilled down her cheek.

The door banged open. Crayle jumped. He turned, ready to protect his love.

In walked two men dressed in Army fatigues. Crayle spotted the shoulder patches, and he knew they were Hekka's brothers. They had returned from the Middle East. They were joking about something until they saw their father, bathed in blood. Dead.

Their eyes snapped to Crayle, but Hekka held up a hand. Then the younger brother saw the coat. He erupted at Crayle, but big brother grabbed and restrained him. Little brother slowed his breathing as he had been trained. He regained control. The two soldiers went to their sister, kneeling on either side of her.

Again, Crayle felt the need to speak. To say the right words. He knew there were none. This was his fault. He had promised himself not to draw her back into the violence of his world, yet his love for her made rational thought impossible to implement.

"We must leave, Hekka. It's not safe here. I know a place where we can truly be safe. *Please*," Crayle begged.

The elder brother stood. He looked at Crayle. "Go, sister. We will see to our father's burial with full ritual. Then we will seek justice for what has been done."

"You don't understand," Crayle pleaded. "These people are fully trained and experienced in the art of death. If they return, they will kill you."

The younger brother stood and faced Crayle. "It is you who do not understand." He tapped the Screaming Eagles patch on his shoulder.

Hekka rose and walked to Crayle. She took his hand, leading him outside to the Cobra. "I will drive," she said, reaching for the keys.

"I have racing experience on mountain roads. We may need it to survive. Another time."

As they left the ranch, Crayle drove, not to Jack's cabin, but to Highway 18 north. To the Quarry.

CHAPTER 16

They headed north from the ranch in the red Cobra, intercepting Highway 18 just before it plunged into its snakelike downward track. The road, plowed of snow, remained wet and slippery. The Cobra, like most upscale sports car, was shod with sport tires that placed a lot of rubber on the ground for traction, but had little avenue built-in for the channeling of water. They were precisely not the tires for use in the prevailing conditions.

They did not skid off the road, although there were many opportunities. Crayle displayed his expertise in handling the car, especially when the tires lost traction. They arrived at the quarry in one piece. Hekka appeared surprised when Crayle turned into a gravel drive.

As the Cobra crossed the rock-strewn landscape, she looked even more surprised when he pulled up to a metal garage and its corrugated door slid upward. There were more surprises in store for the woman whose world, until Magus Crayle, had been confined. Inside, the door closed and the floor seemed to fall out from under them. Down they flew. She grabbed the passenger handle and Crayle's arm. It was dark.

"*Magus!*"

"It's an elevator. For cars. It's okay." He covered her hand with his own.

In the bowels of the covert medical facility, a set of five orderlies encircled them and confiscated their weapons.

Rorschach came next. Then Jack. Crayle removed his sunglasses, but he quickly restored them. The hospital walls had been painted chartreuse, just like Neil Wohlford's office in Manassas.

Jack retrieved Hekka's Bowie knife with a beckoning of fingers to the weapons orderly. Crayle had shown her how to mount her Bowie's sheath in inverted combat style between her breasts. She could release the handle snap with her left hand and draw the Bowie downward with her right. Jack walked her to the waiting room and taught her a quick draw technique. Coat on, coat off. He showed her how to catch the handle strap in the zipper so an outward pull on the jacket with her left hand freed the handle and provided space for her right hand to retrieve the ten-inch weapon in a single move. She practiced, the killers of her father heavy on her mind.

Jack had done all this with purpose. It freed the doctor for some private time with his memory-experiment subject, Magus Crayle. Later, Jack would retrieve Crayle, and Rorschach would be mollified. For a while.

• • •

Rorschach and his orderlies, remembering their last encounter with the martial arts adept Crayle, escorted him gingerly to the doctor's lab.

"Please, Mr. Crayle, lie down on the nice, white bed."

Crayle took a step backwards. Like an animal that had been abused.

"It is alright, Mr. Crayle. I have received orders to delete …" He noticed Crayle stiffen, as if anticipating an attack. "… nothing. And there is some very good news. I now have means to return some of your memories. Memories that will help you defend yourself. And perhaps, understand the work you accomplished for …" He checked his papers. "… uh, Mr. Chin."

Crayle's head snapped toward the doctor. His gaze penetrated. "Chin Yao-wu? Hong Kong?"

"I believe that to be the case. Our … my experiments on you will benefit operatives in a material manner from this moment on. In that way, you will benefit our country." Rorschach eliminated the detail that he was Swiss. "But do understand, Mr. Crayle, we are in cloudy waters. All that I do is experimental. Do you understand?"

"You're sure about my memories?"

"Eighty-seven point nine percent sure, to be exact. I have a degree-of-certainty program developed by the fuzzy logic team at—"

"Do it!"

"Very well. Lay back, and I will administer the requisite instant-acting sedative. If you will first please sign this waiver of responsibility …" He handed his subject a chartreuse tablet. It bore a legal document in fine print with octuplicate copies attached.

"Doctor, we are situated in a CIA covert hospital, domestic, and are 300 feet below the surface of the Earth. I characterize myself as a mathematically-endowed strategic planner-of-consequence entrée with essence of deadly spy operative on the side. A waiver?"

"You must sign."

Crayle signed the document as lightly as possible in order to frustrate the *company* bureaucrats.

Rorschach remembered his previous experience while working on this partially-awake subject. He put ear buds into Crayle's ears and leaned him back on the bed. The last words Crayle heard were, "Some music you liked. Eric Clapton and so on."

"Who is Eric Clapton?" mumbled Crayle.

• • •

After Rorschach gave him a small black alert pill, Magus Crayle was woozy, but awake. The first person he saw after the doctor was Hekka. He began a smile, but noticed something was very different—with him. His mind turned into an Asian kaleidoscope. His conscious mind fought to rationalize memories that were, at the same time, new and old. He grabbed his head with both hands, ready to scream.

"There, there, Mr. Crayle. It will all settle in. It should please you that I am writing in my notes that the experiment was a success."

Crayle's near-term memory recalled the experiment. Hekka took his hand. He calmed. Jack rushed in.

"There's a hiatus in assassination activity in this sector. You have to leave now. To a new safe house." He hustled them to the car park, handed a couple of items to Hekka, and started them to the surface. "I'll keep in touch," he yelled up the shaft.

They reached ground level in the car elevator. Hekka manned the GPS device and the cell phone Jack had provided.

"When it is clear, they will raise the garage door. That will be our signal," he said. "They are monitoring the assassination team's cars. We'll have a clear shot. Don't worry. We'll be safe."

"I don't want to be safe. I would give my life in a heartbeat for my father to be alive."

"I'm beyond sorry, Hekka. I would give mine, too." Consoling was not the thing to labor on at this point. It would take time and distance for her to begin healing.

The corrugated metal door sprang into action. The abrupt noise made them jump, both ultra-sensitive at this point. Crayle drove the short distance to state road 18 and turned left, north, as Hekka directed. They saw sparse evidence of snow in the expansive, flat valley. They traversed the dry roads of the desert floor to the four-corners town of little more than 5,800 inhabitants called Lucerne Valley. After turning left at the intersection, they transited the Victor Valley to California's femoral artery, the 15.

He felt her eyes on him. He also felt her concern. She wanted his welfare as much as she wanted her own.

The trip took them through a matrix of other attached freeways and winding mountain roads to the north of America's third-largest city, Los Angeles—the City of Angels. As he neared civilization, Crayle's driving became restrained so as not to attract notice by the ChiPs—California Highway Patrol—or the area sheriffs.

"We can go fast in this car, Magus," Hekka advised.

"We can't afford to be stopped by the authorities. The animals chasing us would kill us *and* the police with no concern about consequences. They would be halfway to France before anyone found our bodies."

"But there is no one in sight for miles."

"They watch from the sky out here. Then the cars show up, lights and sirens, seemingly from nowhere. Trust me."

"Yes," Hekka acknowledged. She wanted to trust him, forever. But a check of her unobstructed view of the sky revealed no planes, helicopters—nothing but surveilling hawks.

The road ran through the San Gabriel Mountains. It hid from view the 33,954 square mile expanse of monstrous Greater Los Angeles, which included five counties and a population of 17,786,419. The metropolitan L.A. area covered 4,850 square miles and attempted to contain 12.9 million Angelinos.

With no car top and only jackets and mufflers over their street clothes, the bite of the cold air kept them alert. The trip took two hours. They spoke little except for Hekka's directions. It gave them each time to think. To contemplate.

CHAPTER 17

To the casual observer, the innards of the American Embassy at 2 Avenue de la Concorde in Paris seemed ornate. It offered the usual ambience of perpetual traffic in its hallways. The walls appeared a soiled cream color. The floors presented a dull shine and sported the black markings of the thousands of cheap shoes that tread them. The air was stuffy, the smell stagnant. Rather than the attention to first impression one would expect, the feel was reminiscent of the Washington, D. C., Department of Motor Vehicles.

The building itself sat on Embassy Row, expressing its America-ness with the Star-Spangled Banner flying overhead.

Stephen Randolph Norbrunn, America's Deputy Chief of Mission, strode happily along the third floor corridor that led to the Embassy Travel Office. That office supplied travel suggestions and made plans and arrangements for employees. Once in a while, it helped lost American tourists, who easily tracked down the embassy. Randy wasn't planning travel. He visited often when she was in town, and he had quality intel that she was here today.

Inside the doorway, there she was. Cute, petite, smart. With her dimples, she looked to be the identical twin of George Harrison's wife—the one the Beatle shared sequentially with Eric Clapton.

Norbrunn's loving wife sat busily pecking at a keyboard, no doubt preparing another exciting trip for someone lucky enough to have the time off. Or some rich American seeking a grand tour of Amsterdam's renowned red light district. It had happened before, and he had seen her blush. So innocent. He began to whistle the melody to *Walking down Canal Street lookin' for a whore*. His personal licentiousness came to an abrupt end. Damnation would descend him to Hell for letting such thoughts, and images, run amok in his mind. His eyes changed the subject and settled on her. So business-like. So professional. So dedicated. And there was the nametag perched perfectly above her right breast. P NORBRUNN.

"How's it going, Pattie, my love?"

She looked up, embarrassed that she had not noticed his presence. She hid her red face in her hands and jumped to her feet. "Stephen! I just got in." She called him by his given name because his nickname, Randy, meant *horny* to the British diplomats. She couldn't abide their snickering. She ran to him, bounced to her tiptoes, wrapped her arms around him, and pressed her head hard against his firm chest.

He responded to her embrace with his own. He remembered his initial posting to Paris. How she had blushed each time he'd asked her out. It turned him on even more. Then came the *sexual harassment* dictums from the Secretary of State. Lucky for him, she'd said yes to a date and yes to their marriage.

"Hi, love. How was your trip?"

She sighed. "Oh, Stephen. I feel like I have seen everything in France. I travelled to the south on a discovery trip. Churches and ruins, churches and ruins, but no Monte Carlo this time. I so want to see it."

"My dear, Monte Carlo is surrounded by Monaco, a principality. The whole of it covers less than two square kilometers. Three times the size of the Washington, D.C., Capitol Mall. Furthermore, it is politically separate and not a part of our domain, France. It is better that you familiarize with all of France so that our people will vacation here and understand the peculiarities of its people. They are very different, region to region, you know."

"Yes, but there is so much more. Oh …" She hugged him again. "I'm so glad I married you, Mr. Ambassador."

"Deputy," he hushed. "But I have the Ambassador title in my sights. I am scheduled for classes on dealing with the spooks. That moves me closer to the top job."

"You're taking classes about ghosts?"

"No, sweetness. I have to learn about the operatives that the Central Intelligence Agency attaches to the embassy and how to let them do their thing and maintain their covers. They'll show up at the embassy as Special Envoys of the State Department, but can still be difficult to spot."

"Oh, you worry about under cover Special Envoys. Not Travel Agents?" She pouted.

He laughed at her humor. "Pattie, you are just the greatest thing ever to happen to me. You wouldn't believe it, but, in the world of diplomacy, you can't trust a word you hear. Everyone lies. It's *so* un-Godly. And I thank God for sending you to me. You are my base."

"And your rock."

"Look, let's do a little restaurant on the Left Bank tonight. A cozy place down in the Fourteenth Arrondisement. It's called Monsieur Lapin. We'll have something special."

"Whatever we get, I bet it tastes like rabbit." She giggled. "Tonight at eight. I'll pick you up at the apartment." Randy gave her one last hug and spun on his heels. He whistled his tune as he exited the Travel Office. Stephen "Randy" Norbrunn was *très* happy.

Pattie had never shared her dark secret with her husband. He was a strict Calvinist and expected obedience, openness, and subservience from his wife. It would not do to blurt out, "By the way, dearest Randy, I neglected to tell you something. Yes, my love. I'm a spy."

Several cover names from her espionage incarnations passed through her mind as, with a sigh, she watched him leave. Anne-Isabel in Alsace-Lorraine, Sandrine in the South of France. And she loved how the Dutch pronounced her Netherlands *nom-de-coucher*, Angel, with a hard G—as had her ancestors. Her thoughts returned to her husband.

Upon her arrival at the embassy, he'd pursued her relentlessly, despite of the widespread male attention she received. He shared with her that her simple, sweet, girlish approach to life was the perfect counterpoint to his stressed-out, immoral, backstabbing world. Perfect cover. Carrying on two distinct lives had its challenges, but the exploratory jaunts for the travel office provided cover for ops like MITIM. She noted that Randy's devotion to her was immutable and forever. If he ever discovered that she existed in a universe quite apart from his idyllic mental picture of their life together, there was no telling what he might do.

No matter, though. She had given him the bum's rush promise because it was near time for her call. Under normal circumstances, too elevated to handle operatives in the field, her boss at CIA headquarters had subsumed direct responsibility as *her* case officer. She took her orders only from *him*.

She reflected. Neil Wohlford had brought her in person to Paris to show her the ropes. Six months later, he had returned to see that she had adjusted. She was prepared. She escorted him up the Eiffel Tower, past the *Sorry, Closed for Maintenance* barriers of her doing, to the viewing station at the top. She cemented her relationship and status with no less than three erotic versions of lovemaking. Pawn captures Knight.

She stowed her pens and post-it pads, smiling at the orderly nature of her work surface. Her phone chimed a reminder that the call was five minutes hence. She fetched a brocade tote bag from under her desk and flounced out the door, which locked itself whenever no body heat or movement were detected in the room. Along the way, little Pattie Norbrunn practiced her shy flirt several times until she reached her destination. The special elevator had been programmed to accept her at the appointed time. Down in the basement subfloor in the kinetic and acoustic isolation cubicle, she gave a sitrep and received orders for the next phase of Operation MITIM. She squealed with delight at the magnitude and impact of what could evolve. Imagine a remade France. With a new line of kings. The king would need a queen. Mmm.

She entered a four-by-four *clean* restroom at the back of the cubicle. She watched herself disrobe in the mirror, checking her dimples and pushing kisses at herself along the way. She applied makeup and instant hair color, courtesy of the CIA Science and Technology directorate. After one last look at the fabricated red hair and freckles, she swapped the Embassy attire for work clothes. She sat on the stool to complete the task. The black patent leather stiletto heels added five inches to her five-foot-three stature. She dropped the work clothes and her black flats with pink roses into the bag. She stood before the mirror one final time to examine her appearance. The mirror self-adjusted to her new height. She was ready. Ready for a swap-sex-for-intel meet with an agent she ran from France's spy entity, the DGSE. If she hurried, she could just make her dinner engagement with Randy afterwards.

As her last preparation, Pattie Norbrunn installed a false name in her mind which, in turn, invoked an associated spy legend. She tweaked the faucets twice, then three times simultaneously. The room rotated 180 degrees. She hoisted her tote and stepped out into the catacombs of the Parisian sewer system.

Sometimes this job just stinks. She smiled, dimples deployed.

CHAPTER 18

The view from the Dragon Building never disappointed. Yet, with taller structures crowding out the slivers of the clouded Winter sky, his view remained the one to be envied. The golden reflective windows hop-scotched the red-accented, gloss black trim. Beauty and mastery incarnate. The train of thought ended abruptly as his solid gold office doors opened. The two steroid-enhanced eunuchs guided the uniformed visitor inside. Red daughter escorted him to a gold and cardinal chair. Chin flipped a switch and the wall-to-wall HD replica of the outside scenery turned a matching red. He stepped around his desk and down from the riser to the guest level. He strode to greet the most important guest—his colleague in crime.

"Ah, General Li. This is a pleasurable and auspicious moment. Please, sit here at our working table. Red …" He turned to the escort. "… please choose from my thirty-year collection." He turned to make eye-contact with the general. "Nothing less will do."

Red daughter bowed. Shuffling away to procure an appropriate bottle of well-aged single malt Scotch, she concluded that something major was afoot and she needed to "overhear" the dialog. Not to subvert Father or the general, but because she needed to know more at any given moment than Chin's current favorite.

Red's countenance took on a dark hue whenever she thought of Black daughter and the latter's hold on Father. If Black made no mistakes on her own, then Red would need to find a suitable end for her. One in which Red appeared to try to rescue her would play best in Father's eyes. But she also knew that a direct confrontation was out of the question. Black was death touch adept. Two or three pokes from her long, sensuous fingers would kill.

Chin and Li exchanged pleasantries until Red returned and the exquisite amber liquid sat before them. Once she departed, Chin opened the conversation by raising his crystal tumbler in a toast.

"To what has passed, to what is present, to what is future," he announced.

"And to faster horses."

"Such smoothness is beyond description, Li. And that is how our next task must execute. My star is well on the rise with our people. The Boys of Beijing, as Mr. Crayle labeled them, are falling in respect and honor ever faster."

"Yes, Chin. Where none of my peers would speak before out of fear of Beijing, their grumblings intensify. I have promised them, privately, that the situation will resolve. I have promised that the military will be unleashed when the inevitable regime change occurs. I promised it soon."

Chin took another sip, actually a gulp of the fine Scotch. It seemed Li was sticking out his neck in anticipation of the next step. The general was a doer, which was good. But, when requisite patience was the order of the day, he needed him to take a deep breath. Chin knew that any one of the other generals could be spying for Beijing to garner favor.

"Li, I appreciate that you have given them hope. And I sense that they see the top level leadership you embody. The news I have, then, is music to your ears." Chin raised his glass. His military accomplice mirrored the move. "I am initiating the next phase … immediately." Chin clinked his glass against Li's.

Li stood and came to attention as if Sieg Heil and a straight-arm salute would come next. "Chin, I have never been more ready. All aspects of the final solution for the dissident peoples in the western province are in place. I can implement your order to execute within the hour."

Chin felt compelled to calm his fellow conspirator. "In due course. Within the week we will be positioned to close the deal. I have reviewed the Crayle Strategy and have had an epiphany, my dear General. I've discovered a means to combine the next two steps as a composer would imbue the optimum effect into his concerto's final movement. Mark my words, one week from today we shall be positioned to destroy the Beijing regime and to insinuate ourselves in its place."

Li's jaw dropped. He wasn't an emotional man. In fact, the high-end call girls he utilized rarely discerned when he reached his climax. He trusted Chin. Completely. And he was a true believer. The dreams in the farthest reaches of his imagination would come to fruition in mere days.

Chin observed the general's reaction with great interest. If things went bad, the general would fall apart under interrogation. He made a mental note to pleasure him by Red daughter's extreme oral talents at the conclusion of their talk. She would addict him. Then, she would be Chin's assassin of choice should Li become a liability.

"I must travel to Kaohsiung, Li. Our inventory of six mini-nuclear devices will deplete to *new order* levels, and we will require one more. The problem is America. Their president is weak, but his unanticipated reaction to our gambit—the Iranian explosion—has caused the Frenchman to require an additional unit."

"Does this mean you have added a step to the original Strategy? Chin, you've said this man was a true genius. Could this change of yours not derail a plan that has been perfect up until this point?" Li had morphed from elation to abject fear of the unknown. It was his turn to gulp the Scotch.

Chin, as always, parlayed the seeming self-destruction of his necessary colleague into a positive. He placed his hand on the shaken man's shoulder. "Relax, my friend. Mr. Crayle's genius provided for accommodation of the unknowable the future might bring. I have merely input resolution of the new intelligence regarding the American reaction into the Strategy, just as he had anticipated."

The calming effect of the touch and the soft, yet sapient words caused Li to sink back in his chair and expel a sigh of relief.

"Remember. When you travel to Beijing, you will focus on preparations for our next step." Chin's emphasis on *our* reinforced them as a team. "But I must be assured: are you in control now? Can I rely upon you as I have in the past?"

The general extended his glass for a clink. "I am truly ready."

"Then we leave tonight. You will meet Xiang and know exactly what must be accomplished. We will fly to Kaohsiung and receive from the Frenchman's son the new batch of perfect water diamonds."

"Is he not in hiding, Chin? Would you not be at risk? Would we not be at risk?"

"Not at all. He sends his son on these missions to deliver the stones. When we congregate next, I will transfer them to you for the purchase. I have every confidence in you, friend Li. And now it is time for your treat," he said, as if talking to his pet dog. He watched the anticipation swell in the general. Chin knew his thoughts. He punched a couple of keys on a remote. The golden doors swung open.

Red daughter knew from the color of the guest chair that it would be her turn to pleasure the guest. As always, she would excel. When she entered, Chin observed the 'dashing of hopes' effect on General Li. He was certain the man wanted Black daughter more than life itself. Most desired is the carrot just beyond reach. And Chin knew why his comrade wanted Black so desperately. He experienced exactly those feelings himself. Chin reasoned that settling for second best would remind the general of his actual status as number two. And Red could be very persuasive.

The young woman led the befuddled Li off to be pleasured once more. Red intended to remove Black from his thoughts completely. Chin's status-assertion tactic fit Red's personal agenda to perfection.

• • •

With his colleague handled, Chin focused on his own needs. Two more punches on the remote control and his favorite daughter entered, not through the main doors, but through Chin's secret portal.

"We must go soon. To Kaohsiung. But first …"

Black daughter knew her duty. She placed the golden pillow at Father's feet. Before she knelt, she placed a kiss atop the older man's head. For anyone else to take such liberty would have meant instant and excruciating death. She had never gone this far to express her own feelings, but, if death was her reward, she would accept it without reservation.

Instead of a violent reaction, she witnessed the rise of his chest, anticipating a silent sigh as it fell. She took her position at his feet and spread the hinged chair in preparation. What happened next surprised them both.

"No. Not this time." He clasped her head in his hands. For several heartbeats, he scanned her warm, dark eyes. Then, her face. The feelings trapped within him welled. That his mother had been defiled and that he was a product of that rape precluded biblical knowledge of any woman. The intimacy of a kiss, any kiss, threatened the indelible promise he'd made to the woman who had given him life. It posed a threat to his steadfast self-denial.

He spoke, softly. "We must prepare for our trip, my darling. Go."

CHAPTER 19

When her jet touched down on the 6,168 foot runway 35 at Caremont Airport in Avignon, the spy Sandrine knew exactly what to expect. Her charge, Sylvain Lalumière, masquerading as Mitim, the Man In The Iron Mask, would be in his stateroom pouting. He would say he was being treated like a prisoner again. She hoped he had not thrown the historic mask overboard in a fit of rage.

She descended the stairway to the tarmac, pleased that the Provence weather was a typical late Autumn temperature of fifty-five degrees. Deceptive, she knew. The bitterly cold Mistral winds could arrive and peak quickly. Clasping the strap of her Langley-supplied Coach bag, she made her way to the waiting vehicle.

The pickup car was decidedly un-French. A Ford S-Max seven passenger van. Jack. She rarely saw Jack, but she liked him. Not enough to bed and kill. He reminded her of her American father. She stepped through the open passenger door and plopped into the seat.

" 'Lo, Pattie," he said.

"*Je m'appelle Sandrine, Monsieur,*" she replied.

"Okay. Okay. Sandrine, then. I see you have no luggage, so I assume you left it on the boat and, knowing you are all OCD with the details, I assume there's nothing on or in it to give you away. Right?"

"*Oui*, Jack. You know me, outside of the biblical context, in every aspect of my being."

"Speaking of which, kill anyone today?" He smiled her way.

She rubbed her hand along his thigh. "Not yet."

"Moving right along. I've been read-in on the op, so here's the refresher on the mission parms."

"I know the mission parameters, Jack."

"Yeah, but I need to check the box, so listen up. You are to get Lalumière, intact, to Arles. There you'll disembark—"

"*Debark* is the correct word … Jack."

"Your driver will take the two of you into Marseille. It should take …" He checked his S & T watch. "… one hour, six minutes to travel the whatever distance."

"It's exactly sixty-five miles." She required precision and always did her homework.

"Listen. Please. During the transit time, you need to key Frenchy into the next phase. We're going underground in Marseille like we did in Fasd. In Iran? Yeah. Tell him this: it's all being done for him. He can't be up front like he was in Iran, because everyone on the planet is on the lookout for him. You'll pick up a boat at …" He gave her the GPS coordinates. "… under codeword Frogface." He smiled. "I borrowed that from Lenny. Anyway, the boat takes you to the château. Remember, this is critical. He goes in character, Mitim. The whole time. We will exfiltrate in six days."

"A little more detail, Jack?"

"Pattie … Sandrine … this is highly compartmentalized. You're in a cocoon 'til this breaks. Your exfil pilot will take you and Lalumière to the next site. You look worried." He touched her hand. "Trust me on this."

Sandrine rotated the seat back. She looked up at the headliner, nothing really. Trust equaled enigma in her profession. You could only trust someone, anyone, until they killed you. She smiled at the thought of being killed. And then at the thought of killing. She was a long way from Pattie. A long, long way.

• • •

During the trip, Sandrine observed that the provincial walled city of Avignon seemed packed with cars. More so than in the recon trips she'd made to the area. It was not market day, but something special was afoot. She saw tents in the square, perhaps because of the nearness of Christmas. An immobile carrousel seconded that notion.

It occurred to her—she so loved her ops—that any transit time was too much. After what seemed like forever to her, they arrived at the Royale. She gave Jack a peck on the cheek, and he was gone. She felt a calm as she boarded across the gangway. It was short-lived.

"Oh, Mademoiselle Sandrine."

She held aloft her ringed finger.

"I am sorry, Madame Sandrine. How nice to see you. I have a note to tell you, uh, Mitim is not aboard."

"*What!*" Sandrine reverted to schoolgirl English.

"We are sorry. Your instructions that he not be bothered were quite clear. And that the actor suffers from the onset of Alzheimer's Disease and can not be allowed to leave the boat—"

"You let him leave?" She embodied exasperation.

"Oh, but it is no problem."

"No problem?"

Unruffled, the woman explained. "*Oui*. We gave him a very special wristwatch to wear. We told him to return at least one hour before sailing."

"And if he doesn't?" Sandrine considered the person before her a candidate for her Jackson Pollock artist's palette.

"It has GPS. You can locate him." She gave Sandrine a Garmin-like device. "There." She pointed to a green Peugeot 3008 on the dock. "Our driver awaits you."

Sandrine ran down the gangway, sprinting like the athlete she was. The woman on the gangway noted that this one, under duress, reverted to high school English. Perhaps she had been an exchange student. Or, perhaps Mitim was not the only actor.

Sandrine's driver wound through Avignon in pursuit of the errant Lalumière. It seemed all traffic shared their purpose.

"We are near the river again," said the driver. "You will have to find him on foot. I will pick you up at the Hôtel de L'Horloge. It's on the square with all the Christmas booths and the carrousel. We passed it five minutes ago. Meet me in the lobby."

She remembered the hotel well. And the priest she'd introduced to backdoor sex. "May he rest in peace," she mouthed.

The cobbled streets of the old town reflected the wear of centuries of inhabitants and travelers. Sandrine checked her GPS device and proceeded as indicated. As she drew near to her target, she saw a sign: Pont D'Avignon.

"Oh, crap!" She could hear the tune that came from the bridge, a children's tune she recognized immediately.

Sandrine wedged into the pressing crowd, her diminutive size giving her a claustrophobic rush.

A woman yelled, *"Il est là!"*

And then an American, "Yes, there!"

"C'est Mitim!" a young man cried.

They rushed to him, but stopped as if an invisible barrier had been placed twenty feet from the masked man. The intensity swelled.

She realized to its fullest extent that Jack's CIA boss, along with his DGSE colleague, had created a whisper rumor that had gone viral worldwide. The first act of their symphony played out in the fervor of the fully inclusive demographic. The second act would step up the intensity a thousand-fold. A few days hence.

"I am with him!" she yelled in French, waving her fake Mitim Tour ID over her head. She pushed up the stone stairway, through the guarding castelet, across its drawbridge to the arched, twelfth century bridge, and through the crowd to the front. There he was … dancing. Dancing and singing to the children's song. *Sur le Pont, D'Avignon, On y danse, on y danse …*

As she approached, the in-character Mitim danced away from her. The bridge, in its current manifestation, quit midstream. She worried that the crazy Frenchman might just go off the deep end. She slowed. When she reached him, he stopped dancing and, before she could react, gave her a huge hug. The crowd burst into thunderous applause interspersed with the hoots and whistles of American tourists. Then Mitim, fully in character, addressed the crowd.

"You know me. I am Mitim, the Man In The Iron Mask. As you can see, I am no longer confined in the Bastille. Save for my mask, and the government police who seek to return me to my captivity, I am free."

The crowd cheered. The catcalls and whistles barely pierced the din.

"I will only remove the mask when those who would tax us to death and regulate us into oblivion have seen justice."

More yells and screams. A woman fainted.

"Then, and only then, will I come forth to reclaim my rightful throne … and return France to her inalienable glory."

Members of the crowd formed circles. They began to dance to the tune of the well-known children's song.

"We are all now no more than the children of the government. They have subsumed the role of our parents. Our anthem, until justice has accomplished the necessary, will be this song." He led the crowd, "*Sur le Pont D'Avignon …*"

The entire crowd, familiar with the song since childhood, sang the new Anthem of Mitim. Even Sandrine joined the throng. When they finished, a man from the crowd stepped forward.

"Monsieur Mitim. We helped the Americans throw off the chains binding them to the English Crown. They must help us now!" Cheers. "The American president and his congress have raised taxes and, with rules and tariffs, have strangled those who would provide growth and jobs. The rich Americans are leaving in droves. They are taking their wealth to Asia and to South America. Most construction in Europe now takes place in tiny Andorra and Liechtenstein. And in Switzerland. And Germany, which is poised to leave the European Community and its farcical, socialistic ways. What can we do?"

"Our beloved France must have these jobs. We must build these new buildings right here in France. France must grow. France must throw off her chains!" He held his hands aloft, brandishing his Mitim shackles.

Members of the throng jumped and spun, cheering and screaming their delight. Here was their man. Here was their savior. Here was their Mitim.

Gendarmes had been notified of the large, impromptu crowd now being transformed into a mob by a costumed man in a mask. Their lieutenant, who realized that he and his men could not permeate the assemblage, also saw that the crowd could turn on them as symbols of the hated government. He withdrew his force to a nearby schoolyard. He contacted headquarters for instructions.

"Who is proud to be French?" Mitim yelled into the cacophony.

The crowd chanted, *"Vive La France!"* over and over.

"Who wishes with every beat of his French heart, and who wishes, with every beat of her French heart, and every surge of his and her French blood to be proud once again?"

The thunderous applause returned. One man shouted, "Mitim for President!" A woman cried, "Mitim for King!" More applause. The craziest hurled themselves from the bridge into the Rhone.

Sandrine witnessed Lalumière in full swing, propelling the men and women of Avignon and its surrounds to near riot stage.

"Citizens of a new France? Do you see these chains?" He raised them once again, waving his bound wrists. He thrust them toward

Avignon's Eiffel Tower replica, in the direction of Paris. "Do you see these chains?" This time he emphasized each word. "I am the people of France! I am the heart of France! I, Mitim, am the blood of France!"

The crowd, now completely at his command and approaching a bloodlust, began to throb.

"Save me! Save yourselves! Save France!"

"Down with the tyrants!" cried an elderly woman. The crowd took up her chant. "Down with the tyrants!" The final straw. The crowd turned as one. It raced down the bridge through the castelet and over the drawbridge, headed for the Hôtel de Ville—Avignon's City Hall. The irate citizens and tourists blew by the schoolyard, where the gendarmes strove for invisibility. Many of the officers fell in with the crowd, uniform jackets and firearms abandoned.

A stunned Sandrine watched the bridge empty. Although she'd played the seminal role in begetting the op, it now surpassed even her wildest dreams. She saw the potential. The incredible potential. She needed Neil's approval and the next sitrep would make it hers.

She panned the crowd as it disappeared into the corridors of the city. Enrapt was the only word suitable to describe them. Enraptured by the man, or by the man they wished to see. Enabled by a succession of fumbling politicians. Her Mitim owned them as much as she owned him.

"Holy shit," she whispered.

• • •

With the crowd gone, Sandrine and Mitim located their driver and, with little outbound traffic, arrived dockside in minutes. She didn't have time to meet Jack—he would understand. Mitim checked his watch and broke into a run, Sandrine on his heels. They sprinted over the gangway just as it was being removed. Shipboard onlookers, wanting to catch the departure, cheered that their Mitim was back in their possession. Mitim had, indeed, become a factor.

Back in their suite, Sandrine decompressed. Langley had really gotten the word out. Neil must have set up this little op. So why was she, the woman-in-charge, not in the loop. Spying was an imperfect science, she knew that. She also knew that spies must watch their front and their back with equanimity.

• • •

The Royale left the city of temporary Papal residence following daybreak, proceeding downstream. Sandrine kept Mitim under wraps, confined to quarters until the final night and his advertized performance. He did not disappoint. Sandrine and the standing room only crowd felt, as much as heard, the intensity of the man, Sylvain Lalumière. The throng on the bridge had transformed him from "I can do this" to "I will, I must do this!"

Others came to her mind. It was as if he embodied the spirits of Louis XIV and Napoléon Bonaparte—come back to retake their rightful throne. Lalumière no longer *played* the Man In The Iron Mask. He had become him. Sandrine made a mental note: *that* could become a problem.

CHAPTER 20

The guests occupied the small theater, the lights low and conversation lively. A glow of contentment and exhaustion dominated. The eight day river cruise aboard River Royale had taken its passengers to Lyon, Avignon, and was now enroute to its final stop, Arles.

The passengers, having formed alliances during the trip, clustered in their newfound support groups. They awaited the final performance of the Great Mitim—The Man In The Iron Mask. No one had the slightest notion that Mitim was a man wanted throughout France. The gendarmes wanted him. The French spy agency, DGSE, wanted him, and Interpol hunted him, in case Sylvain Lalumière had escaped the boundaries of his homeland.

A small, circular stage had been hastily erected in the center of the room due to the astounding success of the Mitim show. All chairs and eyes remained fixed on the stage, now encircled by an eight-foot high curtain suspended from a ring that closely resembled arc-shaped shower curtain rods.

"Good evening," said the petite woman as she took the curtain and slowly drew it around the rod. The passengers, mostly American, took her accent to be that of a pretty and young French girl—not the well-blooded American spy, Pattie Norbrunn.

Within the curtain, a dark shape stood upon the stage. A bright light flicked on to illuminate the shape. The man, clad in peasant garb, stood with his chin resting against his chest. The light panned up his body. Shifting shadows brought an eerie feel to the scene. Talk amongst the passengers turned to whispers. Then, whispers to silence. Mitim lifted his head, heavy with the iron mask. All breathing ceased.

"For seven days, you have heard my story. I have been trapped inside this … this disguise. I have been captive. Captive of those who fear my truth."

The crowd sighed.

"You will leave soon. You will return home to America, but you will not forget me. Some day, I will remove this mask. You will see me for the man I am. Perhaps …" Lalumière reached up to the mask with both hands. Not a sound from the crowd, save their heartbeats.

As he pushed the mask, Sandrine ran to him. She grabbed his hands. She stood on tiptoes to whisper, "No, my love. This is not the time. Soon will come the time. I will explain when we leave the boat."

The crowd resembled a select bunch of radioactive atoms restrained just beneath critical mass. They burst into cheers so loud, they startled the captain in the pilot house above. He dispatched the First Mate to quell what sounded to him like a riot. The First Mate found a roomful of tourists applauding, hollering, and whistling, but no mayhem afoot. He provided a sitrep over his wireless set and left, hands over his ears.

"You masquerade as The Man In The Iron Mask," yelled a pot-bellied Texan. "You do it so well … could it be you are actually the *real* next king of France?"

Lalumière's eyes opened wide. They beamed. Beneath the mask, he smiled. For the first time in a very long time, he laughed. "I am, of course, the real next king of La Belle France." The crowd cheered again. "But you are the only ones who know." The crowd laughed. "Can you keep my secret?" Cheers and applause.

The battle lantern being used as a spotlight went dark. The diminutive assistant brought the curtain back around to complete the circle. The tourists ordered more drinks, abuzz with the dynamics of what they had witnessed. One man mused aloud of the possibility that a man of breeding and intellect could appear from nowhere and dramatically alter the course of their host country. Could someone remove the socialism and stagnant bureaucracy that had festered over the years, and could he replace it with something that worked? Lalumière, in his guise as the repressed and suppressed prisoner Mitim, knew the answer.

The room lights went black. When they returned seconds later, the actor and his attendant had vanished. Back in their suite, Lalumière discarded the heavy iron mask. Sandrine applied a purposeful neck massage. He normally would have surrendered to his lust and taken Sandrine to bed as his prize, but the Texan's comment had penetrated his core.

"He was right. He saw it. I *am* the next king." He closed his eyes, tilting his head back as Sandrine pushed her thumbs into the deep muscle tissue. "I must know now. I cannot wait. Tell me how I will complete my destiny. Tell me, Sandrine."

Pattie Norbrunn had a knack. She had played many roles, and Sandrine was just the latest, tailored to the Frenchman and his opsit. The operational situation accompanied her scheme to put Lalumière in character to enable his escape, given that his facial image was everywhere. It had blossomed into much more. Now the man believed his own internal press releases. He saw her as his enabler. She bit back a smile. She could manipulate him in any fashion she chose.

"My dear Mitim," she began, "I will tell you how you will, indeed, become king of France, but on one condition. No, two."

"Anything," mumbled the entranced Lalumière.

"Condition One is that you do exactly as I command. No impromptu variations. Your emotions are at peak. We must deal with them. We cannot allow them to interfere."

"How can I suppress my emotions? I am French. I realize now, tonight, that I will … I must … achieve my dream. How can you help me?" he asked, surrendering totally to her control.

"Condition Two, my dear Mitim. Condition Two is that you make love to me while I reveal how you will become king."

She led him to the bed. They undressed. During their expressive lovemaking, Sandrine whispered the plan into his ear. He responded to the beauty of the plan with gasps as she laid out the sequence of tactical moves. She worked him and her story until both reached their points of no return. Her final words, "Your coronation will be the ultimate. It will be … the climax!" As if performing a sexual concerto, both bodies hit the final note ensemble. Each, for very different reasons, felt complete. Within seconds, they drifted off to sleep.

The plan called for Sandrine to escort Lalumière to the southeast, there to commit the next international incident and pave the way for his final run to the throne of France. Tomorrow early, they would disembark. Neil had set up transportation outside of the CIA framework. The intensity of her role made her true self seem like the cover character. She needed grounding. She would complete this phase, then rush back to Paris and her beloved Randy. She couldn't wait.

• • •

When Mitim and Sandrine debarked the Royale in the city of Arles, they did so last. The other passengers, aligned on the dock, refused to leave. Sandrine marched Mitim to the sun deck atop the Royale. The temperature was a cool forty-eight degrees, and a light rain tapped at the mask and cloak of Mitim.

She guided him to a square, separated from the deck on all sides by a one-inch space. After she positioned them at its center, the wheelhouse rose to its fill height, thrusting them high above the crowd. Again, the cheers overwhelmed the two for nearly five minutes. After the wheelhouse returned to its under-bridge configuration, they walked hand-in-hand. Sandrine felt his confidence.

As they crossed the gangway for the final time, it occurred to her that Lalumière had not removed his iron mask since she had aborted his attempt in Avignon. Even when they made love. The fear that he could descend into lunacy seized her. There would be work to do to keep his feet on the ground, while also keeping his head in the air.

Sandrine was quite aware that Sylvain Lalumière lacked a familiarity with the South of France. "Mitim, this city, Arles, is beautiful. It was Greek, then Roman. The river divides in two here and flows to the Mediterranean Sea not far. You must grow to understand these regions as you do your own. You will dominate them." She saw her words take effect. He had become a true believer. Still, she wondered if he would lose his mind in his alternate identity. As had nineteenth century Arles resident, Vincent Van Gogh.

The crowd applauded. Cameras clicked and flashed, even though the morning sun was well above the eastern horizon. The Marseillaise sounded over the boat's speaker system, announcing their arrival in the true south of the French republic. Mitim stiffened. It touched him deeply. He made a crisp salute as if a bearer of the tricolor in wartime. But Sandrine sensed his emotions. She had lived among the French for several years. Inside, the man of the iron mask was choked up.

When he snapped down the salute, she led him to their ride. Next stop, Marseille.

CHAPTER 21

The breeze picked up as the afternoon progressed. By sundown, it had become a wind. The weather prompted most *Marseillais* to spend such conditions indoors, sipping Pastis with friends or enjoying a bouillabaisse repast.

Lalumière, not at all nautical, did not understand the effect wind produced on the otherwise silken waters of the Mediterranean. Not until his twelve-foot water taxi left the quayside of the Vieux Port. Within minutes, he longed for the smooth river sailing of the Royale.

The pilot noticed his consternation. "It is less than a mile to your destination. You will survive."

Lalumière's black-hooded sweatshirt, and the iron mask that Sandrine had darkened with a substance from her makeup kit, assured his anonymity, yet conferred another form of confinement in his mind. The ride would be brief, Sandrine had promised. Soon, he could lay back and relax from the unbearable tension in his new apartments.

Lalumière peered into the rain. "The man I nearly killed at my château. Magus Crayle. I wonder, where is this master strategist now?

Has my assassination team completed eradication of the only man who may remember every step in the original plan? He created it. Perhaps your compatriot has, against all odds, survived yet again. Perhaps I will see him again. I will thank him, then personally execute him for the clothes dryer tumble I am suffering in this tiny craft."

"You are fortunate, " the captain intervened. "There is no Mistral from the north. When it blows, landing a boat on these islands is impossible."

The radical fore and aft, port and starboard roll of the boat assured Lalumière that he was, least of all, fortunate.

Sandrine observed her beleaguered charge. "The trip has worn you. You need some rest."

Lalumière pointed ahead. "The rain is lifting. There is an island. Like the top of a mountain. And atop … a walled monastery. We are going there?"

"That is Hôpital Caroline. It was a quarantine hospital during a yellow fever epidemic. Early nineteenth century. It is quite empty these days."

"There I will be safe?"

Before Sandrine could answer, the captain swerved the boat left. Except for a haze, the new course afforded an unobstructed view ahead. Lalumière's jaw dropped.

"D'If!"

"I can explain—"

"Another prison!"

Lalumière stumbled to his feet. He threw himself toward the gunwale. The heavy mask and turbulent sea would drag him to his fate.

Sandrine intercepted him in mid-air, her arms and legs engulfing his body. They slammed to the deck. Lalumière's feet pushed under a seat, contained against their flailings. The spy held his arms tight. Silently, she thanked Flori for the Brazilian Jiu-Jitsu training. She pressed her head against his.

"You must stay here. It is abandoned for maintenance. There will be no jailer, Mitim. Only me."

The pilot had turned. "Stop! You will tip the boat!"

The man in the mask calmed. He gazed ahead.

Not quite 1,000 feet long, the island, If, was half that in width. It appeared small, confining, to those who had been incarcerated in its château.

They pushed on towards the landing. Yes, the old prison looked its part. Rocks loomed up to encircling walls. Within and to the right, the foreboding three-tower keep. He absorbed the chill.

Lalumière glanced at the pilot. Was he just a man who owned a boat, working for a handful of Euros, or was he an agent, too? When they made landing and the boat's captain gave him a hand ashore, he found out.

"Start up the stone stairway, Mitim. It zig-zags through several doorways. Longer than you would think. You must stop halfway up for a rest. I will be with you presently. I must first take care of the captain."

He turned and trudged upwards, supporting his heavy mask with both hands.

"We have travelled nine tenths of a mile. As agreed, 10,000 Euros per tenth."

When Sandrine extended a packet of money to the captain, his eyes converged on it. A smile came to his lips. As he accepted the packet, she pressed up to him on her tiptoes. Her hands disappeared under his arms. She could see it in his eyes. And his smile. He would receive more than had been agreed upon. He didn't see the long thimbles on her thumbs.

The petite spy forced his head back with her parted lips. A second later, she thrust the pointed instruments of death under the back of his skull, as she had the Bastille jailer. The captain's mind switched off. Bone against bone, life departed his kiss. He tumbled into the belly of his boat. She turned.

"Mitim, go ahead to the top. I'll catch up," she shouted up the stairway.

Lalumière watched her, entranced.

"Mitim?"

He obeyed.

Sandrine turned to her work. She retrieved her purse and unfastened one end of the leather handle. She withdrew a length of cord, placing it in a circle at the deepest part of the boat's hull. Employing an heirloom World War II Zippo lighter, she lit the cord. The nimble spy stepped to the transom, engaged the motor, and leapt to the landing as the boat made for open waters.

Having left the counterfeit currency for Davey Jones, Sandrine was halfway up the steps by the time the circle of det cord burned through the hull. She stopped to see both boat and captain slip beneath the waves.

"Did you have to do that?" Lalumière asked plaintively when she arrived at the top.

"The sea is the graveyard of D'If, it is said, and a captain must go down with his ship, Mitim. Sooner or later."

It startled him as the euphemistic threat took hold.

She took him by the hand and led him across a stoney expanse of ground to the infamous Château. She halted. It was as she had guessed, only more so.

"Welcome home," she said to the man who would be king. "Welcome home."

"From prison to prison in just eleven days," came his plaintive reply.

"You can write a prison-break *Dummies* book in your spare time. Look. Think of it not as your prison, Mitim, but as passage to your dream."

They crossed a drawbridge over a dry ditch, ducked a partially raised portcullis, and entered the château to find its keeper in the meal room. A disheveled man sat hunched over a half-eaten plate of food, a spilled mug of beer next to his head. The commotion of the creaking oak door and the footsteps brought him around. He stood, weaving his way to his new guests.

"You must be the notorious Mitim. I know of you." He patted a beer-stained copy of Le Monde. "They guess your identity. Take off the mask so I may see your face."

Mitim fell back against the block wall, exhausted. The jailer approached.

Sandrine stepped between them, her thimbled thumbs prepared for their next employment. But the jailer grabbed her hands and stripped the thimbles. They fell to the stone floor with a clatter.

He was much stronger than she. He grasped her upper arms so hard, she cried out. As he stepped close, he pinned her arms behind her, but Sandrine hadn't survived by being unprepared.

As he pressed against her, she used her hands at the back of her belt to activate a buckle blade. Blade edge up, she thrust into him and pushed upward using her sprinter's calf muscles for force. The razor edge plunged deep into the jailer. The push upward slashed through his intestines.

He lurched back. He grabbed himself, trying to contain his guts. The blood loss, quick and plentiful, sapped his energy. He sat heavily on the floor, then fell back.

They watched him die.

"Is this your solution to everything?" Lalumière asked. "You have killed the jailers. You have killed the boat captain. You have done it as if you were slicing an apple or making a sandwich. Does it not trouble you?"

"Some people order death, Mitim. Some people execute. When all is done, *yours* will be to order. To get you to that point, *mine* is to execute. It's part of my job description."

"But—"

"It's okay. He is to be replaced by one of ours. Sit down. You don't look so good." She went to a wall table and returned with a basket. She handed him a folded piece of white canvas, a large needle, and a length of cord. "Here. Put him in this and stitch it up. If you have seen The Count of Monte Cristo, you know how it's done. When our jailer replacement arrives later, the two of you can toss him into the drink. Cool?"

Lalumière looked from her to the body and then back. He had no more words.

"Come. Let's go see your new digs." She pulled out a tourist map she had obtained in Marseille and led him along a gallery. "This is your new address." She pointed to the cell number. "Same as the original. And here we have your new residence. Now, the rumors are that the other Mitim was held on a coastal island, Sainte Marguerite, just off Cannes. If anyone brings it up, just ignore them."

"I have seen no one else on this island," said a beleaguered Mitim.

"But, if you do …"

Lalumière inspected the cell. "Of course, you know that I am worthy of much better quarters. I have a château—"

"Okay, it's not quite a spa resort here, but it serves the purpose."

"Spa? Resort? This is a prison. The walls, the ceiling, and the floor are all stone. The bars are flat, rusted iron bars that I could not get through with a special saw."

She used the jailer's key ring to find the proper key. She struggled to push open the door enough to allow them to squeeze through. The horror sanctum sound befitted its 481-year age.

"There is nothing but a stone table, a stone chair, and a small bed. I cannot stay in this place."

Sandrine grabbed his arm. "This is the way it works, Mitim. You stay here a couple of days, put up with the accoutrements as they are, and then move on to the next phase. We are getting very, very close now, and I need you to focus forward. Are you with me? 'Cause if you aren't, remember what happened when I no longer needed the boatman and the jailers."

"I am not like them. And you have made love to me. Many times. You must have—"

"Feelings?" She glanced up at the ceiling. "Nope. Feelings are not specified in the manual. But, hey, you'll do fine. Do you know your number?"

"Number? What number?"

"Check it out." She nodded at the one-person bed against the back wall. "That's a Sleep Number bed. Different numbers match up to your every need. Try it out. I have to find the nearest cold stone potty and relieve myself. I'll be right back." She pulled shut the heavy door and turned the key. "For your protection."

Mitim went to the bed and dialed 92, the year his aristocrat ancestors were beheaded. He laid on top of the gray blanket cover and fell asleep. The next thing he new, the spy was sitting on him. Naked.

"How about an amenity, Mitim. Let's make some noise."

He aroused quickly, and the sex lasted a good half hour. They slept off the pleasure and, when they awoke again, she explained to him what would come next. And she brought him up to speed on the recent past. He could not believe what he heard. He could not believe that his team of assassins, sent once again to Big Bear Valley, had failed to deal a death blow to Magus Crayle.

CHAPTER 22

Motoring through the narrow valley away from civilization gave Hekka Poppi some time to think. To ponder. She viewed the surrounding territory: California scrub, desert flora, the mountains tipped with white, the blacktop, birds of prey circling, forty-degree temperature, and crystal clear air. She glanced at Crayle.

He appeared comfortable in the driving position, his gloved hands placed symmetrically on the steering wheel at what he had called Nine and Three, as with the hands of a clock. He looped his thumbs over the two horizontal spokes. Like her, he sported a black Greg Norman visor with a neon-colored shark outline above the bill.

She realized she knew little about him. What kind of family did he have left? Where did they live? What was his youth like? His sports? His schools? His girl friends? More than one—she thought. And hobbies and career and experiences and principles. Likes. Dislikes. She knew none of this. She sighed. He was her Mystery Man. Her Secret Agent Man.

She asked him a question. He yelled back, "What?" She attempted to lean toward him, but the racing harness restrained her body. It didn't, however, restrain her feelings.

Because of his crash and memory loss, he had become an enigma. In a sense, he was like her tribe, the Serrano. Never telling their stories, their origins, their loves, their tragedies. As far as she knew, there were no Serrano biographies. Oddly, this made her comfortable with his inscrutable nature. It was her normal.

Yet, she had witnessed an attempt on his life and had made love to him twice. He had disappeared, then reappeared in her life, only to be attacked again. And to make love to her again. He had cost her her father. He had taken her to a hospital deep underground. Mystery atop enigma. He was dangerous for her, yet committed. Whatever he was, he was hers. And she—she was his.

They travelled another hour, her hand gestures calling attention to impending freeways.

The red Cobra, replete with its fugitive passengers, reached the terminus of Highway 2, the Angeles Crest National Scenic Byway. As Crayle veered right onto the 210 freeway, he glanced left. Not to check traffic. He knew, somehow, that just a few miles to the south lay the expanse and excessive brainpower of NASA's Jet Propulsion Laboratory. He also knew of the high-powered program managers preparing the next space probes, each managing a concoction of Phds from mathematicians, like himself, to astrophysicists and metallurgists. He was certain that even the janitors had doctorates. The internal conflict between a former scientific life and a covert life worthy of assassination attempts returned to the foreground of his thoughts to haunt him.

Hekka's voice brought him to reality. "The 2 zigs right onto the 210 west. At the city of Montrose, it zags south again." She pointed to a dash mounted gauge. "We need gas."

Crayle exited the freeway onto tree-lined Montrose Avenue, gliding into a gas station to fill the depleted tank. Hekka unstrapped and headed inside, stopping only to catch a glimpse of a Sir Walter Scott festival poster in the window. Whether Jack's Cobra got miles-per-gallon or gallons-per-mile, he wasn't sure. But it seemed thirsty even at docile speeds. In any case, he knew it could run damn fast.

No one at this station missed an opportunity to agree; the comments ran from "Who do I have to kill?" to "Look, dear. God sent Jesus back to show us how it's done."

Just as Crayle completed fueling, Hekka strode out of the associated 7-11 store with a tray that consisted of lunch—Slurpies, hot dogs, and doughnuts. And a lottery ticket.

Crayle glanced at the fare and then at the expensive leather racing seats. "Oh, well," he concluded. They washed down the food with the Slurpies and dumped the trash.

Having spared the Cobra any noticeable damage, they were back on the 2 headed south until navigator Hekka announced, "The 134 west. It becomes the 101."

"Next exit?"

"The 27 south. Half-an-hour ETA."

He glanced at her, ready to ask how she had acquired the vernacular for estimated time of arrival, but she was engaged, observing the sight of the expansive metropolitan monster known locally as L.A. Crayle felt sure he understood how she thought. Trapped in her familial role at the ranch, she had previously only heard of this place. He read her mind.

She was trying to imagine that, before all of the twentieth-century development, her Serrano forebears travelled tirelessly to the Ventura and Santa Barbara coasts many miles away. With a deeper read, he would have realized that the Serrano had traded baskets and mother-of-pearl inlaid vessels with a coastal tribe called the Chumash many years in the past. Without the ubiquitous asphalt, concrete, sheetrock, electricity, and vehicles. With only the natural noises of the animals and carts. Birds and lizards. Wolves. Without White people.

CHAPTER 23

When Crayle glanced at her again, her head was laid back, chin up, eyes closed, and her long black hair trailed behind her like gloss-painted speed lines on canvas.

Crayle made the Topanga Canyon exit and headed south toward the Pacific Ocean. It was not yet in sight, but the smells of seawater and its myriad contents wafted up the canyon, rushing to meet them. Foreign visitors, including those from the East Coast, were forever surprised that the California coast turned west in this area, putting the ocean to the south.

• • •

"The GPS says turn right next chance … onto Lover's Highway."

Crayle pulled the device from her hands. "It says Mulholland Highway. The lover's part is to the left. Mulholland Drive."

"I want to go."

He handed back the GPS unit. "How did—"

Her cat-swallowed-the-canary smile cut him off. Mulholland Drive was world famous as Hollywood's Lover's Lane. How did this young Indian woman, who barely ever left her ranch … what were *her* secrets?

She read his quandary. "I went to school down the hill in San Bernardino. I received an Associate Degree."

He glanced at her, searching.

"A girl in class moved to San Berdo, as we called it, from Woodland Hills. Where we exited the 101. A Valley Girl."

Crayle felt a twitch. He sensed a set up. "What was your degree?"

"Husbandry." A rare occasion, she burst out in laughter, tossing her head to and fro. He could tell she was, at last, relaxed, or at least distracted from all that had preceded. They were safe now.

"Magus. Pull over."

Crayle gave her a surprised look.

"No, I don't have to pee. Pull over."

He pulled the Cobra onto the dirt shoulder. He knew she was not accustomed to traversing winding roads in a firm-suspensioned sports car. She might be getting sick.

Hekka Poppi, the woman known in the Big Bear Valley for her breaking and training of quarter horses, to say nothing of her restored Blood Orange Bronco, exited the Cobra and walked to the driver's side. "I'll drive," she announced. "It is better. You have the gun. You cannot shoot and drive."

Once again, her straightforward assessment of the situation and common sense won out. Crayle suppressed a protest and climbed out.

"You'll be fine. It's not about the power or the speed. It's about control."

"Oh, my." She settled into the seat. It took but a few seconds for Crayle to adjust the seat and the racing harness to fit her five foot six inch frame.

"There. Snug?"

"Yes, but …" She extended her arms and legs, four inches short of the steering wheel and pedals.

"Press the front of the flat wheel on the left side of the seat bottom."

She did as he directed.

The seat and belt anchors moved with her to a manageable position.

"Shouldn't the belts be bolted to the body?"

"It's okay. It was a Bond car," he teased. "Flip the top of the gearshift and push the button."

"And it will eject me?"

He laughed and trotted around to the passenger side, slid her seat rearward to the stops before entering.

"It's no problem. I can drive a stick. I learned on my father's tractor." She smiled.

"This is much more powerful than a tractor, and it handles—"

"Don't worry. Those bad people are far behind us now. There is nothing to worry about. I like to learn new things."

Crayle adjusted to his new digs. After some effort with the heavy racing clutch and spinning of the wide rear tires, the Cobra was once more underway. The car's steering was assisted, but retained a heavy road feel.

She did quite well, even as she struggled with the heavy clutch and the frequent smoking of the rear tires.

They passed one of the many lookout points on Mulholland Highway. Crayle provided commentary. "Couples come up here at night. They look out over the forty mile expanse of metropolitan Los Angeles. It's beautiful. Romantic." The many-colored lights shined and sparkled.

"If space aliens are ever going to spot us, it'll be L.A." He noticed that she had no reaction. She did not look. He read into the non-look her inclination to process. *How does he know about this road? Who has he been here with? Was it before the accident? Or after?*

She broke the silence. "Some day, you must bring me here at night. Will you?"

Before he could answer, an explosion of gunfire sounded from behind. The bee-buzz nature of the fire indicated small arms.

Hekka checked the rearview mirror.

"Oh, my!" she yelled. "It's them." She poured on the gas, leaving a heavy plume of tire smoke in their wake.

Crayle didn't know that the Vestige chip embedded under his skin had not been removed as he had been told. He didn't realize that Dr. Rorschach had replaced its dead battery with a new one. It had left 'Magus Crayle has been here' data on the metal freeway sign posts and cell towers along the way. Associates of the French assassins had picked up Crayle's route and relayed it to the hit team.

With the racing harness holding firm, Crayle couldn't turn around. Releasing it would have thrown him against the gearshift lever and Hekka during a hard right turn.

Hekka withdrew her Bowie knife.

Crayle refrained from repeating the hackneyed phrase about bringing knives to gunfights.

The sun glinted off the Bowie's polished blade, temporarily blinding him. "Angle it so," she said, positioning its point against the mirror. Crayle snatched it from her with care. Using her impromptu technique, he was able to reflect the mirrored image and view the assault team.

There was no mistaking the black Chargers. And there was no mistaking the triangle-jawed killer he had seen on the mountain. This one was bigger and meaner-appearing than his dead twin.

"It's TJ2," yelled Crayle. "The one from Cougar Crest. There's no time to switch. You'll have to outrun him."

Hekka gave fair effort at a task experienced sports car aficionados would find a challenge. Still, the Chargers closed, and her attempts to carry speed through the corners slid them dangerously close to the edge.

The weather had been a beautiful day of sunshine, not atypical of L.A. in the late Fall. But, in a few short minutes, an overcast replaced the blaze of the sun. The temperature dropped.

"Hekka," he shouted over the engine's din, "they put low profile, Summer tires on these kinds of cars. Rain turns asphalt into greased glass. Pick it up a bit so we reach our destination before the showers arrive."

She nodded acknowledgement and stoked the engine.

A whooshing sound caused them both to start. Then, a sound reminiscent of thunder. Not rain. A boulder exploded twenty feet ahead, showering them with particles. Crayle cranked his head hard right.

"It's a Barrett .50 caliber! Hekka, go!"

She went after it like a lioness after an antelope. The Cobra twitched left, then right, then left again. When the tires slid sideways, it was always under control. The young Indian rancher, who had never engaged in other than foot races with her brothers, neared racing speeds. Throughout, her determined demeanor never changed. Cast into the moment, she owned it.

The three passengers in the black, hemi-powered Charger all swore at once. The driver did his best, but the engine-suspension combination of the Dodge supercar proved less than a match to the Cobra.

The Charger had been modified. It sported a sunroof opening over the rear seat instead of the front. The man standing in it manned the Barrett sniper rifle. A bipod with roller feet steadied the heavy weapon, but the side sway, back and forth, of the mountain highway made placing a targeted shot hopeless.

In a second car, the man inside was swearing alone. The three others were required to listen.

"How can we not catch them? The sports car is being driven by … a girl. You are imbeciles!"

Crayle slid a computer out of the glove box. He punched in a code and pressed Function Key One. The panoramic mirror's center section zoomed in on the lead attack car. Jack had the car set up like a dual-seat fighter. Except the pilot and weapons officer sat side-by-side.

He saw a man with an RPG launcher preparing another shot. The telescoping capability of the mirror allowed Crayle to watch the man load a bright yellow round.

"A heat-seeker," Crayle yelled.

Hekka traced the road around a left-hand curve. At ninety-miles-per-hour, she struggled to keep the car tight against the mountain. The speedometer hit 100. She slowed slightly to round a right-hand bend that placed the Cobra beyond the assassin's sight line.

The two fugitives heard the missile whoosh. Another Function Key and a heads-up display appeared on the windscreen. A calm, feminine voice, one Crayle recognized to be Jack's flight attendant, Flori, announced, "Fifteen seconds to impact."

The rocket flashed around the corner behind them, seeking Cobra engine heat.

"Ten … nine …" Flori intonated.

Ahead, a sharp curve left would put them broadside to the missile. It would provide the best heat signature for the missile's tracking system. If Hekka could make the curve.

"There!" Crayle pointed. A tanker truck trundled into sight. Coming their way. "Brakes!"

Hekka stabbed the pedal. The six-pot Brembo disk brakes pulled the car down to sixty in an instant. The racing restraints gouged their skin.

"Three …"

Hekka pushed to the right, scarcely avoiding the jagged mountain wall.

"Two …"

Crayle popped his restraints. He grabbed the wheel and twisted the car left ninety degrees. Toward the road edge.

"One …" Flori purred, as if sex would come next.

He removed his hands. Instinctively, Hekka swerved right.

The missile streaked by, clipping the Cobra's left taillight. The red car skittered along the road edge, millimeters from a deadly plunge.

Having overshot and having a damaged tail fin, the missile lost its target. Designed to re-acquire, its guidance system once again found heat.

The exploding tanker produced a huge ball of flame. The truck, its driver, and the outside half of the road plunged down the cliff in a rolling ball of flame.

Hekka had accelerated the car to ninety. With the road just ahead weakened by the explosion and collapse, the remaining inside lane could give way in an instant. She pressed the Cobra as close to the mountain as possible. More of the road fell away. She screamed …

The chase car rounded the curve, its occupants sure to find the death and destruction to complete their mission. To their dismay, they saw the Cobra thread through the narrow passage. French provided an excellent vocabulary with which to swear. They took advantage.

The pursuit driver followed Hekka's lead. At speed, he pushed to the inside of the curve, but the heavy Charger caused the remainder of the road to collapse. The Charger and its crew followed the flaming tanker, bounding downhill like an elongated eight-ball.

The road destroyed, the remaining chase cars broke off pursuit. A furious Jerome screeched at the skies, "Merde, merde, merde!"

Once again, Crayle, together with yet another confounding woman, proved to be an impossible target.

• • •

Safe now, they detected sirens far behind. The surviving assassins would live to endure the fury of their leader. After the attack on Cougar Crest Trail, it was his second failure. He would be taking it out on them after he finished off any wounded. With no road left to continue the pursuit, he and his men would have to retrace back to the freeway. There, they would have no further Vestige data to collect. That was good news. The Mulholland Highway emptied out at a specific point in Malibu. The question was whether the original Triangle Jaw's brother, Jerome, knew that, and whether he and his killers would find a way to greet them there.

A few miles further, Magus Crayle and Hekka Poppi arrived at a small, gate-guarded enclave indicated as Monte Nido—Mountain Nest. It was not a bastion for assassination escapees, but rather for eating disorders. Crayle motioned to pull over. They exited the Cobra to catch their breath.

"So, Lover's Lane is that way," Hekka puffed, pointing east. She stood two feet away, her head tilted up to him and with the countenance of a prosecutorial parent. "And you know that how?"

"Rorschach must've slipped."

In a flash, the ten-inch Bowie was in her hand. Crayle jumped. She held it up, using its gloss side as a mirror. She moistened a finger and groomed her black eyebrows. The knife returned home as quickly as it had left.

"You know how to send a message, don't you?" Crayle remarked. "As soon as I get the chance, I going to muss up those eyebrows."

She grinned. The first time ever. She jumped into his arms and kissed him full on the lips. "Let's do it now."

Crayle broke loose and pecked her lips. "Soon. I promise."

"Remember my Bowie. It doesn't like broken promises."

He shook his head. "Driver swap." He rearranged the driver's seat and belted in.

Hekka pouted. "You don't like my driving."

"Pilot to navigator. Get in."

She complied and checked the GPS. "Turn right next chance onto Malibu Canyon south. Magus! The GPS shows a checkered flag at the end of Malibu Canyon!"

"It's okay, my precious, knife-wielding partner in crime. From there, I know where we're going."

It had been a long time.

CHAPTER 24

The road known both as N1 and Malibu Canyon dead-ended into Southern California's most famous road, the Pacific Coast Highway. Locals called it the PCH; politicians called it State Route 1.

Hekka's cell phone rang. Crayle heard only one side of the conversation. He interpolated the rest. "Yes. We are at the PCH," she said. "Turn right." Hekka pointed. "I will repeat what you say, Mr. Jack, so that Magus can hear. Yes. We are to continue to a sign indicating a restaurant at the beach." She spelled the name. "A woman will meet us there. She is pretty, a knockout actually, and has short blonde hair with spikes on top." Hekka looked perplexed. "Spikes? Of metal? No, he says, Magus. The spikes are not of metal."

Crayle saw the sign and turned toward the beach, which was not visible from the highway. The Cobra wound through a curving undivided two-lane amongst what seemed a forest of trees that concealed a mobile home park. They passed the entrance to a state or Federal park, exiting the small forest into a large parking lot. Because of the roadster nature of the Cobra, they could smell, as well as see, the beach. They pulled up to a building that divided the parking lot from the sand. A sign confirmed it as the Paradise Cove Restaurant.

To the right side of the building sat a number of beach tables with benches and umbrellas. A woman with close cut, spiked blonde hair occupied one of the tables. She wore an off-white, wide-collared blouse over turquoise Capri's and a pair of red open-toed pumps. With the addition of matching red lipstick and a tanned face, she personified Hollywood. Jack had described her well. She had removed a deep-brimmed, tan straw hat to better enable identification. Once accomplished, she replaced the hat above large, black-framed, movie star sunglasses. Crayle and Hekka took their places next to her.

"Hi, I'm Marilyn. Around here, they call me Malibu Marli," the woman said as she extended her hand across the table. "And you," she said, glancing at Crayle, "are Mr. Treadwell and you …" She turned to Hekka. "… are the lovely wife, Anna."

She spoke quickly, as if there wasn't a moment to lose. She saw their reaction.

"Ha. I'm having a Five-Star day. It stands for five caps—cappuccinos—from Starbucks. I hear I slow down a bit when I talk in my sleep. Welcome to Malibu. I understand you desire to buy a place. I have found exactly the right one. It has space so you won't feel cramped, a large garage, and five acres of prime landscaped land. The ocean view is way past spectacular. You'll love it. And the best part, all of the financial arrangements have been made. Come." She stood up. "It's perched on a bluff not far from here."

"Hang on just a second. How did all this happen so fast?" Crayle stayed in the character of a well-to-do beach house client. "We only made the decision to buy this morning."

The woman laughed. "The magic of Hollywood. Happens all the time. And I, your humble realtor, am #1 in this area. I've got the only lockbox master key. I know all that is available and for what price."

Hekka glanced at Crayle. Her eyebrows pinched together. She had never pretended to be someone other than herself. She was out of her element altogether.

"Come. I'll take you in *my* car. Your's has already been gathered up for taillight repair and will be delivered to the house later today."

They followed her to a black Mercedes S63 AMG with a mirror shine. On the door in off-white script were the words, *JeneriX RealtY*.

"You can sit in back, Mr. Treadwell, and your wife, Anna, can ride up front with me. We can do the lady talk. I'll tell her the woman's aspect on this wonderful property." She handed them each a gold wedding ring. "Everything in Malibu is for show. I now pronounce you husband and wife."

They slipped on their rings, each a perfect fit. Their eyes met. Hekka smiled her minimalist smile. He smiled back. His mind put the prospect of marriage into the context of his life as it now existed. A single tear trailed down his cheek.

The trip lasted only a few minutes. They drove up to the highway, the PCH, and turned north.

"You'll absolutely love this place. It's just up ahead." She provided the name.

"Point *Doom?*" Crayle gasped. He glanced at Hekka.

The realtor laughed. "D-u-m-e."

Crayle saw Hekka's reflection in the windshield. She just stared at the road ahead without expression. He could tell. The realization that they still might not be finished with the assassins had hit her. The prospect of doom had became a much more prominent notion in her mind. It was real, and Crayle realized he'd put it there.

• • •

She crossed traffic as if oncoming cars were irrelevant, pulling up to two large iron gates centered on a block wall that extended in either direction along the highway.

"This is a quite secure property, Mr. Treadwell. Here, you will find the privacy and comfort affluent newlyweds lust after. You will feel ... special."

The interlocking-brick driveway snaked toward a main house that would cause most Hollywood celebrities to drool. Architected in the French château style, it reminded Crayle of Lalumière's home in northeastern France.

"Isn't this a bit ostentatious for a safe house?" Crayle asked.

"No one would ever suspect this property, Mr. Treadwell. But they would not be surprised by the extensive security and the intermittent entry and exit of security trucks from House Safe, Unlimited, which you may recognize as a Central Intelligence proprietary. Oh, and below ground, in the basement, is a CIA triage setup. You simply *must* see it."

"My memory has been lost. I don't remember these things. What is a proprietary?"

"Ah. It is a real-appearing company that is a wholly-owned subsidiary of the Central Intelligence Agency. Think Air America."

"Air America?"

"Never mind. It's okay. Everything has been taken care of, and you and your lovely wife, Anna, needn't worry about a thing."

She pulled the Mercedes into the porte cochère and led them into the palatial estate. Stepping through the large double doorway, they noticed the whisper-quiet granite floors. Not a sound.

Crayle and Hekka were in awe of the jaw-dropping splendor inside. Clearly, no expense had been spared in the elegant accoutrements, furniture or wall embellishments. Just as they regained their senses, they heard a voice.

"Hey, Magus. Welcome to Margaritaville West. Just kidding. I see you've met my wife, uh, former wife. I'm sure she's treated you with the sort of respect that I never got."

"Don't start," said the agent.

"Yeah, we spent some *company* time together in the early days. Mostly in England and Switzerland. We worked so closely together and played our husband and wife cover so well that one day I rolled off her at about seven in the morning and said, 'We should do this for real. You know, have kids, the whole bit' I told her. So, we did. When the gig was over, we came back to the States and did the wedding thing. In a deep cover cathedral."

"Unlike most of what Jack says, there is a small element of truth there." Marilyn smirked at him as if he had just violated the *tell the truth, the whole truth, and nothing but the truth* admonition given to those who testify in court. Before she could provide details, the closet door burst open. Crayle, Hekka, and the realtor took defensive postures.

"It is I," Lenny announced. He stepped out, Phoebe and Micmac close on his heals.

"It was his idea, Mag," Phoebe said, pointing at the P.I.

"The closeness in there was fine. Coulda done without the third wheel," Micmac said, nodding at Lenny.

Jack intervened before Lenny could be beaten or shot. He turned to Crayle, the wrinkles accentuated on his forehead. "I brought the gang in by private jet. We landed north of here at a burg called Camarillo. After we have a little chat, I'll whisk you guys over there. You can have the jet …" He tossed a set of keys to Crayle. "… for the next major op."

Crayle stepped closer to Jack. "Op? What are you talking about? We just survived another—"

"Make that two," interjected Hekka.

"—yes, two assassination attempts. Add to that a night on a very cold mountain, and I think we deserve a breather. Besides, Hekka isn't a trained operative. She doesn't even have a clearance. Or even know what one is."

Jack nodded his understanding of what they had gone through in the last few days, but it didn't appear to matter. "Something's come up."

• • •

Jack gathered the team, now extended to include one Serrano Indian, at the large dining table.

"Oh. Dear?" He glanced at the realtor known as Marli. "You can go now. Thanks for the help. I'll pay you back with *you know what* as soon as I can get back this way."

"I'm getting my *you know what* elsewhere these days, Dear," she retorted in a tone of pure sarcasm. "Did you all know that Jack's real last name is spelled O-U-G-H, pronounced as in cough." She smiled a glib smile as Jack grimaced. "It was nice to meet you all. And please note, for the record, that I will receive no commission for this job. It is just another Jack Ough IOU I will add to the pile." With that, the Hollywood-style realtor departed.

"She didn't really mean that," said an unconvincing Jack. He then explained why they would be traveling to a foreign land and why it was necessary. In broad strokes, he informed them that the fate of the world depended on their success. And how, as before, he'd back them up no matter what. "Take tonight off. Get plenty of rest. And Mag? I told Phoebe these guys are still tracking you by that tracker chip. They were supposed to remove it back at the Quarry, but ole Doc Rorschach responds to a different chain of command than I do. Or maybe you two just ran off before he could get it done." Jack shrugged. "Between the ladies and Lenny, you'll be able to locate it and get it out for good. Because of its short range, it will be near the skin's surface. Shouldn't be a problem. Micmac and I have some weapons planning to do. We'll be in the basement." Jack and Micmac took a spiral stairway.

"Guys? I get sick at the sight of blood. I'll just watch TV. I'll turn it up to cover the screams." Lenny took to the sofa, remote in hand.

"So much for him being a help," said Hekka.

"Woulda been the first time," said Phoebe. "Okay, bub. Off with the shirt."

"And pants," added Hekka.

Realizing that to complain would waste time, time the assassins could use to track him, Crayle complied.

"Where might they have planted it?"

"You know …" They studied his crotch. "… that'd be the last place anyone would look."

"Yeah."

Hekka drew her Bowie knife. Phoebe drew her Glock.

"Wait!" Crayle defended.

"Easy, cowboy," said Phoebe. She removed the clip and popped a .45 cartridge into her free hand. "Here. Clamp down on this." She held it out to him. "It's called, biting the bullet." The women high-fived. The celebration complete, they explored his body. Phoebe finally located the site of the tracking chip. "Directly behind your right shoulder. It's red here on one of your scars from the crash."

"Of course. I wouldn't feel it when I lean back in a chair. And I can't see it no matter how far I twist my head."

"And, lying on your back, you would not feel it," Hekka added.

"Yes, but I sleep on my side …" Crayle winced. Hekka bit her lip to squelch a laugh from her tease. Her eyes watered.

Phoebe offered, "I'll let Hekka do the extraction. I'll mop up the blood."

Hekka gently opened the wound and pried the tiny chip from its home. "Here is an empty sunglasses case. I will set it in there. Don't let me forget. I will toss it over the cliff. But first, a trip to the bathroom." She left the room.

Crayle and Phoebe joined Lenny on the couch. No sooner had they sat down than a female voice called out, "It's me again. Sorry. Don't get up. Just forgot something." Marilyn Sommers, sunglasses case returned to her purse, was in and out before anyone could speak.

Hekka returned. "Hey, naked man. I am not lending you out. Put some clothes on. I want to see the extent of the grounds while it is still light outside."

Crayle re-dressed and they walked the hundred grassy yards to a cliff overlooking the Pacific Ocean. The sun just touched the horizon when it burst into a red-orange sunset.

"It's the color of my car," Hekka observed. "My father had the Bronco restored for me. I could choose the color. I picked Sunset

Orange. He said it was Bright Yellow. It was really called Blood Orange, but I renamed it. We would get such beautiful sunsets over the western end of Big Bear Valley and my father—" She stopped, unable to continue.

Crayle pulled her to him and held her tight. "I understand. Look, Hekka, I'll have Jack take you back to your ranch. Three times now you've nearly lost your life because of my … situation. I know we're in love, but, please, go back and be with your brothers. Bury your father and wait for me. *Please.*"

She cocked her head and peered up at the tall man who was her lover. "I know that you will be in danger until these matters are finished. I was never one to sit on the sidelines. While my brothers played football, I played soccer. And softball. Fast pitch. I, along with the amulet on your arm, am your protector. Three times you have been attacked in my presence. Three times you have been spared certain death. We must fight this fight as one. We will survive as one."

Crayle was out of his league when it came to Hekka's resolve. He nodded. Then he pulled her up to his lips and kissed her. He tasted the salt of the few tears that had escaped her eyes when she'd spoken of her father.

"Hekka, there are some things I need to fill in for you. After I was attacked at the Tack Store, after our escape to your ranch and our evening together, there was another attack. This time, an assault on my cabin. We escaped, the P.I. and I, and we wound up in Hong Kong."

"Hong Kong? What was there for you?"

"A Chinese man. His name is Chin Yao-wu. A very powerful man, he knew what I had done before my crash. I had made a plan for him. One he would use to conquer his country. I didn't remember a thing about it. He had a young woman, he called her his daughter, take me to a place where I was attacked again."

"Chin's people attacked you?"

"I thought so at first, but they weren't Chinese. I killed one of them. The girl saved my life. She was magnificent—no, not in that way." He quelled her reaction.

"Was she pretty?"

"I won't lie to you, Hekka. In fact, I will never lie to you. She was very pretty. She was just a girl of eighteen. Young and innocent, yet deadly enough to kill three bigger, stronger attackers. That made no sense along with everything else. We removed the masks of these men and found them to be Caucasian. In fact, they were led by the same man who led the attacks in Big Bear. He escaped."

"Then?"

"I was directed to France. It turns out I made a similar plan of conquest for a Frenchman, a colleague of Chin's, for the takeover of France. He was the one behind all of the attacks."

"So you and the private investigator, Lenny, flew to France and confronted this man?"

"Yes. With Jack, Phoebe, and Micmac's help, we attacked his château. He had an army of guards—we killed them all with help from Micmac and his truck. In the end, the Frenchman was taken off to be tried and imprisoned by the French authorities."

"You killed them with a truck?"

He smiled. "An extraordinary truck. A Q-truck. With 8,000 rounds per minute flying out of the back."

"And the man who led all those attacks on you. What happened to him?"

"It was incredible. He surprised and captured us inside the château. He nearly beat Phoebe to death, right in front of us. We were helpless. Somehow, she found the strength to kill the man. There was no question he was dead. That's why I was dumbfounded when we were attacked on Cougar Crest Trail. The man giving the orders was a larger likeness of the same man Phoebe killed."

"Then, they are brothers," Hekka concluded.

"That's all that makes sense, but much bigger than all these attacks is that I have set in motion two such insidious plans. And one of the men, Chin, is still alive, untouched by what happened at the château. Hekka, while we were held captive, the Frenchman ignited a nuclear device in Iran. It has affected the entire world. Everyone is arming and threatening war against the Iranians, and some against Islam. I believe it was part of the plan I concocted. There could be more nuclear devices somewhere on the planet waiting to be detonated. It's my responsibility to stop Chin. Before he kills thousands of people. Innocent people."

"How could you stop him, Magus? You are just one man. If he can acquire, place, and detonate these bombs, then he is very powerful. And he must have other powerful people helping him."

"Don't you see? Dr. Rorschach got me part way. He has restored most memories of my activities in Hong Kong. Chin intends to use mini-nukes—small nuclear devices—to take over his country. I know now that I operated under an NOC. Non-Official-Cover. No diplomatic immunity. For the CIA. If the remainder of my memories would just return, I would know Chin's plans in detail. I could stop him. Each piece of the puzzle I assembled for him is critical. I would need to remove just one."

"How can I help?"

He smiled at her courage. "Right now, you can be with me and give me your love." He seated himself in front of a bench, at the bluff's edge.

The night was dark with nary a sign of the sliver of wolf moon that had glistened her hair and skin their first time. In its place, a full moon glowed through the thickening fog. She pulled her top over her head and tossed it onto the bench. No undergarments creased her perfect flesh. Then, her moccasins. Her buckskin trousers were last. Naked, she gingerly seated herself between his legs. His hands moved to her breasts as they took in the cool breeze and the pounding of the surf. The pleasure of his touch forced her head back against his shoulder. His heart rate fueled a physical response in him.

Hekka worked her hands behind, made him available, then moved him inside. "Love me, Magus! Forever!"

In minutes, they had writhed a few feet farther from the cliff, safer territory, their bodies fully entwined.

They finished in the best ecstasy yet, and lay together. Holding, hugging, and smiling for the better part of a half-hour. They had snatched these ecstatic moments of lovemaking as they had become available. Three episodes in all. Internally, each foresaw many more. Each dreamed of private time as it was desired, not as others made it available to them.

Their breathing de-escalated to normal. Crayle held her against him. The heat subsided, but the love strengthened.

They watched the sun complete its exit and the red afterglow fade from the sky. Reality struck Crayle first. "Let's go inside. Let's find out from Jack when this will be over. When you and I can spend our lives in peace."

"Together."

"Hekka Poppi?"

"Yes."

"Will you marry me?"

Her traditional demeanor disappeared. Eyes glistening, smiling broadly, she leaped into his arms and whispered her answer in his ear.

CHAPTER 25

Crayle and Hekka walked in the door. Jack hailed them over to an ornate, carved mahogany, dining table. Lenny, Phoebe, and Micmac were seated with him. Papers were arrayed before them all, and Crayle felt a sense of reality coming back to him. It was not a reality he wanted, but he knew he owned it.

"Here's the deal, all. This Chinaman, Chin Yao-wu, is planning something big. We know that based on Magus' experiences. Plus, Washington prefers the devil we know to the megalomaniac we don't. I just recently received intel from Central Intelligence that puts some pieces together for us." He tapped at a page of a world map. "See this." He pointed at the center of Iran. "This is where the mini-nuke went off, just east of Fasd. Everybody on the planet believes it was an accident, a catastrophic failure in Iran's attempt to build a nuclear arsenal."

"That's not good?"

"Uh, no, Magus. The consensus is that Iran now has the weapon, but that it is unstable—big time. That's the official position of our government, but given our world class failure at assessing Iraq's nuclear progress, we're being super-careful about attacking Iran with land forces over this. That the CIA helped the Frenchman and the Chinaman to utilize this very same size and type of nukes for their own purposes needs to be kept quiet. Way quiet."

"It wasn't Iran's bomb, was it, Jack?" Crayle still felt Jack kept hidden most of what he needed to know. Jack was former CIA, a spy. Crayle knew that spies obsessed about keeping secrets. The CIA had shot itself in the foot more than once as a result.

"No, it wasn't their bomb. We are now 90% sure the bomb was brought there by Chin's military man, a General Li."

"Like the Civil War guy," Lenny opined.

Jack gave Lenny an 'if you say one more thing, I will set you on fire' look. "It's L-i. He is the general in charge of the Chinese nuclear weapon development and distribution effort. He was tracked to Fasd and probably delivered this device."

Micmac furrowed his brow. "I don't understand. If Iran wants to develop a bomb of their own, what would they do with a ready-to-go weapon?"

"We're not sure. We do, however, believe the Iranians were played. Set up. But here's the kicker. Our friends in the DGSE tell us they uncovered in Lalumière's papers the detailed plans for a water tunnel to the Fasd facility. They also established his presence there at the same time as Li. Trust me, this was not a coincidence. And then, at the château, you four saw—"

"Technically, I didn't see a thing. I was trussed up on that head-chopper contraption with a sack over my head," Lenny inserted.

Jack thought of having the team find a suitable sack so he could continue his briefing unabated. "Three of you saw the Frenchman detonate the device. The timing is exact to what the rest of the world saw. It was Lalumière's gig."

Crayle nodded in affirmation. "Lalumière is off the grid. It's just Chin we have to worry about. What's the plan?"

• • •

As Jack reviewed the plan to deal with Chin, Jack's ex-wife sat in her office a few miles south. She had promised herself to keep Jack out of her life, but she'd let him back in. Preoccupied, she didn't hear the slight noise as men clad in newly acquired Malibu sportswear applied their tools to the back door lock. They entered, guns at the ready, and spread out, searching for their quarry. They found no sign of Crayle or the others. They moved into the office without a sound.

By the time she saw them, it was too late. Two men grabbed her as she jumped up and a third spiked her shoulder with a hypodermic needle. The fourth man was big, not particularly handsome, but fearsome with beady black eyes and a pronounced, angular jaw. She struggled at first, then her body failed her. Her chin dropped to her chest and her arms dangled helpless at her sides.

"I have prepared her, monsieur," said the hirsute medic.

"Bon. We must not mark her face, and we must not damage her body. She must lead us to them and provide topographic details for our assault. She is a realtor, so she will have these things." Then the anger spread from his heart to his face. "I will personally kill the woman who killed my younger brother. She will suffer the extreme of Hell on Earth before she dies. Then I will kill the man who has destroyed my employer. I will give you anyone else in the place to do with as you like, but they must all be dead before we leave. And to avenge my brother fully, they must all be raped before they die."

"All? The men?" asked one.

"All."

"Eh, I did not know your plan. There may be a slight problem."

Jerome drew a silenced, black Manhurin from his waistband. He grabbed the back of the man's head with his other hand and jammed the gun barrel against his nostrils. "What do you mean, problem?"

"Ahhhhh! I have roofied her so that she cannot fight us. We will remove her sweater and bra and use the thumbscrews I brought on her nipples until she agrees to help."

"You fool!" the leader screamed into the man's face, spittle striking everywhere. "She cannot feel the pain sufficiently, and she cannot talk. We must now wait until the drug wears off. They could escape. How much did you give her?"

"Eh, two doses. Enough for the sex after she talked."

The shot was barely audible, but the brain and blood spatter frightened the rest of the killers.

"*Merde! Merde! Merde!*"

• • •

They all sat in silence in the House Safe, Unlimited van as Jack drove them up the coast. He stopped alongside the road next to a wind-blown sand drift that extended from the road uphill at a sixty-degree angle and terminated against a mountainside. "Everybody out."

They complied.

"This is the place, Magus," Jack said with a sweep of his arm. "This is where you crashed."

Across the two-lane road, beyond a flowered cross, was a steep drop. Then an expanse of beach and the ocean. There was a gap in traffic and the silence, only punctuated by the intermittent cry of the gulls soaring the skies, portrayed a sense of ultimate peace.

"Enough time for nostalgia. Saddle up."

They returned to the van, proceeding past Mugu Rock and then north to Camarillo regional airport. Jack drove to a waiting jet, its engines spooled up, its crew ready.

"Go on. Pile in. There's no time to waste. You'll catch Chin off guard if this comes off as planned."

"You're not joining us?" asked a surprised Crayle.

"I've got to make some calls. Don't worry. I'll catch up with you in Taiwan. Before the strike. Now, rock and roll!"

They left Jack standing on the tarmac, hands on hips, appearing concerned. The confidence he'd displayed during his planning briefing was no where to be seen on his countenance.

The jet lifted off, heading for a fueling stop in Hawaii. Flori, the flight attendant and vendor of all necessities, supplied them with beverages. Alcohol. With both Phoebe and Hekka on board, Crayle wondered if Flori would kiss-and-tell.

• • •

Back in Malibu, Marilyn was coming around.

"Don't hurt me. Please. I just took those people to a place that had been rented for them." She had utilized her time under the influence of the drug to formulate a story. She reinforced her innocent bystander persona with, "Please don't hurt me."

"Release her hands," the leader ordered. "We will drive you to the site, where you will supply us with tactical information."

"Yes, anything," she promised, manufacturing the requisite tears.

The leader handed her the Hollywood shades. She put them on. She picked up her glasses case and a small, round object fell onto the table.

"The chip!" cried the leader. "It brought us to your office. *Merde!* It is no longer in Crayle!"

A stroke of luck for Marilyn. She had just moved from the *get the gates ready, St. Peter* to the cat bird seat. The killers could not find Crayle without her assistance. She squelched a smile.

The leader continued, "You must be your normal, friendly self. You will be always, eh …"

"Up?" she supplied.

"*Oui*. Up. If necessary, you will introduce us as clients. Understand this: if you help us, you will be set free. Unharmed."

Marilyn had heard every word they had said while she was doped. She didn't need Cliff's Notes to understand the *rape and kill everyone before we leave* command made by the leader. If her plan worked, no one, including herself, would be raped or murdered by this gang on this day. *If* her plan worked.

She led them to an old house in the hills north of Malibu. The yard was overgrown, and the place appeared as if it would collapse if a wrecking ball passed nearby. The last non-Malibu aspect of the property was the bright yellow tape with black writing that encircled it.

"This is a wreckage," said the leader. "No one would stay in this place."

"That's why they wanted it, I guess. A fixer-upper. It's Malibu cheap at 750k."

"You," he motioned to the others. "Check this place out. If you see them, shoot them."

The men entered from the curbside via a short bridge to the front door. The home squatted against a hillside, no doubt propped up by scaffolding below. The lead man kicked in the door. Nothing but black. They moved in like felines single file. Outside the leader gripped the realtor tightly by the arm.

"Ah!" came from inside. Then, "Ah!" "Ah!"

"What has happened?" he demanded from the realtor.

"I … I don't know. The floors need a little work. I don't know!" She winced as he tightened his grasp. He drew back his weapon and struck her on the side of the head, knocking her to the ground. He turned and silently entered the house. He heard only the sounds of his men.

Outside, one of the realtor's eyes popped open. She sat up.

"Ah!"

She smiled, scrambled to her feet, and dashed to the car. In seconds, she was blazing a trail out of there. She smiled into the mirror. "Sorry, guys. Gotta do sumpin' 'bout those rotted out floors. Oh, yes. And Jack, darling? I'm gonna kill you for this."

CHAPTER 26

As the jet disappeared into the cloud cover, Jack returned to the van. With two calls to make, each one worried him for far different reasons. He pulled up his contacts list and made the choice. He wanted this one over quick.

"Herr Doctor Rorschach. May I help you?"

"Doc, this is Jack Sommers. I've got some good news."

"A first, Mr. Sommers. Be warned. I do not wish to hear that my subject, Mr. Crayle, has left Big Bear or that you have spirited him out of the country again. He is too valuable for your games. My memory manipulation experiments must be kept strictly under my control. Dr. Rikki, to whom I report, would be upset in the extreme … hello? Mr. Sommers?"

"I'm here, Doc. Your subject is just fine, but … there's just a slight problem."

"Ahhhhh!" yelled Rorschach. "I knew it. I want him back here in the Quarry hospital immediately. No, sooner than that. Ahhhhh!"

"I'd love to comply, Doc, but your subject is flying west about now. Should be in … oh, shoot. I can't tell you. It's classified."

"Ahhhhh!" yelled Rorschach.

Jack hoped cardiac arrest would soon follow. No such luck.

"You turn him around or … or …"

"There is no *or*, Doc. National Security supersedes your little mind-fuck experiments." Jack winced. He could have chosen a more diplomatic characterization for the doctor's memory work.

"I must call Dr. Rikki immediately to report this breach of protocol."

"Relax, Doc. I'll have him back in no time. Trust me."

"Ahhhhh!"

Jack rang off and fired up the next call. Though he'd struggled with the doctor, that didn't bother him. He needed to get this next one right. It was to his boss.

• • •

"Yes, this is Neil Patrick Wohlford."

"It's Jack. How's it hangin', sir?"

Neil frowned at Jack's pedestrian language. He skipped the pleasantries. "Is it done? Are they off American soil?"

The patrician nature of the man oozed from the speaker on Jack's phone. Neil had retained his high-born nature to the point that he seemed arrogant to his colleagues at the CIA. His love of France and everything French adorned his office. Jack had once quipped that he would check storage for any leftover thrones so Neil could replace his office chair. To his surprise, Neil had pondered the notion.

"Yep. They're gone. I am happy to tell you that Operation Bumfuck is on."

Silence.

"Oh, you didn't give me an op name, sir, so I made one up. Anyway, Crayle and the team are headed for Asia."

"Good. And have you advised the good doctor of this fact?"

"Yes, sir. He was a little perturbed, but he'll be fine. Just to be on the safe side, don't be surprised if you get a little call from Dr. Rikki. She's so into this mind-fuck thing, she's doesn't realize there's a real world out here. With bad guys that must be stopped. She doesn't know Crayle has the survival skills of Godzilla."

"Godzilla perished, did he not?"

"No shit? Bad example. Sorry."

"Jack, your orders are that this team defeats the money supply for Mr. Chin and his general. Bad things could happen if they follow Crayle's strategic and tactical plan. I am referring to the use of nuclear devices as a means to an end. I believe that holding you back was a mistake. I will send my private jet to fetch you and deliver you west. You must catch up with them *in situ* and take leadership of the operation." Neil practiced the insertion of Latin phrases into his dialogs. He felt it put him in good stead with his superior, who used them with ease.

"It'll take hours, sir. And they and their plane have gone dark, comm-wise. I won't be able to talk to them 'til I see them."

"Have a safe journey, Jack. Stay with the operation until it succeeds. Clear?"

"Yes, sir. Sir? Sir?" Jack put away the phone. Three thousand miles away, and Neil remained a pain in the ass.

• • •

Neil regretted that he would probably need to lose the team members as resources. Mick Mackay was a genius in fabricating weapons solutions. And the FBI would scream bloody homicide when they learned their hotshot Annie Oakley type had perished overseas in a CIA-sanctioned operation. The private investigator, on the other hand, would be a welcome loss. His mother and father were deceased and his only sibling, a brother, had expatriated himself to Europe long ago with no likelihood of return.

Crayle's Native American girlfriend, Ms. Poppi, was of no particular interest, but Magus Crayle was another story. The Elder liked and respected the strategic genius. Without Crayle, the worldwide master strategy of the Illuminé could not have begun. The competing knowledge was that Crayle, via Dr. Rorschach's methods or a mere bump on the head, knew every last step in the plan. The cost-benefit analysis took Neil three seconds. Too bad. Crayle would be sacrificed for the good of the planet. Neil would make it seem like Chin's doing in case the Elder felt inclined to vent his displeasure. And pushing Chin down as he had Lalumière would effectively elevate Neil.

Another thought entered his elitist mind. What if he, Neil, could work directly with Dr. Rorschach to recover Crayle's memory of the Lalumière and Chin strategic and tactical plans? What if he, Neil, used that intelligence to throw France and China into chaos? He could save the day. Surely the Elder would elevate Neil Wohlford to Elder Elect, or better yet, to Crown Prince. He could retire from the CIA and live in a Palace. Damn.

He sat back in his newly-acquired throne chair. It was off-white with gold embellishments and red velvet cushioning. He played with a solid gold replica of Louis XVI's royal carriage, imagining himself in such a conveyance. For now, he would report status and receive his global update. He picked up his special phone to make the call.

"Elder, it is I, Neil. How is your day?"

"Ah, Neil, it is good to hear your voice again. May I assume the operation is in process?"

"Yes, Elder. They are enroute to the island nation of Taiwan, where they will cause a break in the money train by interdicting the second shipment of water diamonds, which will leave the remaining five nuclear bombs in play."

"Let us hope they will use wisely their scarce resources. Will your man, Jack Sommers, be running the operation *in situ*?" the Elder queried.

"Why yes, of course." Sweat beaded on Neil's brow. He crossed his fingers that Jack would arrive in time. Neil's life depended on it.

"The global update, Neil, is particularly of interest at this time. I have on my desk today's issue of *Le Monde*. And front page, above the fold, is a picture of our associate and leader of Illuminé in France, Sylvain Lalumière. They explain that he escaped captivity from the remnant subterranean chambers of the Bastille. They note that he had assistance, but are unable to identify who, what, when, how, or why. There are no reports of your young spy or her part in the escape. Well done, Neil. Keep Sylvain under her control for the duration. We are on plan, but he is volatile … like any good Frenchman. Remember, he still has two of the bombs."

"My spy has moved Lalumière undetected from imprisonment in the Bastille dungeon to D'If while also generating a following on the Internet. The mysterious Lalumière now has more friends than the president of France."

"She has done well, but we have only moved half of the distance to our goal. She must assure that the event in Marseille takes place as scheduled. Then, she must help him to escape. That will take us to the final phase. You have briefed her on the entire sequence, haven't you, Neil?"

"Yes, Elder. In spite of her youth, she is a natural for what must be accomplished. And should it become necessary, she is the perfect one to erase the Frenchman from the picture."

"Little *Grietje* has the perfect pedigree, Neil."

"*Grietje?*"

"Her given name. It is short for the Dutch, *Geertruida*. After her grandmother's grandmother. She was the famous spy of World War I, Neil. H-21. The Germans ran her against France. You may have heard of her."

"*Mata Hari?*"

CHAPTER 27

Jack's Dassault Falcon 7X, absent Jack, approached the airport at the Taiwanese capital of Taipei. Crayle and the others were buckled in, but their apprehension had nothing to do with landing. It anticipated running a violent operation on foreign soil. Lenny had advised that Sun Tzu's strategies relied on knowing the lay of the land. Yet, no one on the flight knew anything about the country of Taiwan or any of its cities.

Lenny saw the concern on Crayle's face. "Hey, MC. I've pulled up some particulars on Kaohsiung where we're going to do the nasty. This clown, Xiang, Chin's money man, resides in a building alongside the Love River. Maybe we can give him some love off his rooftop."

"If we take out Xiang, there are too many to take his place. Willingly. Someone from his own operation. We need to find the water diamonds and remove them, like a game piece, from the game. Without them, this mess I set in motion will dry up. We'll keep the stones for ourselves."

"That's what I'm talkin' 'bout!" Lenny grinned.

"Not to get rich. I've thought about this. We rely on Jack and whoever supports him for everything. If we confiscate the diamonds, we can finance our own ops, call our own shots."

"I'm on orders, Mag. I'd have to return to D.C. and get a new assignment."

"Phoebe, think about it. From what Jack told us, there is enough for you and Micmac to retire. Do whatever you want. No more 'will *he* come back' or 'will *she* come back.' And Lenny could spend all of his time with Alona."

"Better check with Alona on that one," Phoebe mused.

"Very funny," Lenny responded. "It so happens I like what I'm doing. And MC got me to my dad's killer so I could help you take him out. I still have a bit of a debt to repay."

Micmac took his turn. "Look. I quit this gig and Jack just finds me another one. What am I going to do? Play music? Phoebe, while fondling her Glock, has informed me that groupies are off the menu. Kinda takes the fun out of it." On cue, Phoebe punched his shoulder.

Flori stepped into the cabin from the cockpit. "We land in thirteen minutes. You will need these." She handed each a fresh passport, which noted their vacation in Belize during recent months.

Crayle examined his and held up his hand to stop her. "Flori, I have a visa for Taiwan, but I also have a multiple-entry visa for China. What gives?"

The rest checked. They, too, had visas.

Hekka spoke first. "Perhaps we need to go into China, too. Maybe it is a Plan B."

"FYI, ladies and gentlemen. I have not been read in on your operation," Flori intervened. "You can contact Jack on a secure line once you arrive at the staging area. I am sure he will tell you all you *need to know*. He will decide when. It protects the team should any of you be captured."

The last statement dampened the enthusiasm of a team that had never failed or lost a member, but each knew that every operation existed on its own and was independent of what had gone before.

A sobered team deplaned to begin a journey south in two hardened Hummers. The charcoal gray exteriors and minimalist interiors did nothing to brighten the mood.

• • •

Lenny, citing a P.I.'s nose for direction and following the GPS device provided by Flori, took the lead. His constant intercom banter became a nuisance, but he did locate a frontage road along the Love River. "The building'll be on the left side, according to its even number."

"They don't do that here. I'll know the building." Crayle hesitated. "Lenny, your brother's involved."

"What? Wolfie? No way!"

"He's a diamond broker. Amsterdam. One of Lalumière's nuclear custodians fenced a few stones. They traced back to your brother's business."

"Wolfie helped finance the bombs? People died, Magus. He couldn't've known. He's the nicest guy. Magus. No."

"Jack pulled down the intel while we were airborne."

Lenny fetched his cell phone. Crayle snatched it away. "A courier's enroute. We'll intercept him here. At Xiang's. That'll cut the pipeline. Then we'll find a means to remove Wolfie from the chain. A covert way."

"Kill? Aw, c'mon. Kill?"

Phoebe exclaimed, "Hey, check out that fabulous building!"

Crayle did. "That's it! Lenny, turn left!"

Eyes widened, Lenny complied.

"Into the alley!"

Lenny pulled up next to a tall, square chimney chase affixed to the back of the building. An ornate, cast iron door, four feet by eight feet, provided access, likely for cleaning, but was padlocked shut. Crayle's voice filled the intercom.

"This is the plan. Micmac, Phoebe, and Hekka stay with the vehicles. Lenny comes with me. We will reconnoiter Xiang's homestead and return. Rationale: Rorschach restored my memories of former events, and a working knowledge of Cantonese and Mandarin. The latter is spoken here. Lenny will play dumb … unable to speak." Crayle clicked off.

As they approached on a side street, Lenny couldn't resist. "You and Hekka, and Phoebe and Micmac seem to have all the personal stuff lined up. I …"

"Listen. Lenny. I will personally find you a nice Chinese girl. Okay?" For a moment, Crayle considered Chin's Red daughter a suitable prospect.

"Why didn't Jack supply intel on Xiang's suite?"

"Someone who finances international coups will take several floors. He may move daily and use encrypted Wi-Fi for comms. With the kind of money in play, all of his computers will utilize hardware encryption—much faster than the software equivalent. Much more difficult to analyze or spoof. And a longer key-length—harder to violate." He noticed Lenny's blank stare. "Encrypted files disguise their contents and keys are needed to unlock and …"

Lenny's stare advanced to a glazed state, then he asked, "It would take the power of the FBI, NSA, or CIA to understand their messages?"

"You've got it." He clapped the P.I. on the shoulder. "Silence."

Crayle and Lenny rounded the corner and approached the entrance. The wall behind a reception desk proclaimed INTERNATIONAL CHILDREN'S RESCUE FOUNDATION. Criminals of Xiang's stature often positioned their operations' behind phony charitable organizations. Those purporting to help distressed children provided cover and a reliable cash flow to cover overhead. Xiang's illicit dealings were gravy.

The receptionist, a Taiwanese national with tinsel-red hair, evidenced an astounding change in Chinese culture. He recalled Ling An-yee in her elegant, traditional black and gold dress. He shook free of his reverie. To his right, he noted a security station with three uniformed guards.

"*Ni hau.* I am the National Asbestos Inspector for the southwest. Our records show this building's top five floors have not been inspected for ten years. As you are probably unaware, asbestos is required for fire and noise suppression." His mind added population maintenance. He nearly smiled.

Lenny, unrehearsed, held still. He caught a security man taking interest. He pinched Crayle's butt.

The young girl checked Crayle's faux I.D. Her dark eyes lingered on his blue ones. She nodded. "Yes, sir. We have the elevators to your left. They service all but the top three floors. You must exit the elevator at Twelve, proceed to the end of the hall, and climb stairs to Thirteen. In the middle of Thirteen, you enter the ICRF special elevator. You will be greeted on floor Fourteen and shown to your destination."

In a pre-arranged dialog, Crayle told Lenny to stay put. He, Crayle, would make the preliminary inspection and return. In reality, Lenny was to create a continuous distraction—something he could accomplish in at least 150 of the world's languages.

The guard approached and, solely by hand motions, informed Crayle that his person and his briefcase required inspection. Body search complete, the guard moved to the briefcase. He removed its sole contents, a package wrapped in red and gold.

"It's a present from the president. An ancient firearm."

As anticipated, the guard took possession of the package.

Crayle rode the elevator to Twelve as instructed. As strode the hallway, he noticed no sounds, no people. Eerie. Out of order. As he topped the stairs at Thirteen, the security door buzzed. And opened.

Something was wrong.

As he entered, the door closed and a bolt embraced the casing. The hallway ahead curved right, taking him toward the front of the building. Then left, like a component of a pretzel. Then right again. He arrived at a Y and paused. He placed his briefcase on the floor and removed the fire bottle from his shoulder. He pulled the safety pin, raised the powder horn, and pressed the pin into the full automatic position. The red canister held three hundred rounds of titanium/carbon fiber projectiles. Light and deadly.

Being left handed, he chose the right passageway, holding the bottle tight to his body. The pure white walls morphed to odd shapes of bright colors. His mind recorded the distraction. Was Thirteen always this enigmatic … or was this just for him.

His head ached, yet no indication of gas entered his senses. His mind clicked. The clever juxtaposition of bright red and blue colorations were responsible. They caused the mind to struggle in its attempt to resolve the far left and far right extremes of the visible spectrum. Distracting. Clever.

He moved forward. Slowly. The walls changed from Picasso to cammo.

"Halt! Stop, Mr. Crayle!" The voice surrounded him.

The cammoed walls came alive. Six men armed with H&K MP5's emerged, their uniforms becoming distinct by their movement.

"Jack!"

But, it wasn't Jack's doing. Xiang had risen through Kaohsiung's criminal ranks. He knew all of the lowlifes. Three who still owed him money informed him about a small parade of Hummers travelling the coast highway. He heard from a source in Taipei that the passengers had deplaned a Dassault Falcon 7X—like Chin's. Criminals, like cops, don't believe in coincidences. To do so meant death.

• • •

Crayle had been removed to a windowless room, its walls, ceiling, and floor a matte black.

"Red, attach the cap to Mr. Crayle's head," directed Chin.

Red daughter, his expert in all things technical, attached the cap. She adjusted the straps for a snug fit.

"Power up the computer."

The new tablet computer booted and engaged its only application: Rorschach's Beta Version 2. The initial screen was a picture that moved as it displayed.

"There is a data file on this tablet, but I found it to be encrypted," said Red.

"Then it is of no use to us," Li commented. He feared that all files of material importance would be likewise encoded.

"Ah, but wait. If you watch the splash page, you will notice it moves from here to here, blending tones, morphing colors."

"I can see," said Chin. "Of what value is it, Red?"

"It is not what is seen, Father, but what is not. A trained eye can notice something is amiss, but not what. My eye exceeds training. It can sense that some pixels are not playing this game. They are steganographic pixels. They are key, so to speak."

"I wish Black daughter were here. She would appreciate the value of these files."

Red daughter's jaw tensed. To hear the name of her chief rival in affectioning Father disturbed her.

"Yes. I wish my adjutant, Gao Bo-da, were here as well. He is an expert in computer technology. He might be a good match for your Red daughter, Chin." Li smiled at Chin. With Gao's assistance, he knew from his prior examination of Chin's psychiatrist Chong Ming-shu's memory that Chin was dead set against intercourse involving his daughters, no matter the reason.

"How so, Red?" Chin asked.

"Watch." She tapped a pattern on the touch screen, and the picture changed. The pixels raced to new positions, forming a 256-character string mid-screen. "That, General … that, Father, is our key to the encrypted file." Victorious, she tapped the character string and sets of thumbnail images covered the screen. Red dragged her finger to demonstrate that the display was merely a window on a much larger tableau of information.

"I have isolated this segment, Father. It depicts the Crayle Archive ..." She tapped the screen again, "... and here is the Chin Yao-wu component." She jumped up and danced around. "Get down, Daddy-O."

"Red daughter! Stop immediately! You have been educated for years to be refined in your manners!" admonished Chin.

"This one," said Li, pointing at Red, "is too Westernized."

Chin's anger stopped as quickly as it had begun. He turned to Li, "She is well-suited to be my technological spy in the Western world. Her education in this respect has utilized some perhaps outdated videos, but more current ones are being copied in Hong Kong as we speak." Li didn't know that a daughter, upon celebrating her twentieth birthday, was led off by his eunuch servants and the filial relationship abruptly terminated.

The general nodded thoughtfully. Chin was either quite the conceptual thinker, having anticipated every contingency, or was able to render a plausible excuse on an instant's notice. The former would be of benefit in carrying out the Crayle Strategy, and the latter would be requisite for the politics that lay ahead. Li hoped both to be the case.

"Shall I take you through the entire Strategy?"

"No, Red. Restore the Chin component to his memory. I need certain details for our next move. Be careful, however, not to restore the Frenchman's strategy. We will examine it in detail when we return home. After Beijing."

"Last call for alcohol," announced Red. She dragged the top image with Chin's visage to a brain icon on the system tray at the tablet computer's bottom margin.

Chin's countenance bore his opinion of her diction. He had sent her to America. To UCLA. They had corrupted her in the ways of the liberal West. He congratulated himself on sending Black to the American university across town. She had been comfortable in the colors of the People's Republic.

Crayle moaned. His face turned beet red. His body shook. He gasped for air. His eyes shut. He went limp.

Dead.

Black daughter, who had just returned from an errand, assessed the situation in an instant. She ran to Crayle, rolled him onto his left side, and employed the ancient revival techniques of her martial art.

She slapped the side of his neck to the left of the windpipe. Again. The artery responded.

Crayle's eyes popped open. She had returned him to life. For good measure, she applied pressure to the acupuncture point, known as Gall Bladder Twenty, at the posterior terminus of his skull. It calmed the subject and the flush disappeared from his face.

A loud bang from outside overtook the scene. Red switched videos to surveillance. Mouths agape, all stared as three men and two women entered the building's ground floor, guns drawn. The screen labeled them via dialog bubbles.

"We are outnumbered!" cried Chin. "Take the computer, Red!"

She yanked free the cable connecting the electronic skull cap.

A second crash. The video showed Jack and the team had penetrated the second layer of security.

"This way!" Chin ran to the wall-width fireplace and yelled an ancient Chinese curse word. In an instant, the entire fireplace leapt into the ceiling, propelled by no fewer than twenty stainless steel pistons. The pistons retreated back to floor level in the next instant. Red was through the opening first, followed by Li. Chin turned to Black. She continued the pressure to Crayle's nerve, keeping him sedated.

"Now, Black! We must give him up for the present. We will make for Beijing. Crayle knows what lies ahead in my segment of the Strategy. He will bring his team to us on more convenient ground. We will be waiting. This time we will kill the others. Crayle will be ours at our leisure."

Black stared at him. She and Crayle had serious history. Severe history. She employed a hemostat and tongue depressor to continue the pressure. She placed her hand on his forehead. As if executing a protective ritual, she pressed her lips against her fingers, then followed Chin out the secret passage. It closed behind them, leaving no indication that anyone had been in the room but Crayle.

Black and Red pressed by circumstance and the elevator confines against Chin. It had been built, disguised as a chimney chase, for the covert, back-door exodus of only one man, Xiang. Each woman apologized in her own way. Chin felt his male member harden. Red wiggled down to take him.

Chin had never been one for confrontations. His heart raced. Black daughter took liberties never taken before. She stroked Chin's hair, then pressed her head against his shoulder, her free hand caressed his chest. She watched his face with a warmth in her heart. She had never been this close, her breath striking his flesh.

Chin sought to reclaim his regal character. He failed. He felt her moist breath soft on his cheek. He turned to her. Their lips touched, softly, lightly.

Red daughter, fully engaged on him, missed the intimacy. She mistook Chin growing ever firmer for her personal skill. She concluded that her plan to replace the more lady-like and sophisticated Black as Chin's number one had taken a step upward.

Chin finished with a flourish and Black backed off. Red rose to her feet and rested her head on Chin's right breast. Black examined her countenance. She read Red's licking of her lips as a display of triumph. Black knew better.

• • •

Xiang had been in the secret first floor vestibule prepared for the elevator to take him to his private floor when the commotion began. He heard the explosions and their voices when Jack and his team entered the building. Xiang stayed put. He listened to them ascend the stairs adjoining the vestibule. Time to flee. He pulled out his phone. Before dialing Chin, a thought occurred. If something happened to Chin, then Chin's worldwide fortune would accede to … Xiang. Holding his blood red Acer Ferrari laptop in one hand and his brief case in the other, he hustled out of the vestibule and into the entryway.

• • •

Outside, a pissed Phoebe guarded the team's rear. She had drawn the short straw. She investigated the only other car in the alley. As she opened the rear door to check the contents, she heard a noise behind her. Expecting to deliver her prepared explanation, she turned. Xiang slammed her abdomen with his laptop. Phoebe doubled over and fell across the back seat, the corner of the computer catching her in the solar plexus. She gasped for air.

A man sprawled across the front seats jerked awake at the noise. Xiang's eldest son. He plunged between the seats to aid his father.

Xiang flipped open his briefcase and removed a treasured pair of handcuffs. He rolled Phoebe onto her stomach, secured her wrists, and then utilized all three seatbelts to imprison her body. He slammed the door just as she kicked out. The door's edge cut deeply into her right leg. Once he closed the rear door, he tossed his briefcase and laptop onto the front seat.

His son, a great fan of old Charlie Chan movies, yelled to Xiang, "Okay. I got it, Pop." He powered open the sunroof, engaged the Mercedes traction control to prevent a telltale squeal of tires, and applied full throttle.

Xiang watched in horror as his Number One Son sped off into the distance.

Phoebe struggled to free herself despite the gash in her leg. She finally reached the nearest buckle. One push and the belt loosened. With similar determination, she freed the second and the third. All of the noise she made prompted Xiang's son to glance in her direction.

Hands still cuffed behind her, Phoebe flipped around and wrestled her arms over his head. As he redirected his gaze to the road ahead, he felt the cuff chain dig into his throat.

She pushed and pulled with all of her strength. Her effort paid off. The son's windpipe collapsed.

While he was trying to die, she freed her hands and grabbed the steering wheel. She now sat atop him and pushed her left foot onto his. She twisted her head, allowing her to view the road ahead with one eye.

The car careened from side to side, leaving the pavement for brief, but terrifying moments. An oncoming truck honked its air horn three times. She barely avoided sudden death at high speed.

Her lips pursed out in combat mode, air whistled through her clenched teeth. Every element of her being told her the end would come soon. Phoebe Bransfield made a command decision.

She released the wheel and flopped onto the passenger seat, the laptop between her and Xiang's briefcase. She grabbed the laptop. Her training, experience, and instincts told her there was good stuff inside. Stuff the team could use. She pushed up through the sunroof. One hundred feet ahead, the road curved sharp left.

She rolled out and down the trunk of the automobile just as it plunged off the road into a sewage canal. She hit the bank hard and, with no way to control her momentum, followed the car. Thirty feet. Twenty feet. Her hands still cuffed behind. Ten feet. Her leg bleeding. The pain severe. Five feet …

Xiang's car slammed into the sewage and exploded. A methane cloud hugging the foul liquid enhanced the destructive force tenfold.

The blast hit Phoebe like a locomotive at speed. It flattened her to the ground, and the leading edge of the flame singed her hair and eyebrows. It also stopped her progress toward the canal.

She caught her breath, placed the laptop on the ground, and fished out an international handcuff master key provided by Jack. The Taiwanese S & M cuffs popped off with ease. She pitched them into the channel, an afterlife gift. She reclaimed the laptop in time to hear a familiar voice.

"Hey, you okay? You look a little banged up," said Lenny, his head poked out the window of Jack's vehicle.

She walked the twenty feet to the passenger side door, grabbed his face with both hands, and gave him a big kiss.

"Holy shit!" Lenny exclaimed. "Seems I'm getting lucky tonight!"

Phoebe felt for her Glock.

CHAPTER 28

Phoebe. Get in!" Crayle shouted. "We've got a tracker on Chin's vehicle—he's headed for the airport."

Phoebe stumbled around the car and pushed in next to Hekka, who sidled up against her man.

"We have to catch Chin," Crayle said. "Something huge is planned for Beijing ..." Crayle's memory restoration regarding the strategy he'd created for Chin extended only so far. The rest was kept on a second storage unit, and Jack had grabbed Crayle before Rorschach could finish the job. Rorschach had informed him that there was a "burn-in" process, then a "read back and compare" process, to assure the memories had been stored onto the brain correctly. The nascent technology considerably slowed the process. In addition, Rorschach had stopped to null the targeted memory cells before the restoration could begin. More time.

But, mentally, Crayle had to thank the good doctor. The restoration had given him a prescience not otherwise possible. He knew what would take place before it happened. He knew where Chin was headed, and he knew why.

• • •

Chin, the general, and their entourage were enroute to Beijing. Chin's personal jet would span the distance in two hours and twenty-six minutes at a cruising speed of 500 miles-per-hour. As Chinese citizens, none of them needed to produce the multiple entry visas demanded of foreigners. Chin hoped the American "hit" team had only prepared visas for Hong Kong. He knew that, assisted by America's Central Intelligence Agency, appropriate visas could be created on the fly. It bothered him that their Falcon was exactly the same model as his. It was as if all players operated under the same umbrella.

Before he could take the notion farther, Red daughter appeared. They had been given privacy in the cabin. She took his pulse, knelt before him, and provided another dose of sedation. Afterwards, Chin drifted off. He dreamt of Li arriving in Beijing, to be greeted by the military and an emissary from the Party elite. He would thank them for their kindness, and then steal away to carry out his mission. Chin lapsed into a deep slumber.

In the bedroom similar in layout to Jack's, Black daughter, Ling An-yee, sat with the others. She had never been to the Chinese capital. She wondered what wonders she would find. Whatever Father's needs, she would fulfill. She wanted to be closer to the man, the genius. She wanted his every wish as if it were her own. More.

Her thoughts shifted. Red daughter had beaten her to the punch when it came to providing Father with his manly needs. She had noticed Red pushing ever closer, at once endearing herself to Father and pushing Ling farther away. Ling would have to consider remedial action with regard to Red. The notion of employing death touch to the young woman brought a faint smile to her lips. It disappeared just as quickly.

CHAPTER 29

Jack Sommer's aircraft departed half an hour after the would-be emperor. The many-talented flight attendant, Flori, distributed suitably seasoned passports to all, complete with requisite multi-entry visa stamps. She then produced a tray of drinks.

She turned to Hekka. "Punch?" When she returned to the bar, she stowed all of the liquor bottles, including the tasteless, 190 proof Everclear. A little boost for the Serrano girl. To liven her up. One shot. No, two. She retreated to the flight deck to provide company for the pilots.

Lenny felt the need to retrace their book of knowledge. "Listen up, people. We need to prepare for this one. Kaohsiung did not go well. So, we'll talk through what we learned, and then Magus can dump the rest of Chin's plan on us. Agreed?"

There was no dissent.

Lenny began. "We know that Mr. Chin gets his funding in Taiwan. From that Xiang character. And we know that the water diamond money from Frogface is used to buy these bombs. So, this recent trip of his means he's buying more bombs. But why? What is he planning to blow up next?"

Crayle inserted, "I didn't get everything from Rorschach, but Chin will use his own bombs in China."

"But why?" asked an unwinding Hekka. "It is his country. We do not blow up our own countries, do we?"

Phoebe turned to her. "Remember the Oklahoma City thing? That was one of our own trying to change political reality with a bomb."

Crayle nodded. "That is exactly what Chin plans to do. Remember what Lalumière said to us at his château? They plan to replace their countries' governments."

"I recall," said Phoebe. "But how do these bombs play into … your strategy?"

Crayle winced at her use of the possessive. His possessive. He quickly made the bombs and the consequent assured mass destruction and death not about himself. He employed abstraction.

"These men are deploying the small, radiation-free, nuclear devices they've created. The Iranian blast …" He closed his eyes and pinched the bridge of his nose. "… twenty-two days ago turned the world's attention to that country and its leadership. People who will kill solely for an ideology are quite dangerous, but fanatics who wish to die in the process to achieve a perceived paradise, far worse. A world already pre-disposed to hate the Iranians and their radical Islamist leaders witnessed their worst fears."

"But why them?" asked Micmac. "Iran has nothing to do with France or China, so it's a distraction. An atomic diversion. I've experienced enough to know that, if you create a little noise over here …" He gestured to his left. "… then no one sees what you're doing over here." He gestured to his right. "Employing nukes indicates the degree of the stakes involved."

Crayle tied it all together. "There's more. The Iranians appeared to the world to have created a nuclear weapon so unstable, it self-detonated. Chin and Lalumière can use Muslims as their fall guys.

And there are Muslims in both Western China and in Southern France."

"So why are we going to Beijing? To refuel? Why aren't we headed West to where the Muslims are?" Lenny looked and sounded non-plussed.

Crayle shook his head. "The Rorschach restoration didn't get that far. I don't believe there is a Muslim presence in Beijing or in its surrounding province. All we can do is track Chin and Li."

Lenny tapped on his computer. "Less than two percent of the Chinese are known to be Muslims. And those that are … live in an autonomous, make that semi-autonomous, region known as Xinjiang." He sat back, folded his arms across his chest. Smug.

"Whew!" Phoebe exhaled. "I had no idea!" Sarcasm fairly dripped from her lips.

Hekka, the biggest fish out of water and the only non-drinker on the team, attempted a voice of reason. "We do not know their ul … ul … ultimate des …" Her head bobbed. "… tination … or what they'll do. We think their chess piece, a bomb, might be used. We need to find 'em. Watch 'em." The alcohol in the punch made her woozy and giddy. "We need to get on this horsey and ride." She held her hands up in front as if riding one of her quarter horses. Then, she slid from the chair.

Crayle and Phoebe lifted her from the floor and returned her to her seat. Crayle tasted the punch. "Flori!"

The plane hit an air pocket. It plunged. Since no one wore a seat belt, they all grasped their chairs to keep from pitching to the floor. Hekka bounced from her seat, and giggled.

The pilot regained the jet's horizontal attitude and the ride smoothed. Crayle glanced at the too effusive Hekka. Not normal. Her normal was solid. She was like the large rock a farmer sees in his field and decides to remove. He presses against it. Nothing. Expected. He employs his tractor against it. Nary an inch. Undaunted, he calls in a crane at great expense. Nothing. He steps back. No shaking of ground or howling of hurricane or tornado could budge this rock. It became symbolic. The farmer left it in place. And so Hekka Poppi was Crayle's rock. And rocks don't giggle. He would have a talk with Flori.

Pushed to its limit for the duration of the flight, Jack's Falcon made an uneventful landing at the same airport as had Chin's. As the team deplaned, the errant flight attendant bade them farewell from the top of the stairway in her inimitable Brazil-sexual style. The team noted the new landscape and layout of China's premier city and capitol. Lenny spoke first.

"There it is! It's the one with Chin's chop painted in red over his Golden Dragon logo!"

"There goes a limo. Chin's gotta be on board," Micmac apprized the team. "Either they're both inside, or one of them has already left."

Crayle frowned as he studied Chin's aircraft. "They're refueling. Chin doesn't plan to be on the ground for long." He shouted up to Flori, "Have the pilots surveille the Falcon with the dragon logo. Call me the minute someone returns to it. It will likely be the same red and yellow limo."

"We will comply, Mr. Crayle," came her sultry reply. "Your transportation is an American school bus. They have replaced Chinese buses and vans due to safety concerns. Your Central Intelligence designer version is infinitely safer, given the armaments and the integral, cocoon-like safety cage. And you will take precedence in the Beijing traffic."

Crayle considered the intel transmitted by Flori. He made a mental note. She was more than a flight attendant. One of Jack's operatives, perhaps.

Appearing to be quite old, the bus driver was a local operative under Jack's control. His English sported a New England accent, product of the Massachussetts Institute of Technology. He seemed unusually calm. "Do you wish me to follow the limo transporting Mr. Chin Yao-wu?"

"Hurry!" yelled Lenny. "He's getting away!"

"Tut, tut, Mr. Lipschitz. We are tracking him via his personal GPS. He can go nowhere—almost nowhere—that we cannot perceive. And relevant customs and political officers are well in hand." He rubbed his forefinger and thumb together.

All officers at the airport exit stepped back as the school bus approached. Huge iron doors swung open, and the team was through to the streets of Beijing.

"And, as a backup, we have placed an industrial strength version of the CIA Vestige chip on Chin's vehicle. Without a need for satellite availability, the chip will plant tracking information on nearby structures for us to follow."

The driver's confidence passed itself on to the team, all unaware that one of Chin's daughters had discovered the tracking device and it had departed Chin's hangar with General Li.

They entered Beijing on Dongzhimennan Dajie, the Second Ring Road. A name change later, the driver turned west onto Jinyu Hutong. The three gawked at the eclectic architectures, built over centuries, the entire distance. There were always aspects of red and gold, but there also existed a common thread that was felt rather than seen. The Peninsula, Raffles, and Grand Hyatt—all upscale hotels—returned them to the modern era.

• • •

Across town, not far from Beijing's Forbidden City, General Li and a team of fifteen men and women drove slowly toward an unguarded entrance to another city. The Underground City. A vast array of tunnels and quarters constructed during the Cold War as a nuclear bomb shelter for the city's population. Li had most important business here, and luck was beginning to turn Li's way. His counterespionage lieutenant now possessed the Vestige chip secreted in Chin's limo by one of Jack's people. Li would employ it to lure Crayle and his team into the catacombs. He planned to impress Chin once again.

• • •

"We have a problem, Mr. Crayle. The Vestige chip indicates right, the GPS left. How do you wish me to proceed?"

"Pull over and stop. It's okay. Distance-of-follow is not a factor with either tracking device." He gathered the team at the rear of the bus. "We must be extra careful now. It's possible Chin has detected us and has plans of his own. We must split up."

"I'll stay with the women," offered Lenny. "They'll be safe with me."

Hekka and Phoebe closed their eyes in unison.

"Thank you, Lenny, but Micmac and I are an item," Phoebe extolled. "We'll take the Vestige signal. Okay, Mag?"

"Not okay. Team Alpha: Phoebe is with me and the GPS. Omega: Micmac and Hekka track the Vestige signals." Crayle felt it best to alleviate members of each duo from having to choose, under fire, between mission and lover. Dividing Phoebe and Micmac also provided serious firepower to each team.

"Hey!" Lenny jumped up. "What about me?"

"You stay on the bus. I know from Rorschach's reconstruction of my memory that we're going to require surveillance—right down your alley, P.I. We just don't know where, yet."

Lenny appeared to take the news well. He nodded approval of the best use of his skills and experience. He sat down, sporting a look of contentment.

A loud rumble grabbed the team's attention. All jaws dropped. Through the windows, they saw what had to be a mirage. An exact replica of their bus driver sat atop a genuine Harley-Davidson trike. Red, white, and blue.

"My twin," confirmed their driver.

"Omega," Crayle announced and pointed to the motorcycle.

Micmac and Hekka jumped out of the bus and into a back seat, replete with feature-fitting black tuck-and-roll and wide enough for two adults and a child.

While force leader Crayle engaged Phoebe, putting the past in the past, Lenny snuck off the bus and jumped in between Micmac and Hekka. "Magus changed his mind," he lied. "Let's roll!"

They followed the track past Beijing's famous Forbidden City. Lenny consulted his computer, shouting color commentary to his wedged-in colleagues.

"Completed in 1420 for the succession of emperors, it contained all necessities including a special palace. You'll like this one, Hekka. The only non-castrated dude who could mess with the concubines was the emperor. If one of his women got knocked up, he wanted to be sure it was him."

Hekka frowned. Intel was a strange concept.

"The final Chinese emperor, Pu Yi, abdicated the throne in 1912. Wow. Hey, I'm gonna take a little break here to check things out and let you two digest all that history."

The driver kept a close eye on his special tachometer. He stopped abruptly. "The Vestige trail stops at this point. It is likely that the bearer of the chip has gone to ground."

"This," he said, pointing a frail finger, "is the entrance to our Underground City. During the Cold War, special leaders were designated to move the population away from atomic bomb destruction to safety. Only the ignorant believed they would survive. The layout is unknown to most and requires a special guide, like myself. We will deploy at this point."

Omega piled out and, one-by-one, entered the prospective nuclear tomb.

Micmac supplied detail on the tracking technology. "The CIA's Vestige technology denies the possibility of track-back. Its range is quite short, and it operates in a burst mode. Location information is transmitted to a surrounding infrastructure's metallic members in an instant. A tracker would have to be scanning exactly the right location and frequency at exactly the right time. Computer models have demonstrated the operational impossibility of accomplishing that task." Micmac's face expressed pride.

Hekka stared into his eyes. "You invented this, didn't you?"

He smiled, unaware that Crayle's movements had been tracked via one such chip and had led to her father's grisly murder. She looked away.

Micmac turned to the other two men. "Stay here. I need you to keep anyone from coming in on our six … our behind."

The old man shook his head. "You need me to guide you."

"If any of Chin's people came in behind us, we'd all be screwed. Besides, I follow directions well."

The old man reached under his cap and handed him a small map. Micmac nodded thanks and turned to Hekka. "C'mon," he said as he pulled open a second door. He drew his weapon from his backpack and peeked inside.

Hekka held her submachine gun like the former demolitions man, barrel angled down. She followed him inside. They walked quietly down the subterranean corridor. The cold and damp produced an eerie feel, but heightened their senses. The City's uneven flooring and dim lighting, the latter provided by metal-structured lamps, challenged their sense of balance at every step. He led them to the left side of the tunnel, Hekka to his right and slightly behind.

"Your weapon looks so bizarre."

He whispered. "It appears to be a pretzel, but it's an FN P90 bullpup carbine. Its 20" length makes it a perfect submachine gun for close quarters."

"And mine?"

"Your Uzi is perfect, too."

She took some comfort in his reassurance, and the rest from her ten-inch Bowie, attached jungle-style to her vest.

On the bus, he had taught her operational hand signals. He raised his fist. They both stopped, her close behind.

He whispered, "Hekka—maintain separation. In case of a grenade or automatic weapons. The stakes are high … at least one of us must survive an attack."

In silence, she crossed to the opposite wall.

In his operational days, his senses had been honed and spot on.

An echo of distant voices.

Micmac stepped forward. Too far.

One of Li's guards sent automatic weapon fire his way. He stepped from sight, but the hard tunnel construction and shape focused ricocheted slugs to where he stood. With no place to hide, Micmac was struck.

The force slammed him into the wall. He hit the stone floor hard, his weapon clattering beside him.

Hekka unleashed a fusillade into the tunnel, emptying her clip. A distant cry, then another, were followed by anxious shouts.

Crouching, she traversed to where Micmac lay, blood oozing from his left arm and right shoulder.

More gunfire from ahead, resounding off the walls above. She reloaded, protecting her fallen compatriot with her body. She knew he would do this for her. She was resolute. When they finished here, she would return him to Phoebe. Alive.

When the gunfire ceased, she placed her weapon on the floor, ready. She pulled feminine hygiene pads from her slung purse and strapped one tight to his bicep. The other she pushed against the more severe shoulder wound. "Hold this. Press hard. If you lose too much blood and grow weak, your hand will drop. I'll know to help." She retrieved her weapon.

He had been wounded in combat before. He knew the drill.

The next moments were accompanied by excited lowered voices ahead. Then, a loud clunk. Then another. Then, quiet.

"Can you hold this?" She retrieved Micmac's weapon and placed it on his lap.

"Yeah." He winced. "Flesh wound."

"I'll check ahead."

"Be careful," he groaned. "I gotta bring you back in one piece."

She moved forward and peeked around the corner. No one. Just a large doorway with a bank vault-like steel door. She retreated and informed the former UDT man.

"Hi, guys!" The P.I., running and stumbling, arrived out of breath. "We heard the firefight." He glanced at the man propped against the wall. "What happened to Micmac?"

"Here, Lenny. Hold this against his shoulder. Press hard."

"Wow. Looks bad. And where are the bad guys?"

"I'm fine and they're gone," Micmac advised. "Hekka, open my satchel."

She emptied the items on the floor. "These are Disney characters. This is not funny." She picked up Minnie Mouse as an example. Several remaining characters, strings of small cylinders connected by cord, and a TV remote remained.

"It's C-4. I like to amuse myself when I'm not blowing up things," came a deadpan retort.

"Another Mickey Mouse operation." Lenny's howl echoed down the tunnel.

"Please, Lenny. You're not making friends here."

"Tell that to the group of local tourists who walked in after you left," Lenny intoned. "I learned Chinese on the plane from Taiwan, but when I tried it out, the people got angry. That's when I heard the gunfire. I was lucky to escape with my life. Jack's dead-man-walking agent is setting them straight. He'll be along shortly."

Standing behind Lenny, the referenced old man considered friendly fire. Instead, he helped Lenny apply pressure to the wounds while Hekka, following Micmac's coughed and moaned instructions, pasted three of the Disney explosives onto the door. The last item was a string of wireless blasting caps.

With everyone a safe distance away, Hekka pressed Mode on the special remote control. It enabled the Wi-Fi detonators. She moved her thumb.

"Okay. *Play!*"

CHAPTER 30

While Team Omega battled in the Underground City, Team Alpha's yellow school bus pursued Chin and his daughters across Beijing. But something was wrong. Their driver had brought the bus to a halt and remained stationary for minutes that seemed like hours.

"What's wrong!" Crayle yelled, his pulse accelerated by the jackhammer sounds outside.

The old driver hollered into the back. "Construction is blocking the road! It's nearly cleared! They will allow us through soon!"

"This is our last chance," a gloomy Crayle advised Phoebe.

"Last chance?"

"Chin should've flown back to Hong Kong, not here. He's meeting someone … or doing something. He brought General Li, so I believe he plans to set up the military for a coup. Li has probably gone to organize the meeting. Someone for Chin to charm."

"Didn't Rorschach provide you with Li's role?"

"He couldn't. Li came on board with Chin *after* I left for France. How Chin linked up with him, I don't know. Jack informed me that Li was the one who took the nuclear weapon to Iran. CIA intel puts him in charge of the Chinese nuclear miniaturization effort, so that fits, but there's nothing on the radiation-absorbing shroud. That's new."

"So you can now flatten, kill, and move right in with your family," Phoebe reasoned.

"It allows for a very small device. Easy to transport and conceal. The absence of fallout traveling on the prevailing winds eliminates collateral deaths, destruction, and contamination—bad politics. But where will they strike next? They could go anywhere. I now know that I had advised Chin to pack the Chinese Communist Party leadership into a closet and lock the door."

"The Iranian explosion. It made the Chinese government the bad guys. They had helped Iran with nuclear weapons technology—in exchange for oil."

"Chin has them in the closet, Phoebe. He needs to shut the door. That's got to be next."

"If we take him down, we won't need to know about *next*, right?"

"Yes. That's what we must do."

"Topic change. If we survive, you gonna propose?" Phoebe asked, deadpan.

"I'll address that when Chin and his minions are history. It doesn't do to plan a future while bullets are flying."

• • •

Inside the Palace of Heavenly Purity, Chin Yao-wu observed as General Li pushed his way up through a trapdoor from the bomb shelter tunnel below.

"My dear General. Please, fill me in." Chin provided a warm smile, disguising the intense trepidation he felt inside. It was best to exhibit the calm of a true leader.

The general took a seat next to his fellow conspirator. "As you directed, I have placed our second bomb. In addition, I have lured the Crayle team into the tunnels. When we have departed and activated the device, they will perish."

"Are you certain?"

"It is a labyrinth below. They would require a very senior guide not to be lost forever."

"Excellent. We must leave quickly, but first, I wanted you to see this." He turned his gaze to the 54-inch flat panel television attached to the primary interior wall. "Of course, the real-time effect during my press conference in the Dragon Building training room was much more dramatic. Consider this a replay."

After providing the men with a suitable Scotch and popcorn, Red daughter connected a pair of deep-bass earphones to the television via a wireless splitter.

"Ah, yes. We must preserve the tranquility of the Forbidden City. For now."

"My ears are sensitive, Black, but turn up the volume so we may receive the dramatic effect." After she complied, Red daughter handed him the remote control. He motioned them close, and whispered orders. The daughters picked up gear as if going on a mission, and left through the trapdoor.

Chin breathed deeply, and pressed the *Play* key.

Boom!

Both men jumped to their feet in awe. Shock waves pushed out to either side from the surface blast and the Uighur autonomous region capitol, Ürümqi, turned to paste from the intense heat. They were elated. The general held up his hand for a high-five and Chin, relenting from his anti-West attitude, gave a slap.

"This follows the Iran blast by just seventeen days," said the general.

"Yes. The world has been duped. It believes that the Iranians developed a nuclear device so unstable as to self-detonate. Now the world, in our sphere of interest, will accept that the Nuclear Jihad has transported a similar weapon to Xinjiang. It is ironic they would attack those who provided them with nuclear weapon technology in the first place, but such is the Muslim bond. Now, our people will demand that Beijing's assistance end."

"Brilliant! With nuclear technology assistance rendered impossible, Beijing has nothing to trade for Iranian oil." General Li's countenance lit up as he realized the impact of Crayle's masterful strategy.

"Exactly. Beijing is between a rock and a very hard place. Any additional nuclear technology to Iran, and the people, fearing that the West will attack China, will revolt. And if Beijing prints Yuan to buy the oil, they will ruin our currency and the people will revolt." He gazed at his tablet computer's image of the People's Congress building. "Heads, we win. Tails, we win."

"And now that capitalism has made more of our countrymen rich like you or well off like me, Beijing must keep the supply of oil steady. If not, the people will revolt."

"It is called a dilemma—a problem with no acceptable solution. Rumblings from the people are already being heard. Beijing cannot survive another Tiannenmen Square fiasco. Neither can they shut off Internet access in order to suppress the news and popular interchange."

"You are a genius, Chin. The noose is tightening and, with your rise in popularity as King Capitalist, there simply must be a dramatic change in leadership."

Chin ignored Li's attempt at ass-kissing, the former's mind already elevated to his ascendance. "The Communist Party elite will wish to make deals. I will circulate photographs of Genaralissimo Mussolini hanging outside an Italian fueling station. Put there by the people of Italy. Beijing will make any deal I dictate. There is but one step left. Our president truncated his meeting with the leader of the Democratic People's Republic of Korea and has returned from Pyongyang. He has ordered an emergency session of the National People's Congress to discuss the crushing chain of events. Everyone will attend."

The general nodded his agreement, and pointed at his watch.

"Yes," said Chin. "We must gather our things and proceed to the jet. We will pick up my daughters and your men on the way."

• • •

Magus Crayle's black ops Team Omega came through. As soon as Hekka, Lenny, and the old spy pushed the door open, Micmac regained the Vestige signal on his watch. Easy. Too easy. No alternative, though. They followed the signal for what seemed like a few hundred yards. It stopped.

Before them sat a crate made of glass. Inside, what looked like a rugby ball. Next to it lay a dead military man, a lieutenant, with a bullet hole in his head.

Micmac removed his watch and handed it to Hekka. "Here, move it over the dead guy. The date window displays signal strength."

As she did, the numbers increased. She stopped at his head.

"The chip's in the wound. We've lost them, and found their bomb."

Hekka, shocked at first, regained her composure. "We must disarm it!"

"Explosives could trigger it. I don't see a timer. Some kind of remote trigger, then. We have to chase them down."

"The tunnel is a dead end here. They must have gone through there." Hekka pointed to a door, heavier and more formidable than the last. It was a far better bet than the previous one to withstand a distant nuclear detonation, but not the perfectly placed explosion Micmac instructed his Serrano compatriot to deploy.

"Do it, Hekka," a much weakened Micmac wheezed.

"I want to do it," Lenny whined.

"Here." Hekka held the remote firmly. "Press here."

Even though they had retreated a hundred feet and around two corners, the blast from the remaining characters knocked them to the floor. A thick cloud of dust blew by.

When they regained their vision, they moved with caution to the door. Even the best efforts of the three intact team members could not budge the steel monstrosity.

The old man produced a can of knockoff sewing machine oil labeled Four-In-One, and lubricated the hinges. It required the effort of the healthy Omega members to swing the door open, lift Micmac through, and push it shut. They traversed a long tunnel and arrived at their third steel door.

"You must blast this one, too, Micmac," Hekka observed.

"No more juice … uh … explosives."

Lenny walked to the door, and rapped it with his ring.

In seconds, the door mechanism gave a loud groan. The door opened.

• • •

Finally through the construction zone, the school bus pulled up at the East Glorious Gate of the Forbidden City. It was not unusual for special tours to be granted. The primary guard, his Mongolian features from China's Midwest causing him to appear much more warrior-like than he was, approached the driver's window. At first, he tried to peer into the windows, but the one-way paint, proclaiming this the People's Prototype, barred examination. Certain the elderly man posed no problem, he assumed the best, smiled, and received the duly-prepared entrance and exit papers from the driver. He waved the Q-bus through.

The City appeared to Crayle and Phoebe to be in excellent condition, mindful that it was constructed between 1406 and 1420. Its 980 structures amazed them, even though Lenny had prepared them. While the Celestial Emperor of ancient China resided on the North Star, this was the home of the Terrestrial Emperor. A fitting place to find Chin. It would have been of interest to the FBI Agent had she known that the wood used in construction was of the precious *Phoebe zhennan* variety. Lenny's intel had stopped short of that tidbit.

As the bus lumbered across the southern Outer Court, Crayle and Phoebe watched for signs of life. They saw none. The City appeared quiescent on this day, but Crayle felt sure that particular circumstance would soon change.

"I'm thirsty. I wonder if they have a Starbucks," Phoebe mused.

"On the jet, Lenny told me they had one, but protests caused it to close. In 2007. Sorry." He smiled at her. Micmac was indeed the lucky man. That she was massaging the brace of silenced Glock .45s on her lap indicated her mental readiness.

The old man brought the bus to a halt. "We are stopping at the Palace of Tranquil Longevity. If you view to your left, you will notice the most precious building and fifteen men. Armed protection for Chin and Li. I will step outside, appear to be confused, re-board, and take us to the Palace of Heavenly Purity. You will find Chin and Li inside." Using a four-legged walker, the old man exited the bus. He glanced around, scratching his head and seeming lost. Crayle and Phoebe had a private moment.

"We're trusting this guy with our lives, Mag."

"Yes. Jack provided his backstory. He has every reason to help us, and he's provided vital intel over the years. He swears on his own life the old man is not a double agent."

"I'm good to go," Phoebe replied.

The old man re-boarded and drove the bus across an expanse. The guards alerted until the man pulled up and explained his quandary. One of the guards, the obvious leader, laughed. He commented to the others regarding the nature of risk to China's school children with such an old and feeble bus driver.

Before the guard could say more, Crayle and Phoebe burst out of the rear door. The old man stepped from the bus' front step and rotated his walker to horizontal. The first button push flipped open its rubber feet. The second opened fire. Crayle's and the driver's weapons were silenced and fully-automatic. Phoebe had positioned the fader on her internally-silenced Glocks to Dead Quiet. In less than five seconds, every guard was dead.

Their movements were quick, but stealthy. Inside, they became aware that the rooms were alive acoustically, and they followed the noise. They located Chin and Li in the family room.

"Freeze!" Phoebe yelled.

The men froze.

Crayle glanced at her. She shrugged.

Chin pleaded. "Please, Mr. Crayle. Please, Miss. Do not shoot."

The two arch-criminals, stunned, gave up without a fight. Still, they acted as if they knew something that Team Alpha did not. Phoebe checked the rest of the Palace, shouting "*Clear!*" from time to time until *"All clear!"* She returned to find Chin and Li seated on the floor, their hands being bound together with a fourteenth-century Ming Dynasty silk scarf. She had seen Jack's elder asset fight and observed his deft manipulation of the cloth.

Seconds later, Micmac, Hekka, and Lenny emerged seemingly from nowhere.

"Trap door," Lenny informed. "They're all over the place under ground." He went for credit. "We tracked Li up here."

Micmac shook his head and pointed at his watch. "I got a read on someone's Vestige. This trap door had to be the one."

Shoving Lenny and the antique spy out of her way, Phoebe rushed to her injured lover. Tears welled. She looped his left arm over her shoulder. "We're stickin' together, babe. I've got your six." She glanced at Hekka and mouthed "Thank you."

Lenny plopped into Chin's chair and quickly discovered its ability to spread open due to the hinged back. "Way cool." He grabbed the nearest set of earphones, fitting them to his head. "This is high-end shit, Micmac, my man. Hey, I can work one of these." He picked up a remote control and increased the volume. "Yeah." He pushed the *Play* button.

Frump!

The muffled explosion expressed itself through the P.I.'s skull.

The building shook just as the nuclear shockwave hit the Palace, scattering people in all directions. Chin and Li bounced into the Royal bedroom.

The Palace swayed back and forth. Two-thirds of the floor gave way, as if opening a pathway to Hell. Then, the roof sagged, crashing down and covering the hole.

Crayle rose to his knees, but an aftershock knocked him down again. He took a quick glance, trying to locate team members through the dust. Groans allowed him to find and uncover them, one-at-a-time. Everyone was banged up, but accounted for. Everyone but Chin and Li.

"They must've fallen into the tunnel. Help me pull away the debris."

"Damn!" cried Phoebe. "I needed to impart extreme justice."

The TV had been jarred from its mounting and lay, end down, against the wall. The image righted itself. On it, a hardened surveillance camera displayed the center of Beijing. Flattened. Smoke and heat rose as if fueled by the core of the earth. The camera panned up and back to reveal a mushroom-shaped cloud.

"We will die!" cried Hekka. "We survived the explosion, but the radiation will kill us. Magus …"

Crayle grabbed her to him. He needed to comfort her. "This bomb is from the same source as the one in Iran, and in Western China. Ensconced in a radiation sponge. It will suppress radiation below danger level."

"What?" said Lenny. He stood facing them, his hands cupped over his ears. "*What?*"

"Lenny! You set off the bomb!" Crayle yelled.

"*What?*"

Magus Crayle yanked his cell-sat phone from his pocket, not expecting a signal. He pressed speed dial 1. "Absent the radiation, I might be able to contact Jack." He placed the call. Jack picked up seven seconds later.

"Yeah?"

Crayle enabled the phone's speaker. "Did you hear what happened in Beijing?"

"I, and the world, Magus. The blast took out most of the Central Committee. Intel says that the president has been taken to a Beijing hospital. Not expected to live."

"What now?"

"Uh, we have to get you out of there. Find your way to the jet and head out. I'll vector your exfil to Taegu, Korea, or to one of the bases at the north end of Japan. Maybe Hokkaido." Jack rang off.

• • •

Below the Forbidden City, a disheveled Chin Yao-wu and Li Yafei found themselves in the bomb-shelter tunnels. To their west stood a door three feet thick, built to withstand a distant nuclear blast. Unlike most things created during that era, it had done its job well.

"What will become of them, Chin?" Li asked.

"They will be removed. Exfiltrated, Crayle would say."

"Listen!" Li warned in a whisper. "Someone approaches." He pulled his Chinese Makarov pistol.

Around the next bend came Chin's daughters, pulling a gurney that bumped over the uneven stones. Disheveled and dirty, they appeared to have been not far from the epicenter.

Li recognized the squat, chubby, and bloodied man strapped to it. "President Hau. Nice of you to join us."

The man tried to speak. Only bloody spittle emerged.

Chin spotted a sinograph painted on the wall. It made no sense in Mandarin, but Chin had studied an ancient dialect—from his homeland at the headwaters of the Yangtze. "Black daughter anticipated our escape. Quick," said Chin, waving an arm. "This way."

The entourage followed Chin northeast to a rendezvous point. A squad of Li's troops met them, escorted them to a large, rusted, and apparently defunct elevator. Li's men manned the manual cranks and, slowly, the platform screeched and groaned up to ground level inside a hangar. They scrambled aboard Chin's jet. Within fifteen minutes, the aircraft turned onto the runway.

The pilot, a refugee from the North Korean Air Force, checked out the radar returns. Most of the debris had fallen to Earth. The flight tower, laid out on its side like a giant meat tenderizer, provided no resistance to Chin's impromptu flight plan. The brakes fully applied, the engines raced to three-quarter revs and the pilot released the Falcon to a partially blocked runway.

• • •

The team cleared away the rubble as quickly as possible. Finally, there below, the Tunnel of the Heavenly Purity was quite unlike the tunnels for the masses or the elite. It was gilded in gold, the air fresh, and mother-of-pearl flooring stones glowing in perfect harmony. Phoebe stepped to one side and pulled a gold wheel chair from a wall recess. Micmac now had proper transportation.

But, to Crayle, it seemed to project forever into the ether, like his quest for justice. And his identity.

He snapped out of it. "No time for chatter," he said as he reasserted command. "This could be our last opportunity to catch them. Follow me."

The team followed a trail of discarded chewing gum through the maze. One of Chin's younger daughters apparently indulged a nervous habit of chewing the flavor from the gum, then replacing it with new. The trailing technique worked until they reached the tunnel's end. It terminated at a hand-operated lift perched high above. They heard a roar overhead.

Lenny offered the obvious. "This is the only means of escape. Chin must have used it."

The cranking mechanism was on the lift itself, so no one had to be left behind. It also precluded followers.

"Lenny, shinny up the supports and crank it down," Crayle ordered.

Absent his usual repartee, the P.I. retrieved the platform as directed.

Just as they had winched themselves to the top and could see into the hangar, they spotted a squad of five of Li's men, dead ahead, weapons raised.

Phoebe jumped in front of Micmac. The rest fell to the floor.

A spray of gunfire.

Silence.

Surprised to be alive, they glanced up.

Atop the stairs to Jack's aircraft stood Flori, her Heckler & Koch MP5 blowing smoke rings. "Clear," she said.

Lenny, on an uncharacteristic roll of success, found a remote in the hand of one of Li's soldiers. He pushed its large, chartreuse button. Instead of another catastrophic explosion, it started the entire hangar up to runway level.

They reached the surface just in time to see Chin's Falcon catapult down the damaged, rubbish strewn runway.

"Eat some slag, asshole." Micmac hoped the jet engines would suck in some of the ambient debris scattered across the tarmac. It didn't happen.

Crayle clenched his fists as they watched the plane circle the former Chinese capital, Chin's pilot wagging the wings in victory.

Flori assisted them aboard. The beleaguered five embarked, too exhausted to ask even obvious questions as they collapsed at random. The reunited spy twins bade them farewell.

Their pilot taxied from the hangar onto the only viable runway, one that had elevated in concert with the hangar. They were aloft in two minutes.

Crayle made the only observation necessary. "We failed."

CHAPTER 31

Chin and Li escaped the carnage and destruction. Although their special guest, the People's Republic president, was head-to-foot bloody and broken, his vital signs remained intact. Neither Chin nor Li informed the old man. Best he believe he needed them for survival. That notion would provide value once they arrived in Hong Kong.

"What we are witnessing, Li, is the result of Crayle's strategy. Crayle computed expectations of two outcomes: the president dies or the president lives. He utilized an expected value system, calculations of expectation of regret, and many other attributes beyond my comprehension. His plan covered every contingency."

Li nodded. He also took note of Chin's excellent mind. The general now comprehended how Crayle, though damaged, still represented a formidable opponent.

• • •

Two daughters, one certified in acupuncture and the other in Western medicine, kept the president alive. Chin had apprized them of the man's critical position in the grand scheme. They also knew that, if the president died, they would soon follow, an endless supply of younger, more avid daughters waiting in the wings for their opportunity.

Chin and Li, alternately, sought privacy in the jet's lush bedroom. Privacy for Chin included his Black and Red daughters—Black, his protector and favorite, and Red, his technical guru.

"Red. The television."

Red selected the Chinese language news. The flat panel television embedded in the bedroom wall came to life, first displaying videos of Beijing, and then the various news anchors of the world.

"Many opinions, Li."

"None correct. I have given orders to avoid busy Hong Kong airport and land at the airbase—my home."

By the time they landed, global journalists had presented new and definitive information that, as is common in the media, debunked most of what had come before. It was clear, though, that the bomb had been placed directly beneath the People's Congress meeting place. The absence of radiation detection for an explosion that only could have been caused by a nuclear device forced governments to clamor for the heads of Iranian leadership. The notion of a worldwide nuclear jihad took a leap forward. Jay Leno referenced Ahmednukejihad.

• • •

The entire ensemble of Chin's inner circle had returned to his Dragon Building in Hong Kong's Wanchai. Blue and Gold isolated the Communist Chinese president in the Learning Center. Normally utilized for indoctrination of his daughters, it was perfect for the sequestration of Hau. Should government forces attempt a rescue, all bolts would fire simultaneously, covering every square inch of the room's floor. The president and his rescuers, in perforated format, would transcend this life and enter the next in no more than a few seconds.

Chin smiled once again at his own genius. Perhaps he could have accomplished all this without the Crayle plan. No. Even his huge ego couldn't make that leap. He bade Li good night and retired, eager to recharge. Tomorrow he would enter the home stretch.

CHAPTER 32

Flori provided Crayle with a sealed envelope. "New orders, Mr. Crayle," she provided in her smooth-as-silk, sexy tone.

Magus Crayle's jaws clenched. His hands invaded the envelope.

Magus,

Sorry about outcome. Bad mission. Refocus. Lalumière loose. Boss says Rorschach might be able to restore French mems. See you after short hop. IYDGFJDH.

JAS

Crayle didn't know what to make of the message or of Jack's use of his initials. The Lalumière news and the Rorschach mention didn't improve his demeanor. He was not finished with Chin, and he knew that he would be putting Hekka in greater danger. He deciphered the final word.

"Destination: Hokkaido. Lenny, check it out," he said before he informed Flori that he wished to be alone in the bedroom. She sighed, then smiled her understanding.

In minutes, Lenny had destination intel. He leaned over to Hekka. "Indigenous folks are like yours. Called Ainu. Similar to Inuit. Lost their language to Japanese."

His comments took her home. To her people, to her brothers, and to her dead father.

• • •

Despite a recent heavy snowstorm, Jack's jet landed at an air force base southeast of Sapporo, the largest city on Japan's northernmost island. A short, stocky man dressed in heavy wool and hip boots met them as they deplaned. The team piled into a heated, stretch Snow Cat, which set off over the feet-thick snow layer toward craggy, snow-draped mountains at the island's center. In twenty minutes, they arrived at a CIA quiet house.

Crayle's words, "I'm sorry," were the only words spoken. Throughout the ride, Phoebe glared at Lenny, hoping he would say, "You win some, you lose some." Instead, Lenny moped, probably saving his life.

The single-story quiet house appeared to be no more than approximately 1500 square feet. The charcoal-colored tile roof was still laden with snow and seemed to harmonize with the mountains.

"Welcome to my old stomping grounds," Jack greeted. The team, unprepared for the intense cold, hustled inside. A pretty fifty-something woman in traditional dress smiled as she worked at a kitchen counter. Jack waved his thumb at her. "She's cleared."

The woman with no name placed white porcelain cups on a dining table, one for each guest.

"It's good stuff," Jack informed. "Rice and fish products."

The woman spoke. "Rice with toppings of uni and salmon roe."

"The fish eggs are the color of my Bronco," Hekka observed.

"I recognize the other color. I see that when I throw up," added Lenny.

The woman's hand slid imperceptibly to a large butcher knife.

"It's excellent, Lenny. Turn you into a man."

They ate the brief repast, Lenny included, then turned to Jack.

"Follow me." Jack gathered them into a secure room. He opened a closet door and pulled out a CIA-perverted Dyson vacuum. He plugged it in and flipped its switch. Anything that could vibrate, was made to vibrate at frequencies that disguised conversations.

"Yeah, I know. The guys that built this room had good intentions, but the noise from the vacuum makes conversation impossible. Thank you S & T." Jack referred to the CIA's Science and Technology directorate. He glanced at Crayle, who sat on a blood red couch with his fingers in his ears.

"Do you mind, Magus? The noise doesn't mean we don't listen at all."

"It's a trick. I learned it in a noisy nightclub in Big Bear Valley. The Sugarloafer." He nodded at Micmac. "He plays there and taught me this. See this little flap in the ear opening. Press it back so it just barely touches flesh. It blocks out noise, but let's the conversation through."

Each member of the team tried Crayle's trick. It worked. Each understood every word spoken. They appeared to be a human version of the fabled *hear no evil,* minus siblings *see no evil* and *speak no evil.*

"A groupie told me she taught it to all the guys she met so they wouldn't misunderstand her intentions—her availability." Micmac glanced around the team for confirmation. His eyes stopped at Phoebe's. "Yeah, well, groupies were a long time ago. Gave 'em up for Lent a while back."

A bare nod from Phoebe was all he received for his explanation. He sat next to her. He tried to rescue that which couldn't be rescued. "Hey, groupies aren't bad. You were once one of my groupies, huh?" He smiled into her glare.

Phoebe squirmed her hand under his leg and poked.

"Ow!" The pain was evident on Micmac's face as he bent over.

Phoebe switched from self-defense to nurturing mode. "Oh, my. I'll kiss it. It'll feel better."

Jack chimed in. "There will be no testicle kissing on my watch. Look, I just got off the phone with my boss. We're headed for France. Looks like Lalumière escaped and may cause a little mayhem. I'll get us all on the plane and we'll make the long trek. Get as much sleep as you can during transit. We don't know what's ahead, and it might be a long stretch before we can rest again."

Throughout Hokkaido, the particulate debris from the blast in Beijing was thick as a fog. With Jack's driving, it only took twenty minutes to reach the refueled Falcon jet at the airbase. The pilot transitioned the jet aloft by instruments, heading towards Hawaii. Then mainland America. Then Washington, D.C. The final refueling would take place in Ponta Delgada, Portuguese Azores, close to the European continent. The team slept, ate, and joked. Just one more hop.

As was apropos of Lenny and Phoebe being in the same confined space, a verbal battle ensued.

"Ya know, Annie Oakley, this would be a good time for us to mend our fences. Perhaps a little history would help—what was that?" he asked. He was unable to pick up the word "Crap" the agent had spoken under her breath. "The folks who treated us Jews best weren't the Christians. No. We had to exodus to Europe and then survive in the new world. We prospered. The Christians decided that was a hell of a way to repay their hospitality, so they threw us into ghettoes, some with high walls. No, it was the Muslims. They treated us best. We're all made by the same God, for Christ's sake."

"That's scary," said Phoebe.

"You're a Christian. You owe me. You need to treat me better."

Phoebe turned to Micmac. "As part of our targeted oppression, didn't we sacrifice Jewish P.I.'s?" Her eyes panned to the overhead, seeking a benevolent God for confirmation.

"You two! Cut the crap! Lenny, I need you on the 'Net to research … here's the wireless access code." Jack handed Lenny a blue three-by-five card.

"I'll help." Phoebe rose. "You look tense. I'll massage your neck."

"No, thanks. I can feel your fingers tightening already."

Jack stared at them, livid. "Stop the fucking—"

"*Five bucks!*" they chimed.

"God … ern … anh," Jack choked. His face glowed red.

Lenny Lipschitz and Phoebe Bransfield hurried from the main compartment to the sanctity of the bedroom.

• • •

Phoebe waited fifteen minutes to see if the coast was clear. No Jack in sight meant he must be forward in the cockpit, running comms with his boss. She came out of the bedroom and whispered in Crayle's ear. Crayle headed for the bedroom.

"There's something I didn't tell you, MC. You need to know this."

"Lenny, if there's one thing that I've learned about you, it's that you're the Imelda Marcos of always having another shoe to drop."

"Who's she?"

"A one-time First Lady of the Philippines. She had 2,700 pairs of shoes."

"Oh."

"Come on, Lenny. Out with it."

"It's about my brother. Turns out dad, who loved my mother very much, had another love. He got 'em both pregnant. Turns out Wolfie and I were born on the same day. We're half-brothers. When mom found out, it was the end for her. After she died, Wolfie split for Europe. He went to school in Holland—University of Leiden."

"Why should that have meaning to me?"

"Turns out he roomed with a guy named Desrochers … Jean-Marc."

"Sylvain Lalumière's bastard son."

"That was what I kept from you. Wolfie must have supplied diamonds to Lalumière through Jean-Marc. Yeah, the Frenchman used his own son as the goat. Wolfie knew our dad found the memory stick in your things at Langley. About what you had done. And that our father tried to extort millions from Lalumière and his clan."

"Did he tell you how Lalumière got the cash to pay for the diamonds?"

"He manipulated water rights priorities and services in the Middle East. Those sheikhs had beaucoup petro bucks. Made Mr. L. rich."

"So Lalumière provided his son the wherewithal. The son exchanged the water money for diamonds from Wolfie. Why, of course. A small, lightweight, untraceable store of value." Crayle glanced around, excited, as if more puzzle pieces loomed in plain sight. "The international currency of weapons traffickers. That's how Lalumière bought the nukes!" Crayle reached full animation. "Stop the source … and this whole mess comes to a screeching halt."

"That's why I kept quiet. I was afraid you'd kill him. My brother."

"Your brother is just doing business. He probably has no knowledge of the nukes. He's safe … for now."

"Thanks, MC." Lenny's eyes welled up.

"I want you to think hard. Any more shoes?" Crayle was dead serious.

"No. That's it."

Crayle heard more shoes. On the other side of the door. Thinking like an operative, his last thoughts were not to kill Wolfram Silberweiss, but to co-opt him. For now. He filed away this new option.

• • •

Santa Maria Airport in the Azores was their last refueling stop before Europe. Everyone wanted to exit the jet and stretch their legs. Jack forbade the luxury. The Azores were an Atlantic crossroad, the likelihood of surveillance and facial recognition high. Jack made the rules. He pulled on a Halloween mask and a gray Sorbonne University hoodie he retrieved from the armoire in the bedroom. Flori let down the stairway. He descended to the tarmac. She returned the stairway back to its flight posture.

"This is Neil Wohlford," said the voice in response to his call.

"They're getting antsy, Mr. Wohlford. It's been tough going. For most of them, this is duck soup. It seems a lot of Crayle's training at Camp Peary and field experience have stuck with him, probably in his subconscious. The P.I. is always a question mark, but the Indian maiden, Poppi, is the real surprise. She's a trouper. I'd think of adding her on permanent except she looks like a … a … Indian. Maybe if we had to attack Indian-a." Jack laughed.

"Not funny, Jack. You are going to Marseille."

"That wouldn't be the Marseilles in Indiana, would it?" Jack refused to abandon his attempt to humor the humorless Wohlford.

"That Marseilles is in Illinois." Neil paused to appreciate his well-studied breadth of knowledge and its utility. "You are going to the one that ends in *e*—in France. But you know that. You are fairly good at what you do, Jack, but instances like this one assure me that you are not trainable."

Jack gulped. Neil kept the fun jobs and the generous, tax-free money coming in—to say nothing of the luxurious cabin compound in Fawnskin. Jack needed to present a more professional persona. He struggled to read Neil in person, let alone on the telephone. The next operational phase of The Strategy was timed to accomplish just that—when the jet reached France's number two city. Jack was not able to observe Neil's call to his boots-on-the-ground spy to provide her with the timing.

• • •

Crayle used Jack's absence to commandeer the bedroom. "This dialog is meant for Dr. Rorschach. Ears only. The memory restoration seven days ago was insufficient to prevent the separate detonations, per the Blackstone Strategy, of two mini-nuclear devices. 35,725 in human collateral. Lost. These are estimates. Actual numbers are expected to be ten times higher. Doctor, in today's version of myself, I have no intention of orchestrating such abominable acts. How could I be capable of that? Based on memories you restored, I qualify as an international terrorist. A hideous monster of a human being. These notions are in opposition with my naturally acquired memories. The current Magus Crayle wishes peace, not destruction. He wishes hope—a better existence for every worthy human being. The battle between good and evil exists not only in the world as we know it, but within as well. For me, it is particularly intense. Please, Doctor, find a means for me to preclude further devastation and suffering. Bring to me the Lalumière memories that I may complete this devious puzzle I've created. Please."

Lenny burst in the door. "Hey MC, we're outta here. Buckle up."

• • •

As Jack's Falcon jet entered French airspace, team members exhibited signs of apprehension. Nervous twitches, failed attempts at humor, frequent glances out cloud-shrouded windows. What was Lalumière up to? What were his next plans for the conquest of the country below? And after? They'd all studied history. They all knew of an Austrian nobody who, against all odds, rose to the leadership of the German Republic. Touting National Socialism and a need to regain respect, the man built an enormous military power, suspended all human rights, and came within an atom's distance of conquering Europe and, perhaps, the world. Lalumière had to be stopped. At all costs.

Phoebe and Micmac held hands. Their dreams of spending a lifetime together could end abruptly, and soon. Their permanent union might take place in eternity. Lenny might never spend another moment with his professed love, Alona. And Crayle. He and his Indian love stared silently into each other's eyes, their breathing elevated, but controlled. Circumstances had sent all of his plans askew. His pledge to protect her from his violent and unpredictable life had vanished on Cougar Crest Trail. Her father had been butchered, her solid, predictable life forever altered, forever linked to his.

Lenny surveyed the cabin. "Where's Jack?" His eyes came to rest on the closed bedroom door, closed. "Shhh," he said as he tiptoed to the door. Private investigators know how to open a door with no sound. Lenny did. Jack stood with his back to Lenny, his voice hushed. The P.I. heard 'sir' which meant Neil Wohlford.

"Yes, I am aware that Crayle's father was killed in Hong Kong. They found the murder weapon on scene, a Russian Makarov. The Russian's figured his father's work with the Chinese might upset their apple cart in Nam. What? A Type 59. But, that was Chinese. Sir, are you saying that it wasn't the Russians who killed his father?"

Jack listened for a few seconds, then spoke again, in a hushed, intense whisper. "Oh my God! A young Chicom lieutenant pulled the trigger?" Jack fell silent. "The lieutenant was … our General Li? Shit! If Crayle finds out, he'll go right off the reservation."

Lenny eased backwards, closed the door, knocked, and reopened it.

Jack turned and glared as he signed off with Neil. "Do you mind, Lipschitz? A little privacy?"

Lenny stepped inside and closed the door. "Your boss knew about this all along. He didn't want MC and me to dismantle this General Jerkoff into his component subsystems in Hong Kong. Wouldn't serve his purpose. That about right, Jack?"

Jack tried to respond, to defuse the situation, but the P.I. was in a rage.

"And I'll bet the deal with Dr. Bumfuck was just to experiment on Mag's memory. Magically, he visits the doctor and, poof, his memory of making Chin's strategy reappears. Did the doctor have it all along. Was Mag's memory dumped to disk before the car crash … or—Jesus Christ! There was no amnesia! Bumfuck removed all those memories as part of his experiment! Wow!"

Jack reached slowly for his weapon.

An oblivious Lenny panned the bedroom, deep in deductive thought.

"Whatever these clowns at Central Intelligence want, they want bad, and don't give an eternal crap about who gets hurt. Like I said, that about right?"

Jack took a breath. His hand eased back. He couldn't risk breaching the fuselage. But, being confined in the jet with an informed Crayle would be every bit as bad. "Don't say a word, Lenny. There are reasons for everything, but I just can't tell you," Jack lied. "If Magus learns of this, he won't stop 'til he kills Li. We—America needs Li. If that changes, I'll tell Magus myself," he lied—again.

CHAPTER 33

On the fifth day after being incarcerated in the infamous Château D'If prison, Sylvain Lalumière awakened to the screech of his opening cell door. He wiped away the cobwebs, and there appeared both his mistress and his master.

The diminutive spy wore a long, blood red skirt and black leather boots. Above the waist, she wore a navy blouse and peacoat. He judged that the early Winter weather had turned chilly, but the absence of an umbrella implied there was neither rain nor snow. The CIA had seen that insulated, double-pane safety glass graced the cell's outside and courtyard window openings. Besides keeping out sound, they assured a perfect 68 degrees Fahrenheit inside the cell. Sandrine's coat was the first to go.

"Good morning, my Mitim. How are you feeling today, my prisoner friend? Look, I have brought some things for you." She placed food items from a canvas tote bag on the stone table. "And, as did the minstrels of old, I bring you tidings." She removed several newspapers.

"Finally," he said, "news of the world outside." He lunged at the papers, but she pulled them back. He sprawled across the floor.

"I felt that you have gotten a little behind in your reading."

"But I love your little behind," he said with a devouring smile.

"This is some serious stuff," she continued. "Your partner in crime, Mr. Chin Yao-wu, has struck. Here. Check it out."

He had picked himself up and the spy handed the English language International Herald-Tribune to him. He poured over the front pages for the next ten minutes while the spy known to him as Sandrine watched patiently.

"It says there was a bomb, a nuclear bomb, in Western China. Xinjiang. It also says China and the West are blaming the Muslim Uighur inhabitants." The Frenchman struggled to pronounce *wee-gur* properly. "And look, another! Chin has struck Beijing! It says that most members of the high council have been killed. The public blames the government for its lax attitude—one of appeasement toward the Uighurs. There are demonstrations everywhere. Chin has spoken publicly in Hong Kong, proclaiming an immediate need for new leadership." He read silently for a few seconds. "There are unconfirmed reports that Chin has offered refuge to the remaining leaders. Sandrine, he can and will dictate terms. I know the plan." Excited, he looked up. "This is Magus Crayle's Blackstone Strategy."

She handed him the French language papers, Le Monde and Le Figaro. What he saw wiped the smile from his face.

"But how can this be?" he said, astonished at the front pages. "They talk of nothing but … me. Of Mitim. I was well received on the river boat … and Avignon, but this is much, much more."

"You could say we've been working overtime at Langley. Social media, it's called."

"The French government has made the socialism even worse. My beloved France is doomed to the same consequence as Greece, Spain, and Portugal. We will default on our debts like some homeless soul in the street. How can this be?"

"They also say that the political prisoner known only as the Man In The Iron Mask, Mitim, is the only one who can save them. They are so desperate at this point, they see no possible help from those they elected, or their opponents. True, I have just spent a few days thwarting attempts by those leaders at any solution, but it is all for the best. For your France and for you."

"Several of our leaders have committed suicide," he read. His head snapped up. *"You?"*

"Assisted suicide. Or, they died of natural causes, abruptly. All for the best."

"But the people of France must be suffering. I must help them."

"The best way to accomplish that is for you to become king, my Liege." She curtseyed.

"Sandrine, it also says that the American president is barring my way. He says that America must now help France the way France helped America against its former oppressor, the British crown. If they help, my plans are doomed."

"Yeah, well, there has been a change in plans. We will deal with the meddling American president later. There is someone in the White House who will help, but we must complete our project here in Marseille."

"It is my time!" His voice echoed off his stone confinement. "I must act! Now!"

Lalumière looked like a bomb ready to explode.

Sandrine stepped into the middle of his fantasy. "We are not quite ready."

"We?" said Lalumière, appearing lost.

It was then that she reached inside the bag and handed to Lalumière a present. It was wrapped in 18th Century paper. "Go ahead. Open it."

Lalumière removed the ribbon and paper as if he would later frame it for posterity. He pulled open the gold leaf inner wrap and removed a black object shaped like a small fish.

"It functions the same as the one at your château, just a little nicer." She pointed at one of the gemstone inserts. "This one, the sole diamond, marquis cut, is Play," she said.

"Do you know my son?" the Frenchman asked.

Mainly in the biblical sense, she thought. She had bedded Jean-Marc in Amsterdam as Angel and in Luxembourg City as a nameless Czechoslovakian script girl. "I worked with Jean-Marc to design this wonderful device. He procured the stones from Wolfie at CIA expense. It's a present and a reward for all you've been put through."

"How do you know my son, Sandrine? And how do you know his friend, Wolfram?"

"Honey babe, I've fucked them both." She made the statement as if saying it's all in a day's work.

Lalumière had to process her words. Not the meaning, he got that. He needed to see behind the words. But more questions surfaced. How long had she known the two? Had she been manipulating them all along? If so, was she manipulating him now? He refocused on the clicker.

"The LED for power is off. The remote control is beautiful. A work of art, but the batteries, they are dead!" A note of panic sounded in his voice. To the spy, any sign of weakness in a subject represented an opportunity for her to assert control. For this, she was never unprepared.

"Not to worry." She produced a package of charged batteries she'd purchased in Marseille on sale. Then, as if to add an exclamation point to her skill set, she pulled a rabbit out of the bag. She placed it on the ground between them and pressed its tummy. The Energizer icon padded energetically about the cell.

Sylvain Lalumière considered himself a man of strength. But the advent of the energetic toy caused him to stand, then fall back against the stone wall. Sandrine's bunny, as if sensing weakness, changed direction and headed directly for him.

Before she could reach out and grab the aggressive toy, Lalumière lifted his foot and stomped it into oblivion.

"Oh!" was Sandrine's plaintive exclamation.

Lalumière retreated to his bed, never taking his eyes off the bunny remains. He sat, hoping to retrieve some sense of calm. Sandrine sat next to him. Close. She removed the battery door from the back of the clicker. As she removed the batteries, Lalumière's heart raced. Her petite fingers, so deft. Her touch, so soft and sensual. He grabbed her shoulders and pulled her onto the uneven stone floor of the cell. They made love, the pain from their bed of opportunity hurting them more with every motion. Fueled by the pain, both of them screamed out their pleasure. The screams could not be heard outside. By design, they only echoed within.

The completed lovers snuggled together on the narrow bed. One was convinced he was the next king of France, the other confident she was the world's deadliest female.

CHAPTER 34

Jack didn't have to lie anymore. What happened next took precedence.

Flori spoke in a soft and sexy voice, "We are approaching the Marseille Airport zone. Please fasten your seat belts. The westerlies are clashing with the late Mistral from the north. It will be a bit rough coming in. We will bypass the airport on the south side. You can view the port city of Marseille on the port side. As we bank and enter the pattern, you will see a small island and its prison, the Château D'If. I have it on good account that the fictional Count of Monte Cristo slept there. As did, some believe, the veritable political prisoner, the Man In The Iron Mask. That the latter was domiciled in the cell bearing his name is speculation, but it draws tourists."

The cabin lights dimmed as Jack emerged from the bedroom. "Just a little mood lighting for the orgy," he announced.

The team glanced at one another, questions all around. Phoebe broke the silence.

"Orgy, is it? Let's see. Four guys and two gals. Hmmm. Sounds like an even fight."

Everyone's attention shifted as the bedroom door reopened. Flori stood in the doorframe, the door held open by her left arm with the rest of her leaning against the sill. She did everything but purr. Phoebe appealed to her clever word muse, but was denied. Flori was sex incarnate. Every cell participated. For a moment, Phoebe wished for that. The Brazilian was as different a persona from her own tomboy childhood as could be imagined. The addition of Flori would make the orgy-fight more even. Much more.

Jack peered out into the dark blue hue that had supplanted the creamy-white cabin glow. "Calm down, team. The orgy's been postponed. I've changed the lighting to give everyone a better view."

A sigh of relaxed anticipation pervaded the ensemble.

• • •

The spy, Sandrine, awoke first, but stayed in the comfort of the situation. She was used to leaving a sexual conquest without so much as a goodbye. Or a heartbeat. Then again, she never heard any complaints. She considered the Frenchman, who now shared his bodily warmth with her. What if this all worked out as planned? What if Sylvain, as she now called him, got his way? What if he actually became king of France? Wouldn't the new king require a new queen?

"Off with their heads," she commanded under her breath. "Let them eat cake," she said. Then, a sigh. She drifted back to sleep.

It was the chime of Sandrine's cell phone that brought them both awake. Quickly, she checked it for messages. The crypto segment showed one FLASH PLUS message from her stateside controller. It took only one second to decrypt the terse message. "*Maintenant!*" it said in French. Now!

She moved to the chair and installed the charged batteries. Lalumière scratched his scalp and then, due to the abrasions from the iron mask, his face.

"Here." She handed him the bejeweled remote. "Take this and follow me."

Lalumière did as instructed. Only when they arrived at the barred window did he realize both of them were still naked. Still holding the clicker, he lifted her, back to the wall, and began to press inside her.

"No. I have to watch." He lowered her and she turned, facing the wall. A foot too short, she threw "Up" over her shoulder. He lifted her once again and pressed inside. His heart pounded. He panted so hard, his breath blew her hair against the wall. She moaned, barely able to keep her eyes open.

Lalumière held the remote in his left hand, his right hand wrapped around Sandrine. All of his fingers were in the right places. Their breathing accelerated together, propelled by the circumstances.

"Now!" she cried.

His finger reacted.

It all happened at once. At the instant their sexual embrace bore its fruit, a huge rumble followed by the ground bowing upward in the old part of Marseille. The neighborhood inhabited by North African refugees exploded skyward, sending shock waves. Building and human debris exploded in every direction.

The lovers, awed by the sight and the experience, collapsed to the floor. Seconds later, pieces of brick and human collateral damage blew through the glass above. The giant prison shook, but stood firm.

The two conspirators savored the moment. They embraced. All of their work, the Mitim impersonations and the transport to D'If, had not been in vain.

"Mitim. Listen up. When the winds abate, we will make our escape."

Again, Lalumière would have to rely on the spy. But she had come through on every occasion. His mind wandered. He drew a mental vision of his coronation. He looked at her. He would need a queen.

• • •

Inside the jet just seconds before, the words over the intercom had done nothing to quell the nervousness. Jack and his team used the opportunity the verify the pilot's visual. The city of Marseille was quite large and the island known as *If* was inverse in proportion. Lenny, against the admonition of the pilot, just had to see. He popped his seat belt and bent over Phoebe, pushing her head to her chest. Before she could react with appropriate violence, a sound like thunder gone mad reverberated inside the cabin confines. Everyone covered their ears.

The jet hurtled across the sky. To the east. It tumbled sideways and head-over-heels, as a bug caught in the stream of a fire hose. Anything that was not tied down turned into an airborne weapon.

The G-forces became so intense, neither the pilot nor the co-pilot could grasp the controls. No matter. The whoosh of the underground explosion in the Marseille center rendered all control surfaces irrelevant.

The occupants were thrown in all directions, the seat belts cutting them in all places they touched. The unrestrained Lenny flew about like an errant billiard ball, making outcries for only the first few seconds. *No Smoking* and *Fasten Seat Belt* signs dinged like a Las Vegas casino gone amok.

• • •

The explosion in Marseille's old quarter continued to shake the D'If castle. Even the heavy stones moved with the shock wave. Huge blocks fell to the cell floor, just missing its two denizens. Flung by the huge pressure wave, seawater splashed high enough to penetrate the shattered window, high above the normally placid Mediterranean.

When the debris ceased to funnel through the barred opening, Lalumière and his accomplice pulled their few things together, tucked them into two of the 600-thread-per-inch Egyptian cotton sheets, and ran down the gallery. The stairs took them to the courtyard and across to the door, Sandrine leading the way.

They stepped around cars, bodies, and all sorts of items Marseillaise before they reached the south side of D'If.

A 30-foot statue of Madonna and Child, blown toward the heavens from atop the hilltop Notre Dame de La Garde basilica on the mainland, whistled through the air like a missile. The fugitives dove behind a structure. The gilded form slammed into the Vauban governor's building, sending side walls and roofing in all directions. As if protected by an unseen force, they survived.

The cliff, behind the building and away from the city, was steep, but protected from the blast and its aftermath. A landing had been cut into the rock to afford access protected from the northerly Mistral. Due to the sheet-bags slung over their shoulders, the steep stone stairway down the rocky cliff to the sea proved nearly impossible.

• • •

Jack's Falcon jet finally blew far enough from the explosion epicenter for the pilot to utilize his fighter pilot skills. He had been read in on the experimental parachute riggings at both ends of the jet. He lifted a protector and stabbed at a button marked FORWARD. The front 'chute deployed. The diminished force of the nuclear winds pushed the nose away from the epicenter. A second push and the triple-layer Kevlar sucked back into the nose. With the plane now approximately trimmed, he pushed, pulled, and toggled the wheel to regain a semblance of control, and avoid one of France's highest maritime alps.

Headed now, by no intent of their own, northeast toward Geneva, Switzerland, the team released their restraints and rushed to the immobile, possibly dead, Lenny. Phoebe and Hekka shoved the men out of their way.

Each took up a position on their knees next to the fallen P.I.

Hekka placed her hands on his sternum.

Phoebe felt his neck. The carotid artery still functioned. She pressed her ear against his lips, searching for a sign of breath.

"Jeeesus Christ!" Lenny's voice was so loud, Phoebe jerked her head away. "WTF just happened? And what is that I smell. Oooo ..."

He glanced at the FBI agent. "… Phoebs and I have dibs on the bedroom."

Before Phoebe could enact her rage on the private investigator, Crayle and Micmac each grabbed an arm and brought her to her feet.

"I'll kill him!" she struggled.

"What if I push here?" A supportive Hekka moved her layered hands to Lenny's crotch and shoved.

Lenny cried out and grasped at his private area as Hekka moved back, pleased at the justice deployed by her off-label employment of the CPR revival technique.

"Everyone," intoned the pilot over the intercom, "Marseille just went up in smoke. Nuclear, I'd say. Get buckled in. We're having to divert. I'm going to be busy for the next several minutes finding a place to land. I'll let you know when I have substance." The smoking sign flickered off.

Flori gave Phoebe a sedative to relieve her of further homicidal intentions. Micmac knew a distraction would help. She responded to his lips pressed tightly against hers, nearly pulling him to the floor with her embrace. Lenny's "I never have any luck" was a distant drone. Crayle and Hekka smiled at the couple. As Phoebe relaxed fully, Micmac picked up the substantive agent like a piece of balsa and seated her on the couch.

"We are cleared for an emergency landing at Nice Airport. Well, not exactly cleared. We may have to dodge an old 747 heavy and an Airbus 380, oh, and a maiden voyage Dreamliner … we'll be fine."

The jet, not exactly shipshape after the catapulting, creaked and groaned in complaint. The smiles and embraces faded. Everyone jumped back into their respective seats and pulled the belts pain-tight, the pilot's assurances disregarded.

Crayle glanced out the window. It seemed the concussion from the bomb blast had blown the clouds into cartoon character shapes. There was Daffy Duck. Elmer Fudd. And that … that was Foghorn Leghorn. Crayle knew these characters. He asked the others, "Did I know about them before my crash?"

No one answered.

He turned to Lenny. "Did I know about them before my memory restoration?"

Blank stare.

To Hekka, "Did Rorschach implant them … for fun?"

Not one answer. They just stared at him. Had the cartwheeling through space scrambled his brain? Or had the doctor damaged Crayle's mind?

CHAPTER 35

At the bottom of the D'If cliff, a power boat awaited the would-be king and his spy-cum-facilitator. The landing and boat were located on the south side, protected from the nuclear explosion. It was clear to Lalumière that Sandrine had brought the craft back with her goody bag. And since she had sunk the boat that had brought them to the island, one boat must have been staged here much earlier. His thought was reinforced by the lack of any other person in sight. He recalled the sailor who'd transported them to the island in the first place. The dead one. His mind quickly moved on.

As usual, the petite spy had thought of every detail. Once again, Sandrine would take him onto a far-less-than-friendly sea. She tossed the tie-down into the boat, and they tumbled aboard after their linen cargo. She knew it would be better for him to be topside with the wind cooling his face and with his eyes fixed on the horizon. But he would have to wear the mask to avoid recognition. It would negate the cool air. A no-brainer. Secret trumped seasick. She ushered him into the cabin.

Back at the wheel, she stripped off her outer garments to reveal a French *Garde-Côtes* uniform, the chance that her boat would be searched diminished by the simple forethought. She pointed them out to sea and east, past the *Îles D'Hyères*, past the Frollywood town of St. Tropez, toward Cannes. For her charge, she knew it meant freedom from the Château D'If and would allow his mind to refocus.

She avoided what seemed like a myriad of official coastal patrol and navy vessels, her Coast Guard attire not being given a second glance. At one point, she swerved to avoid an airliner literally blown from the sky.

• • •

Cannes at this time of the year was far from its mid-May sunny, half-naked International Film Festival configuration. There were no producers, directors, nor celebrities to be found. And as the town received the news of the blast and ensuing catastrophe in Marseille, the sight resembled a Chinese fire drill of metropolitan proportions. People ran from their offices, restaurants, and bars to awaiting transportation and attempted, ensemble, to simultaneously depart. Traffic ground to a standstill. More so than normal, the French yelled obscenities replete with energetic gestures to show their frustrations. All to no avail. A Frenchman who had lost track of time would interpret the scene as typical August, the month during which all of France went on vacation.

Sandrine guided the boat past Cannes, stopped momentarily, and rushed into the cabin. "Mitim, there it is!"

"What?" he moaned.

"Golfe Juan, Mitim!"

His head perked upward. "He landed here. After his escape from exile. From Elba."

"That's right, honey. Napoléon himself and 1,000 of his trusted personal guard."

Lalumière forgot his undulating environment. Excitement captured his face. "He marched them north, through the maritime alps to Grenoble. And on to Paris. He became emperor, Sandrine. I can do this! Please, I beg you, put me ashore!"

"Uh, not quite that simple, kemosabe. We have a stop to make a little ways east. Almost to Italy. You need to meet someone."

"But—"

"All part of Magus Crayle's plan. We okay?" Sandrine placed her hand behind her back and embraced her pistol.

"You are right. I can't allow impatience to destroy my destiny. But we can't let the living legend, Mitim, recede from the public eye."

Sandrine's hand eased. "My orders are to ensure your success." She stepped to him and kissed him full on the lips. Then a smile. She returned to the bridge.

The boat bobbed and weaved past several small towns until the Riviera centerpiece, Nice, came into view. The scene was no different than Cannes, only larger in proportion. Eighty-four miles east of the nuclear epicenter, the sea roil had mitigated to a slumber-inducing roll. In fact, a check of the cabin revealed a slumbering Lalumière with no signs of breakfast expelled onto the deck or bulkheads.

She guided the boat into Fontvieille—the downscale harbor just west of Monte Carlo. It was, like its expensive neighbor, part of the Principality of Monaco and seemed to be unaffected by the mayhem and chaos taking place in its French neighbor.

"Where are we?" asked a blinking Lalumière, popping out of the cabin.

Sandrine pushed him back inside. "You must not be seen. Here." She withdrew attire from a closet for each of them. "Put this on. Take the bandages from the pockets. Put our things in these suitcases."

He did so, discarding the kingly white sheets from his former cell. The two exited the boat onto a quay and traversed the seaside boulevard to a purple Mercedes 600, former transportation to the Emir of Abu Dhabi. The driver needed no directions. In less than five minutes, he had driven uphill to the top of the main promontory of Monaco. To the service entrance of a giant and elegant building. With the bandages in place, Lalumière could not make out the signs leading to a resupply loading dock. He could only tell that this place was very, very important.

CHAPTER 36

The Great Mitim, now outside the borders of France and once again Sylvain Lalumière, was ushered into a square, semi-lit room. There was just enough light for occupants to move about safely. In the room's center sat a large spherical object that, as Lalumière was led near, gave itself up to be a bean bag chair, covered in royal blue leather, and adorned with golden bees and fleur-de-lis. A single beam of light cast down from the concave ceiling upon the chair. Lalumière's name translated to *the light*, and his membership in the secret organization, Illuminé, defined him as enlightened. It all converged for him as he stood next to the chair. The beam illuminated his countenance in a dark, dramatic fashion.

"Be seated," ordered a voice from behind an ornate Louis XVI desk.

Lalumière's heart stopped. He recognized the voice and its authoritative tone. The Elder. He sank into the chair. It molded around his body like a smothering embrace. He fought off a claustrophobic reaction and forced his mind to the instant respite from the multiple aches and pains engendered by his D'If residency.

"Ah," he sighed.

"Yes, Sylvain. We meet at last. Relax, I have use of the Yellow Room as long as I require. As long as *we* require."

"So, you are tight with the Prince?" Sylvain attempted to employ as much street vernacular as he could recall from his conversations with his son, Jean-Marc. He needed to move from mere fluency to a mastery of colloquial English. He needed to impress the Elder.

"Let us say we are of like mind. We have a great deal to discuss, Sylvain. Let us begin."

The speaker was in the shadows and Lalumière could not make out his face. "Yes, of course, Elder."

"Sylvain, you have performed as I expected. Against odds, you have escaped the French authorities, you have initiated a necessary bomb from, of all places, the Château D'If. You have escaped undetected, and sit now in my presence."

"I have succeeded only with the assistance of the young woman, Sandrine. She appears delicate, but has strengths and courage beyond imagination."

"Sylvain, the Illuminé left the shadow of the German-founded Illuminati prior to your country's revolution. Its members were the Enlightened of the French-speaking world. They drifted into historical oblivion simply due to a lack of persistence—a rare French trait. I have that trait and, when you have taken the crown, will have demonstrated to the Francophile world that you possess it as well."

Lalumière noted that Elder was being far less terse than in the past. He felt himself being sucked into the rarefied realm of supreme leadership.

The Elder observed his prodigy's reaction. He thought, *Yes*. "If you listen, Sylvain, you shall hear your murdered ancestors, aristocrats all, and their chorus shall be *revenge!*"

Engulfed by the bean bag, Lalumière jumped from within.

The Elder caught his breath. He was an intellectual, unused to emitting passion through his lips.

By any measure, Lalumière was not a timid man. Still, the sheer power of this man, his mentor, astounded him. "About the young woman ..."

"Our reach extends into the American CIA. It is only one of the many tentacles of our Illuminé. But, hear me, Sylvain. You must be careful of this one. Our CIA operative at Langley has advised: do not sleep with her. He described her wiles as those of a witch whose spell, once insinuated, cannot be denied by mortal man. If allowed, she will take ownership. Once you have succeeded, she will be ... removed."

"I will remember, Elder." Sylvain knew his son would have said, "Oops."

"In the East, Chin has completed his task and has, like you, entered the terminal phase of his quest. For completion at your end, the young spy will lead you to your destiny. With Marseille, no one of the government will be searching for you, nor will they challenge you. The full beard and long, tangled locks, and unkempt clothing will not be of interest. They are, in full force, seeking our dark-skinned pawns. And, Sylvain, should you doubt my reach, my power, the man Crayle and his eclectic team of misfits were manipulated onto the scene and destroyed in the skies above Marseille by the blast. It was I who arranged for the coordination of their demise."

"There are no doubts, Elder." Lalumière was beyond impressed. "Marseille was your symphony."

"Why, yes, so it was. Thank you." The Elder nodded approval ... and continued. "With the world already turned against Iran after the first blast, this one, taking place in the Arab district of Marseille, has led to summits and likewise clandestine conferences regarding actions to be taken against Muslims. It has come to pass as the American, Crayle, predicted. The Iranian blast turned the world against the Shia, which leaves the other primary component of Islam."

The Elder had implanted the epiphany. Lalumière picked up on the notion. "And now, the blast on French soil has turned them against the Sunni."

"While the world governments plot and scheme and huff and puff, the French soil aspect plays right into your hands. Our hands. The French have elected a president of the radical left ideology. He is compelled by his ideology to further constrain businesses and to tax the rich. And the middle class. The government has, in desperation, hitched itself to the socialist star. France is nearing its weakest point. Its incontinence regarding the European debt crisis has astounded every Frenchman. They have no one to turn to, Sylvain. Chiraq and the Socialists failed miserably. Sarkozy and the Conservatives likewise. Their political replacement can do none other than fail."

"I agree, Elder. The people require a superhero."

"Yes," the Elder smiled. "Your escape has become the Legend of the Mitim. You have played and have become that captive hero. Our final move will take place to the north. Near Paris. You will be escorted by Sandrine to Normandy and, from there, will orchestrate the *pièce de résistance.* The *coup d'état.* Paris will burn. And with it, those who would defy your arrival and installation as the next emperor of France."

Lalumière was fine up to the last point. "Elder, I was under the impression that I would be named king. That I would be crowned Louis XIX."

"Of course, Sylvain. A kingdom would assure the right of succession for your son. That would, of course, not exist as emperor."

Lalumière was more than relieved. The Elder did understand him and his needs to their exactitude and magnitude.

"My apology, Sylvain. I misspoke. You will be King Louis XIX—the Symmetric King. Your coronation will require a high cleric. We shall have the Bishop perform the ceremony. You have met him, I believe."

Sylvain sighed relief. "Yes. He presided over the initiation of Jean-Marc into our society. I will be most honored."

The Elder smiled. Aided by CIA-supplied, low-light contact lenses, he read the expression on Lalumière's countenance at the mention of the Bishop. The Frenchman could not know that the

Bishop was not a man of God. In fact, the Bishop was the premier Illuminé assassin, used only for presidents, emperors, and kings. As an ordained Bishop, the killer could travel in any circles and never be suspect. The Elder smiled again. Whatever Sylvain wanted to be called was acceptable, though short-lived. The conquest of France by Crayle's methodology and strategy would set up the final coup. The Elder's coup. A reunited France would begin his new empire.

"Sylvain, you must go now and initiate the final stage of your conquest. You may expect to achieve your dream by year's end." He pulled a lanyard and a uniformed assistant appeared as if by magic. "You must be exhausted. Gaspard will show you to quarters where you may rest. I have dispatched Sandrine to deal with an issue. Later, Gaspard will take you to the underground *porte cochère.* She will join you there. Sylvain, whatever you do, follow the Crayle Strategy to the letter, and heed my warning about the girl."

Gaspard led Sylvain from the room via a hidden doorway at the back of the room's massive fireplace. The Elder smiled a knowing smile this time. Everything moved according to the Strategy. The infallible plan was, indeed, perfection. The Blackstone Strategy was, instead, The Blackstone Perfection.

CHAPTER 37

The young woman, perched atop the castle's clock tower at dusk, peered down at the world's richest harbor. Yellow and red slivers of light that sliced through encroaching storm clouds provided little visibility. She pulled her peacoat tight against the chill breeze. The task at hand would have seemed impossible to a lesser spy, but night-vision binoculars, one of her everpresent resources, enabled her.

"I see him," she said into her headset. "There is no mistake. The facial-recognition system indicates 100% certainty. I understand his itinerary to perfection, and I understand what you wish done." She listened. "Thank you for your faith in me."

• • •

Hamid Mohammed, a slender five-foot-nine Arab, arrived by power yacht in Monte Carlo. He drove his Arabic-licensed Mercedes to the iconic Fairmont Monte Carlo Hotel, whose zig-zag balconies pushed out over the Mediterranean. Inside his first-floor room, a bucket-chilled bottle of carbonated apple juice greeted him. A quick call to the concierge, and fine champagne was on its way. He smiled. He'd provided very special delivery instructions.

He stepped onto the balcony and peered out over the Mediterranean Sea. Although there were mostly power boats this time of year, the most vigorous wind sailors displayed filled white sails in defiance of the cold. The peacefulness provided a moment to reflect.

Hamid's Saudi parents, illegally in Iran, had been butchered by the Imperial Guard. By the grace of fortune, a wealthy couple had rescued him and his brother, adding them to their childless family. Following an excellent education and his ascension in the army, he'd discovered his ancestry. Not Shia Iranian Muslim, but Sunni Arab. Hamid had destroyed the records, and those keeping them. It had been his first blood.

The twisted nature of Hamid Mohammed caused him to prepare himself, not by cleansing and praying, but by ordering delicious, relaxing, and inspirational sex. He was rumored by some to take women to his bed, then to kill them. No one knew whether he derived more pleasure from the sex or the murder. Speculation centered on the latter.

Because money was no object, he had requested the finest prostitute in Monte Carlo. His champagne would be delivered by a Monegasque girl—hair other than black, please. He would use her to release all of his tensions and ready himself for the assassination he would soon commit, with pleasure. A soft knock came at the door.

"Room service," said a French-accented voice.

Hamid had replaced the security eyepiece with a camera. Her picture popped onto the high-definition television. He opened the door, her presence superseding his first glimpse. He smiled. Money talked in Monte Carlo.

"*Monsieur Mohammed?*" asked the cute young woman with a dimpled smile. "*Je m'appelle Sandrine.* I am Sandrine."

Hamid was at once taken with her. She was delectable as a young, innocent female would be. That she was experienced in the needs of men made her undeniably attractive. His face displayed the apprehension that he might not be able to kill her.

"There is no worry," she said. "I will make it all you could want."

Hamid felt overwhelmed. She was no more than 5' 6" in heels with glistening red hair. Freckles dotted her face. He couldn't wait. He reached for her, but she deftly evaded his hands and brushed by him into the room. She placed the iced champagne on a nightstand and positioned herself behind an antique, stuffed chair adorned with green and gold material.

"Please, Hamid. Please sit. I must prepare you for what is to come." She belabored the final word.

Hamid did as he was told. In his regular life, he was a general in the Iranian army. An expert in atomic weaponry. Yet, in the presence of this child-like goddess, he had turned powerless. She began a neck massage that took his mind away from his mission.

"It is best that you speak your mind. We will remove all anxiety and distress."

Yes, he thought. He would talk. They would have sex. She would die.

"You may have heard of the nuclear explosion in central Iran. Only by fortune, did I escape the underground blast. Still, the scars and bruises, and the nagging body pains, keep the memory present."

"Why was there a bomb, my love?"

"The purveyors of wisdom in Tehran craved a nuclear capability. Clearly, had we attempted to truck nuclear bomb-making equipment to the remote valley, the operation would have been discovered easily by American look-down surveillance. The Israelis would have justified a strike. Boom, boom, boom."

"Yes. I believe the Israelis would have attacked you."

"The Chinese came to us with a plan, created by American Magus Crayle, that enabled our scheme. The cover story, to create for Iran an international playground superior to Dubai, was brilliant. The parched valley we chose required water, and a Frenchman named Lalumière would construct an underground pipeline to furnish it.

The publicity had placed the endeavor beyond reproach. The world believed."

Neil had never provided her any detail, she noted. "What then?"

"By the grace of Crayle's genius, bomb-enhancing equipment would be 'packaged' and floated the distance via Lalumière's pipe, uninspected. No one would know."

"So you had your water and materials, but what about the nuclear part?"

"A Chinese, General Li, supplied a small nuclear weapon. All the cards had fallen into place. Then, on the next day, it exploded. Instead of becoming a national hero, I became an international patsy. Lalumière and Li betrayed me. Tehran believed that I, General Hamid Mohammed, handed the decadent West, and the Israelis, a smoking gun."

"They concluded that Iran had a nuclear weapon. I see."

Sandrine understood the complex plot better than ever before. The Iranian blast put the world on notice. Next, Marseille. More blame on the Iranians. And France was at risk. More pressure on the French government. She smiled. Crayle must be quite an intelligent man. "Where is this American now?"

Hamid ignored her question, pulling a throbbing phone from his pocket. "Yes, brother … It is good that you are well. How is my favorite nuclear physicist? … Good … Yes, I am aware the world has concluded in error that our first nuclear bomb failed catastrophically. Listen, brother. I have received intelligence via backchannel. The American CIA wants Lalumière pulled down. Yes … the Frenchman detonated both the Fasd and Marseille explosions. Co-conspirators hide this infidel in Monaco's Presidential Palace," the general fumed. "I will obtain access. I will find Lalumière, make him suffer, and kill him." He listened. "Escape? With my credentials?" Hamid rang off.

"Your muscles have loosened, but you are mentally tense." She walked to the bar and poured two drinks. She placed them on the table in front of him, then reached down into her black cocktail dress and removed a silver, metal cylinder. From it, she extracted a capsule, and dropped it into her drink. "It is calibrated to dissolve slowly, Hamid. When you see it start to affect me, you must place me on the bed. The chemical will disable my ability to move, to struggle, to fight. But not to feel. You may then do whatever you like to my body. You may even kill me, if you so choose."

She saw Hamid's sex push hard against his trousers. She had studied his psychological profile in the sanctity of the embassy's isolation room. She knew the scenario she had depicted provided more desire in him than he had ever experienced.

"You are here on business. Something dangerous. Quite dangerous. Danger excites me, Hamid." She stared into his brown eyes. She knew the general would tell her anything, knowing he could have her and then kill her. "Tell me quickly while the drug begins its journey."

"I am here to rectify a wrong. A wrong done to Iran, and to me personally. A man named Sylvain Lalumière has escaped from a French prison. He promised to provide water to our secret nuclear plant near Fasd."

"He failed to do this?"

"He and his people built the tunnel. Our people laid the piping at his direction." His breathing accelerated.

She could tell he needed to tell someone his feelings, but they were so intense he struggled to do so.

"And then …"

"A Chinese general brought us a weapon. A small nuclear device to power our secret electrical facility."

"A weapon? Why a weapon for a power station?"

"It was a …" He searched his mind for the arcane word. "… a ruse."

"And then …"

"They left. One day later, the bomb exploded. Lalumière betrayed us. His goal all along was to turn the world against Iran. I was just miles from the facility. Sandrine, it was magnificent and frightening at the same time. The ground above the facility lifted into the air like a child throwing playground sand. All were killed instantly—melted into the rock and steel below the ground."

"You must have lost people close to you. People you cared deeply about."

"Yes. My brother was away and spared. But two cousins were turned to paste by this madman. I will see him tonight and take revenge."

The prostitute caught his attention.

"Please, Hamid. Prepare our bed. When the drug takes effect, you will have little time."

Hamid rushed to the bed and drew back the covers. He ran back to the chair and watched her every move—searching for the first indication of the drug's effect.

"Please, Hamid, drink with me. That is all I ask."

Hamid took the champagne flute and, defying the will of Allah, took a gulp. The liquor scorched his throat more than the desert's burning sand. He elated in the feeling. As the woman who had introduced herself as Sandrine took her next sip, her head appeared unsteady.

Hamid leapt from the chair and scooped her up. Once on the bed, he undressed her as she moaned, "It's happening now, my darling." He jumped up and tore at his clothes. He must hurry.

He climbed onto the bed on his knees beside her. Something wasn't right. *His* head. The alcohol, he thought. The feeling took him over like a wave takes over a beachfront. He fell onto his back. He tried to move his arms but to no avail. Same, his legs. Her face came into view above his.

"It's alright, Hamid. Your pill was a very special pill," she said in English.

"You … when I ran to the bed …"

"Yes, my darling. Americans, such as myself, call it the old switcheroo."

The last expression Hamid managed was one of utter shock. Then, horror.

Sandrine climbed atop of the Arab and put him inside her. “The drug? A blend of roofy and the hard-on drug. I can move on you and pleasure myself and watch you struggle, mentally. You, the magnificent General Hamid Mohammed, are terrified.” Her breathing intensified. She reached behind her and massaged the soft flesh between his legs. She felt him grow harder.

“It’s a whore’s trick. The part I have in me is only 2/3 of what you have to give. Few men even know that.” She removed the Spanish comb that gathered her hair in back. Using both hands, she popped it open and pivoted it at the hinge on one end to reveal a razor sharp blade.

She felt his progress toward the standard male sexual conclusion. She drew the blade across his neck. The blood pulsed softly from the nick in his jugular vein onto the white sheets. Neither Hamid nor his eyes moved at all.

“You will not kill my Mitim tonight, General. Or any other night. It would be good if you make your peace with Allah.”

Climaxes came to them both at the same time. But while her body racked with pleasure, his did not move. When she finished, she looked down. Hamid’s eyelids traversed from wide open to full shut in slow motion, a gauge depicting the lapsing of fuel in a tank. She experienced her most intense and satisfying sex ever.

She cleaned up and wrapped his body in the bedclothes. She used a desk chair to wheel the Arab outside. The balcony light remained off. Walls on either side of the balcony assured privacy. She struggled to get his heavy corpse over the rail. Waves crashed against the rocks below. Hamid, the feared general and assassin, went quietly into oblivion.

• • •

The little spy stretched around the balcony divide and entered her own room, one she had taken after dropping off Mitim at the Palace. She stripped, showered, and washed the red from her hair. A special cream, also from S & T, removed the freckles. Her phone rang.

"Is it done? Is he dead?" Neil Wohlford's voice seemed calm.

"Yes, he is dead."

"I should have informed you earlier. It became necessary to remove him from the field. My goal required it. When I rise to the top, I will take you with me."

"And Chantal?"

Silence.

"I see."

"There will be a backlash. The people of France will mourn the loss of their Mitim—"

"Mitim? Mitim is fine. He is in good hands at the Palace. It is the Iranian general who is no more."

"*What?* No! That's not possible! Hamid was to kill Lalumière. For me. Oh, my god!" Neil's voice trailed off.

"I need to leave. Let's talk later. 'Kay?" She silenced the phone.

"Oh, my god," squeezed through before she clicked off. She pressed speed dial.

"Elder."

"I just spoke with Neil."

"Ah, yes. It seems he initiated a hit on dear Sylvain. It happens that I need him a while longer."

"And me?"

"Return to the Palace." The Elder terminated the call.

After a quick swap of outerwear from her favorite brocade tote bag, she departed. Sweet Pattie Norbrunn.

CHAPTER 38

That is the last time I fly," Phoebe announced as their pilot taxied the weary aircraft to a remote hanger.

"Not as bad as the little château thing," offered Lenny.

"You mean where my hands were bound behind my back and that thug with the triangle jaw …"

"TJ?" Lenny interrupted

"… beat and kicked me half to death. Yeah. TJ."

"And you caught the gun I threw and pumped one from behind your back straight up and out. Between the eyes once again, AO." Lenny added the Annie Oakley tag.

"I'd do that again to avoid Jack Air."

"I heard that," said Jack as he emerged from the bedroom with the flight attendant. "I've arranged ground travel for you, but there's a little detail I need to impart. Listen up."

He garnered their attention.

"Good news, bad news. The good … I have two reports on Lalumière's whereabouts. The bad? They have him in two locations. A place called, I spell, *A-i-x,* and a country called Monaco."

"Where is *aches*?"

"Thank you for the interruption, Lenny. It's pronounced *ex*, like my wife. Speaking of Marilyn, I received a note from her. Seems Lalumière's men captured her in Malibu … thanks to Magus' Vestige chip winding up in her glasses case. Tried to get her to lead 'em to us. Big mistake. No weapon, took 'em all out. You can imagine what *I* had to deal with." Jack's cell phone dinged. "Uh, oh. Her again. Says she purchased a super-duty cattle prod. Ends with, *We need to talk.*"

The team observed his weak smile. Jack's ex-wife sounded serious. Given what he'd put them through, they sided with Marli.

Jack followed a deep breath with, "Okay. Same teams as Beijing, except equal opportunity requires Lenny to change teams. Micmac and Hekka get a two-seater. The other's a four."

"I drive this time," said Lenny.

"First team to Aix, second to Monaco. I'll supply intel en route. You'll have to reconnoiter and surveille and stuff. Let me know if you spot him. Before you take him out. 'Kay?" Jack tossed one set of keys to Micmac, the second to Crayle. Hekka and Lenny received telescoping, push-to-talk walking sticks. "Rock and roll!"

Heads bobbed. They fell into line.

Lenny elbowed Phoebe. "Last time Jack got us a Volvo station wagon. Don't expect much," he whined.

Flori lowered the plane's stairway. The team deplaned. Jack leaned against the side of the door opening. "Micmac, you'll take Hekka. You'll have to backtrack over some pretty hairy landscape, given the bomb aftermath. There's a safehouse in Aix. You'll be 16 miles north of the epicenter, so the roads'll be strewn with all manner of shit. There's your ride. I hereby declare you qualified on that spankin' new Ducati Diablo."

Phoebe glanced at the Italian motorcycle. She pictured the beautiful Serrano girl pressed tight against Micmac's back, her arms clutching him, feeling the unsubtle vibrations of the blood-red bike through her private parts. Still, she smiled. She now owned the trust game and Micmac possessed all the honor necessary. "Keep her safe for Magus." They would be fine.

Micmac noticed a special GPS attached to the gas tank. He pressed Favorites—the device lit up a course to Aix-en-Provence. He ignited the throaty rumble of the Ducati, shot an I'll-be-back glance at Phoebe, and they were off.

The road to Aix-en-Provence, littered with blast debris, proved just doable on the Ducati. Exodus traffic jammed the other side of the divided road, with Micmac and Hekka the sole westbound travellers. The carnage included bodies of all sizes, shapes, and ages.

Micmac enabled the intercom. "Bad stuff. Like a war zone."

"You've been to one?"

"A few."

"Did you ever stop to help?"

"No."

Silence, then, "How far?"

Micmac checked the gas-tank-mounted GPS. "At normal speed, a little north of 70, we'd cover the ninety-one miles in an hour-and-a-half. We'll only average 40 or so."

Stopping and starting, bobbing and weaving, it took them close to three hours to complete the journey. Aix no longer appeared to be a town of 143,000 inhabitants. Now, it resembled a ghost town. They passed a string of collapsed buildings, one bearing the sign Poste. Next to it was a roundabout with a large fountain base, its fifteen foot disk frisbeed into the side of a nearby building. At the circle's outer rim, a statue of the town's most famous inhabitant, Paul Cézanne, had been ripped from its mooring and thrown, whirling like a flung crowbar, through the restaurant *Le Cintra*, a site for meeting and watching in calmer times.

"I only witnessed this order of devastation from the air as we left Beijing. This is too close. Too personal. I need Magus."

Micmac heard her tears. "This is tough time, Hekka. This is where we take it all in, then refocus on our mission." The former underwater demolitions and weapons specialist knew the drill. It never was easy, but you forged on. Always.

He started up *Cours Mirabeau,* Aix's main tree-lined drag, only the trees had all been uprooted or blown flat. Some had turned into spears, impaling the windowed shops lining the street. Micmac parked the bike. Once they removed their helmets, the smells hit them. None of them good. He gave Hekka a long, tight hug. She smiled her minimalist smile. It was enough. She was good to go.

"We'll search the rubble for survivors. This is a long shot, but we have to stop this guy. There's no telling how many of these bombs he has."

"We must check in. Can you call Magus?"

Micmac checked his phone. Zero bars. "I'm afraid not. We have a rendezvous point and a time to meet."

"How long?"

• • •

Near Jack's jet, in its concours-finish shine, sat a brand new Porsche 9ll Carrera S Cabriolet. Its gloss black, layered cosmetics simply glowed.

"Oh!" cried Phoebe. "Oh! … Oh! And my color."

"I'll drive," Lenny announced. "She can orgasm in the back."

"Over your dead body, P.I." Her love for her man, her Glock, and 911's was no secret.

Suppressing a grin, Crayle handed the keys to Phoebe. "You and I will be the eyes here, Lenny. Jump in the back. A perfect fit."

Lenny's short stature made him the best fit of the three in the baby-sized rear seats. Pouting, the P.I. scrambled in. Crayle took shotgun.

Lenny wasn't done. "My dad told me the S stood for Stud. This ain't no ladies car."

"Oh, you are so right, Lenny. But, I do really love the 7,400 RPM whine of the three-point-eight liter, 400 horsepower, horizontal six. Let's see … PDK paddle-shifters for the seven-speed tranny. Doesn't that stand for Porsche Doppelkuplung, Lenny? Over 100 large in the States, and I get it for free."

"You made all that up," Lenny pouted.

Phoebe adjusted the mirror to lock eyes with Lenny. Smiled. She fluttered her eyelashes and punctuated with a middle-finger salute. Finished with the P.I., her mind re-acquired focus. A 911 was on her one-item bucket list. The seat had been adjusted to perfect. She sat there for a moment. Savoring. A turn of the key, and the engine roared. A few foot-to-the-floor revs. "Just getting her oiled up." She giggled her delight, tapped the right paddle into first gear, and headed east toward the principality known as Monaco. On Jack's expense account. "Whew! Monte Carlo, here we come!"

Crayle directed her into the principality and onto a road that climbed to the world famous casino. He knew the road was used in the once-per-year Formula 1 Grand Prix races, he imagined the trip at speed.

Phoebe topped the hill and turned left, in front of the celebrity lodging known as the Hôtel de Paris. She passed a massive fountain and headed downhill to the Mirabeau turn and through the following hairpin. She stopped at a 'T' intersection with a road bounding the Mediterranean. She turned to Crayle with a shrug.

He pointed left. "Thelasso-therapy massage there, if you have the Euros." Still on the Grand Prix course, he pointed her right toward the Fairmont Monte Carlo tunnel. "We won't find him in there," Crayle said, knowing that race cars blasted through the curved, two-car wide cylinder at 180-plus miles per hour. "Speed it up."

Phoebe jammed the volume pedal to the floor. Billows of smoke flared from the rear tires. "Oh!" Phoebe cried with delight.

"Jeeesus!" Lenny wailed in fear.

The Porsche's engine wound to a screaming, red-line ecstasy. It surpassed 150 miles-per-hour as it blasted from the tunnel into bright daylight. Phoebe blew around terrified motorists and set up for the sharp left hand tobacconist corner.

"Oh!" This time from Lenny. "I gotta pee!"

Phoebe eased off the throttle. Her lips pursed. Her jaw tightened. "Okay, Private Buzzkill. There's a place ahead. A restaurant. *Rascasse*, the sign says. We'll go in there." Phoebe parked the Porsche.

While Lenny found the W.C., Crayle showed his computer-generated likeness of Sylvain Lalumière with a twenty-two day beard to a short, stocky bartender clad in 1000-wash whites. Finally, luck. Crayle listened hard to permeate the man's thick, local, Monegasque accent.

"Zis man stopped for a dreenk. Beer, Seven-Up, Grenadine … eh … *tout ensemble*. Hees daughtair 'ad absinthe … eh, Mata Hari was thee brand. Like zee spy."

Crayle did a double take. "Did she, the daughter, have dimples?" He pushed his forefingers into his cheeks.

"Eh, oui. *Très adorable*." The bartender blew out through his lips. He regathered himself and continued. "Ee sought zee *Route Napoléon*. Ee said ee 'ad raison to travel zat route. I told heem, go west. Golfe-Juan. Eet ees where Napoléon and ees followair landed after ee escape from exile on Elba. Follow zee sign. Zey weel take you north into zee French Alp. To Grenoble."

Crayle whispered in Phoebe's ear. She left in a hurry.

Lenny returned, still zipping his trousers. "Wow, this has been a bust. Where's the Fibbee?"

"C'mon, Lenny. She's in the car. We know where he's going."

"Nobody tells me nothing." Lenny glared at the bartender for being the same size. He tossed a ten centime tip on the bar. By the time the offended man retrieved a barb-wire wrapped cricket bat, the two were gone.

The entire group was beat. Crayle knew the signs because he felt them. He checked-in with Jack.

"Okay, team. Listen up. Jack says we're not much use in the shape we're in. He wants us to backtrack and spend the night at the

Fairmont. The place with the tunnel. Oh, yes, and he may have lost his mind. He wants Lenny and I to man the room while Phoebe picks up necessities. Clothes, stuff like that."

Phoebe wore an ear-to-ear grin. "Forget any shopping list. All you guys need to know is that everything in Monte Carlo is way beyond expensive, and I've got Jack's card."

• • •

Lenny awakened everyone just past dawn. Surprising to all, he even arranged the delivery of a sumptuous breakfast. They departed by ten. None knew they'd just shared the same room that Sandrine had vacated. Or that Jack had afforded Phoebe privacy when he'd made the reservations. She occupied the room next door. Hamid's room. It still smelled of blood.

• • •

Phoebe drove the crew the twenty miles west past Nice to the much smaller Riviera town, Golfe-Juan. Along the way, Team Alpha listened intently as Crayle enabled the high-end speaker system and called Jack.

"Jack, everyone is here, and we're on speaker. Can you hear me?"

"Yeah, but tell Agent Bransfield to turn down the revs on her dream car so I can hear … thanks."

Phoebe upshifted two gears.

"Okay, guys, here's the deal. Head up Highway N85 at Golfe-Juan, go about thirty miles to a burg called Digne-les-Bains. The Frenchman will have to pass through and, by my calculation, it's likely they'll stop for food there. Check at the gas station first. Those folks see and hear everything. Ol' Sylvain appears to be on his way to Grenoble, just like Napoléon, and that's another place to check. Especially at the airport. Okay? Gotta go."

Click.

The Porsche, under Phoebe's command, processed up into the alps, taking every curve with grace. "Oh, yeah. I had evasive driving at the Farm," she informed the crew.

At Digne-les-Bains, Crayle signaled Phoebe to pull over. "We are all hungry and tired. We need to stretch. Lenny, reconnoiter a place to take in food and caffeine-enhanced French coffee. Check for Wi-Fi. We'll keep an eye out for signs of trouble. Two beeps and you come running."

After Lenny unwound from the back and set off into town, Phoebe said, "I never told you this, Mag. I never told anyone. I understand how you feel about your dad."

"He's dead, Phoebe. I had no memory of him after the crash. Before Rorschach's latest magic, I could only learn about him through others. Chin. Jack. In restoring the work I did in Hong Kong, the memories overflowed with memories of my father. I can't see how can you understand how I feel?"

"Oh, my God."

"I now see him as a little boy saw him. In his uniform with the silver oak leaves, going off to war. At the time, I didn't realize he was with Army Intelligence or that he was travelling to Hong Kong, not Vietnam. Now, each time I look into a mirror—"

"You see his eyes," she whispered.

"How—"

"Mag, my dad's eyes were just like mine. I was every bit Lt. Col. Bransfield's daughter. It's the same for me. Every time I look into a mirror, I don't see *my* eyes looking back. I see his. At first, it frightened me—now it gives me strength."

They leaned across to each other and embraced.

"Jeez-Louise! Leave 'em alone for a moment, and they behave like rabbits. Room for a threesome? No?" Lenny planned to continue his monolog, but the glare back affirmed the 'hell, no' status of his fantasy.

"It's about our dads, Lenny."

Had Micmac been there, Phoebe would've leapt from the car, run to him, and thrown her arms around him.

They grabbed a quick lunch at *La Chauvinière*, and stared at their likeness of a bearded Lalumière. The waiter noticed. "Oh, you know thees man?"

Heads snapped up.

"'e was 'ere thees day. Goeeng to Paree, 'e said. Like Napoléon."

Crayle tossed a 100-Euro bill on the table, and they ran for the door. Outside, the weather changed. An alpine storm encroached on the beautiful day, the temperature having dropped twenty degrees Fahrenheit.

"I'm cold," Lenny whined.

Crayle understood. His arms had puckered up as well. "We're all tired. If we raise the top, Phoebe could fall asleep. Over the side is a drop of hundreds of feet. Certain death. Neither we, this country, nor the world can afford that." He popped the door pocket lid and retrieved a black sun visor. At its peak was a multi-colored, neon outline of a shark.

"Greg Norman," Phoebe observed. "The Bureau found him a person of interest after a questionable score card." She laughed. "Daddy golfed." She pulled two more visors from the driver side pocket.

"Won't keep us warm," Lenny groused.

"Jack knows what he's doing. Caps will be sucked off at speed. Visors are the only way to go." Crayle cranked up the Germanic-force heater.

"At speed?" cried Lenny.

Phoebe demonstrated the speed she felt necessary to catch Lalumière even as the snow began to fall.

• • •

They moved ever higher into the mountains. Phoebe varied in temperament from controlled to edgy, her multiple past traumas still working their way out of her system. "This has got to be the road to nowhere. Mag, we just keep wiggling our way higher into these hills—"

"Alps," corrected Lenny.

Phoebe hit the brakes, popped her seat belt, and was over the top of her seat in an instant. She grabbed Lenny by the neck as if staging a final assault.

A following police car snapped on its noise and lights. The French gendarme ran to the Porsche in time to see Crayle pull the two apart. He turned to the officer and shrugged. "Brother and sister." The officer returned the shrug, retreated to his car, and put the dysfunctional siblings behind him.

"Not good, children," Crayle said, sounding like Jack. "Think nuclear weapons. Think a hundred thousand grisly deaths. Think deformed survivors that could number in the millions. You're both on time out 'til Grenoble."

• • •

The Porsche-borne group reached Grenoble by mid-afternoon. Crayle felt they had little chance of catching the Frenchman here. He played a hunch.

"Phoebe, follow the signs with Aéroport de Grenoble-Isère." She did.

The airport sat high in the rarefied Alpine air a few miles from the ski village of Grenoble.

"Over there." Crayle pointed. Phoebe stopped near a man who carried two flashlights, the kind used to direct aircraft. Crayle hopped out.

"*Pardon, monsieur.*" Rather than ask the man if he spoke English, Crayle dove in. "Have you had any Dassault Falcon 7X's depart today?" Crayle had deduced that everyone involved seemed to have such a jet. His hunch paid off.

A restored German Me-109 fighter lumbered not far away, so the man had to yell and keep sentences brief. "Eh, yes. Just one. Bound for, eh, Normandy. Rouen."

Crayle showed him the picture.

"*Oh la la!* Yes, that man was a passenger. They left not two hours ago."

"Damn!" Crayle cried out.

"*Monsieur?*" The man looked concerned.

"*Merci, beaucoup, monsieur*. Yeah, *merci*." Crayle stalked back to the Porsche and informed his colleagues.

"I get to drive my dream car from Grenoble to Rouen? Oh!"

"Jeeesus!" from the back seat.

At that instant, a rumble overtook them from behind. Heads snapped around. Micmac and Hekka, aboard the lightning fast Ducati, streaked across the tarmac, pulling up next to them.

Hekka pulled her helmet first. "You must try this, Phoebe. It vibrates."

"Just a sec." Crayle stepped away from the car and punched in the cell phone code for Jack. He returned in less than two minutes. "Good news. Most of the scheduled flights have been appropriated by the French government for aid assistance in and around Marseille. Jack pulled strings and obtained for us the very next flight out. We will vector to Rouen, Normandy. Sorry, Phoebe."

"Well, that's a relief," Lenny chimed just seconds before Phoebe popped her safety belts, spun in her seat, and clocked him.

CHAPTER 39

Transportation of Lalumière to Normandy, a circuitous endeavor, avoided detection by the still active dragnet in France, which had been extended to Interpol and the entire continent. Sandrine and her charge completed the final leg of their journey aboard a Eurocopter Hermès EC135. It now circled a château with crenellated walls and four turrets, three of normal size and one larger. The property's empty parking lot suggested an absence of tourists—not unusual in such hard times.

As they hovered over the large turret, Lalumière watched the crenellations bend outward. A lighted circle inscribed with an 'H' atop the tower showed it to be the landing target. The pilot held the chopper in the breeze and touched down as if landing on a large, down pillow. Once the blades had spun down, they collapsed inside themselves and the tail rotated to a vertical position. The crenellations angled back to their normal vertical positions.

The heliport disc descended to a subterranean level. A conveyer moved it sideways to a giant double doorway. Its occupants were no sooner off the pad than it began its trip in reverse. It was a clear enough sign that future transportation was likely to be other than airborne. The veritable dungeon caused Lalumière to grasp his chest. Sandrine moved to moderate any panic attacks, but the problem proved short-lived.

Sandrine smiled as a man and woman greeted them. "*Bonjour*. We are the château owners, Monsieur and Madame Defarge."

The Defarges led them to a Great Room much larger than at Lalumière's château in eastern France. A large flat panel monitor ascended from the stone floor. Mr. Defarge initiated a channel and motioned the two to a Louis XV sofa set against a far wall.

"We have a lovely vineyard," Mr. Defarge offered. "Our wine is quite good. I sell it myself. I will fetch a bottle." He soon returned with a cart bearing glasses and an unopened bottle of his finest vintage.

Television images varied from scenes of the panic evacuation in the south to riots in the streets of Paris. Delivered by an Italian broadcasting company, the satellite feed was too excited for comprehension. Closed captioning blazed by at breakneck pace. Only the images made sense.

"We support you, Monsieur Lalumière, or you would not see this in our home. It represents the destruction of our homeland, *La Belle France*. In reality, we view it as a tearing down so that new construction may commence."

Madame Defarge added, "*Oui*, our country, like so many democracies, has arrived at an impasse with respect to leadership. The politicians have decided that we, the people, are no longer relevant. We are only important for two reasons: money for them to spend, and our votes. We have voted out the incompetent and corrupt to replace them with further incompetence and corruption. We have lost the battle, Monsieur Lalumière, but we must … and with your leadership we shall … win the war."

Sandrine watched intently as the video played, but she also glanced frequently at their hosts. She had not been taken by surprise thus far in her career. She didn't intend to begin now.

"We will leave you to watch the happenings. I am afraid I cannot permit you to operate this remote control. It is special." Mr. Defarge nodded for emphasis.

Both guests understood the global reach of the Langley remote.

"Rooms have been prepared for your visit. You may use either or both. Robert, our butler, will show you to them when you ring." Mme. Defarge pointed to a bell on an end table. "Robert is a relic of the war. He is both deaf and blind, and he can be trusted implicitly."

"That's some bell," said Sandrine, avoiding any sarcastic intonation.

"When you have rested, there will be a guest to see you."

With that, the Defarges—most assuredly not their name—departed the Great Room.

"The Defarges were a figment of Charles Dickens imagination, Sandrine. He placed them in the *Tale of Two Cities,* regarding the last major shift in France's management style."

"I know. Didn't I mention. My last name is Manette."

They watched as much of the chaos as they could stand, then summoned Robert. He performed as promised. Sylvain Lalumière and Sandrine Manette examined each other's faces for an explanation. Finding none, they dozed off in the larger of the two bedrooms.

• • •

"Hello, Dad!" boomed a familiar voice. The bedmates sat up in the next instant.

Standing in the doorway was a man Lalumière knew well and Sandrine had, in her current guise, never met.

"*Jean-Marc! Comment ça va, mon fils?*"

"*Ton fils bâtard,*" replied the son. "And who is this fine young lady, Dad?"

The two were naked from the waist up. Jean-Marc felt compelled to check the woman out. "Is she French?"

"What are you doing here? You are to be meeting with the royals of the Nordic countries. They must be brought on board with our grand plan. I bet you spent all of your time in Amsterdam with that Dutch whore, the one you called Angel."

Sandrine, a.k.a. Angel, blushed.

Lalumière had never met Angel, but his son had described her in intimate detail. Especially the beautiful blonde hair. He wanted his son to excel in the art of love, but surely he must have mastered it by now.

"Get dressed, Dad, I'll meet you in the Great Room. I'll fill you in on the Nordics."

• • •

Somewhat disheveled, the man who would be king and his prospective consort shuffled into the Great Room. Jean-Marc sat mid-sofa, sipping a Calvados Cocktail just handed him by the butler. They took positions on either side. Their intense glances indicated that he needed to proffer a good reason for shocking them awake.

"I've travelled the north since your, eh, incarceration in the *sous Bastille,* and I've met with the Baltic royalties of Norway, Sweden, Finland, Estonia, Poland, and Denmark. Separately. To my surprise, they all voiced their acceptance of our plan. It was as if they had been prepared in advance. In any case, they have agreed to a summit to be held in either a Polish or Estonian castle at a date I will coordinate with them." Jean-Marc glanced back and forth, as if anticipating applause.

"What about the Russians?" asked his father, who noticed their absence from his son's list.

"Yes, the Russians. The descendants of the Romanovs were a little tricky to track down. They're next on my list. I'm looking forward to some of that Nyevskoya beer."

"One, you must learn to drink fine wine and malt liquor. Beer will not do. Second, without the Russians, we court disaster. Do not forget, my son, we still have the Dutch, the Belgians, the Germans, the Czechs, the Italians …"

"I get it, Dad. You just stay right here with … her." He glanced at the half-naked spy. "The cops are searching for you and your photograph is everywhere, but that's good news, too. The people of France have made you into a hero. You've proclaimed the danger of immigrants from the south for years, and those chickens have come home to roost. That mushroom cloud in Marseille blew away any doubts."

Neither Lalumière nor Sandrine reacted.

"Jean-Marc, you need to get back on the road."

"I'm looking forward to more of that Estonian beer, Soku, as well. A nice suite in the Hotel Telegraph. Ah, I can feel my fingers wrapping around the blue and cream label—"

"Jean-Marc! Forget the beer. Your job is critical."

"Just pulling your chain, Dad—as the Americans say."

Lalumière briefly shut his eyes. "Before you go, it is most important that I know, how are the Americans taking this?"

"Not well. Their president is talking about intervention and the need to restore order here."

"They feel no threat? They don't prepare for an attack such as Marseille?"

"No. The president must prop up his socialist pals. I'm sure of one thing, though. If an attack occurs in America, they'll forget about us in a heartbeat."

"You are right. Stay well, my son, and only contact me when the Russians are ready to jump in bed with us."

"I expect to have good news soon."

Jean-Marc departed. The room turned quiet. Sandrine had learned more than did Lalumière.

• • •

Sylvain Lalumière awakened in an empty bed the next day. He donned a robe and went in search of Sandrine. He found her with the Defarges at a breakfast table overseen by Robert.

"*Bonjour*," the trio chorused.

"You must hurry," counseled Sandrine. "Today we prepare for the next phase of your journey. We're going skydiving."

Lalumière stiffened beyond horrified. The only thing that frightened him more than water was elevation. If one stood on the ground and fell, one would likely recover. If one fell from the sky …

He refused to complete the thought. He would go. He would do anything for France.

• • •

The plane, a replica of the aircraft Charles Lindbergh had flown across the Atlantic, had been modified for skydiving. Despite poor visibility, Sandrine repeated over and over that Lalumière must learn to jump—a necessity for the next step in his journey.

The pilot took them to the skydiving range and to jump altitude. The two jumpers donned the proper suits and parachutes.

"We'll go tandem," she told him. "We'll connect together. It's the simplest, fastest, and most failsafe means of teaching you to jump."

At the pilot's signal, Lalumière followed her to the plane's side door. She held it open while he poked his head outside. He turned, ready to say, "I can't do it." Just as she shoved him. Out he went.

She turned to the pilot and grasped his hand. Her dimpled smile mesmerized him. With her other hand, she slammed the steel butt end of a combat knife into the radio controls. With the business end, she severed his jugular vein. The crash would distract onlookers.

The plane bobbled. She fell back, her mind not on the logistics of getting out, but on the disappointment Neil Wohlford would express that she'd terminated yet another CIA asset. In the next moment, she leapt from the aircraft and plunged in bullet configuration toward the flailing Frenchman.

She expected his heart to be beating like a jackhammer. She crashed into him, nearly knocking them both unconscious.

Her alarm sounded.

Two thousand feet.

She fumbled with the connectors, brushing aside the panicked Lalumière's attempts at assistance.

Fifteen hundred feet.

There. Connected. She pulled the ripcord. The drogue chute popped above them. The main chute deployed, yanking them upward, further escalating Lalumière's drumbeat pulse.

A thousand feet.

Sandrine never wasted an opportunity to enjoy a man's heightened senses and galloping heart rate. She unzipped her way into his suit. In seconds, they merged.

Five hundred.

She worked him and controlled him, all the while gazing into the distance. The pair climaxed just as their plane exploded into the ground.

Two-fifty.

She restored his clothing and prepared for their landing.

Robert awaited them at the specified landing zone, as planned. Sandrine elected to drive them home in the castle's Mercedes. There would be no rest. The new schedule called for them to be in the air headed toward their next destination by nightfall. They would need to dress warmly.

CHAPTER 40

St. Nazaire, a port on the northwest coast of France, played home to a giant shipyard capable of producing elite passenger ships such as Britain's Queen Mary 2. That the ship needed to be built in France remained a sore spot for the English. The French, of course, pointed out the paradox at every opportunity. At a World Cup Soccer final, English fans were treated to a scoreboard that read *Vivre La Reine Marie Deux*. Fights broke out.

Besides shipbuilding, myriad companies depended upon the outfitting of these fine ships, including life craft. Though most would never be deployed other than as shuttles into shallow harbors, they were crafted to close tolerances and high quality standards.

The owner of one of the major suppliers, unknown to his employees or colleagues, belonged to a secret society long thought to be extinct. The society maintained as its philosophy that intellect and personal loyalty were the necessary components for governance of a people. The owner, pleased because his mentor and superior sounded pleased, had just informed the man known for his omniscience and high class bearing on the phone that the preparations for the next phase of the French operation were now complete.

To the east, the driver and his blue van sped across the hills, bypassing Châteaubriant. From the Brittany capital, Rennes, it was a short drive up the 175. There in the distance, through the morning fog, it stood. Mont St. Michel was a wonderment for this man, but he couldn't linger. He drove up to the land bridge and the large parking lot.

The pyramid-shaped town had graced more post cards than any other. Thierry Jacquard entered the old city. He passed shopkeepers and restauranteurs, preparing for another busy day, even this late in the Fall.

At last, he found the place he sought. He lit a Gitanes, and glanced around. No one gave him a second look. Above, a large sign brought a smile to his oversized face. He stepped inside La Mère Poulard, home to the legendary whipped omelet. He paused at the sight of a chef beating air into an egg mixture in a copper bowl, as had been done for countless decades. He smiled. She winced.

"Soufflé," he told the waiter. "Sugar topping, light. To go."

The waiter, hearing genuine French-accented English and knowing that only American tourists would top anything with sugar, returned with a wrapped steel box.

Minutes later, Thierry continued east on the 175. He wanted to divert north to the village of Bayeaux to view the tapestry of William the Conqueror's accession to the throne of England, but his brother would have his head if he was late.

Three hours after his trip had begun, he arrived in the Lower Normandy port town, Ouistreham. He locked the van and proceeded into the lobby for Brittany Ferries. He would have wondered why the ferry service was in Normandy, but named Brittany were it not for the fact that his blue and white, magnetic striped ticket listed his ride as the *Normandie Express*. Above that name, another name identified him as one *Bowen D*, thus matching his 'borrowed' passport. Still, he wasn't home free. Any facial recognition software would quickly identify him by name and his extensive Interpol history. He sported a days-old beard, large sunglasses, and wore a hoodie to defend against profile recognition. His Gallic nose protruded, but he figured the coverage was sufficient.

He stepped into the lobby, surveying the layout as his brother had instructed. To his left sat rows of benches. To his right, a full-service bar with its requisite stools, and a set of waist high, round tables and stools. Back to his left, past the benches, he spotted a cubicle with the ubiquitous lower-case ***i,*** indicating tourist information. He checked the schedule. *On time.*

He traipsed across the lobby to the bar for a bottle of Desperados 5.9% beer. He needed the infused tequila kick. From there, he moved to a table and bided his time. He tried to flirt with the female passersby, but they visibly recoiled at first sight of his oversized jaw.

The ferry was on time, and he moved the van into line.

The Normandie Express appeared James Bondian from stem to stern. On the quite large passenger catamaran, a softly undulating stripe of blue and red on a hull painted Arctic White underscored near-black window panels across the top. It looked very, very fast while standing still.

He reached the front of the line. An attractive brunette took his blue-trimmed ticket, and he felt a surge. He was ready. He would get this right. Once aboard his ferry, he parked the van and headed upstairs.

The view from the passenger compartment was wondrous. He peered east, toward Honfleur and Le Havre. Toward the mouth of the Seine. Toward the pathway to Paris.

Big brother Jerome would be proud.

CHAPTER 41

It was late evening before the team consisting of Magus Crayle, Hekka Poppi, Phoebe Bransfield, Mick Mackay, and Lenny Lipschitz touched down just outside Rouen. They squeezed into a rust-metallic Peugeot 3008 and proceeded through the city's cobblestone streets and squares, which were outlined by half-timbered buildings. Even the air of Rouen seemed imbued with historic richness. To imagine horses and carriages and period-costumed residents provided no challenge.

Crayle had directions to a stately home. They found the front door unlocked, and a search of the residence produced nothing other than a caged cockatoo. Lenny quickly motivated the large flat-screen television to deliver up a French-version marathon of *The Simpsons*. Their wait for Jack lasted less than twenty minutes.

Jack waltzed in the front door, giving no indication of his means of transport. He enjoyed being a man of mystery, even to his team. He told them that an agency asset was following every clue from Monaco and the Riviera north.

"I've got intel, folks. There've been several probable sightings of this popularized character Mitim in the region. I'm thinking it's Lalumière. We need to split up." He produced CIA file photographs of Lalumière as he'd appeared at the château, then modified to include a beard and long hair, as befitting descriptions in the press.

"The press has no pictures," Crayle said. "They've assumed the beard, based on the Man In The Iron Mask characterization by Alexandre Dumas."

"He won't be wearing the mask in public," Jack explained. "A passenger on the river boat snuck a shot and the mask photo went viral shortly thereafter. His jailer was murdered during his escape from the Bastille, so no one has seen him since his capture without the mask, except for these claims."

"I've been pulling all the news stories from the 'Net," said Lenny. "He had someone with him on the boat. An attendant, they called her. Yeah, some petite little thing brought him in to do monologs and then led him away, chains and all."

"Thanks, Lenny," said an insincere Jack. "I got the same info from Langley. They think this young woman helped him escape, too. Where you're going with this, Lenny, is that she saw his face back in their cabin when he took the thing off."

"Do we have a photo of her, as well?" Crayle asked.

"I have this grainy photo from Avignon," Jack answered as he produced the likeness.

They all looked. Crayle was skeptical.

"The other photo is digital and clear, under the circumstances and lighting. This one … I think this one has been doctored …"

Jack thought of his source for the photos. Neil had ordered that Pattie stay in the shadows. It was like a wild goose chase where someone, namely Neil, kept moving the goose. "Well, at least we can see that she is about 5'3" …"

"And, give or take, a hundred pounds," Phoebe deduced.

"Guys. I've got a plan. There are three areas of this region reporting sightings. We'll split into three groups. Crayle, you and Hekka work well together. Phoebe and Micmac—a dream team." Jack paused. He glanced at the P.I. "You're stuck with me, Lenny."

"It could be worse. You could be stuck with me." Lenny laughed.

Everyone turned to Jack to see if he would finally go postal. No such luck. Instead, he shut his eyes, tilted his head back, and breathed in slowly as if whiffing heaven in a gourmet kitchen. He exhaled even more slowly. Opening his eyes, he managed a pleased expression.

"I've divided the reconnaissance into three areas, which I'll go over before we all head out. First, we need a class in modern intel gathering. Magus, because of his amnesia, and Hekka, because she's new to this. And Micmac, well, this is a beta-male effort—no termination with any kind of prejudice. Phoebe, you've not done undercover with the bureau. Lenny actually knows a lot of this, so he can back me up." He put his hand over Lenny's mouth to forestall all commentary.

Jack proceeded to give the compact lecture on the intel necessary for tracking down Lalumière and how to collect it. "There can be no wasted time, and we can't afford to lose anyone. Each team member has the other's back. Try to act like this guy is your long lost cousin, but, if force is necessary, use it. Hide the bodies. Leave no trail. We have little to go on, so hope for the best. Play tourist. Ask locals questions that appear innocent. Had they seen a man similar to the computer-generated, bearded likeness? An old friend. Travelling with his niece. About five-three."

"And blurry," Lenny added.

Jack impregnated his lecture on tradecraft principles with real-life examples—names changed. After three hours, he observed the collective brain saturation of his acolytes. "Don't bother to stand." He waved his arm. "You are now apprentice spies."

Although he had been read-in on Crayle's backstory, the situation forced Jack to keep it from the former operations man. He wondered if Dr. Rorschach would someday slip up and restore the wrong memories *and* Crayle's deadliest pre-crash skills. With those mental updates and a realization of what had really been done to him, Crayle could turn on them and take them all out. Jack considered the removal of the problematic doctor to assure his own longevity. He packed those thoughts off for another day.

He produced a map of the 11,772 square mile Normandy region and placed it atop a table of polished black onyx with ornate gold edging and legs. The three subdivisions were colored in blue, white, and red—the famous tricolors of the French flag.

"Consider yourselves two-man … uh … two-person sub-teams numbered in the same order as I specified the team makeup. We'll use Sierra Bravo to designate sub-teams. Use Sierra Bravo One-Seven, Sierra Bravo Four-Three, and Sierra Bravo Six-Nine in any communications. If you have to specify just one of a team, follow the designation above with M for male or F for female. Clear?"

Lenny raised his hand. "We don't have a female on our team, boss."

"You'll be my bitch, Lenny. Please bend over so I can f … ffff … fffff … ahhhhh!"

"Good save, boss."

"Get some sleep."

• • •

At first light, Sierra Bravo One-Seven, Crayle and Hekka, left through a side door. It led directly into the stables, where traditional horses had been supplanted by horses of a more powerful nature. The three black Mercedes were exactly alike. Crayle picked the first.

"Perhaps I should drive, Magus," Hekka teased, aware that he had the chops for chase and evasion that she didn't. She had learned to place total confidence in him. Love and confidence go a long way.

Hekka monitored the GPS as Crayle headed them for the Lower Normandy beach areas at Honfleur, Deauville, Caen, and Bayeaux.

Sierra Bravo Four-Three, Phoebe and Micmac, left for southeastern Normandy on route E402 toward the towns of Alençon and Falaise.

The Odd Couple team, Sierra Bravo Six-Nine, took the Autoroute A13 for western Normandy to a location past Avranches. Jack had been provided this lead by Neil himself. Neil had stressed that the site was classified over everyone's head, because it related to the mini-nuclear bombs that had surfaced in mid-Iran, western China, and in Beijing. Jack knew in his gut that Lalumière was wrapped up in this to his eyeballs.

"It'll be a while, Lenny. Catch a few winks."

Lenny snored compliance for the next four-and-a-half hours.

• • •

Now through Avranches, Jack cranked the radio. French rap was just the ticket. Lenny jumped as far as his seat belts allowed.

"Jeeeesus Christ! What just happened?" Lenny pulled his Walther and fired one shot through the offending device. His gun might as well have been silenced. Jack laughed so hard, he nearly ran off the road into the flatlands.

"Check that out." Jack pointed to their right side.

"Holy Mary," exclaimed Lenny. The view in the distance was of a pyramid made of buildings surrounded by a high, stone wall. Mt. St. Michel was everything the travel folders promised and more.

"Man, I'm makin' an offer," said Lenny.

"Yeah, my ex-wife would love a realtor commission on somethin' like that."

"Maybe she'd share."

Jack laughed. "The time when she'd share passed long ago, Lenny." The thought of her almost evoked a tear. Jack didn't cry much, just when she came to mind and the great days they'd experienced as an ops team. Before spook loves spook became spy versus spy. Oh, well. Life goes on.

"We'll cross the causeway that links landmass France to that otherwise island, topped like an ice cream sundae with a cathedral. Before the causeway's construction, travelers in or out had to wait for low tide like we have now." He pointed to the right. "Check out those expanses of sand. On both sides. The sand is close to billiard table flat. Every now and then, you'll see small pools of seawater, trapped in little indentations like shallow dimples." Jack remembered Anne-Isabel, the CIA's number one spy in France. Petite and hopelessly magnetic. The quicksand symbolized the woman. Deadly.

The walk to the portal in the walls didn't look like a quarter mile, but it felt like it. Jack purchased entry, and they began their trek up the winding cobblestone street. He concluded that an assaulting army would be winded in short order and the road, lined with shops and restaurants on both sides, could become a death spiral. Lenny just followed, gawking at the wares on display.

"This is it," Jack announced. "Madame Poulard's famous egg soufflé restaurant."

"We came all this way for breakfast?"

"It's a meet, Lenny. Someone has intel for us. Whoever it is will locate us inside."

"How will we know who it is?"

Jack started to become upset once again. "I'm the only one with a dummy. Now keep quiet."

"Yes, boss."

They stepped inside and briefly glanced at the egg maiden, who vigorously whipped a mixture in a large, copper tub she held tight against her midriff. She smiled, as if recognizing old friends. Her whipping continued unabated.

A man in his fifties seated them, as requested, so they could observe through the outside windows and view anyone entering the front door.

"Monsieur D'Estaing?" startled them both. Neither had seen the middle-aged man who had hobbled up from behind, carrying a shopping bag.

"*Oui, je m'appelle D'Estaing.*" Jack concluded the handshake. He, of course, bore no resemblance to the former president of France. But the name was uncommon, and it worked for the purpose at hand. The man hooked his cane over the chair opposite Lenny and sat down across from Jack.

"I will speak English. Forgive me, it is not my first language."

Jack nodded.

"I have been ordered here to meet you, but I am afraid I have little information," came the raspy apology.

"We are seeking a large-jawed man named Thierry. Do you know him and his current whereabouts? We're in a hurry, monsieur. Give us the intel or …"

"I am afraid … oh!" came from deep inside the man. Not loud enough to disrupt the fervent conversations at other tables. It was the item pressed against his private parts that drew his attention.

Lenny spoke with pursed lips. "I was forced to acquire a very long silencer in order to make very little noise. The intel, please." Lenny had a most serious look on his face. Jack had not seen him in draw down mode before.

The man leaned toward them. "This Thierry has been seen here on the Mont. He is transporting a device of some kind. He is bound for Honfleur," the man lied. "On the coast."

Jack knew in an instant precisely what kind of device was in play and remembered that Honfleur sat at the mouth of the Seine River. "How big is the device?" The bent man's answer shocked him to the bone.

The man pulled a ball from his bag. A rugby ball with a honeycomb covering. He leaned even closer. "This size. Five kiloton."

Lenny whistled under his breath. Jack leaned back. "Crap," was all he could manage.

The man had been so engaged with Jack, neither had noticed Lenny sneak the cane under the table. Erratically resourceful, Lenny had used it to portray a silenced firearm.

The waiter arrived. "Your soufflés, monsieurs."

Jack had more questions. "I need to know the final destination for the device. And why trek the bomb to a coastal town? And where is Lalumière?"

Without answering, the man rose and searched about for his cane. Lenny produced it. The man's jaw clenched as he padded off in the direction of the bathroom.

"Lenny, follow him. Make sure he comes back for round two."

Lenny forked a wad of egg mass into his mouth and headed off with, "It's okay. I need to drain the lizard, anyway."

When Lenny arrived at the W.C., there was no one inside. He heard a motorbike, an electric one, out back. A secret door, no doubt. He returned to inform Jack, who wanted to yell and scream. Instead, he calmed himself. "Finish up. We're outta here." Jack jumped up and race-walked to the door. Lenny grabbed a handful of soufflé and followed. The Egg Maiden continued to furiously beat and smile.

"There's some serious arm strength there," Lenny deduced. "Wonder if she needs a boyfriend."

Jack headed them back through the portal and along the roadway toward the car. "That's twice, Lenny, you've proven your worth. At Lalumière's château, and here."

"Jack, I told you that first day at the cabin. I didn't need the FBI version of Annie Oakley … or you, for that matter. I got the chops."

Jack sought an absorbing topic for his thoughts. Phoebe, hands lashed behind her back, beaten to near death, grasped the gun Lenny had tossed to her, flipped upside down, and put a .45 Hydrashock clean up the bad guys center, ruining his *chi* as well as his day. Lenny had gotten lucky, that's all. Jack vowed never to compliment him again. As for Phoebe, she had exhibited skills, courage, and tenacity he had only seen once before in his entire career in CIA operations. The Magic Man. Magus Crayle.

A tour guide and an entourage of about twenty cut across their path. Jack knew enough French to get the drift.

"*And, at last, we will tour the infamous quicksands that wreak peril on unguided souls.*"

Jack felt inspired. But, no. Neil required that he keep the P.I. safe. Damn.

Jack summoned the entire team back to the safe house. Crayle reported he had acquired intel that couldn't go live over the airwaves. Critical intel. Micmac related a similar finding. Astounding was the word he had used. Jack couldn't wait to hear and to relate his, and Lenny's, finding at Mt. St. Michel. He hoped two plus two plus two would equal six—or something close.

The team spent the remainder of the day sharing their experiences and tidbits of information. Jack summarized.

"What we know, and we know this in spades, is that Lalumière plans to use a nuclear weapon to take over France. We know that. We saw Chin do it and these two are peas from the same pod."

Hekka whispered into Crayle's ear, "What does that mean?"

Crayle answered her to everyone. "Lalumière will use the same basic strategy as Chin. Only here. My restoration at the quarry hospital reminded me that Chin's was the Blackstone Strategy, East version. Then, Lalumière's must be the West version."

Micmac leaned forward. "So, what do we have?"

Lenny turned on the television with a remote that had been left within his reach.

"Turn that down!" Jack ordered.

Lenny complied.

The TV droned in the background. "… and the French parliament, its president, and premier are meeting tomorrow at the National Assembly."

"Turn it up!" Crayle demanded.

Lenny complied.

"… and due to the wanton destruction centered in the Muslim sector of Marseille, the entire government will meet in special session to discuss the matter and a proper course of action. Given the recent incapacity of this same body to resolve or even address the enormous European debt crisis, little is expected."

Crayle analyzed the situation first. "This is it. Do you see? It's all clear now."

Jack shook his head. “This is France, Magus. Nothing here is clear. Ever.”

“No, Jack. Check this out. Chin and Lalumière explode a bomb in Iran. The world reacts. It appears as if Muslim Iran finally has gotten the bomb. Next up, Chin and Li explode a bomb in Xinjiang. Do you see the Muslim connection?”

“You have two incidents that may be connected.”

“Scapegoats. The strategy turned Muslim fundamentalists into scapegoats. In the aftermath, the Chinese hierarchy was driven to assemble in Beijing. So Chin could blow them up.”

Phoebe picked it up. “So the Frenchman blows up Marseille’s Muslim neighborhood. More of the same. A nuclear religious war.”

Then Micmac, “A jihad. And every bit of it believable.”

Jack asked the operative question, “What’s next, Magus?”

“The strategy is symmetric. Marseille produced the same effect as Chin’s bomb in Western China. All the French politicians, Lalumière’s foes, are forced to assemble in Paris. That’s it!”

Micmac added, “And that goon with the bomb is gonna take it …”

“… up the Seine river … to Paris!” Crayle took a deep breath. “Lenny, we need intel on when and where the French government will meet. Jack, we have to warn them. These bombs take huge tolls in collateral damage.”

Jack was on the move. “I’ll get on the horn to Neil, uh, my boss. He’ll alert Langley and they’ll tell the whole friggin’ world.”

“Jack, we’ve all seen world leaders at work. They couldn’t stop a toothache. We have to take the team in. Catch these clowns still in the water. Shit!” Crayle, who rarely swore, exclaimed. “They’ll take the bomb into the catacombs. Or the sewers. Lenny, pull up a plan of the sewers. Superimpose the catacombs.”

“Right into my wheelhouse, MC.”

“Cross-reference with the hall the government plans to use. Lalumière’s people must have expertise on the sewer system and subterranean burial chambers. Our embassy would have the details. Jack's boss can get that for us." Crayle glanced around. "Jack?"

Jack returned from the bedroom. "Neil's onboard with the operation. Let's rock and roll!"

• • •

The team departed within thirty minutes. They anticipated that CIA and French security forces would be at their side. They did not know that Neil's next call, after Jack, was to his real boss. The head of the ultra secret Illuminé. "Yes, Elder. I fed them the bait."

• • •

"Listen up!" Jack shouted above the helicopter's roar. "We can't set down anywhere near the National Assembly. Airspace is tight there, so we're taking our act to suburbia. Northern suburb of Paris called St. Denis. Primarily a Muslim enclave, so traffic in and out will be nonexistent."

"Jack, the Muslim enclave, as you call it, in Marseille was the blast epicenter. How about south—"

"Negative, Magus. There is a mass exodus from major French cities. The roads are jammed. Except one. No one is headed toward St. Denis and no one is allowed out. We'll have a clean shot into Paris central."

"How close to the Assembly?" Hekka glanced at Crayle.

"Half mile, maybe less," Jack guessed. "My travel agent put us on the island next door to Notre Dame. Lenny, when does the Assembly meet?"

"Computer says two days from now."

"We're getting some sleep. Then, we're on. Seriously. We'll have about 24 hours to find the madman and his bomb … or Paris, and everyone in it …"

The landing and transit put the team into a row hotel, *St. Louis-en-L'Isle*. A subcompact elevator transported two at a time to their rooms. Exhausted, neither couple enjoyed the rare opportunity for lovemaking, but slept entwined. Lenny took up snoring. Jack took sleeping pills.

• • •

Morning light pierced the curtains like a laser. Lenny popped up, shook a beyond irritated Jack awake, and proceeded to the other two rooms, rousting the rest of the team. By 7:30, Jack had trooped them the short distance to *Le Lutétia*, and commandeered a corner of the small restaurant. Floor-to-ceiling windows afforded a view of all avenues of approach, and of the legendary Seine River.

He spoke in a hush. “Like I said, we’re a half mile east of the Assembly. The same distance west of where Lalumière escaped the Bastille. That’s where we collect if we know a bomb is gonna go.”

“How will we know that?”

“Intel, Phoebe. Very lucky intel.” He pointed to his right. “If and when I give the word, get yourselves up river to a water channel on the left bank. Fast. Grab a boat and proceed underground. It’ll take you to the Old Bastille dungeon—where they kept Lalumière.”

“And that will protect us from a nuclear blast?”

“Micmac, it’s what we’ve got at this juncture. Years ago, they collapsed the Bastille fortress, but the bowels wouldn’t go. So, they covered it up with dirt and asphalt.”

“Oh, we can make slow, delicious, moist love in a dungeon, sweetheart.” Phoebe flashed her eyelashes.

“Too much information, children.” Jack’s demeanor betrayed his true assessment—their chances of escaping another nuclear catastrophe pressed close to zero. “Crayle, you’re the planner. What do we do?”

“The odds that Lalumière will change his mind are also close to zero. So, we assume he will take out the French leaders with the bomb he picked up in Victoria. The one being muled by TJ3. I see three possibilities. One, he’ll float the bomb up river and when it’s next to the Assembly, boom. Two, he’ll take it into the catacombs, underneath the building. An upward burst will do the trick." Crayle paused. "The last possibility is that he will attempt something more spectacular. World class."

"The Tower?"

"I just don't know. The tower symbolizes Paris to the Parisians. It symbolizes France to everyone else. I think he'll spare it."

"To tell you the truth," Micmac interjected, "I'd rather spend the hours I have left with Phoebe. Making love. Over and over."

Jack turned somber. "Not a choice. Fifty thousand or more innocent human beings to say nothing of leaderless chaos—"

"There *will* be a leader, Jack. That's what this is all about."

"You're right, Magus. Okay, I need to know. Everyone in?"

They all nodded affirmative.

"Micmac, Phoebe, there's a boat outside. You'll patrol, looking for the jaw guys. And their bearded leader. Invert your coats, and you'll find DGSE on the back. French law enforcement have never seen such jackets. They'll be impressed. They'll leave you alone. Magus, Hekka, the north shore promenade. My girlfriend and I will take the catacombs."

"For how long, big guy," Lenny chided.

"Until I bend you over something painful, and have my way with you... alright... I'm a little tense. Okay? You've all got communicators. Bomb's in a metal box. Call us in if you spot something."

• • •

It fell softly at first. In fifteen minutes, the snow commenced in earnest. Each player, along with false ID, carried a no-limit black Eurocard that vectored through the DGSE to Langley. Thanks to the travel agent's foresight, their closets had been replete with hoodies, heavy coats, and boots. With Micmac and Phoebe away in the boat, and Jack and Lenny off to the catacombs, Crayle and Hekka walked along the river.

"You're shivering. Here, put the scarf this way, then swing one end around your neck … like this."

"Hekka … I don't want you to die."

"I—"

He put his gloved hand to her lips. "As much as I want you to run from this place as fast as you can, I know you won't."

"Can't."

They stopped. He kissed her. His piercing blue eyes penetrated to her heart. "Hekka, with all that's gone before, with what could happen next, I—"

This time, it was she who covered his lips. No more words spoken. They knew. Nothing, not even a nuclear bomb, would separate them. Ever.

"That's the *Musée D'Orsay*," Crayle pointed across the river. "By the crowd waiting outside, Lalumière wouldn't go there. The next building is the most likely place."

The National Assembly blazed with illumination, its columns and façade proclaiming substance into the night. "There is a temporary fence surrounding the building. And gendarmes guarding. Perhaps they have been warned."

"No, Hekka, this is normal. Sadly, old, well-architected government buildings are targets for extremists. We'll cross at the next bridge. With a 5 kiloton device, being a hundred yards closer to the target won't matter."

"What are we looking for?"

"An older man, 6-foot-6, with a beard, or a young man with the big jaw. Like the one on Cougar Crest Trail."

"And, then …"

The man jumped from the shadows. He went for Hekka, knocking her to the ground. Crayle pulled him off, but the man was strong. His eyes were fierce as he renewed his attack. He grabbed her purse.

Crayle yanked him away a second time. He spun, nearly slipping on the snow base, and propelled the man over the railing into the river.

He stepped back. "They're hungry. Times are very, very hard."

• • •

After the politicians had broken up for the night, the team reassembled at the hotel. Beside a small protest group at the Assembly and the purse snatcher incident, no one had seen or heard anything out of the ordinary.

"Lenny. See if they're meeting again tomorrow. Get the timeframe. We're up at daybreak anyway. Same surveillance. Same teams.

• • •

On the team's second day in Paris, Crayle realized something had gone wrong. Horribly wrong. Their information and deductions had sounded reasonable and rational, but had no relationship with reality. The ministers, president, and premier had met and adjourned. No conclusions drawn, they had left town. No nuclear explosion. Nothing.

The team sat on the few available surfaces in Jack's European-sized hotel room.

"Jack, we're at the end of our rope unless your boss can come up with some actionable intel. Lalumière wants—no, needs—to blow up Paris. It's in the plan. No deviations, other than any Plan B's I might have created, are allowed. The bomb has to be here."

"Maybe he just couldn't get it here in time, Magus. Maybe the damn thing went off."

"We'd know if it went off. We'd have felt the rumble and seen the cloud. No. It's still out there. The only good thing—we're still alive."

• • •

Chartreuse was not his favorite color—it made his head hurt. Neil Wohlford chased a handful of Advils with Napoléon brandy. Walking the halls at MUG, Manassas Under Ground, had disabled him again. He would give his right arm—no, his wife—for Jack's magical sunglasses. He mulled recent events.

His attempt to assassinate the Frenchman at Monaco had failed. For some reason, the Elder needed the man, perhaps as a nuclear martyr. That had required a countermove to place Jack Sommers' team, Crayle included, in harms way. In Paris. The bomb would explode, the French leadership would be incinerated, the team and all it knew would be history. And, with luck, so would Lalumière.

His phone vibrated him back to reality.

"Good evening, Neil. Do you know where your team is?"

"I've sent them on a snipe hunt. Lalumière is free to do our … your bidding." Neil winced. Little mistakes did not go unnoticed by the Elder.

"As we are Illuminé, *our* bidding is the appropriate choice."

"Of course."

"The agenda has changed, in drastic fashion. The Frenchman has gone rogue, Neil. He will not attack the French leadership in Paris. Listen carefully …"

• • •

Jack left the room to provide a sitrep to Neil. Ten minutes later, he returned, appearing as distressed as any of the team had ever seen him.

"Y'all want the good news first or the bad news? Let's start with the bad news, 'cause, frankly, there ain't no good news." He drew in a deep breath, then began. "Just chatted with the boss at Langley. He has apprized me that one Mr. Sylvain Lalumière is not to be found in Paris or anywhere else in France. That's because he has changed plans and now intends to blow up—are you ready—America."

The team members expressed astonishment in gasps, hoots, and "Son-of-a-bitch!"

"Yeah, Neil managed to obtain, through his various world resources, intel that Lalumière is sailing on the Queen Mary 2, which is past its halfway point between Southampton and …"

"New York. Jack, it's New York."

"That'd do it. Cook up our top city, blame it on the Arabs, and America's outta France in a New York minute. And we have nothing but conjecture. *Shit!*"

"What now, Jack?" Crayle demanded, his anger evident. "The entire intelligence community of the Free World missed this one by a mile. Thousands, actually. Why is he … of course! He needs France to fail. That must've been my plan. Just like China. And America is riding to the rescue. An attack with one of his mini-nukes removes our country from the playing field." He turned to Jack. "What can we do?"

"We proceed as if he's on the ship and has spirited the bomb onboard. Man, if he simply wanted to explode a nuke in the U.S., he could have done it a whole lot easier."

Crayle put it together. "The guy with the bomb, the third triplet, wasn't taking it up the Seine. He was ferrying it to Southampton, the QM2 port. Lalumière's feeding his ego. He'll ride the ship in, debark, and then detonate when he's out of harm's way. America's plate will be full. We'll be at war."

"If you're wrong, Magus … if he's given up and sees America as the cause of his defeat … this could be a suicide run."

A silence of more than a minute followed as everyone absorbed the potential consequences. For the ship. For their country.

A glassy-eyed Jack scanned the team. "We've got to catch the ship. It left Southampton three days ago."

Lenny looked and sounded perturbed. "How do we get on the ol' QM2, which is thousands of miles west of here in the middle of the Atlantic … Jack?"

Jack pulled a device from his pocket, placed it in his mouth, and selected a special number in his cell phone. The device emitted electronic sounds when he spoke, unintelligible. He listened. He terminated the call.

"We're out of here to a French airbase. They'll transport us, post haste, to a little burg in Nova Scotia … Glace Bay. We'll chopper out to the Mary. *Capisce?*"

Crayle performed a mental calculation. "If we hurry, we'll arrive on board on the ship's fifth day at sea on a seven-day cruise. I know of the ship, Jack. It has no helipad."

"Not a problem. En route to Nova Scotia, I'll explain in detail how to repel from a chopper onto a luxury liner tooling along at flank speed. Any questions? No? Saddle up!"

CHAPTER 42

The Queen Mary 2, a masterwork of craftsmanship, boasted the outward appearance of a great ocean liner that possessed the accoutrements wealthy passengers would expect. It sailed from Southampton harbor with the usual hoopla and spraying of fire boat water cannons, and the crew and passengers quickly settled into life at sea.

The passengers occupied their cabins, stowing luggage contents, medications, ditty bags, cosmetics, and such items necessary for instant-access fashion. The first-timers placed that night's finery on the beds as if an emergency claxon would sound and they would have a mere fifteen minutes to dress for supper. Although designated a non-formal evening, those who'd bought tuxedos and ball gowns for the trip would wear them tonight just for the fantasy buzz. Few noticed the five men who jogged the outside deck, one carrying what appeared to be a rugby ball. They all feinted left and right, puffing air into their tired lungs and working up a sweat until the one with the ball called the group to a halt. At the exact location of Lifeboat Station Twenty-One.

With two men covering at either end and two others monitoring the doors, Thierry accessed the Zodiac compartment next to the rail, unhinged the port-side, aft end of the Zodiac, and placed the football inside. He secured a special clamp to hold it in place. Last, he buttoned up the pod and peered all around and at the balconies above. Good. No observers. Everything in place. He and his team would dine in their cabin, right after he crowed to Jerome that he, in charge, had completed his dark mission.

• • •

Each evening, the male passengers, looking like a swarm of mutant penguins, dressed in tuxedos. The women, as if anticipating discovery by Hollywood, donned their be-baubbled best. Dinner on the fifth night included a gourmet's menu, consisting of numerous entrée choices. Those with special requirements, such as gluten-free, received the functional equivalents of the standard fare.

The man and woman seated in the corner of the Queen's Grill would have been notable had not the lighting in that area been lessened to a mere blur. Escorted via a secret passage from their special stateroom, they'd been seated first. Lalumière failed to perceive how he would manage to eat in public and not remove the iron mask. The petite American spy intruded on his musings.

"Listen up, Mitim. Since you can barely see through the mask, I will read the menu and you may select your preference. Then I will summon the waiter and place our order. Clear?"

"I feel like a child. Will you cut my meat, as well?"

"Behave, Mitim. If you do not follow my instructions, I will definitely cut your meat." With that warning, she began.

"APPETIZERS.

River Trout Mousse, Waldorf Salad and Chive Crème Fraîche.

Sautéed Chicken Livers, Warm Poached Egg and Madeira Jus.

Yum. I'm having that.

Frogs Legs Provençale.

Twice Baked Goat Cheese Soufflé.

Escargot Bourguignonne in Garlic Herb Butter—"

"I will have this one. The escargot."

"Well done, my celebrity friend. We move on to the entrees."

"Why don't you just order? This is tiresome."

"Patience, my Sylvain. My orders are that we dine in public, in the most expensive restaurant aboard. Then, we rise to meet the richest of your worldly fans. After waiting a few minutes for our food to settle, I will escort you back to the cabin and fuck your brains out. Sound good?"

Lalumière's knowledge of English, including colloquialisms, was excellent. Still, he couldn't quite grasp the concept and what was to become of his brains. But he understood only too well the degree of authority and control over the situation Sandrine exhibited in both speech and demeanor. He responded with, "Okay."

Sandrine made a mental note to not make him too weak and obedient. She needed to direct Mitim, not destroy him. He must exhibit strength for his fans. She could overpower him at will, and that knowledge pleased her.

"ENTRÉES.

Pan-Seared Cod, Wilted Bok Choy, Mustard Grain Sauce.

Herb-Roasted Lamb Rack, Grilled Eggplant, Anna Potatoes—"

"The lamb."

"DESSERT.

Vanilla Napoléon, Cherry Compote—"

Lalumière turned to her, reacting emotionally to her last words. Of course, she realized. The mention of Napoléon. A tear dripped from the bottom of the mask.

"Hey, sweetie," she whispered, moving close. "We'll both honor the last great Frenchman. When we have completed the Blackstone Strategy, you will move into that honorable title, Emperor of France. *Comprenez?*" She kissed the cheek of the mask.

Sylvain Lalumière sat erect, back arched, chin elevated. The spy always produced the right words at the right time. She motioned to a waiter, nearly invisible as he stood in the shadows, and repeated their supper order verbatim. She also asked him to provide suitable wine pairings.

Within an hour, they finished dining. She led him out of the shadows to the various tables. Jaws dropped as each person recognized the man who graced the cover of every news magazine, every newspaper, and every international television news program. Before they departed the Queen's Grill, Mitim had received checks totaling €375,000, plus £175,000 from the expatriate French residing in Britain and an additional quarter million in American dollars.

"These checks are written to Mitim. There is no such man. I cannot sign them."

"Sweetie, we'll take care of that. It will go against your advance."

Barely inside the suite's doorway, the little spy stripped him of his mask and clothing. She led him to the bed and began a slow motion striptease that aroused him within the first ten seconds. The Elder's dire warning was forever lost. Then, true to her word, she provided the sex he would never forget.

CHAPTER 43

The team mounted up for yet another operation. At top speed, Jack's refurbished Falcon jet whisked them across the Atlantic to a covert site near Glace Bay, Nova Scotia. From there, on cruise day five of the QM2 crossing, a man known only as Darryl hustled them aboard a specially-prepared helicopter. Cold and windblown, their flight exceeded unpleasant by several magnitudes. Hours later the team was delivered to the ship.

The top deck in front of the smoke stack was dressed out in teak planking. Glazed, perforated wind screens protected open air strollers from the heavy sea breezes encountered in the North Atlantic at this time of year. There were no passengers in sight, the top deck having been declared off limits. *Maintenance.*

In the wheelhouse, the captain pressed one of the hundreds of buttons. A special one. The windscreens rotated to flat, emulating a skyscraper helipad. Jack, who had hinted at a rappelling operation in response to one of Lenny's annoying comments, didn't intend to rappel onto anything. He knew from Neil that the QM2 could be reconfigured, in the event of a need for special operations by Britain's Strategic Air Services.

The aircraft, painted in forged Cunard livery, landed just forward of the smoke stack, the same location on which the Frenchman and his accomplice had landed a day earlier. Although fatigued, everyone knew to expect some heavy lifting ahead. Crayle, Phoebe, Hekka, Micmac, Lenny and Jack ducked and ran beneath the swirling blades. In the next instant, the chopper lifted off and away. Then, it happened.

"Hooooooonk!"

The powerful horn aside the stack gave one long blast. By the time their hearts restarted, they encountered a trio, two men and a woman, who moved in every aspect like SAS operatives instead of their cover as uniformed ship staff. Inside, they led the team down stairs to an off-white passageway that seemed to disappear into the distance, terminating a quarter mile away. Everyone knew the Queen was big. This provided the underscore.

"There must be thousands of places for people to hide," Crayle observed as he considered the giant vessel.

"That's great, if you're the ones trying to hide. Unfortunately …" Phoebe didn't need to finish her sentence.

Lenny sighed. Hekka glanced around, appearing as if she'd arrived on another planet. The bells, whistles, and accoutrements possessed an unfamiliar level of luxury and substance. Ranch life, and the care and feeding of the horses, seemed light years away—as did her warrior brothers and dead father.

The female SAS operative, who appeared like she would have been comfortable in black leather and swastika, took charge.

"Everyone you see here, including our room steward, food delivery staff, and anyone else who comes into our rooms, are MI6 assets. They are compartmentalized and know nothing about our operation. We may, however, utilize them for black ops as they all have the proper creds for that role. I will be liaison for any such operations."

"Our GS-15 travel associate, Ms. Pattie Norbrunn …" Jack nodded at the young, suited, and bespectacled brunette who appeared at his side. "… of the American Embassy in Paris, will see to our needs. She has situated us on the starboard side of the ship, away from the morning sun. Phoebe."

"Doesn't matter. The crack o' dawn is embedded in my genes." Phoebe saw that Lenny was about to respond. Her simulation of an eye-borne death ray precluded his response. She glanced back at the travel associate. Beneath that French-style short hair and bangs, and thick red plastic-rimmed glasses, she sensed something familiar about her.

Little Pattie Norbrunn inspected her nails.

"I'm a night person." The FBI agent continued her retort as she searched her personal FBI Computer Aided Facial Recognition database for a match.

Jack intervened. "Your room keys are also your boarding cards. Normally, you would use them to leave and return from excursions. Our trip across the pond, as the Brits call it, is non-stop. No excursions. No one gets on or off 'til we reach New York."

Lenny had held quiet for too long. "Oh, man. You mean the only thing we can do is get wet?" He glanced at Phoebe.

"The only wet that you gonna get," she rapped, "is seawater wet."

Jack, the man who would be in charge, sighed.

"Your cards were issued at the highest passenger level of the Cunard cruise line. The Diamond membership is normally reserved for passengers who have taken many trips on the Cunard line's three ships. None of you have cruised Cunard before, and you won't have the answers that fifteen voyages or 150 days at sea would provide. If anyone tries to engage you in conversation about previous cruise experiences, don't fake it. Change the subject or excuse yourself. Get away." He handed each team member a Diamond membership pin. "This level affords you eight complimentary hours on the Internet. Since Lenny will provide all of our Internet research, your time is his time. Understood?"

All heads nodded comprehension and acceptance. Except Lenny. "What else do we get?"

Jack ground his teeth. "You will get priority disembarkation. That allows me to throw problem team members overboard. And a complimentary meal in one of the alternative dining venues."

"What does alternative mean … in this context?" asked Lenny.

"It means, when I disembark you early, we will all watch the sharks dine." Jack held up his hands to either designate surrender or that he would take no more questions. He regained his composure, sent the travel agent on her way, and gathered Crayle, Hekka, Phoebe, Lenny, and Micmac in the Princess Suite he had commandeered for the operation. There was only one more elevated class of accommodation—the Queen's Suite. Surely Lalumière stayed in one. They each took a seat. Then a petite woman entered from the bedroom. She was dressed in emerald green silk pajamas, but her hair was styled and she wore full makeup.

"Lady and gentlemen, this is Sybille. She works in Europe for us and is a *company* asset. She's quite familiar with Mr. Lalumière and his quest, and she will be helpful in bringing him and his cohorts down."

"She's not Sybille!" Phoebe shouted. "That's Anne-Isabel. She was in the farm house near Lalumière's château."

"I am Sybille, and I would kindly ask the blonde girl to use that name," said Sybille.

It was déjà vu. Sybille parted her lips, looking a quantum less innocent. She ran the tip of her tongue slowly across the bottom of her upper lip, just as she had at the assault staging house.

This time, Phoebe, unhampered by a healing shoulder wound, leapt from the sofa. She charged the little spy, knocking her hard to the deck. But the multi-faceted operative used her legs to propel Phoebe up and over. Phoebe crashed onto the carpet behind. Both women were up in a second. Crayle and Micmac jumped between them. To restore order.

Lenny, watching from the piano bench, couldn't remain silent. "Here kitty, kitty."

Both women turned their heads toward him, having acquired a common enemy. Before they could launch, he threw up his hands, palms outward. "Just sayin'."

"Stop!" Jack yelled, as if trying to ward off a heart attack. "We have a world-class enemy in Lalumière. The stakes are defined by a nuclear weapon somewhere aboard this vessel. He will use it to strike our premier city, New York, unless we stop him."

"Isn't Washington, D.C. our premier city?" queried Lenny.

For an instant, Jack reconsidered his restraint of the women. In fact, he pondered joining them. Certainly, Lenny Lipschitz ran a close second to the Frenchman as a threat to humanity. Jack regained his composure and focus. "Everyone, cool it. Sit down far enough from each other so this shit won't happen again. Okay?" He struggled to excise the word 'children' from his admonition.

He nodded at Crayle.

"This is how I see it," he started. "Remember that Rorschach did not restore any memories of Lalumière or the strategic plan I customized per his macro goal. But he didn't become the premier choice of the French people by being other than smart, perceptive, and adaptable. He will follow the general approach and tradecraft I would have imbued in any … uh … customer, such as Chin."

"So where do we find Mister Smart, Perceptive, and Adaptable?" probed Lenny.

"We don't know where he and his troops are, but he will put them in compartments."

"Yeah, like this one," said a less than perceptive Lenny.

"I mean he will keep his human resources compartmentalized per each individual task and separated physically, one from the next. It's like a Venn diagram." Crayle drew virtual circles in the air. "Such that each task's members are represented by these circles, but they only intersect here, at Lalumière. The size of the intersection must be minimized to insure maximum program integrity."

His mathematical explanation left stares on his students' faces that gave blank a bad name. Clueless on the Queen. Hekka realized he had regained his mathematical self, whatever that portended.

"The less each subset knows about the others and their tasks, the better."

"Oh," reverberated from the team.

Jack retrieved control. He delineated the tactical plan in detail, giving each person his or her role. Everyone but Sybille was to see without being seen. "She is to infiltrate Lalumière's party, one-at-a-time. With respect to extreme prejudice, her rules of engagement are that each of Lalumière's team is expendable. All except him."

She smiled her innocent, dimpled smile at the assignment. She winked at the FBI agent.

Phoebe fumed.

• • •

The spy, cover name Sybille, had intel no one else had. Not even Jack. Hers came directly from her handler, one Neil Wohlford, at Langley. She had distanced herself from the rest of the tactical team and had arrived on the top residence deck. Neil had provided a suite number. She took up a position on the opposite side and just down the corridor. It would have been bad luck if extraneous inhabitants had been inside or returned during her operation, but ship's intel had them located in the casino. The captain would alert her if they headed toward their room.

She had reasoned that, although Lalumière would have compartmentalized the various components of his team, he could not leave to meet them. Further, he could not trust wireless comm or the ship's system to give orders and receive status. Sooner or later, each member would have to come to his suite.

The door opened and one of them stepped out. As he surveyed the corridor, all he could see was Sybille's back. She was inserting her door key in a lock, but insured that her body did not block the red *invalid key* response.

"May I be of assistance?" he asked in French-accented English as he approached.

She turned and offered a blushing smile. "The card does not seem to work," she said in French.

He was taken with her in that instant. Magic. His defenses fell to zero. He shrugged his shoulders in the French manner. "You could knock."

"Yes. Someone is inside, but, you see, my sister is asleep." She flirted.

"It is too bad," he flirted back, "my compartment is occupied as well."

The necessary repartee complete, she turned her pretty head a little to one side. "I know a place …"

She led the Lalumière minion down the corridor and up a couple of flights of stairs. The force of the howling wind required the strength of both to open a door to the open deck. Despite the chill wind pushing and pulling, they engaged fully in seconds. When he was dead, she took a moment to appreciate her craftsmanship and the intense pleasure of her fingers and the kill, then helped him over the side. His compact size made it easier for her. "Splash one," she said as she verified that he was indeed 'pulled down.'

As the dead henchman fell, a man on his third Singapore Sling saw the body flash by. Just a glimpse. His head bobbing to the beat therein, he yelled, "Man oh … man oh …" and then fell to the deck.

"He's passed out," someone exclaimed. "Get him to the lounge."

Sybille smiled. She thought about the men who had come into her life. She considered cutting notches in the appropriate part of her anatomy for each such victory. Ah, but someone would discover them at an inopportune time and ask a difficult question. She sighed. She hoped for a large number of men.

CHAPTER 44

A new day dawned. Jack and his investigator minion proceeded down a breakfast buffet line. Jack had set up a one-on-one—he needed the P.I.'s help as much as he needed him out of the way.

"This here will put you in the right frame of mind for what we need to do, Lenny. You see those?" He pointed at bins of various food items as if Lenny were a dunce. "We're having the MI5 breakfast."

"I've heard of that bunch. The Brits call it Intsec. My dad said so."

"Intsec. What's that?" Jack realized he had stepped again inside Lenny's event horizon for trivial nonsense.

"Simple. Short for internal security."

"I know some Fivers. Nobody calls it Intsec."

"Well, they should."

"Look. During the Second World War, it was short for Military Intelligence—Internal. MI6 stood for the external stuff—the spies. Here, take some of those beans." Lenny did. "And some of that."

Lenny checked the sign by the food bin. "You want me to take a leak?"

The people in line moaned.

He pointed. "In there?"

Groans escalated to laughter.

Jack shut his eyes, pinching the eyelids. "And boiled eggs and bangers." He held up his knife to preclude any more of Lenny's flaccid witticisms.

They found a bay window alcove and ordered coffee. Black. Jack peered out into a morning fog that engulfed the ship. With recurring frequency, blasts from the QM2 horn punctuated the clinking of silverware and glasses.

"Y'know, I researched the ship. Did you know that the horn making all that racket is attached to the starboard side of the smoke stack? The Brits call 'em whistles. Yeah. It made its first voyage on the original Queen in 1936. It's run by diesel, but they make the steam come out like the original *plume*." He pronounced the 'u' as 'eeoo.' "What can I say, I'm a research hound."

Jack seized the segue. He bent toward the diminutive investigator as if to supply classified intelligence. Lenny leaned in.

"Lenny, we're heavily focused on what is happening here—and for good reason. The downside is unspeakable if we can't stop Lalumière. He can make 9/11 seem like a non-event. It wasn't. It was huge. And if there's such a word, this is much, much huge-er. We'll be back to the suite by nine. I want you on the 'Net full bore. I want a briefing every half-hour on what's happening in China."

"I'll be on it, boss." He forked a boiled leak.

"Really, Lenny. We know these two guys are connected and that this whole mess is orchestrated for synergy. If Rorschach had been able to repair Magus' whole memory, we'd be in the catbird seat."

Lenny sat back, looking pensive. "What I don't get, Jack, is how Doctor Bumfuck got all those memories on disk in the first place. I mean, if Magus lost his memories 'cause of the crash ..."

"I wish I knew. Remind me. When we get out of this ... if we do ... I'm going to take Magus back down the hill and stand there with a gun to Rorschach's head until he has everything put together again. Magus is like a mental Humpty Dumpty right now, and he's also a man heavy in love. He needs to have it all back so Ms. Poppi can really know what she's getting. And so he can know what he's able to give."

"I volunteer to shove my gun at the doctor's other head."

"That didn't sound right." Jack sighed.

They finished their MI5 meal and returned to Jack's suite. Time for the QM2-6 briefing.

• • •

Jack called a briefing rendezvous in the team suite. The entire team was present: Crayle, Hekka, Micmac, Phoebe, Lenny, and the three SAS operatives. The small talk ended abruptly when Jack began.

"Everyone. Sit," sounded more like a command than a request. "We're less than twenty-four hours from New York, and we still haven't found the bomb. The SAS leader scanned the Mitim drawing into the ship's system. The captain will provide us with Lalumière's whereabouts from shipboard surveillance. We could take him at any time. That does no good. He may well have gone nuts, and we can't rely on interrogation providing what we need. And he might not survive a kidnapping, anyway. So, we're gonna keep tabs on him ourselves and put in some of our own bugging devices."

"I will interrogate him," said Sybille, examining her nails.

"It seems everyone you interrogate dies, my dear," Jack observed in a fatherly tone. "We can't afford that. Our country can't afford that."

"After we find the bomb?"

Jack ignored the spy who left no witnesses and continued. "There's a performance in the theater tonight."

"Oh, boy. Opera," came Lenny's sarcasm.

"Everyone just shut the f—" Jack noticed heads spin his way. He realized he was entering the vulgar toll booth. "Just be quiet, okay? I've got upscale outfits for Phoebe and Micmac. They will attend the performance. I expect the Frenchman to be wearing a mask—the Man-In-the-Iron-Mask mask. Now, he saw you both at his château after our assault. I've made arrangements through my high-level contacts for tonight to have a Masked Ball motif."

"That's a winning idea, Jack." Crayle intercepted the thought. "So everyone in the theater will be wearing a mask."

"Crap." Jack turned to the private investigator. "Lenny, fetch a picture of the original iron mask. From the copy of the *Le Monde* I bought. Phoebe and Micmac can study it. No one else will have that particular mask." Jack glared at Crayle, as if blaming him for the blunder. "Look. We've got this guy. As long as everyone keeps his head and stays on point. We've got this guy."

Jack's last statement instilled more doubt than confidence.

• • •

Jack dispatched the lovebirds to dress and get to the theater on time. He decided to take Lenny out for a walk and asked Hekka to come along. He figured Lenny would respect the authority embodied in a ten-inch Bowie knife.

When the last of them had departed, Crayle turned to ask the operative Sybille for her backstory. He needed to understand her capabilities. To his surprise, she had disappeared. The only other person in the room was Pattie Norbrunn. Before he could speak, his cell phone rang. Pattie could only hear his part of the conversation, but she blushed at her unintended intrusion.

"Yes, I know that Phoebe, my agent protector, is gone. You sent her on a mission." Crayle listened. "*Who's* going to protect me?" He glanced at the shy Embassy employee, her face still a pale shade of red. He turned his back to her and walked toward the balcony window, his voice lowered. "How about someone with experience and some heft. She's …" He glanced back at her. His mouth dropped open. He stared.

The facial redness was gone. In its place—the most sexual look he'd ever seen. She held a French MAB PA-15 9mm automatic, fitted with a four-inch silencer. She held it sideways just in front of her lips and ran her tongue in slow-motion to the business end.

"Crayle? … Crayle!" came Jack's voice through the earpiece.

She brought the gun around and inserted the tip of the quiet-kill device between her lips. Her eyes moved from the gun, in slow-motion, to Crayle's as she worked the visual. Slowly.

Crayle deduced the mental process she had traversed. She had recognized that he was in doubt due to her diminutive stature. In an instant, her mind had taken her to the farthest outer reaches of her personality. Everything she had just done—in mere seconds—answered his question, his doubts.

"She'll do fine, Jack."

Jack's silence indicated he knew the petite spy had worked some sort of magic. But, how? Crayle could almost hear him shake his head. "Signing off." Click.

Pattie put away the weapon. She pulled the knee-length skirt up to her hips. Any further, and he could have seen her black panties with the white scorpion. Seduction ensued. She curled her legs under her. Then, she patted the cushion next to her.

Crayle could not read her mind. If he could, he would have been worried.

As she watched him approach, she wondered if the ship with its extensive electronics could enter New York and dock on its own. She smiled. That would mean everyone on board would be fair game.

Killing felt so good.

So erotic.

So climactic.

She could establish a record. She could kill everyone.

• • •

The two love birds, Micmac and Phoebe, departed their suite in tux and evening gown. Micmac's ripped torso did not lose much in the finery. And, courtesy of Central Intelligence, Phoebe wore her first diamonds ever. The necklace, earrings, and bracelet came in at just under $200,000. "Can I keep 'em after?" had been met with a humorless stare from Jack.

They fell in line and entered into the mid-level of the tiered seating. Jack had indeed gotten his way. As Crayle predicted, every person in the theater wore a mask. A master of ceremonies strode across the stage to a microphone at stage left. His accent was decidedly English.

"Ladies and Gentlemen. Welcome." He glanced around. "This is perhaps the scariest audience I've ever had." The crowd laughed, releasing the normal, up-front tension. "We have a surprise band tonight, as advertised. They are from the colonies, and they are excellent. In fact, you have heard of them many times. They will play some of the Classic Rock tunes you grew up with. And for the younger amongst you, they will finish with their latest worldwide hits."

The high velvet curtains pulled apart at a steady pace to reveal the band set up.

"Marshalls and Les Pauls. And an Ampeg—"

"Shhh, Mick. Look for Lalumière." She tugged at his sleeve.

"Oh, I know where to find him. While you were in the bathroom getting gussied, Mag and Lenny found the theater layout on the web."

"I was only in there for a minute or two."

"Uh-huh. Well, where do you think an egotistical, megalomaniacal king wannabe would sit?"

"Come on …" she urged.

"Crayle figured it out. The Royal Box. Right up there." He pointed to their right and up two tiers. Sure enough, the gold encrusted Royal Box held bodyguards, a lady—elegant in her period finery, and the man with the mask that mattered. Lalumière.

"And now, without further ado," yelled the MC at fever pitch, "Colin Gleese!"

Phoebe's head snapped to the stage. She jumped to her feet. "It's him! It's him!" she screamed.

The crowd picked it up. They all stood and filled the theater with a jet engine level cacophony.

Micmac grabbed her hand, "Calm down, Phoebs."

"It's the rock star," she turned to Micmac. "The one who …"

It hit him. Like a ton of bricks. She had told him the entire story in all its horror. She had experienced the criminal act in every detail, yet the drug had rendered her powerless. He understood. Out of all possible fortune, here was the man, the rock star, she had guarded with her life, who had drugged and raped her not two years before.

He looked to the stage. There he was, waving and bowing, center stage. Micmac's jaw clenched. The crowd expressed its awe and admiration with thunderous applause. Micmac hated him.

Phoebe turned her head to him, her lips pursed out. "I can take him from here." She reached into her Glock-sized purse.

"No, Phoebe. Listen to me. Everything goes down the tubes if you whip out your .45 and put a bullet in his head."

"But …" she pleaded.

"Here's the deal. We'll get him later. We're on a ship out on the ocean. He's not going anywhere. We just gotta make sure he doesn't recognize you by accident. Before we can find this nuclear bomb."

Phoebe Bransfield, known internally at the FBI as Annie Oakley, had gotten past the tears. She was in full self-control now. She just wanted to take the shot. But, she had joined the Federal Bureau to serve something bigger than herself.

"Him recognize me? Not a problem. I heard that he didn't even remember … the next day." She kissed Micmac on the cheek. "Let's go." They left to the rock star's first number, a Stones tune, *You Can't Always Get What You Want.*

• • •

Lenny came running in from the balcony, waving the computer. "Jack, Jack, Jack!" he howled. "Have I got some shit for you."

Jack's interest overwhelmed his desire to fine Lenny for the language. "This needs to be good."

"Oh, it is soooo good. I took your advice on the international web news and got three confirming reports. They all line up in a row like the famous ducks."

"Lenny, early reports sometimes have only one source, and are all in error. Give it to me anyway."

"The official Commie news agency was blown up by the bomb. So this stuff is all foreign reporting and Hong Kong. Chin is on the move. Not physically, but in implementing his plan. He's cut a deal with the remnants of the party leadership, and they've been boat-loaded to Hainan. It's the big island on the way from Hong Kong to Vietnam. He's promised them they can live like kings and can turn the island into a real worker's paradise by doing all the work themselves."

"I'll be …"

"Watch your language," Lenny advised, cocking his head. "But, wait, there's more! Remember General Li? He's the guy with the mini-nukes. He's now in charge of the armed forces of the—wait for it—*New* People's Republic."

"That's not good. Not at all."

"I'm just arriving at the best part. There's going to be a major announcement from Hong Kong about the future governance of China. Chin called for calm. He also called for prayers from the religious folks they haven't put in prison."

"Jesus Christ, Lenny. The Chinese Communist Party, like all communists, have denied religion and persecuted the religious since they took over. If religion is starting to be good again, that means …"

"Oh, shit! That means the Party is over!"

"Get back out there and keep after it. Remember what I said? A report every hour on the hour. Now!"

Jack attempted to consume what he knew. His history with Central Intelligence as an operative and then as an outside project manager did not provide him a practiced set of skills for conceptualization. But, he knew who had the chops in spades. Magus Crayle.

• • •

Later, the team re-assembled in Jack's suite. He told them it was important for this operation that they each have a code name. He went around the team, handing out names. Lenny was last.

"Beetle Juice," said Jack.

Phoebe nodded up and down. "That one's easy. It's like when a beetle walks in front of you and you *stomp it.* Out squirts the beetle juice. Here, Lenny, get down on all fours. Crawl in front of me."

It was clear Phoebe was losing it. The rock star sighting had hit her right between the eyes.

"Give us a moment, guys," Crayle asked.

"I'll stay," said Micmac.

"To the arcade," said Jack, grabbing Lenny by the arm.

Phoebe sat on the sofa. She cocked her head back and pursed her lips. Not in anger this time, in anguish.

Micmac settled next to her, on his knees on the deck. Then, the tears. She dropped her head into her hands, her fingers digging into her scalp. Crayle sat next to her.

"Let it out, honey. You can't bottle it up any longer." He rubbed the back of her neck. Micmac put his hand on her thigh and squeezed. "Yeah, baby, it's okay for a tough kid like you to let loose. There were times, awful times, when one of the SEAL team or UDT team would just bawl. Not a lot, but intense. It was like throwing up after a hard night at a club. It didn't feel good, but it was necessary."

She sniffed and tossed the tears from her cheeks with her thumb—as she had the night she observed Crayle making love at the fountain with Hekka.

"It's purging," said Crayle. "Take your time—get it all out."

"I promise you this," said Micmac, "we'll get the son-of-a-bitch. Karma has its rules. And we're the enforcers."

She glanced at Micmac, and then at Crayle. She hugged Crayle first.

"I'll give you two some together time." He took his mask and left.

"Mick, I'm okay now. I need a little alone time. Going for a walk." She put on her mask, picked up her purse, and was out the door. Micmac knew no more words would help her.

• • •

The long walk down the passageway helped. She fished her QM2 *Welcome Aboard* location map and unfolded the two-inch by three-inch packet. It revealed a side-view diagram of the ship, and, for each of the thirteen decks, the locations of restaurants, lounges, bars, restrooms, stairways, elevators, and cabins. She chose a destination, vectored into the nearest transverse passageway, and headed up the stairway. It was intuitive to her that the two flights of stairs per deck level would dispel some of her anger and grief. She arrived at the top passenger deck, Twelve, and a notion struck her. This was the deck for Queen's Grill passengers. Lalumière would be on this deck, of that she was sure. And so, too, the rock star.

Her emotional state was such that she was out of character for a black ops team. Rogue. Her mind was a mess. She was unaware that she was being followed. The tracker had followed her onto the stairway, but kept two landings back so as not to be discovered.

Phoebe walked down the hallway the best she could. Her CIA-issue stiletto heels had been designed for discomfort—probably by the cross-dressing management at Langley. A couple emerged from a suite ahead. They glanced her way with the paranoia typical on a luxury liner that allowed the Great Unwashed to tag along. Fortunately, the high-heel wobble gave her a semi-drunk appearance and the sparkle of the baubles were all the creds she needed to be on the top floor. As she neared them, she stumbled. The man caught her and sank down with her to her knees. The woman removed the mask—fresh air would help.

"Darling, take her into our suite. She can sit on our balcony until she's ready to continue her journey." As they crossed the threshold of the suite, one of Phoebe's shoes detached. The door closed on it.

"Put her on the couch instead, darling. I'll get a wet wash rag and wipe her brow." No sooner had the man placed Phoebe on the couch, than the woman returned with a soaked white cloth. She pressed it against Phoebe's forehead. It had a strange smell. The woman quickly moved it to Phoebe's mouth and pressed with all of her might.

"Chloroform, Dolores?"

"She's the one Colin did after that concert. Remember? The FBI protector. It's her. If she recognizes him, we're screwed."

Phoebe fought, but the man put all of his strength into holding her wrists. Her strength failed due to the chemical. Then, she heard another voice.

"Hey, my manager man. You brought me a snack? Hey, that's the one … I'll be damned." He yanked the cloth from her mouth. "Hold her down. This time, I want her to struggle."

Phoebe, half out of it, knew exactly what was happening. Her legs free, she kicked and twisted for all she was worth. The rock star, undaunted, dropped his pants and began to push his body between her legs. Her dress was already up around her waist from the struggle. He stopped only for a second when he saw her cammo panties. She screamed for help in a suite already soundproofed for the rock star and his music.

No one heard the door open. Due to the suite's layout, no one saw the person who had trailed Phoebe from below. Moccasins made no sound.

"Hold her!" commanded the rock star.

The woman threw herself across Phoebe's mid-section, so she couldn't arch up. The man bent over her head to force it against the sofa cushion. The rock star sat up on his haunches. He shoved his shins down across Phoebe's thighs. He was ready.

Hekka Poppi slid the Bowie knife from its scabbard like a combat veteran approaching a sentry from behind. No sound. She reached around and grabbed the rock star's forehead for leverage and plunged the ten-inch blade into the back of his skull. To the hilt.

He tumbled to the deck, dead. Hekka grabbed the Dolores woman from behind, pulling her off Phoebe. The man looked up, shocked at what he saw. He relaxed his grip. Phoebe was up and into her handbag in an instant.

The rock star's manager and his assistant panicked. They ran for the balcony. As they slid the door open, the ship's last night fireworks display began. From inside, neither Phoebe nor Hekka saw the glitter and glare. Only the sounds, like gunfire, pierced their night.

The two who had held her down realized their plight when they reached the balcony railing. They turned—to plead for mercy.

The two shots that boomed inside Colin Gleese's sound-deafened suite could not be heard anywhere inside the ship nor above the din outside. It didn't take the two women long to toss the three bodies into the Atlantic. This night, Phoebe achieved closure. Cleaning up the small amount of blood spatter that remained was nothing more than a wind down period for her. She stopped only long enough to give Crayle's main squeeze a squeeze of her own. Magus had chosen well, indeed.

Hekka closed and locked the sliding balcony door. She moved to one end of the sofa. Phoebe took the other. Decompression time.

"I hope that helps. That man was the extreme opposite of our men."

"Hekka, I'm so in love. I almost lost him tonight."

"What you must lose is that thought. You will both continue to live in dangerous ways. You are warriors. You could not be otherwise."

"Yeah, you're right. Holy hell, Hekka. I killed two unarmed people. I'm supposed to bring their type into custody. I could be sent off forever. I wonder if I can swim back to Europe."

"We are not yet inside the territorial waters of the United States. What you have done would be for the British to decide, if someone told them."

"Secret?"

"Secret."

They caught their breath. Both appreciated the perfect silence that surrounded them. Then, without words, they rose to their feet, placed the masks of the manager and his wife on their faces, and left for the sanctuary of Jack's suite below.

CHAPTER 45

The sign read: BROOKLYN LUMBER, INC. It was perched atop a corrugated, steel building rectangular in shape and built with the long side's wide sliding doors faced onto the lumber yard and then to the Atlantic. A man dressed in denim overalls and an eponymous cap, its bill tilted to one side, squinted out to the South as if to discern the face of a friend.

The sun itself glimpsed from the Eastern horizon and the light barely cast a glimmer on the yard and on the man's dream state tableau. He wore a hunter's flannel shirt under the overalls—late Autumn proved chilly without the sun's warmth.

"William, William," came the southern drawl of Harry Wilcox as he approached from behind.

"Waddya want, Harry?" said the overalled man, his stare still engaged.

"Y'all stand there, gawkin' at that boat, that long list of to-do's is gettin' longer."

"It's not a boat, Harry … it's the Queen."

"The Queen Mary 2, to be exact. Still don't get the work done."

"Yeah, you're right. Gotta be two miles out—still looks magnificent, don't she? That's one classy boat, Harry."

"I hate to break up your love affair, William … I need you to make that phone call."

"What call?" Eyes transfixed, William stood beside a giant pile of sawdust.

"I pay you to work, William. Get after that Sawdusters bunch. They shoulda removed this pile a week ago. It's up at twenty feet high with a ground-level girth of thirty feet. We cain't saw wood 'cause it's at maximum big." Harry managed to extract two syllables from the last word.

"Someday, I'm on that boat, Harry, goin' t'other way. No list, no problems … and no boss."

"Git to work or I'll fix the *no boss* problem right quick. Better yet, I'll hav'em make a coffin box out o' this here pine dust—'bout yer size."

"It's just so peaceful," William remarked as he wheeled around and headed for the office. "You wanted the dust pile removed?"

CHAPTER 46

Only one person on board was a member of both teams. Pattie, as Sandrine, used her skills to inform Lalumière that Magus Crayle and his minions could be found in an otherwise empty cabin. They were ready to make a deal. Give up the bomb, and Lalumière and his men could go free. And she provided a key.

As Sybille, she whispered in Jack's ear that Lalumière could be found in that selfsame location, and he wished to strike a bargain. Jack received a second key. Her plan was simple, but exquisite. Once the assemblage was complete, she would enter as a non-threatening neutral party. Pattie Norbrunn travel agent would facilitate the end to a madness in which everyone died. She would ride off into the sunset with Mitim and formulate a new plan. France weighed heavily on her mind.

• • •

It was a standoff, pure and simple. Jack's team and Lalumière's team were weaponized to the hilt. It was a modern, albeit light version of the Mutually Assured Destruction of the Cold War. If anyone fired, all would fire.

No one made a sound, lest it incent the destruction. If someone could have synchronized all of their heartbeats, the din would have been thunderous.

Then, a slight sound from the door. Heads turned. The handle rotated slowly. The door opened. In through the threshold stepped someone that none of them expected, but all of them knew. She looked different. Her dark brown hair was pulled back into a librarian-like bun. The glasses framed in dark red plastic added to the lack of mystique. Most unusual were the black patent leather flats. Her 5'3" stature made her appear smaller than one would expect. All of it was encased in a gray pin-striped, tailored suit.

"Hi, I'm Pattie. Pattie Norbrunn." She had introduced herself, but the visage of the sweet, friendly-but-business-like embassy travel agent evoked other, more visceral interpretations.

"Angel!" cried Lalumière's son, Jean-Marc.

"Anne-Isabel!" Crayle and Micmac chorused. They saw the CIA operative who'd helped to stage the château assault just twenty-seven days earlier.

"Anne-Isabel!" Phoebe cursed through combat-pursed lips. Her outstretched arms rotated from the Frenchman until her sights, in perfect alignment, settled on the bridge of the petite woman's nose.

"No, no. This is my Sandrine," opined Lalumière.

"Sybille," Jerome gasped.

Lenny glanced up from his laptop, "Let's see. Sybille is French for … Cybil. Ha, like the chick with all the personalities."

"Oops."

At that defining moment, Pattie Norbrunn's multiple cover characters collided inside her brain. Her eyes spun skyward as she weaved in a tight circle before landing full force onto the carpet. The men rushed to her.

Phoebe's face clenched, expressing itself with a "You're doing this on purpose, you little …" glare.

"I will get help," shouted Lalumière as he ran for the door. TJ2 and the others rushed after him.

"Hold it!" yelled Phoebe, her Glock ready to take down the first one to touch the door knob.

• • •

The First Officer rushed onto the ship's bridge, waving a piece of paper. "Emergency comms just in on the GMDSS, Captain! Origination: American Homeland Security!"

Well aware of the severity of Global Maritime Distress and Safety System communications, the captain snatched the paper. Her face portrayed an intensity the FO had not seen before.

"Emergency back," she commanded.

The quartermaster obeyed.

The front two propulsion pods came to an abrupt halt. The two rear azimuthing pods, starboard and port, rotated 180 degrees in an instant. Now they thrust full force toward the front of the ship. Their 21.5 megawatt motors responded to the full astern command from the bridge and spun the 18 foot diameter propellers at maximum speed.

• • •

Inside Lalumière's cabin, the drastic change in momentum caused mayhem. Bodies crashed heavily to the floor. All that was not tied down was slung in all directions. Phoebe slid to the forward bulkhead, slamming it so hard she lost the firm grip on her Glock. Lalumière and his minions recovered first, scampered through the door, and darted down the hallway.

"I'll take care of her," yelled Lenny. "Catch the son of a bitch and turn off his lights."

"Now!" yelled Jack as he led all but Lenny and the down Paris operative after the Frenchman and his gang.

The door slammed shut, and Pattie's eyes popped open. "How'd I do?"

"C'mon," Lenny said, dragging her to her feet. "We've got to stop the crazy Frenchman. He's got a bomb somewhere on board. He plans to blow up New York."

"I know," Pattie's Sybille personality said, pointing her automatic at Lenny. "Sit down, please."

Shocked, Lenny was still quick to assess the situation. "If I'm going to die, can I at least have a little—"

"*Sit!*"

• • •

Lalumière and his men mercilessly pushed through the panicked passengers. They reached the Zodiac pod just aft of starboard Lifeboat Station 21. Precisely 1.7 miles after the captain issued her command, the QM2 came to a complete stop. They heard the sirens of a fleet of approaching American Coast Guard cutters and helicopters. Jerome and Thierry grabbed the aircraft quality tie down ratchets with KINEDYNE stenciled on them and loosened the two-inch straps holding the bobbing Zodiac.

A crewman yelled, thinking they were just passengers in full panic mode trying to save themselves. Jerome turned and, with one swift motion, drew and fired. The man slammed into one of four-foot-long mahogany chests affixed to the deck. He posed no further threat.

The Queen had been built with lifeboats positioned forty-five feet above the standard height. It protected them from damage due to the high, and sometimes violent, Atlantic seas. Lalumière hyperventilated, waiting for the boat to be lowered. As it hit the sea, Jerome spoke to his younger brother, "You must stay. Protect us if you can. You will process through the U.S. Customs, just as the terrorists do, and return home. I will contact you when we are safe. *Au revoir, mon frère.*" They hugged. Thierry stood guard while Lalumière and Jerome descended on bosun's chairs to the Zodiac.

No sooner had they taken their positions in the front and rear of the boat than they heard gunshots from above. Jack and his team had arrived seconds too late to stop Lalumière. Thierry disappeared into the panicked throng, taking himself out of the scuffle. In seconds, the remaining henchmen were dead. Crayle reached the rail first.

"He's getting away!" He pointed at the fast moving Zodiac.

Phoebe arrived second. She settled into a combat stance and took aim at the fleeing Zodiac.

"Forget the headshots! We've got to stop the boat! Mick, go for the right air chamber! I'll take the left! Phoebe, stop the motors! Don't hit the bomb!"

Numerous shots punctured the Zodiac's right and left air chambers.

Phoebe shifted slightly and fired. She emptied the seven-round standard clip in less than five heartbeats.

The two men in the boat saw and heard the gunfire. They dove for shelter behind the twin high-output, Mercury outboard motors. Under normal circumstances, they would not have heard the shots. They would've been dead. But Phoebe hadn't aimed at them. She had followed Crayle's lead and dismantled the motor.

The boat slowed to a halt and became awash with seawater. In spite of his limited swimming ability and fear of water, Lalumière jumped. His killer lieutenant caught his leg in the boat's tie up line. He stood to pull free. He neither heard nor felt the first .45 slug from Phoebe's second clip. She watched the boat sink quickly as the combined weights of the engine and bomb overwhelmed the diminished buoyancy.

The light water chop had been accentuated by the sudden halting of the QM2, and she found it near impossible to pick up a swimming megalomaniac under the circumstances.

"There he is!" yelled Micmac. He pointed to a man fifty feet north of the Zodiac's final position and struggling in the choppy water. "He's headed for Coney Island!"

Phoebe took aim.

Before she could fire, another Zodiac powered across her line of sight. Anne-Isabel. The petite spy turned and blew a kiss. Another taunt. Phoebe swung the Glock to her right. "She's getting away! I can take her from here! No sweat!"

Crayle grabbed her arm and pulled it off target. "No, Phoebe! She's on our side!"

"Damn!" Phoebe's jaw clenched. "Another time," she whispered.

Micmac reached around Crayle and yanked her arms. "Get Lalumière!"

Back on target, she waited for the Frenchman to be turned about by the current, to get the ideal headshot.

Out of sight and out of mind, the nuclear Zodiac reached a depth of twenty-five feet. Unknown to all, the bomb maker had installed a Plan B pressure-sensitive trigger device. Just five more feet.

CHAPTER 47

Sylvain Lalumière's nuclear bomb exploded in thirty feet of water. The upward surge pushed the entire Queen Mary 2 up and out of the water, twisting it sideways. A city-size funnel gushed to the sky, carrying with it thousands of fish killed instantly by the enormous concussion.

The fish rained down as a wall of water pushed over the Coney Island amusement park. The giant wave slammed vacationers, caught gawking at the awesome sight of the Queen Mary 2 lifted from the ocean surface, into amusement kiosks, killing them instantly. Fish tore through windows and walls, some hitting people and knocking them dead.

Then, the ship returned to the turbulent sea, rocking hard to starboard. Phoebe slid across the slick deck. She impacted the railing and started over. Had she dropped the Glock in her right hand, she could have stopped herself. She flipped over. Before dropping the distance to the roiled brine, she thrust her arm between the rail and the safety glass just beneath.

Crayle and Micmac heard a sickening snap. Her arm, trapped, was all that kept her from plummeting several stories to a certain death. The men were to the rail in an instant. Crayle grabbed her. Micmac extricated the broken arm. Crayle pulled her to safety. Micmac grabbed a ratcheted tie down from the Zodiac container and strapped her arm tight against her body.

Phoebe grimaced at the pain, but fought the tears into submission. She was tough. And Micmac loved her for it. He pried the Glock from her grasp and poked the business end into his waistband.

"Careful," she croaked, mustering a smile.

• • •

To the east of the amusement park sat Brooklyn Lumber, full of cut timber and a pile of sawdust twenty feet high. So high it was a landmark. The body of Sylvain Lalumière fell from the sky. It hit the top of the pile with such force, it felt like a stone wall. Yet the sawdust gave just enough to spare the Frenchman's life.

Seconds later, a seawater surge reached the lumber yard and washed the man and the sawdust pile beneath him away—away to the North. Away from the ocean.

Three black cars, Chargers, were positioned nearby, their occupants atop a brick building. They had orders to photograph the entire scene: before and after the ship exploded in New York Harbor. They saw something completely different—the crash landing of their leader. Their jaws dropped.

• • •

A man dressed in a tweed three-piece suit and wearing custom Swiss Bass shoes padded down the beach, surveying the flotsam and jetsam left by the bomb surge. He carried a special cell-phone. One with the Top Secret Vestige tracking app. As the detail HD map indicated, he was within fifty feet. He stopped. Through the mist, he saw her. The Vestige capsule embedded in his favorite operative had performed to perfection.

She had clawed her way along the beach and had stopped just short of a shallow effluent that split the beach. Her suit, soaked through, clung to her perfect body. Tears in the material gave her a survivor goddess appearance. She rolled onto her side. Petite, yet beautiful. And in dire need of assistance. She looked into his eyes, her lips parting with the little strength remaining.

"May I be of assistance?" he said.

"Please," she pleaded as the scorpion to the frog, "carry me across the river."

Neil Wohlford lifted his favorite operative into his arms. She wrapped her arms around his neck, pulling herself tight to him. As he forded the effluent stream, a glisten could be seen on her face. And a dimpled smile penetrated the mist.

• • •

"News just in," yelled the excited news anchor. He read a handwritten message that replaced the normal and mindless teleprompter. "There has been a serious event in New York City. Videos are in transit from Fox News." No one had to tell fans of CNN that this was serious enough for the two networks, often at odds, to share. "We do have exclusive reports from the area. Our citizen reporters." Budget cuts disallowed more than a token in-the-field staffing. He left that out. "From Queens, 'What's all the fuss?' Oops. From Newark, New Jersey, 'WTF?' Oops. From somewhere in Central Park, 'Fishin's never been better.' Okay. So much for that," came the frustrated voice. "Ladies and gentlemen, please tune in to Fox News where Shepard Smith will provide timely and verifiable news reporting. Me? I'm outta here."

The newsroom shot went black. The CNN logo filled the bottom right corner in its place. A country song played in the background. The network's motto, *The Most Trusted Name in News,* popped across the screen. Those who switched channels were apprised of the situation by an animated and informed Smith.

"Manhattan and other area restauranteurs are acquiring fresh fish from mongers, who are utilizing the Internet to get the word out. Because of the high density of seawater, most fish died of a concussion versus their impact with the ground—hammer fresh. I hear that O'Reilly's headed that way. He always wanted to open up a fish chowder, seafood stew, and chalupa restaurant. I think I'll join him. I'm good for the bouillabaisse and jumbalaya. But, before I do, here's a note in from our CBC affiliate in Toronto, Canada. A huge water plume has been spotted from a restaurant atop the 1,151-foot high CN Tower near the Lake Ontario waterfront. Whup, here's more. Fish carcasses have landed on the observation platform of the Empire State Building. Oh, and in Palisades Park, New Jersey.

"Check this out. This just in. It seems that Marcus Dubie, out of Manhattan Beach, California, wanted to try surfing the East Coast. Unfortunately for him, he caught the first nuclear wave ever. Yeah. Paramedics picked him up in New Jersey, five miles inland. Holy cow!

"And this. Reminiscent of a maritime version of Vlad the Impaler, the statuesque lady who welcomes newcomers to America's shores, the Statue of Liberty, is now sporting a number of skewered sea creatures on her crown. Through the mist, she appears to be smiling at the representative incarnation of the British Crown, now settled back upon the sea." He pushed his hand against his ear. "I am told the QM2 is verily swarming with NRC, state and local law enforcement, and bomb detection. Might have wanted to detect the bomb before it went off, guys.

"Finally, breaking news: the Cardinal of New York has released a statement. 'Holy Mackerel!' Just kidding." Smith followed with his trademark cat-that-swallowed-the-canary grin. The station cut to an ambulance-chaser commercial. Appropriate.

• • •

ESPN coverage of the annual Giants-Jets game at New Jersey's MetLife Stadium was interrupted by the aerial influx of sea life. The organ player, caught by surprise, queued up a slightly modified version of a crowd favorite. Ducking for cover, the teams and crowd heard 'It's Raining Fish.'

By the time the projectile-filled sky emptied, most power and communication lines and most satellite dishes had been destroyed. The indestructible cell-phone system provided communications linkage at all levels. Within hours of the disaster, a new app appeared searching for the farthest fish. A claim from Bermuda would have taken the prize, but it could not be confirmed. Later, the app owner and sole judge disallowed the entry. The particular fish mentioned was not indigenous to the vicinity of New York City.

CHAPTER 48

The giant Queen Mary 2 settled, at long last, on the calming sea. Of the capacity complement of 2,620 passengers and 1,253 crew, nearly every one had been injured in some way. Miraculously, no one was killed. The captain ordered them all back to their cabins, per the order she'd received from the American president less than five minutes before. The Illuminations theater become an amphitheater waiting room for medical treatment. The huge Brittania restaurant turned into a gargantuan sick bay and the U.S. Navy hospital ship, USNS Comfort TA-H-20, was enroute from its home port in Baltimore, Maryland.

"Captain. Another call from the president." The First Mate handed her the ship's phone.

"Yes, Mr. President. Can we proceed?"

The president of the United States had cut back on all forms of national defense. Now his decision hit him like a ton of lead. Circumstances beyond his control now forced him to re-engage the security spectrum abandoned by his office.

"I'm afraid not, Captain. I understand that your power plant, generators, and steering apparatus are all in working order."

"Yes, that is the situation at this end. The passengers are damaged and in great emotional distress. May we make port as planned previous to the incident?"

"Madame, a nuclear bomb exploding just offshore from America's premier city is hardly an incident. No. I must ask you to make way to a position ten miles off our coast. There might be a second device aboard. The hospital ship will pull alongside, and you may transfer the wounded. Yes, Captain. Understand that, with whomever is responsible, we are at war."

"I will need permission from the British Admiralty," the captain advised.

"I see you didn't get the memo, Captain. We colonists are no longer under the authority of the British Crown. You must depart our near waters as soon as is possible."

"I will make ready, Mr. President. Perhaps you could make the call. It will speed up our departure."

The president established ownership. "I have dispatched a team to scour the ship for other weaponry and terrorists. I have put our Vice President, Kimbel Stones, in charge of that effort and the process of caring for your American passengers. He will also see to the vetting of all passengers, their transport to our shores, and return home for those who are not U.S. citizens." He wanted to say *colonials*, but thought better. Britain was one of America's few friends in these troubled times. "We will send choppers out to fetch specific citizens, those who have specific knowledge of the terrorist act. We must have our version of MI-6 and MI-5 interrogate them at once. Often, there are several coordinated events, not just one."

"Yes, Mr. President."

The president rang off. The captain breathed a sigh of relief. Her staff had already contacted the Admiralty, which instructed her to do whatever the Americans wanted. The Americans were, contrary to the public relations 'leaks' they put out, the most adept at signals intercept technology and the resources to deal with terrorists. This was not a time to be petty.

• • •

The executive assistant stood at attention beside the lanky captive.

"I want you to leave him … here … in my custody, Billy."

"But, sir, he's the son of the man who's been tagged with the QM2 affair. Shouldn't …"

Neil Wohlford's head swiveled at the pace of a lighthouse beacon. His chin, now pointed directly at Billy Scramble, tilted up no more than an inch.

"Yes, sir." Billy exited in a hurry.

"So, Monsieur Desrochers. Have a seat. Please."

Jean-Marc moved in slow motion to a chair not unlike those at the family château.

"Brandy?"

• • •

United States Vice President Kimbel Stones alighted from his VH60N Marine One helicopter. He was forced to take the president's whirlybird because his own, Marine Two, was in the shop. He and a small entourage were greeted just beyond the prop wash by the ship's captain, first mate, and two Cunard security men that Kimbel took to be SAS, British Special Air Service, operatives in disguise. He and his team were hustled to one of the available Deck Twelve suites. It had been prepared as a safe and secure room. The sound-isolated room permitted no communications, verbal or otherwise, in or out.

"Mr. Vice President, welcome to the Queen," the captain said with a stiff upper lipped smile. "Admiralty has authorized me to pass on the Prime Minister's apology for the mishap. Our two countries—"

"Please," Kimbel held up his hands. "Not necessary. Let's move on from here. Tell me what you know."

"I am not sure I am authorized …" She saw Kimbel's unaccepting twist of the head. "We believe that a man and his cohorts smuggled the bomb on board in a Zodiac replacement. He attempted to escape, but some operatives … I assume yours … shot the boat out from under him. He swam toward shore, but the device must have had a depth sensor. It exploded beneath the sea."

"Did you find this man's body?"

"No, but we're certain he did not survive."

Kimbel took her measure. He would have preferred undeniable evidence of the head perpetrator's body. Being an expert in reading body language from his days at the NSA, he perceived her to be telling the truth. "And his people …"

"All dead. As well as we can ascertain, of course."

"Very well. Could you have the operatives who thwarted the bombing of New York City brought here?"

As if by virtue of Divine Provenance, the bedroom door opened and the battered members of Jack's team entered the room. Jack brought up the rear.

"It is best that we don't talk here. You will be escorted offsite for a formal debriefing."

"She isn't a formal operative," Crayle said, pointing to Hekka.

"I understand, but national security, especially at this level, trumps anyone's job title. Including mine."

Kimbel thanked the Brits for their assistance, reiterated the standing Presidential Order to lay off the coast for further inspection and orders, and led the team to the helicopter. Under other circumstances, there would have been media helicopters blotting out the sky, but the vice president had also ordered a no-fly zone over an immediate ten-mile radius. Nothing was to fly in or out of JFK, La Guardia, Newark, or any of the small airfields or helipads in the vicinity. F-18s were on stand-by alert, the media had been told. In fact, F-18s currently performed a tag-team overfly with all weapons armed. Great concern remained for a second or third attack as experienced on 9/11.

Besides the fighters, the only flight in the area was the helicopter ferrying the vice president and the team to Maryland. On Kimbel's orders, preparations were effected at Crypto City in Maryland and the chopper touched down without incident. The sky was dark now and nearly-invisible black-attired sentries guided Marine One's occupants into the OPS-2 building and through security, though no team member had clearance for the NSA's hyper-secure campus. The NSA Director ushered them into his personal twenty-five person conference room. The four walls, adorned with twenty high-definition flat screens, displayed both news feeds and the NSA's own satellite and extended surveillance videos. The NSA chief muted the sound. A perfect quiet dominated as everyone took chairs at the conference table.

"The president has put me in charge of your safety. And security. I know, from my stint at this institution, that you are a wealth of information. I have the president's ear to the point that it is I who will dictate who else receives your intel. That includes the defense intelligence agencies, the CIA, and the FBI." He glanced at Jack and received an affirmative nod. Then to Phoebe. Another nod. "Due to my association with NSA, I have full dossiers on each of you. Even you, Miss Poppi."

"Then you know that I operate … operated … a quarter-horse ranch. You know that my father was killed by these savages. You know—"

"Miss Poppi. Please. You have my sincerest condolences for your father. I have seen to it that your brothers have everything they need to continue what you and your father created. You can trust my word that we, meaning America and our allies, will bring all people responsible to justice. And by that, I mean dead."

Crayle volunteered. "How can we help?"

Jack intervened. "Sir, on the Queen, I confiscated the rock star's place. It was double soundproofed for the noise. I debriefed them all. And everything matched up. Uh … was consistent."

"Then, Jack, fill me in. If anyone hears something that Jack has misinterpreted, I expect you to correct him. Understood?" All nodded.

Jack proceeded to tell the vice president everything he believed would not get his neck chopped off. He omitted his conversations and content with Neil from the debrief.

When he completed his tale, the vice president excused himself, returning a few minutes later. "I have something for you all. I'm sure the president won't mind. Please stand." He depressed a button on a remote control and stepped through a doorway. The floor descended with a barely noticeable smoothness.

Twenty feet later, all members took in a new interior. The ceiling above had transformed into a cupola. The walls were now baroque ornate, replete with brilliant light beaming through stained glass windows. Each told a religious story.

The team took seats in the front row of the large cathedral. The stained-glass windows, twenty feet by ten feet, had survived the tremendous blast of air and water. Crayle glanced around. Something caught his eye. One of the windows pixilated. He turned to Jack. "It's dark outside. Your boss?"

"Yeah. Neil puts everything underground. The hospital. His office. Even a cathedral. Like some kind of mole."

Crayle mulled over the last sentence.

"The guy's a Roman Catholic. He was married here. I was best man. Yeah, married his girlfriend from Montreal. Just six weeks after his wife died."

"Too bad about the first one," Lenny interjected.

"Yes, it was. Remember Pattie? She was the one who found her."

Crayle processed the intel.

"But the biggy here?" Jack smirked. "The guy who performed the ceremony."

"That's easy," Phoebe deduced. "It's a cathedral, had to be a bishop."

Jack teased. "Neil has extreme connections ..."

"Wow!" cried Lenny. "A fucking cardinal?"

Jack shook his head. "The Pope."

To the left of the altar, a side door opened. The vice president entered. "I'm here to thank you. There has been loss of life we've not yet tallied, but those numbers would be far worse had you not performed as you did. For obvious reasons, I can't stay, but I—"

A door to the altar's right burst open. A man rushed to Kimbel Stones and whispered into his ear. Stones turned ashen. His jaw clenched. He tilted back his head and sucked in a breath. His eyes stared down at the bearer of bad tidings.

Micmac mumbled to Phoebe, "Now there's a Whiskey-Tango-Foxtrot."

At that moment, a trio of black-robed individuals entered.

Lenny said in hushed tone, "Magus. The tall black one? I bet he's the pizza guy."

Phoebe, "The short woman, the one with the book? She's the first Hispanic—"

Hekka, excited, "The last one, the red-complected one. I know of him. Chief Omygodi of the Sioux Nation. The first—" She went silent.

The woman stood with her back to them, but she seemed to be presenting the book to the vice president. The tall one spoke, his words muffled. The red man handed papers to Stones. The three left.

The vice president turned to the team. "Something has happened. Something serious. I have to run, but first …" He held up the sheaf of papers. "… I have one of these for each of you." He handed each a parchment document with calligraphic writing on the yellowed paper. "You saved millions of lives. Your country's gratitude is off the charts. I am beyond grateful."

With that he approached the gathered team and placed a medal suspended from a red, white, and blue ribbon around each person's neck. He shook their hands, one recipient at a time.

The team, looking more than surprised, held their medals as if having just won an Olympic event. In point of fact, they'd been awarded Presidential Medals of Freedom—the nation's highest civilian award—for bravery and selflessness in preventing the nuclear destruction of America's premier city. Well-deserved.

"This is awkward, but due to the nature of your, uh, unofficial capacity in this near-catastrophe, your awards must remain secret." Again, he shook hands. "I really have to run." He turned. "If you ever need anything …"

Lenny opened his mouth to speak, but the new president of the United States quickly disappeared.

• • •

The floor rose to standard height, the cathedral a memory. Then, a voice. "You can watch whatever you wish," said the NSA Director. He held out a clicker, which Lenny grabbed. "The buttons near the top, numbered one through twenty, control the screens. Push the button twice for the sound feed. I'm going to go catch some lunch. Remember, everything that happened in Asia, Europe … and here, is above Top Secret. You'll receive a lecture before you leave on how to handle the information you've obtained and how to handle any requests for it from the media or anyone else. Jack, STU-V secure phones have been installed, one in your cabin and one in your big house for communications directly with me or Stones. Have a happy," he said as he stepped to the door. "Oh, Mr. Lipschitz. Don't press the red button." Lenny dropped the clicker like a hot potato.

Phoebe seized both the opportunity and the clicker before Lenny could recover. The Director chuckled and exited the room.

"How did he know I call the master cabin the big house?" Jack scrunched his eyebrows.

"Yeah, and how did he know Lenny was dangerous with a clicker?" queried Phoebe.

Lenny, in a funk, sat with his arms folded.

"Phoebe," said Crayle. "Switch us to the world feed over there. I'm betting button five. Double-click."

She switched the audio, and they all took in the surprising sight. The scene was of a huge outdoor square populated with a standing crowd. A series of broad steps led from the square to a flat surface barren except for a pair of chairs suitable for royalty. Banners of gold and red gleamed and whipped in the breeze. A man, dressed in First Century B.C. formal wear, ascended the steps to the flat surface. He turned and raised his arms toward the heavens. The crowd of many thousands moved from their standing to kneeling positions.

"It's the Chinese man," Hekka said, the first to speak.

"No shit," said Phoebe.

"OMG," said Lenny, not to be left out.

"He's done it," exclaimed Crayle under his breath. "The Blackstone Strategy. To perfection."

• • •

Eight-thousand-one-hundred-forty-eight miles from Fort Meade, General Li watched the proceedings from the honored place, the foot of the stairs directly below the thrones. No one, save he and the new emperor, knew of Chin's resolve, in his mother's honor, to never defile a woman. He was certain Chin had never been with a woman in a way that would produce an heir. A wedding night would be most interesting. As for Li, he was Chin's, and China's, number two. A smile came easily to his lips.

EPILOGUE

Jack Sommers and his team returned to the Fawnskin cabin bruised, but not battered. They all toasted the success of their mission. New York would live to fight yet another day and their nemesis, Lalumière, had perished in the explosion. Lenny joked about the New Yorkers getting a free supply of pre-nuked fish. He got a laugh and that pleased him no end.

In the bedroom, Jack had made his final report to Neil and was ready to call the Crayle project complete. Just one more call to the good doctor and the return of his precious subject. Prying Crayle and his Indian maiden apart would require some doing. They seemed every bit an item, like Phoebe and Micmac.

"Looks like we're done with the Frenchman, Magus. You can continue on with the doctor, if you like. With what just happened and with the vice president, uh, president, on your side, you pretty much can do whatever you want. I have to say, though, that it has been a pleasure being associated with you, and I'm very happy you're on our side."

Crayle smiled and acknowledged with a half bow. "And thank you, Jack, for putting me through all that. Seriously, your jet is one serious vacation ride and, were I not somewhat attached …"

Hekka's ears perked. "Somewhat?" She drew her ten-inch knife slowly, thoughtfully, holding it up to Crayle. He responded by drawing his father's slide rule. For the first time since it all began, everyone laughed. The tension of the past several dangerous, violent months expelled itself in a manner of seconds. It was over now. Truly over. They could all move on with their lives in search of normal, whatever that was.

• • •

Far to the north of Washington, D.C., a trussed and bandaged man awoke in a small island hospital facility, not knowing what had happened. Pain assaulted him from all regions of his body. It caused him to grimace. He remembered neither the nuclear explosion nor the flight, the landing, and subsequent rescue. He recognized a brown-eyed woman with dark brown hair protruding from a cap as a nurse. And he recognized that she spoke his native language, French, to a white-smocked man who stood beside her. A doctor. He felt at home. But, where? Devoid of answers, a pang of anxiety welled up inside him.

"*Ou?*" he mumbled.

"*Vous êtes à Miquelon, Monsieur*," the nurse answered. She switched to English for the doctor from nearby English-speaking Newfoundland, but in hushed tones. Lalumière heard the word *Elder*. The doctor turned to him.

"You've had a boating accident. Do you remember?" Receiving no answer, the doctor emptied a syringe into a drip feed. The doctor's eyes followed the fluid up the arm and to the heart, as if it was visible. The patient pulsed.

It came back to Lalumière now. The bomb had been deep-sixed by the American sharpshooter woman. With a handgun. Still, after the blast, everything was blank. He wanted to ask what had happened to the Queen Mary 2, its passengers, and the people of New York. And what had become of the American president and his plan to interfere in France? He didn't dare.

"Who brought me here?"

She smiled. "Fishermen found you. One of them is here. Perhaps you will recognize him."

On cue, a tall, slim man entered the private room.

"*Jean-Marc!*"

Lalumière's son asked to be alone with his father for a few minutes. He watched the doctor and nurse leave. When the door closed, he explained to his father all he had learned from the media in the past twenty-four hours.

"Dad, I have news," He relayed news of Chin's ascension, but he read his father's impatience. "And France. The public is rioting in the streets. The new president's pacifist core disallows engagement of the mobs by police. The people feel betrayed. They believe that Mitim, in their stead, charged into the fray, to remove American interference in the domestic affairs of France. They blame the American president for Mitim's demise. They have surrounded the Embassy in Paris."

"And what of the Americans?"

"Their president internalized what happened outside New York harbor. He … he has taken his life. It has calmed the peoples of both countries, but I suspect a severe and revolutionary undertow has absorbed the massive energy. Both countries will demand true, alpha-male leadership. And very, very soon."

The son excused himself for a bathroom break.

Since the doctor's drug had fully relieved the pain and brought his mind back into focus, it gave Lalumière a few moments of solitude to reflect. "Mitim lives," escaped the tarnished gauze.

• • •

In his subterranean lair, a worried Neil Wohlford paced the floor. Events had overtaken him in a manifold and historic manner. The good news was, with all that had happened, he had not been found out. His employer, the American intelligence agency, still thought him, head of the Other Specialized Staffs office, loyal and dedicated. No linkage connected him to the Illuminé, its director known as the Elder, or his rival, Sylvain Lalumière. The ostentatious exit of the Frenchman had left the secret society without a prospective leader of the New France. It did, however, elevate Neil to a higher level as the prospective heir to Illuminé leadership. He smiled.

He swished the liquid in his French-crystal glass. One sniff of the unadulterated, dark amber essence confirmed its power. The recent event here in his home country occasioned a special toast to the future. Nothing French would do. With no one observing, he had gone to a special desk compartment and withdrawn the American whiskey. Rye. Perfect, considering the extreme happenings in New York. While he still loved his French food and drink, the Americans were to be admired for the unrefined power that Rye whiskey embodied to perfection. Of course, he had poured it into an old fashioned glass made in Baccarat, a town close to Lalumière's château.

Neil relaxed. He had learned early to always have a backup. What manner of cunning and subterfuge could result in him replacing Lalumière, positioned for a *coup d'etat*? He tilted back his head and wondered. Certainly, his deep cover training in an estate near the small French town, Rodez, had prepared him for his role. That Rodez, a long stones throw east of his biological birthplace in Carcassonne, was the source of his American-ness caused a shake of his head. He glanced at his CIA credentials. *Birthplace: Bar Harbor, Maine*. Oh, the irony.

Time to turn his attention to the Chinese, one Chin Yao-wu. He and Chin could benefit from a closer relationship. A Beijing-Paris axis might be in their future. For now, it was time to call it a day. Tonight, he would attend the opera with his lovely French-Canadian wife, Chantal. Sometimes, life seemed like such a dream.

• • •

On May 4, 1814, Napoléon Bonaparte had been exiled to the island called Elba just off the Tuscan coast of Italy. There, he had been visited by special people. Supporters. Those who would return him not just to his beloved France, but to his rightful throne.

In his mind, Sylvain Lalumière had been exiled to the French Overseas Territory known as St. Pierre and Miquelon. As he recovered his damaged parts, he received a message from his son's lips. Whispered into his tattered ear. The quest for global dominance was not over, only suspended. Lalumière regained confidence and reserve. He would throw every energy he could muster into his recovery. Back into the fray. It was far from finished. March 1, the day that Napoléon first set foot once more on French soil, would soon be at hand. Lalumière made it his deadline. Mitim, like Napoléon before him, would return.

• • •

It rang. The special phone.

"Neil Wohlford speaking …

Yes …

Yes …

Yes, Elder …

Plan B."

ABOUT THE AUTHOR

Novelist Dennis Bowen has a long-standing commitment to international affairs, and has traveled to more than 50 countries. Given his martial arts training, classified defense and intelligence community background, and wartime service with amphibious forces, it's not surprising that he pens thrillers. *The Blackstone Perfection* follows *The Water Diamonds* as Book 2 in his International Thriller Series. When not traveling the globe to research his next book, he resides on the Southern California coast.

http://www.twitter.com/DBowenThrillers/
http://www.facebook.com/#!/Dennis.Bowen.90
http://www.dennisbowen.com/

THE CRYSTAL SEDUCTION

BOOK 3:
International Thriller Series

Available: Spring 2014

CHAPTER 1

It looks fabulous in your hands." The tall young man, having given the football-shaped object to the older man, stepped back.

"It rightfully belongs to the both of us, my son." The older man pushed in the ends, as if to plump up a rugby ball.

"Please don't do that," admonished a third man. "Five megatons, you know."

"I'm sorry, General. I thought these miniature nuclear devices were only unstable in the hands of Muslims."

The men laughed. A fourth, a second Chinese, spoke. "The world is only in danger when we possess one of these." He raised the CIA's version of a universal TV remote.

The men laughed again.

"I, Chin Yao-wu, next emperor of China, propose a toast." He raised his glass. "To better bombs. To better governance. To mutual success." He glanced at the general.

"And faster horses."

"Boom!" teased the young Frenchman.

The older men glared.

The young man's father supplied redirection. "Your castle is quite beautiful."

"Hong Kong is my home. I have purchased Craigdarroch as my home away from home, where I visit my offshore wealth."

"The stained glass windows are legendary, are they not?"

"The finest in North America, Sylvain."

"The structure, positioned atop this hill, commands the area. I'm sure the general appreciates its defensibility." The bandaged Frenchman glanced at the uniformed man seated opposite.

"Yes, easy for my small force to protect."

"And protection is key, gentlemen." An unexpected participant strode into the room.

"You!" cried the Frenchman. "What are you doing here? I never expected you to leave your subterranean lair."

"Manassas? As you said, home away from home."

"This is Canada. Your specific role is to be our, Illuminé's—"

"My role, today, is to provide secure transportation for you and your football to the European continent. While Interpol and the rest of the world's forces stand down, believing you are quite dead. We mustn't disappoint them."

"What we must do is attack before the nuclear bombing of Marseille loses its effect. It has been three weeks."

"Had you not gone terribly rogue," Neil Wohlford added, with typical arrogance, "we would not find ourselves in this awkward situation."

"I had to attack America. New York was perfect. The Americans, one of which you are, Neil, have withdrawn support for my France. That was essential. Now, *I* can return with *my* bomb and finish *my* work."

"Gentlemen, we are on the same team. We are the necessary components of the American's master strategy, are we not?" Chin diffused the escalating interplay. "Sylvain, it has been too long since our first face-to-face meeting in Scotland."

Lalumière came back to Earth. "Yes … at the Elite Single-Malt gathering."

Apropos of that comment, two young women dressed in black and red cheongsam dresses wheeled in a cart topped with a 30-year-old Scotch and five crystal glasses. They poured three fingers each.

"To our success in China!" Chin beamed.

They drank.

"To our success in France!" Lalumière tilted his chin upward.

They drank.

"Then Europe."

They drank.

"We'll require more mini bombs, General," the Frenchman advised.

"I now own, in all respects, the People's Republic Armies and all of their resources. You shall have bombs."

They drank.

Chin Yao-wu, swept up in the moment, turned somber. "Gentlemen, my country continues to reel from the Beijing explosion. The chaos must be dealt with. General Li and I must, regrettably, depart your company. But we shall gather again soon … when France is ours."

"Here, here," Neil declared.

Lalumière sipped his drink. *Sharing* France appeared no where on his mental map.

"Well, we must be on our way." Li stood.

"You will return to Manassas, Neil?" a concerned Lalumière asked.

"My movements are, of course, classified. Need to know, and all."

Lalumière sucked in a breath. The arrogance of this man rivaled that of Parisian waiters.

"Dad! Come see!" came a holler from a large, antique glass window.

"What, my Son?"

"A gorgeous Rolls-Royce, maroon over beige, just pulled into the porte-cochère. Royalty incarnate."

"Impossible!" gasped Li. "My sentries—"

"I must see this. Jean-Marc, push me to the window."

The son complied.

"That automobile is perfect. I want it for my coronation."

"Dad, we're far from any coronation. You've survived an atomic blast, for Christ sakes. It will take months to recover. Well into the Spring. Out of sight of Interpol—"

"Look, Son!"

The front window of the Roll-Royce opened, revealing a black-clad figure, an MP5 machine-gun, and a face.

"Crayle!"

Spring 2014

THE CRYSTAL SEDUCTION

From International Thriller Writer
DENNIS BOWEN

www.ingramcontent.com/pod-product-compliance
Lightning Source LLC
Chambersburg PA
CBHW020606310726
48979CB00008B/1369/J

* 9 7 8 0 9 8 8 1 8 4 1 5 2 *